A R

A bold and dashing Jade Falcon MechWarrior might have jumped straight up at the *Catapult*, to negate its tremendous range advantage by coming to grips. At close range the *Black Hawk*'s Streak missiles and hands would give it all the edge over the armless support BattleMech, heavier though it was. But a bold 'Mech jock would also have been painted against the sky by the *Catapult*'s FCS and blasted off its jump jet drive columns to crash to ruin in the boulder-lined streambed below.

Instead, Jorgensen took a short, fast, flat-trajectory jump straight across to the opposite slope. He hit the ground running. The ridge's mass now masked him from the Lyran's potent long-range battery.

The *Black Hawk* rocked as a heavy short-range missile fired from a man-portable launcher slammed against his right torso, just forward of the 'Mech's massive coaxially mounted shoulder and hip joints. Red lights flashed on his heads-up display: his right-side laser's primary control circuit was gone. He ignored both the shot—that was what redundancy was for, and a green light told him a secondary circuit had kicked in—and the grounded infantryman who launched it. With his battle-hardened elementals to back them, he trusted even the green *solahma* foot soldiers' fire-and-moving-forward to police up stranded enemy infantry.

In his three-sixty viewstrip he saw one of his battle-suited giants flipped over in midair by a burst from the *Catapult*'s twenty-millimeter gun. It dropped straight down into the trickle of stream. As he charged upslope with what in any 'Mech-driver less supremely proficient would be mad recklessness, Jorgensen registered from his eye's corner that elemental Dot's tag now flashed yellow. She was no doubt out of the fight, thoroughly stunned and probably sporting broken bones, but telemetry showed she still lived. *A good thing, for I can spare no front-line warriors . . .*

DARK AGE

A RENDING OF FALCONS

A BATTLETECH™ NOVEL

Victor Milán

A ROC BOOK

ROC
Published by New American Library, a division of
Penguin Group (USA) Inc., 375 Hudson Street,
New York, New York 10014, USA
Penguin Group (Canada), 90 Eglinton Avenue East, Suite 700, Toronto,
Ontario M4P 2Y3, Canada (a division of Pearson Penguin Canada Inc.)
Penguin Books Ltd., 80 Strand, London WC2R 0RL, England
Penguin Ireland, 25 St. Stephen's Green, Dublin 2,
Ireland (a division of Penguin Books Ltd.)
Penguin Group (Australia), 250 Camberwell Road, Camberwell, Victoria 3124,
Australia (a division of Pearson Australia Group Pty. Ltd.)
Penguin Books India Pvt. Ltd., 11 Community Centre, Panchsheel Park,
New Delhi - 110 017, India
Penguin Group (NZ), 67 Apollo Drive, Rosedale, North Shore,
Auckland 1311, New Zealand (a division of Pearson New Zealand Ltd.)
Penguin Books (South Africa) (Pty.) Ltd., 24 Sturdee Avenue,
Rosebank, Johannesburg 2196, South Africa

Penguin Books Ltd., Registered Offices:
80 Strand, London WC2R 0RL, England

First published by Roc, an imprint of New American Library,
a division of Penguin Group (USA) Inc.

First Printing, June 2007
10 9 8 7 6 5 4 3 2 1

Copyright © WizKids, Inc., 2007
All rights reserved

ROC REGISTERED TRADEMARK—MARCA REGISTRADA

Printed in the United States of America

PUBLISHER'S NOTE
This is a work of fiction. Names, characters, places, and incidents either are the product of the author's imagination or are used fictitiously, and any resemblance to actual persons, living or dead, business establishments, events, or locales is entirely coincidental.
   The publisher does not have any control over and does not assume any responsibility for author or third-party Web sites or their content.

For Mike and Denise Wernig,
for keeping the faith.

Prologue

The Falcon's Reach
Portmeirion, Skye
Jade Falcon Occupation Zone
3 August 3135

"**N**o!" the little girl in the rubble cried, clinging fiercely to the arm of her teddy bear. It had soft, curly brown hair, button eyes and a nose of yielding tan synthetic.

The *solahma* infantryman was a tall, hard man in green-and-black Jade Falcon battledress. He carried an assault rifle. His web belt and harness were hung with grenades like metal and plastic fruit. His blue eyes showed no mercy, nor did they react to the blue smoke and dust that hung in the air like pepper gas. He had washed out as a youth in his Trial of Position and would never be a MechWarrior. Combined with the normal Clan contempt for Spheroids and their soft ways, a lifetime of bitter disappointment that he would never be a true Falcon warrior left him no sympathy for the child. These soft, crawling grubbers of the Inner Sphere had no sense of discipline. They must harden or die.

It was the Kerensky way.

He backhanded her almost casually. She dropped the arm of her soft toy and somersaulted backward to sit cowering and weeping and holding her face in what had been the corner of the family room of her suburban home. It was now the joining of two stubs of wall, foamed concrete broken off to no higher than a handspan over her head if she stood upright.

The house had been shattered by a volley of short-range missiles fired from a *Gyrfalcon*. Several off-duty members of the Falcon garrison had been attacked in the small town on the rainy, heavily forested southwestern coast of New Scotland two nights earlier. One mixed Star of medium and light BattleMechs and another of mechanized infantry in combat cars had come through the neighborhood and flattened everything as part of a routine reprisal against Portmeirion. The girl and her bear had been playing in the backyard when the attack came; they hid in a subterranean storage space, else she would have died along with her parents and her older sister, who had been studying for an exam.

Had she stayed in the bunker-like storage space she might have escaped. But instead she ran out at the height of the barrage, screaming in terrified concern for her family.

The walking machines strode heedlessly by, with the hovercraft prowling beside their gleaming metal feet. It had been left to the infantry to mop up any survivors.

The hard-faced soldier unlimbered his rifle. "What are you doing?" asked a squadmate.

"What does it look like?"

"Orders were to bring in all children for proper indoctrination," the infantrywoman said. She herself had briefly been a MechWarrior, and been Dispossessed in a battle that not only cost her her left arm but saw her performance deemed so unworthy she was denied regeneration. She would never pilot a BattleMech again. Despite the fact that she, unlike the taller man with the perpetually blue chin and cheeks, had tasted the fierce joy, the sense of unbridled power enjoyed by a MechWarrior, she never displayed his sullen bitterness. She embraced her lot, and was content seeking the lone honor left to her: death in combat.

He glared at her. "What difference does it make? It's just a Spheroid."

"She's a child, Huber."

"Nits make lice," Huber said. He shouldered his weapon and aimed at the sobbing child's head.

The girl lowered her arms and raised her chin. With tears drying on her child-chubby cheeks, she stared without blinking at the small black circle of the muzzle.

"Stop."

It was a female voice from beyond the compound oblong of the rubbled house. It was not a loud voice. But it was a voice that commanded—and that was obviously accustomed to being obeyed.

Huber scowled. But he lowered his rifle. "Who speaks?" he asked.

A woman stepped into the space that had been the family room. She was tiny, scarcely larger than the child. She wore Jade Falcon dress uniform, but nonregulation, more black than green. She wore a combat knife on one hip and a handgun in an open-topped holster of hard synthetic on the other. Ice-white blond hair cascaded over the padded shoulders from beneath the flared helmet, stylized and enameled to resemble a falcon's head. Blue eyes blazed forth beneath the helmet, intense as a bird of prey's.

"Your Galaxy commander," she said.

Huber frowned in suspicion, but lowered his rifle to his hip.

"The orders were, children found alive after the primary action were not to be harmed."

"She resisted, Galaxy Commander," said Huber.

"She clung to her toy when he tried to take it away from her, Galaxy Commander," the infantrywoman corrected. "She was terrified by the bombardment. It was no more than reflex."

Huber stared insolently at the newcomer as if sizing her up. He seemed little impressed. His *solahma* Trinary had recently arrived on this former world of the Republic of the Sphere, conquered not long before on a second attempt by a Jade Falcon expeditionary force. Though they were replacements for the Delta Galaxy, dispatched grudgingly from the Jade Falcon Occupation Zone, continuing trouble on Skye meant they had been deployed before being introduced to their *ristar* Galaxy commander.

Galaxy commander or no, *ristar* or no, it didn't matter to Huber. Obedience to orders was deeply engrained in Clanners from their crèche days. Respect for rank was not. Only strength should rule; that was the law of the Clans.

But he could not bring himself to openly defy someone of such exalted rank. Not quite.

A brisk breeze off the nearby sea lifting her hair like a battle pennon, the woman walked over to the child. "Stand up, girl," she said, not unkindly.

The girl stared up at her for a moment. She sniffled once. Then she obeyed.

"What is your name?" the woman asked.

"Cynthy."

"Well, Cynthy. Do you fear me?"

Huge blue eyes regarded her for a beat. "Yes."

The helmeted head nodded crisply. "You are honest. You are brave. You will come with me."

"Brave?" Huber could not keep from scoffing. "You should have heard her sniveling for her toy, Galaxy Commander."

"I want my bear," Cynthy said. "I won't go without my bear."

"Bravery is facing fear," the woman with the ice-white hair said, "not lacking fear. In the absence of fear there is no bravery." Her voice dropped low, so low her next words almost got lost within the whistle of the rising wind. "I have no fear. So I cannot be brave."

She walked to where the bear lay sprawled against an edge of a blond-wood end table mostly buried beneath the gray dust stirred up by the BattleMech's barrage. She knelt, picked it up, stood. Brushing away the dust and grit, she brought it to the little girl.

"Here," she said, holding it out. The little girl hesitated. Then she took it and hugged it fiercely to her chest.

Huber glared. "Since when is it the Jade Falcon way to coddle the weakness of these stinking mud-crawlers?" he demanded.

The woman's right arm snapped level with her face. In her small gloved fist she held the black handgun.

It flashed red light.

Huber's head jerked. His eyes rolled up to his forehead. Between them, as if centered mechanically on the midpoint of a line connecting them, a blue hole had appeared in the bridge of his nose. It drooled a thin trickle of blood.

His knees buckled. He dropped to them, then fell on his face. Dust *whoomp*ed up around him.

The woman raised her hand, tipping the black handgun backward. "Does anyone else wish to question me?" she asked in a quiet, penetrating voice.

No one answered.

She looked at Cynthy. The child had winced at the laser's crack but showed no other reaction. The woman holstered her pistol, then knelt and held out her arms. The girl came to her and slipped her arms around the woman's neck.

The diminutive blond woman stood up as if the child in her arms was no more substantial than the toy she clutched between them.

"Remind your comrades," she said to the surviving troopers, "that in Gyrfalcon Galaxy, the will of Turkina *is* the will of Malvina Hazen."

Then she turned and carried the child from the ruins to a waiting hoverbike.

1

From opposing ridgetops the two light tanks faced each other across a kilometer of hard, sandy soil broken by bitter, thorny scrub and granite outcrops. Standing on the top deck of the tank's hunched, flatiron shape, Galaxy Commander Malvina Hazen regarded her opposite number through electronic binoculars.

He stood on the khaki dirt of the ridgetop beside his own Scimitar MkII, identical to hers. He watched her with his own optical gear, she noted with amusement. He was, she knew, handsome in his way: a tall, lean, dark-complected man with his hair shaved on the sides and a long, brown horsetail scalp lock blowing out in the wind. He wore a whipcord uniform in tan and dark brown, with a web belt for a sidearm. The hilt of a short, curved sword jutted up over his right shoulder.

"Warriors of the Hell's Horses are romantics," Malvina Hazen said. "It is good to know. We will be able to make easier use of them." That she would fail to triumph in the coming Trial of Possession did not cross her mind.

Her driver, Wyndham, peered up at her with enormous owl eyes from the open driver's hatch. He was a tiny man, not a centimeter taller than the minute Galaxy commander herself, and possessed a disproportionately large head. By breeding and birth he was an aerospace pilot, as genetically optimized to his role as were the Clan elementals, at the far end of the size spectrum. He had failed his Trial of Position, and rather than become a flight technician with the fleet he had taken the step—to him less painful than dropping in caste—of volunteering for combat with Turkina's ground forces.

Once, Malvina knew, his failure would have forced him into a non-combat role. But the great drawdown of Battle-Mech forces into which The Republic's founder, Devlin Stone, had shamefully cajoled the Clans had forced them greatly to expand their armor and infantry branches. They desperately needed warriors. The flash-fire spread of war through the Inner Sphere after Stone's long peace had caught the Clans flat-footed, the same as the Spheroids themselves. More and larger sibkos were being percolated and decanted throughout Falcon space. But years would pass before those warriors could join the fight, and the crisis was upon Turkina *now*.

Those who lacked the extraordinary combination of physical and mental attributes and skills needed to pilot a 'Mech or a fighter were still more than capable of filling the ranks of the less prestigious combat arms. Probably Wyndham intended to expiate the shame of failure by seeking glorious death in battle at the first opportunity.

But no Spheroid had yet proven good enough to give him the death he wanted. He had become by consensus the best driver in Malvina's Gyrfalcons. His fighter pilot's eyesight, reflexes and cryogenic nerve might not have sufficed to win him a position in the service for which he had been bred and trained, but they made him so proficient a driver that even MechWarriors accorded him respect. Especially given the dearth of qualified officers that accompanied the great drought of Clan warriors, Wyndham's exemplary annual proficiency retest scores and battlefield record would suffice to win him administrative promotion without the need to issue a Trial of Grievance to seize a position from a superior. Yet he repeatedly had refused advancement, not just in rank but to the more prestigious position of gunner or vehicle commander.

Such behavior was at odds with Clan character, to say nothing of the hot-blooded Falcon nature. Malvina wondered if having failed his aerospace Trial of Position, he deemed himself dead to honor and chose to seek death in the way he felt would best serve the Falcon. Or perhaps he simply chose to continue serving his flamboyant *ristar* commander in his current role.

Neither he nor Malvina Hazen, of course, labored under any illusion that he was as good a combat driver as his Hell's Horses opposite number. They were the Clans' acknowledged masters of vehicular war.

But his huge dark eyes were eager and falcon-intense as Malvina nodded to him. "You know what to do, *quiaff*?"

The great head nodded once. "*Aff*, Galaxy Commander."

"Then let us prepare," she said. "The flare to commence will go up in sixty seconds." She dropped lithely down her own hatch into the turret and sealed it over her head.

"Do you feel fear, Beckett Malthus?"

His skin crawled. The answer was *Of course*.

Overhead ravens, imported from Terra centuries before for reasons obscure, circled in the morning sun, croaking like prophets of doom. Not for the first time in recent months Galaxy Commander Beckett Malthus felt exceeding gratitude for decades of practice at keeping his emotions from his face.

Bec Malthus was an altogether exceptional Clanner, in that he was adept at masking all his emotions. And in that he, indeed, felt fear.

And now his fear of the great black destroyer hurtling toward them from the Skye jump point was overlaid by the keener and more immediate fear of this tiny, nearly naked woman with almost-white hair.

Malvina Hazen punctuated her question with a grunt of

effort as she yanked the kettlebell left-handed from the hard-packed white sand of the exercise ground. It resembled a black cannonball with a simple handle welded to it. It weighed sixty kilograms. In one smooth move she cleaned and thrust it above her head to the extent of a stiffened arm.

It was a prodigious lift even for a Clanswoman. Malvina's left forearm and hand, and her right leg from midthigh down were black polymer: prosthetics driven by servomechanisms far more powerful than any muscle. But Malthus suspected that, even more, it was the awful elemental force of her *will* that enabled her to perform such feats.

There was very little Bec Malthus put outside the scope of Malvina's will to accomplish.

For a moment she held the black sphere upraised against the cloud-crowded blue sky of Skye. Her arm began to tremble slightly. She threw the kettlebell. It landed two meters away with a thud Malthus felt through the soles of his boots, raising a white sand crater that halfway obscured it.

"A Hell's Horses WarShip approaches Skye, Galaxy Commander," he said. "Our jump point observation station identified it as the *Bucephalus*, a *Congress*-class frigate. It carries missiles that can reach the surface from orbit. They can blast us from the face of this planet within a single rotation."

"*Aff,*" Malvina said. "And if they so choose, no force I possess will stop them."

Though their rank was nominally the same, Jade Falcon Khan Jana Pryde had made clear when she dispatched the invasion force into the Republic of the Sphere that the senior in grade, Malthus, should command, and that Malvina Hazen and her sibkin Aleksandr Hazen—a rare pair from the same sibling cohort who won Bloodnames—should be subordinate. While no one, not even Malthus, would contest that Malvina and Aleksandr were his betters as field captains, he was by far the more experienced and deemed the wiser by the khan, who showed her own famous unorthodox streak by honoring age and wisdom over the youthful savagery Clan culture exalted.

Khan Jana Pryde well knew Malthus' wisdom and seasoning, and his cunning. He had been her right hand—or perhaps her left—during her own brutally contested rise to power.

Yet despite the death of her beloved brother Aleks in the first attempted taking of Skye, and her own injury to the bleeding edge of death, Malvina had emerged from the catastrophe stronger, in both will and political position. Even before that devastating campaign her personality had come to dominate the *desant*, as the invasion was called: from the ancient Russian word for "descent," meaning in that context a paratroop assault. Now both she and Malthus were well aware her will ruled supreme within the *desant* and the Falcon's Reach, as the Jade Falcon Occupation Zone had come to be called.

It was a role Malthus felt comfortable with: working from the shadows. He had no ambition to sit a throne. No one, after all, called a Trial of Possession for the rank of *éminence grise*.

He sighed. "You are correct. Still, it would be a bitter irony to have your glorious achievements nullified in the space of a day and a night."

She laughed, crinkling the long scar that curled through her eyebrow and toward her mouth. It was a relic of brutal injuries sustained during the first invasion of Skye. Dressed as she was in an ivory sports bra and brief trunks of the same color, the substantial scarring of her body and limbs also was visible.

Her face had largely been restored through plastic surgery and skin grafts. Malvina had declined to spend the time out of action that having her lost arm and leg rebudded and regrown would have cost, but Malthus had on his own authority directed that her appearance be restored as much as possible using procedures which cost mere hours. For all its utilitarian rhetoric, Clan culture worshipped youth and perfection. A savagely scarred Galaxy commander ostensibly bore the evidence of her courage and service to Turkina. In reality, Malthus knew, she would be seen as *damaged*.

And Malthus had plans for Malvina. Although not, he had grown to suspect, half so ambitious as her plans for herself.

He knew she had not missed how he evaded her original question. Malvina Hazen was at once the most traditional of Clanners and the most violently unorthodox. The skill of reading other humans was neglected to the point of non-existence in all the Clans—at least the fanatic Crusader Clans, among which Clan Jade Falcon prided itself on being paramount. Yet he feared that she was learning to read *him*, who would be opaque to even the most Machiavellian Lyran diplomat.

"Those were not glorious achievements, Bec Malthus," she said in a cheery voice. "It was death, devastation and horror. No more nor less than it needed to be."

A chill trickled down his spine, a distressingly common occurrence in this young woman's company. "Very well, Malvina. What then do you propose?"

She reached up and pulled out the fastening in her hair, letting it fall like an ice slide about her shoulders. Evidently she was done with exercise for the day. "Wait, of course. Transit from the jump point takes four days. We still have more than seventy-six hours before she shapes orbit around Skye."

"And then?"

"We shall see."

"Galaxy Commander."

The chime of the communicator in her room in the planetary duke's palace on the outskirts of New London, the Prefecture IX capital on Thames Bay, roused her from sleep in time to hear the words. Not that she had ever been a deep sleeper. Since suffering her injuries, she slept longer but even more fitfully.

She sat up, the sheet falling from her. Beneath it she slept naked. "Malvina Hazen here," she acknowledged. "Speak."

Next to her, the pair of Delta Galaxy MechWarriors, male and female, with whom she had amused herself earlier in the evening, stirred in bed. She ignored them.

"Warrior Tyrrell, communications center. We have received communication from the inbound Hell's Horses War-Ship, Galaxy Commander," the disembodied voice said. It was male and obviously fighting to suppress excitement.

"What does it say, Warrior Tyrrell?" she asked, amused at the notion of a spacecraft saying anything. From an early age she and her beloved sibkin—brother, lover, ally against the rest of the *sibko* and against the universe—had been secretly amused by their kin's tendency toward extreme literal-mindedness.

"The communication comes from Galaxy Commander Tristan Fletcher. He wishes to conduct a *batchall* for a Trial of Possession."

"What prevents him?"

"He wishes to bargain with you in person, Galaxy Commander."

"Very well," she said. "On my way."

She jumped to her feet from amidst rumpled sky-blue satin sheets. The erstwhile planetary duke, Gregory Kelswa-Steiner, had lived in a manner fairly Spartan for Spheroid nobility. Which, with the immense silk-canopied bed and the Star League–era oil paintings on the wall, made it merely *sumptuous* by Clan standards. And this was only his secondary residence, not his hereditary holding in the planetary capital of New Glasgow to the north.

By longstanding habit Malvina kept both clothes and weapons close to hand wherever she slept. Given Jade Falcon temperaments, such habits could be risky when entertaining sexual partners. But only Aleks had ever fought Malvina and lived. She gave the matter little thought.

Her current partners sat up now, blinking at her. "What?" she snapped. "You are still here?"

"You wish *what*?" Malvina asked in disbelief. *Is it possible the signal is so distorted that the communications software is garbling the meaning? Is the solar storm that bad?*

"*I said,*" the voice of Galaxy Commander Tristan Fletcher repeated stiffly, popping with static, "*I wish to challenge you to a Trial of Possession for the Mongol doctrine.*"

Malvina stared at the viewscreen in the palace's communications center. All it showed was the image, relayed from astronomical telescopes orbiting Skye, of the *Bucephalus* itself, with starlight glinting from its armor plate and ominous turrets. Still over forty hours out at one-gee acceleration, the

WarShip was too distant for visual communications, especially with the planet's G8 primary—the larger member of a rare planet-possessing binary system—acting out the way it was.

"The Mongol doctrine?" she echoed.

"The modern Mongol mode of waging war," the disembodied voice said. *"The use of high mobility, the* mangudai *and the* tulughma. *It originated with Clan Hell's Horses. You have wrongfully appropriated it. I will see it returned to its rightful owner."*

Malvina drew in a deep breath. When she used the term, "Mongol doctrine" meant the deliberate use of terror to force enemies to submit, both during and after conquest. The Clans had long eschewed attacks on civilian populations as contrary to honor; the devastation from orbit of the Draconis Combine world of Turtle Bay by Clan Smoke Jaguar vessels had been a factor in bringing on the Trial of Annihilation that had wiped them out.

But times had changed, as the hated Devlin Stone had never ceased to remind them. One such change: Malvina and Aleks had defied Clan cultural disdain for the past by assiduous study of military history. Of course, they had come to almost diametrically opposite conclusions about the lessons that history taught. . . .

What Malvina's followers, among the *desant* and increasingly throughout Clan Jade Falcon, came to call the Mongol doctrine was also, ironically, quite at odds with Hell's Horses practices. Indeed, they were known for their shocking indulgence of conquered Spheroids by integrating them as greatly as possible into their strange and un-Clanlike system of emphasizing teamwork over individual drive, thus turning away from the Darwinian struggle of all against all that Kerensky in his wisdom had surely intended for his cauldron-born children.

He thinks I'm copying their battlefield tactics, she thought. She laughed. *No one ever said the Horsemen were bright.*

"As you will, Galaxy Commander Tristan Fletcher," she said aloud.

"With what forces do you defend, Galaxy Commander Malvina Hazen?"

"Myself, alone with a driver, in a single vehicle. You determine its class. I shall specify the Circle of Equals."

A stifled gasp ran through the dozen or so warriors and technicians who were either on duty in the communications center or had found plausible excuses to be there. A pause, then: *"But are you not a MechWarrior, Galaxy Commander?"*

The implied insult brought snarls from the listening Falcons. Malvina showed no reaction. "I am. But you do not fight in a BattleMech by preference, do you? You Horsemen love your armored vehicles. That is your specialty, Tristan Fletcher. *Quiaff?*"

"Aff."

"Then I shall defend in a vehicle."

"Have you experience in vehicular combat?" Fletcher asked after another pause.

"Only insofar as I have commanded formations of vehicles. Not as crew."

"You are . . . most honorable, Galaxy Commander Malvina Hazen. I accept. We shall fight in Scimitar MkII tanks."

"Seyla. I will inform you of my choice for location of the Circle of Equals within twenty-four hours."

One more pause, while the blustery solar winds sang their crackling song. *"Bargained well and done. Tristan Fletcher out."*

Malvina turned to her staff. "Get me maps of every desert and steppe on this world," she commanded.

They stared at her. To take on a Hell's Horses warrior in a ground-vehicle duel was akin to offering to wrestle an elemental barehanded. If she lost, it would bring *dezgra* upon the whole expeditionary force. It would also leave them all stuck inside virulently hostile territory, bereft of her superhuman wit and will, which had driven the *desant* so deep and kept it there.

She smiled at them. "My sibkin Aleksandr *did* wrestle an elemental barehanded," she reminded them. "He won, too."

Her expression changed to an incandescent glare. "Now perform your tasks. I have no intention of losing!"

2

The Falcon's Reach
The Desolation, Skye
Jade Falcon Occupation Zone
3 August 3135

Just ahead and to the left of the speeding Scimitar, sand particles spurted into the air, driven by residual ground moisture and various organic matter flash-heated to steam by the kiss of a blue-green laser beam. As if seeing the shot by precognition, Wyndham had already sent the 35-ton hovertank skidding sideways, throwing up its own cloud of dust.

"You disappoint me, Malvina Hazen," Tristan Fletcher's voice said in her headset. *"I had hoped you might at least put up a fight. But if all you do is run from me, you do no more than delay the inevitable."*

She had already spotted her opponent's plume of yellow dust, streaming from the flank of a hill half a kilometer to her left. By reflex she rotated the turret to bear on him. She had no intention of firing. She possessed only one volley of four rockets, no reloads, and the other Scimitar was outside their short range. Her other weapons fired forward along the hovertank's long axis with very little play. Fletcher was well outside her covered arc.

And all went according to her plan.

Wyndham arrested the Scimitar's sideways skid with blasts of its steering jets. The vehicle scooted forward, rocking Malvina back against the rear of her padded command seat. Her headset howled at the ionization track left in the air as another small extended-range laser shot cracked mere meters behind the stubby little tank's stern. The Scimitar plunged into the broad sand-bottomed mouth of an arroyo. A rocky ridge shielded them from further fire.

The gamble had paid off. Malvina once again knew where her enemy was. And he was inexorably getting closer.

Pylons flying the green-and-yellow pennons of Clan Jade Falcon and the black-and-orange of Clan Hell's Horses marked a ten-kilometer square, called the Circle of Equals regardless of its shape, amid the desert known as The Desolation in the southern hemisphere of Skye's supercontinent of New Scotland. Air-dropped radio beacons emitted tones that became audible at a quarter kilometer and grew louder as the combatants neared the boundary.

Overhead drifted helicopters from various Skye civilian news services, and even a dirigible like a fat, white sausage with red and black stripes that the Herrmanns AG media group usually used to cover sporting events. For all Malvina Hazen's fondness for calculated frightfulness—her *actual* Mongol doctrine—once she had smashed Skye, her hand lay upon the populace with surprising lightness. Which she knew from history was also, ironically, the Mongol way.

The one iron prohibition was against media commentary directly bearing on the occupation or the occupiers, especially anything that might encourage resistance to the Clan. After a minor breach, a Falcon elemental in full battlearmor had invaded a Skye One studio and ripped a popular female news anchor limb from limb during the *Live at 1800* tri-vid cast. The media got the message.

Today, the reporters and their holocams were out in

force—not by Malvina's permission but by her command.
The images and sounds they captured would be carried as
recordings by JumpShips throughout the Inner Sphere and
beyond. It was Malvina Hazen's way of putting all of humanity on notice for what was in store for it. She doubted
many, if any, would fully appreciate the import of her
message.

But soon or late, they would learn.

"You are mad" had been Bec Malthus' comment when
he learned of the *batchall.*

"I thought we had established that long since."

Holding her arms out to her sides, Cynthy walked along
the rampart of the New London ducal residence between
two crenellations, a space of about a meter. For her it was
two steps and turn about. She wore a blue-and-white dress,
black shoes with white stockings. Her blond hair was tied
in pigtails; the pink tip of her tongue protruded from the
side of her mouth as she concentrated.

The two Spheroid women on duty from among those
Malvina had assigned to the girl's care went rushing toward
her with cries of alarm. One was small and lean and dark,
the other big, broad and redheaded. Both were Skye na-
tives. Malvina wanted the girl raised under as close to locally appropriate conditions as possible.

The big red-haired woman got there first. Crooning in
some unfathomable local dialect of English she plucked the
girl away from the twenty-meter drop and folded her to her
substantial bosom. By her tone of voice she was alternately
scolding and soothing. Cynthy looked at her blankly.

"Fascinating," Malvina said as the big woman set the
girl down, faced away from the rampart and gave her an
encouraging little pat on the behind. Malvina wondered
what the fuss was about.

Irritated, Malthus shook his head. A MechWarrior of his
Turkina Keshik had sneered at Malvina Hazen's coddling
of the Spheroid child two days before, not long after the
Galaxy commander had returned with her. Malvina called
out the man on the spot. Fortunately, it had been out of
doors, outside a barracks at the edge of town used by the

occupiers. *Fortunately*. Because she had opened his muscle-ribbed belly with her knife, yanked out several meters of his intestines, scaled his back and throttled him with a bloody, gray-green loop of his own guts.

From birth Jade Falcon warriors were trained—brainwashed, Malthus would have said, not necessarily with disapproval—not to fear death. But he had learned early on that even for such men and women there were still things to fear. One of them was a disgraceful *manner* of death.

Malvina, it seemed, also had learned that lesson. Which meant she was learning from *him*. Which meant he must watch her very, very carefully indeed.

But then, he thought sourly, *it is not as if I did not know that, now, is it?*

"But to consent to duel to the death over a copyright infraction?" he said.

Malvina shrugged. "I perceive it serves me."

"Challenging a Hell's Horses *ristar* to a single-vehicle duel? Why not a game of Russian roulette with autopistols, and you going first?"

Perhaps no one else alive would dare speak to the highly volatile Malvina in such a way. Certainly Malthus trod closer to the edge than he liked. But he also knew that if he deferred too much, Malvina would lose respect for him. That was the most dangerous outcome of all.

Instead of flashing off, she smiled. Despite the twisting of the scar, it made her look disturbingly beautiful; worse, almost friendly. "I will win," she said in a tone that closed the door on further discussion. "When I do, I will enhance my standing in the *desant* and of our Clan as a whole, and reinforce my image as an invincible monster in the eyes of the Inner Sphere.

"More importantly, I bind the Horsemen to me. By winning the right to what they call the Mongol doctrine, I harmonize our destinies, even in those Hell's Horses minds less dim than Tristan Fletcher's. Thus that Clan becomes available to my use, when I am ready."

"What do you think to gain from this hypothetical usage of the Horses?"

"Eventually?" she said. "Everything."

* * *

Red lights flamed in Malvina's heads-up display as a laser stabbed into the Scimitar's right rear with a shower of coruscation and a nasty buzzing in her headset. She was thrown against the left side of her harness as Wyndham broke right.

She checked her display. The enemy hovertank rounded the flank of a hill behind them. With remarkable skill, Fletcher's driver kept the machine at the same angle as the slope, using blasts of the steering jets to prevent it from sideslipping downward instead of moving upright on a column of downblast, which would make it slower and vulnerable to strikes against the weakly armored belly and to being toppled by explosive near misses. It came rapidly through a tunnel of dust and vegetation bits swirled up by powerful fans.

By slewing the 35-ton tank sideways and then accelerating forward at full throttle, Wyndham avoided twin streams of slugs from the enemy tank's miniguns. Confident of his unanswerably superior skill, Malvina's adversary conserved his heat by firing less potent weapons, just as he withheld his single volley of short-range missiles. She expected him to use his extended-range laser and miniguns to herd her, then close for slashing attacks with the short-range lasers and the powerful rockets.

Damage indicators showed a chunk of armor blasted from her Scimitar's stern. *First blood to Fletcher,* she thought.

Wyndham's maneuver had set the tank skidding across the flat at forty-five degrees to its previous course. He kicked up the right-side thrusters to kill the lateral vector. In her 360 display Malvina saw the other vehicle, not a quarter kilometer distant, lining up another shot from the left rear.

"Halt!" she rapped. Driven by hot Clan egotism, many expert drivers might have questioned the order. Wyndham instantly complied. He hit full-power reverse. The tank's nose bucked up, and a shudder ground through the vehicle as its stern skirt scraped hardpan.

Fletcher's long-range laser slashed a brilliant green cut

between land and sky ten meters ahead of Malvina's Scimitar. His paired miniguns plowed furrows in front of her, throwing up short-lived dust curtains.

The dust was still falling to earth as Wyndham powered through the impromptu screen with a roar of motors and scream of fans. Clods flipped up by the bullets pattered on the top and turret armor. Malvina could smell the hot, dry soil through the air intakes.

She had not ordered Wyndham to drive on. But he had successfully anticipated her intent. Had he *disobeyed*, she would have treated him with abrupt mercilessness. Otherwise, only results mattered.

A burst of ammunition raked the Scimitar, jackhammering along its left flank. Lights flared. Klaxons blared. Despite the cleverness of Wyndham's stutter-step maneuver, bullets had holed the rear left-side armor. No internal systems damage registered.

Fletcher is almost as good as he thinks he is, Malvina thought dispassionately. She hit a rocker switch preprogrammed for this battle. Then they passed behind the shielding jut of a gray-green granite extrusion covered with spiky brush.

3

The Falcon's Reach
The Desolation, Skye
Jade Falcon Occupation Zone
3 August 3135

The instant before she vanished behind a rock ridge, Galaxy Commander Tristan Fletcher saw black smoke billow from his prey.

It wasn't just that he had already damaged his opponent without taking a scratch on his paint in return that shaped his lean, dark features into a smile. It was the map displayed on his own HUD from satellite imaging taken from Skye orbit. His quarry had bolted into a box canyon.

In her panic his prey had trapped herself.

"I hoped for better from you, Malvina Hazen," he said aloud. He broadcast it, in case the outcrop did not block his signal. It hardly mattered.

"Now, Jebe," he told his driver over the intercom. "This is all the sport these pitiful Falcons can give us. Let us finish this."

"*Yes, Galaxy Commander!*" his driver responded eagerly. Though he was new—Fletcher tended to use up drivers at an alarming pace—Warrior Jebe's personality and his vehicle commander's meshed very well. They became a true team, a concept far less developed among other Clans. So far less developed, in fact, that some hard-core Crusader MechWarriors not-so-secretly regarded the Horsemen as scarcely Clanners at all.

Destroying the vaunted White Virgin, scourge of The Republic, will go far toward refuting that lie, he thought, his joy as fierce and hot and nourishing as blood drunk straight from a slash on his horse's flank on a long steppe ride.

He checked his own readouts as Jebe wound up the engines. All nominal; his heat was low, despite his driver quickly punching the Scimitar to near its full 162-kilometer-per-hour speed across the mostly flat terrain. It was risky, but Hell's Horses teammates trusted one another implicitly.

Jebe rotated the tank widdershins around its vertical axis, throwing Fletcher violently sideways in his five-point harness. The fans outboard of the turn howled to prevent the 35-ton mass from heeling over. If the skirt kissed ground at this speed, even a rise of soft loose soil, the hovercraft would flip and bounce itself to flaming pieces across The Desolation.

It did not. With artistry, Jebe kept a finger of high-pressure air between the steel skirt and the steel-hard dirt. The Scimitar righted, then continued to slide sideways at over a hundred kilometers per hour as it passed the outcrop with all weapons bearing on its target.

Which loomed as large as a Rommel assault tank in Fletcher's display. His enemy was not floundering helplessly at the far end of the long U-shaped cut. Instead, it was poised just inside it. It no longer vomited smoke; only a trickle streamed upward, blending quickly with the dust cloud remaining of its wake.

Fletcher shouted in inarticulate surprise as it accelerated straight toward him.

There was a moment in which Jebe might have spun the machine clockwise again and darted to escape the charging Scimitar. But that would have let their quarry slide out of his main-battery firing arc. Jebe held his maneuver, braking his sideways slide as Fletcher fired his whole battery in a furious spasm that spiked his heat meter to the redline.

And then Fletcher knew what was happening. He had time only to scream, *"Dishonor!"*

Then impact.

Noise ravaged Malvina's ears even through her headset. Her Scimitar's multiton mass shuddered like an Inner Sphere child's toy struck by a sledgehammer as three SRMs smashed the turret launcher to flaming ruin just over her head. Heat soared in the cockpit as she triggered off all surviving weapons in reply. But her gambit did not depend on winning an exchange of fire. It only required her machine to survive her enemy's full fury for a few crucial seconds.

A laser penetrated the hovertank's thick frontal armor. Coherent green light-needles stabbed through the cockpit and would have burned out her retinas had she not been wearing protective goggles. Metal screamed agony as it sublimated away beneath laser beams, was battered and torn by bullets. The Scimitar began to slip sideways as even Wyndham's iron nerve and raptor reflexes could hold it no longer.

But Fletcher's craft filled her display, the driver's viewscreen dancing with a reflected hell of green glare and yellow muzzle flame. She braced.

Her tank struck its gaudily painted twin at a good fifty kilometers an hour. Even though most of the velocity was its own, the enemy tank still skidded across her bow. Avalanche roar and an abominable shrieking deafened Malvina. Then she was shaken as if by a giant's hand.

The impact could have knocked one or both tanks tumbling across the steppe. Instead, the armored flesh and foamed-steel bones of both craft interpenetrated, locking them together. Both hit the dirt with showers of sparks visible through Malvina's still-functioning heads-up display like maddened fireflies swarming round them. Boulders banged against the interlocked hulls like Gauss slugs as they bucked across the land.

At last they ground to a stop. With a near-supersonic screech they broke apart at last, coming to rest in clouds of dust and smoke not ten meters from one another.

For a moment Malvina sat stunned. Not even her catlike

constitution and demon will could force body and mind to yield to her command.

The weakness passed. She took quick stock of herself. Her body felt as if it had been fed through a hammer forge. Every square centimeter was bruised down to the bone. Her left eye was blind, causing her a stab of panic. Rapid blinking brought a sensation of gumminess, then blurs of light impinging on her optic nerve: blood from a cut on her forehead had flowed into her eye socket. She wiped it out with the back of her hand and blinked the eye clear.

Around her the ruins of her light tank pinged and hissed and creaked as stresses relieved themselves and heat overloads equalized. *"Galaxy Commander,"* Wyndham's voice said in her ringing ears. *"I am afraid I am pinned and my right leg broken."*

It surprised her he had survived. That had played no part in her plan, one way or another. She did feel brief satisfaction that he had lived: he had proven himself most useful indeed.

"Your performance makes Turkina proud," she said. "Now your task is done."

"Aff."

She hit the button to open the hatch over her head. Nothing happened. She scowled in frustrated fury: it was simply *not acceptable* that she be trapped in her broken vehicle at the very moment of her triumph.

She reached up and yanked the manual release. It resisted, causing her to fear the frame had buckled. She punched out of her safety harness, took the lever in both hands and, doubling in her seat, braced both boots against the compartment overhead for leverage. She pulled with all the strength of her muscles and powerful prosthetics.

Grudgingly the lever gave. Then it popped open. Dust-laden, sun-heated air streamed in as the hatch seal broke, seeming sweet and cool compared to the oven the cockpit had become. So focused had Malvina been on the battle that she had scarcely noticed the stinging heat and choking smoke until now.

She pushed the hatch full open and scrambled out. Movement soothed her aching muscles, as it usually did. A fresh surge of adrenaline did the rest, rushing like a tidal bore through her veins as she wriggled beneath the smoldering wreckage of the SRM turret and slid to the ground.

Swaying, she put a hand to her tank's steel flank to steady herself. After a few heartbeats she smelled burning as the synthetic palm of her glove melted on the hot armor. By now she no longer needed the support. She took her hand away.

The enemy tank's cockpit had been blown open. The Horseman driver's whole right side was blood. Shining scarlet in the sun, it streamed from a metal splinter driven into his eye socket and from a shoulder crushed to pulp and white chunks. Still he struggled in his harness, left hand clawing at his sidearm in its holster beneath the same armpit. A blue eye glared at her with almost insane fury.

Walking forward she drew her own sidearm, pushed her arm out to full extension and shot him through his good eye. His head jerked back, driven by a jet of organic steam, then lolled to the side.

She holstered her laser. The casual killing was already forgotten. The Hell's Horses machine's top hatch lay open. A bloodstained hand moved about it like a blind spider. Malvina scrambled up, nimble as a monkey, disregarding how the burning-hot wreck scorched her skin where it came in contact through her uniform.

Fletcher's head, with its shaven sides and smoldering topknot, emerged from darkness. Grabbing his scalp lock, Malvina helped haul the much larger warrior out onto the top deck. He snarled something inarticulate. She lifted her foot and shoved him off the vehicle.

Red flames began to wave out the open hatch like tiny tentacles.

Malvina slid down the Scimitar's flank. Her boot soles crunched on sand.

Fletcher faced her, feet beneath him, legs coiled. It pleased her to see he was resilient, as befit a high-ranking Clan warrior and *ristar*. It also pleased her that, bloody, bruised and scorched though he was, he appeared largely intact and fully functional.

Her vision dimmed. The temperature dropped around

her, almost imperceptibly. It took her a moment to realize a shadow had fallen across her and her enemy. She looked up in annoyance to see the Herrmanns blimp occulting the sun. She scowled, promising herself to stand the fat, useless German against the wall of his own mansion if his airship's blunderings made it difficult for the other media to get good shots of what came next.

Fletcher reached behind his right shoulder. His curved-bladed sword slid free with a metallic slither, a ringing Malvina heard beneath the crackle of the flames from his tank.

"You have not won yet despite your coward's trick, Malvina Hazen," he said.

He screamed with fury and lunged at her, slashing down diagonally from right to left.

She ducked beneath the stroke. Then she sprang at him. Her battleknife flashed in the sunlight as she passed.

He spun, clapping a hand to the side of his neck. He looked at his palm. His eyes narrowed at a bright smear of red on his scorched glove.

"Such a mosquito sting will do you no good," he said. "You must do better."

"I think not," she said. She stood facing him with her arms at her sides, apparently relaxed. "Your every step I have controlled, from the moment you began your *batchall*. You are brave, Tristan Fletcher. But you are a fool. And brave fools are but culls, unworthy of the memory of Kerensky."

His face darkened, then went white. "What?" he screamed. "You dare—?"

He stopped. His eyes flew wide before he could ask *what* she might dare. A feather of pink mist, scarcely visible in the sunlight, sprouted from the right side of his muscular brown neck.

"My cut went through your skin and halfway through the wall of your carotid artery, Tristan Fletcher. When I taunted you, your blood pressure soared. It was enough to force the tiniest of ruptures."

He put his hand back to his neck. This time red sprayed it like paint from an aerosol can. He reeled.

"I first learned of that cut from a Kuritan samurai holovid we watched in the crèche, my brother and I. At the time I failed to realize it was merely entertainment, not meant to be real. So when I came into my first rank as Star commander I began to practice on prisoners.

"At first I had them immobilized. These were rebel laborers, and the means of their disposal was of no account. After many, many tries I found the cut could be made—for I learned to do it."

He took a halting pace toward her, raising his yataghan.

"Then I began using it on opponents able to move. I was fair: if they managed to defeat me they would win their freedom. None did.

"After more than thirty fell to my blade in such duels, I learned to make that cut consistently against a mobile opponent. You are the first to feel it in true combat.

"And now the strength drains from your body and limbs. Your eyes grow dim. And *now*—"

She stepped quickly forward. He tried to lift his sword arm. It rose but a centimeter, slowly, then drooped. The hilt slipped from his limp fingers. The blade bit with a crunch into the sand by his feet.

She caught him behind the head with both hands and pulled his face toward hers, ignoring the dwindling arterial spray that drenched her flesh hand in his life's hot blood. Her lips crushed his. His brown eyes stared as her tongue probed deep into his mouth.

Then she broke away. Stepped back. Her mouth was a brilliant crimson smear.

"—I drink your soul."

He toppled dead at her feet.

She turned and raised bloody arms to the sky, and to the watching cameras, and pealed forth a mighty falcon scream of triumph.

4

Tshombe, Mkuranga
Province of New Katanga
Jade Falcon Occupation Zone
3 August 3135

"I apologize, my lord," the functionary said nervously. She was a small woman, pinch-faced, with pale hair pulled back in a painful-looking bun, wearing the coverall of a Jade Falcon laborer. Her garment's russet color and her badges, however, identified her as a Spheroid in service to the occupying Clan. Her half-defiant, half-apologetic manner likewise marked her to the man she addressed. As did her use of an honorific, which few true Clanners would have bothered with. "The border with the Lyran Commonwealth is closed. Your vessel must turn back."

Heinz-Otto María Manoel de Soares zu Mannstein, *Markgraf* von Texeira, nodded his ponderous head. He was a big, stout man in his fifties, with a snappy cream-and-brown uniform immaculately tailored to his expansive frame and a short maroon cape about his wide shoulders. He leaned on a thick cane of Santa Marta blackthorn that had a great gleaming silver ram's head for a crown.

"I understand, Laborer Katya," he said, reading her tag. "But I am accredited to Khan Jana Pryde on Sudeten as an official emissary from the archon. My duty remains to get to Sudeten as expeditiously as possible. Can you provide me transport within the occupation zone?"

It was a bit unkind, and he instantly chided himself: *she* could do nothing at all without consulting a Clan superior, who might or might not deign to comprehend the issue and might in fact decide to punish her for troubling him. Or her: Clanners, he knew from a lifelong experience, were equal opportunity bastards.

Bullying a subordinate is unworthy of a merchant prince, he told himself sternly, *much less a member of the Lyran Diplomatic Corps.* He thought thoughts about his long-time acquaintance, the Archon Melissa Steiner, which, had they been spoken aloud, might have been construed by some as seditious. *I should never have let her bully me into taking this* verdammte *assignment.*

He smiled at the woman, hoping to draw the sting from his ill-chosen words. Instead, she shrank from him. Racial and ethnic hatred were alive and well, and stalking the Inner Sphere, but seldom based on the color of one's skin. Still, she was tiny and pale, and he was enormous and very, very black. The smile he showed her was full of great big teeth, almost blue-white against his skin's darkness, and his eyes were a vivid blue. They customarily held a merry expression, which he had practiced for hours in a mirror in his youth. In fact he usually *was* merry. Usually.

But he'd lost two days already wading through the impenetrable swamps of Clan Jade Falcon's bureaucracy on Mkuranga. It would have tried the patience of Saint Theresa. Although Saint Theresa, come to think of it, hadn't actually *been* patient, if he remembered his lives of the saints correctly. It depended on which one, perhaps.

"I—I—I," the woman in the russet jumpsuit said.

But von Texeira was back in charge of himself now. He increased his smile's candlepower, which if it did not visibly reassure the woman at least helped get him in the proper state of mind. "Forgive me," he said. She blinked. *Those* weren't words you heard very often from Clanners like her world's rulers. "I know that my difficulties are not your fault. Nor do I wish to make them your problem."

They were in the offices of what once had been, he suspected, a school for junior pupils. Students were now probably educated in a former factory, while what the factory had made was now produced in an erstwhile ice-skating rink. The Jade Falcons had, as always, disposed their military assets with skill and obsessive precision according to their doctrines (which in the real world were not always the most effective, thank the saints, or otherwise everyone would be born out of an Erlenmeyer flask and strut around saying *quiaff* and *quineg* all the time and never, ever, using contractions). In all else they might as well have been birds, in truth: crows or pigeons, indiscriminate and sloppy in their roosting.

"Why don't you call your superior and say that I insist on seeing him or her," he told the frightened functionary. "If it would help to imply that I threatened you, please feel free." And he smiled as nonthreateningly as he could.

It must have worked. She brushed at a stray wisp of straw-colored hair and smiled tentatively. He had given her an out: a Clan warrior would expect nothing but timidity from a mere laborer, especially one who still belonged ethnically to the Inner Sphere. As did many, especially on the fringes of the occupation zone, despite decades of attempting to assimilate subject populations into the all-encompassing Clan way.

Trust the feisty, bucket-headed Falcons to spurn the course Clan Ghost Bear had taken—of mutual assimilation, both cultures merging into a reasonably functional whole, he thought. Turkina's brood preferred to play the role of occupiers, decade after decade, trying to ram their way down their Spheroid subjects' throats. And always puzzled by their indifferent success in doing so.

Turning away, the laborer woman spoke softly into a communicator.

"You walk with a limp," MechWarrior Billy said. "You are a wounded warrior?"

Von Texeira smiled broadly. *MechWarrior Billy?* he was thinking. *Do these people breed for a tin ear for language, along with superhuman strength and reflexes?*

"Ah, no," he said, "nothing so heroic. I lost my right leg"—
he slapped himself on the thigh, which produced an impressive synthetic clack even through his uniform trousers—"in an
unfortunate encounter with a spaceport front-end loader. I
have spent my life as a merchant, you see."

MechWarrior Billy didn't bother to conceal his sneer. He
had not invited his guest to sit down. Then again, his narrow rump occupied the only chair in the small office, posi-
tioned behind a metal desk painted an unattractive olive
drab.

"I see," he said, as if, like an incontinent spaniel, von
Texeira had just deposited something on the thin, puke-
colored carpet. Billy was tall and lean, with close-cropped
blond hair and features that looked as if they'd been flayed
from a normal man's face and stretched over an adze. "You
are Lyran, *quiaff*?"

Von Texeira beamed all over his big face. "Of course,"
he said. Since he couldn't do a music-hall German accent—
he *was* speaking German—he affected his best Hayseed
Parvenu, like a Nova Suevian pig farmer whose father had
won the lottery. The Jade Falcon, of course, spoke perfect
German, having been raised to it along with the usual Clan
English. Except he made it even more soulless and mechanical than it was supposed to sound. *It's uncanny,* von Texeira thought. "We're all merchants at heart, you know. Not
great warriors like the Clans."

MechWarrior Billy nodded with solemnity as preposter-
ous as his name.

"You are a spy?" he asked.

For half a second the smile on von Texeira's big face
froze in place. Given his years of experience in negotiations
with heads of state and boardrooms, half a second was a
very long time.

Then his laugh boomed out. "I am a member of the
Lyran Diplomatic Corps!" he declared with a renewed
smile.

"Whose members are notoriously spies."

Von Texeira shrugged. "All diplomats are spies. At least
we are honest about it."

The MechWarrior said nothing to that.

"I carry accreditation to your khan, Jana Pryde, on Sude-ten," von Texeira said, bending ponderously forward, dropping a plastic datachip on the metal desktop and pushing it forward with a broad fingertip. "Unfortunately, I find myself unable to get to the planet."

The MechWarrior looked at him. "What has that to do with me?" He wasn't being arrogant or sarcastic, von Texeira knew. He honestly didn't understand.

"If my ship cannot cross the frontier," von Texeira said, "then I must request transport aboard a Jade Falcon vessel."

"That is impossible."

It was so impossible the Falcon neglected to be snotty about it, just as if the Spheroid diplomat had suggested he put the sun in his jumpsuit pocket.

Von Texeira smiled wider. "Nothing is impossible, my friend. All it takes is the requisite will."

MechWarrior Billy frowned. It was a pensive frown, von Texeira was pleased to see, and not an angry one. "There is much to what you say," the MechWarrior said.

Von Texeira reached into his tunic. The Jade Falcon didn't flinch, but his eyes narrowed. A big hand came out with a square-sectioned bottle. "Scots whiskey," von Texeira said. "Glengarry Black Label. Accept it with my compliments."

"Is this a bribe?"

"Of course not. It would be dishonorable to offer you a bribe. I would never dishonor a brave Clan warrior. You would most certainly kill me. Consider it, rather, a freewill token of my esteem."

Billy accepted it with a scarred hand and examined it carefully. "Difficult to come by now."

"Yes," von Texeira said, "since your Clanswoman Malvina Hazen caught Glengarry in her talons."

His haughty Jade Falcon self-control unable to keep a look of regret from his aquiline features, the MechWarrior thrust the bottle back at von Texeira. "I cannot accept this. I cannot help you."

"It wasn't a bribe, remember? It's yours regardless."

Billy set it back on the desktop. "A state of tension exists between the Commonwealth and Clan Jade Falcon," he said. "This is why the border is sealed."

"I'm well aware of that, MechWarrior." The *desant* led by the siblings Hazen and Galaxy Commander Beckett Malthus had panicked, and angered, the whole Commonwealth by raiding Porrima and brutally conquering Chaffee.

"It is forbidden for Jade Falcon vessels to transport outsiders."

"Even one with a safe-passage from Khan Jana Pryde herself?"

"There are no exceptions."

"It has taken me three days to find you, friend Jade Falcon," von Texeira said. Billy's eyes widened; von Texeira was reasonably sure no one had ever called him that before. "With great respect, I ask: is there anyone on Mkuranga who can grant me this permission?"

"There is not."

Von Texeira nodded briskly. It wasn't the Clan way to lie, and the Jade Falcons prided themselves on being the *ne plus ultra* of all Clanners. He didn't take that to mean they *wouldn't* lie. They were human, despite the lengths to which they went to conceal the fact. But they were no bloody good at lying.

And one had to be very good at lying indeed to slip one past Heinz-Otto von Texeira. He knew that without the least scrap of doubt or vanity.

"Travel across the Jade Falcon Occupation Zone," the MechWarrior said, a bit ponderously, as if uncertain whether he was speaking out of turn, "is not proscribed."

"In other words, if I find my own transport, I won't be hindered?"

"Precisely."

He nodded. "I thank you, MechWarrior Billy. May you soon win your Bloodname."

The warrior stood. He was almost as tall as the diplomat. Which made him tall indeed. "I have something I wish to say," he said. "I am Jade Falcon. I am a Crusader. I believe in the vision of Kerensky and our duty as Clans to bring order and peace to the Inner Sphere.

"But what is being done in our name in The Republic—this so-called 'Mongol doctrine,' the deliberate devastation of your world of Chaffee, the use of chemical agents—" He shook his narrow head. "It is dishonor."

"Do you really think so?" the female elemental asked. She had a cap of curly, dark blond hair, tanned skin, green eyes. She was a dainty 215 centimeters or so tall.

"Absolutely," said Rorion Klimt. They stood on the steps of the occupation headquarters speaking English. The Clanners here in occupied Steinerspace tended to speak flawless German from childhood, and so did he. Whereas he spoke English, the Clan lingua franca, with what most Anglophone women considered a charming Brazilian Portuguese accent.

When it served his purposes, anyway.

"The somewhat somber green of your tank top accentuates the emerald green of your eyes." *Among other things.* "It's really most fetching."

He was a man of average height for a Spheroid, or even below, which meant he was dwarfed by the off-duty elemental wearing shapeless tan cargo pants. He had dark olive skin, a narrow head with slanted eyes, and cheekbones and a forehead rendered expansive by the hasty retreat his dark brown hair was beating to either side of a thin salient. He had about him the easy, wiry, slightly feral grace of an alley cat. Closely tailored to his lithe form, even the grayish-greenish Steiner *Feldgrau* uniform trimmed with forest green looked natty. His chauffeur's cap rested on the seat of the armored limousine parked at the curb in front of the drab brownstone.

The elemental frowned. "I never really thought of it that way." It was hot out on the street of the capital of New Katanga, and humid. Whereas his keen features were dry, her face, which really was quite pretty in its way, shone with sweat. Just as he and his boss looked right at home among the sparse street traffic of dark-skinned local inhabitants, both felt perfectly at home in the climate. The Clanners, predominantly though not exclusively of Northern

European ancestry, suffered here. They preferred colder worlds—more suitable to their chilled-glass-decanted souls, he felt.

"You simply don't understand what a beautiful woman you are."

"We are not encouraged to think in such terms," she said. "Do you really think so?"

He nodded. "Has no one ever said that to you before?"

"No."

"Truly?" He shook his vulpine head. "A monstrous shame. Is not physical beauty, after all, both a product of a good bloodline and disciplined cultivation and maintenance, like combat prowess? I should think your fellow Clansmen would honor it."

She pursed out her lips in a little moue, considering. It made her look as adorable as a person over two meters tall *could* look. *Don't let your prejudices gull you*, Rorion reminded himself sharply: it was easy to dismiss Clanners as dim by reason of their ponderous and clunky speech, like elemental battlearmor with poorly maintained bearings, and especially easy to disregard their giant gene-engineered power infantry precisely because of their size. Still, he found himself suspecting that elemental Elaine was not the sharpest polycarbide cutter in Turkina's toolroom.

"There may be something to what you say," she said pensively.

"Of course there is, my sweet." Then, glancing around, he said, "But I see my boss approaching. I fear I will have to let you go about your business, dear child."

She smiled. "Very well, Ho-ree-*own*," she said, carefully pronouncing the name the way he had taught her.

"*Tschau*, baby."

His eyes followed her admiringly as she swung down the street. A moment later Heinz-Otto von Texeira came gimping with surprising alacrity, given his prosthetic and cane, down the broad steps between the cement lions weathered into pug dogs.

The diplomat's gaze followed his chauffeur's. "You're incorrigible, Rorion," he said.

He spoke Brazilian Portuguese, one of two native languages they shared. The odds of any Clansman or woman understanding Portuguese approximated the odds of von Texeira's being hit by a meteorite as he stood here on the sidewalk, which was heaved and cracked by the roots of Mkuranga's overly-energetic flora. Abstract interest in languages was a Clan preoccupation to about the same extent as knitting and dancing cotillion.

Rorion flashed his brilliant smile. "My family has been incorrigible for generations," he said. "Usually in service to yours, Heinz-Otto."

"It's a partnership that works," his superior acknowledged with a mammoth shrug. "I envy you the role, sometimes: you get to let yourselves be *seen* to be scoundrels."

"I don't know," said Rorion. "Remember your cousin Waldemar."

"I try not to. Take me back to the consulate. We can cool off and consider our options."

Von Texeira breathed a sigh of relief as his broad behind came to rest on the limo's broad, cream-colored leather rear seat, taking his not inconsiderable weight off foot and stump. The machine was a Fury armored limousine provided by the Lyran consulate. With six big, independently powered wheels, armor plate and a remote-controlled pop-up turret containing two Browning-Sperry machine guns (cleverly concealed in the extra-thick roof of the passenger compartment) it was for all intents and purposes a ten-ton light combat car. While assiduously trying to stamp out private ownership even of small arms—a hallmark of tyranny, to von Texeira's mind—the quirky Clan sense of honor permitted official representatives of the Great Houses and The Republic wide leeway in possessing combat equipment, up to and including BattleMechs. Von Texeira suspected it was precisely *because* any of these representatives might turn into full-blown combatants at any time, given the way Devlin Stone's peace was dissolving.

Rorion turned up the air conditioning. Similar though Tshombe's climate was to their homeworld of Recife's, it didn't mean either man *enjoyed* the sticky heat.

Cargo and utility vehicles made up the bulk of traffic. Pedestrians thronged the sidewalks. Clan Jade Falcon discouraged private vehicles almost as vigorously as they did firearms. The foot traffic walked rapidly; their masters discouraged dawdling by Clan laborers and locals alike. They kept their gazes down, lest they be deemed to challenge some passing warrior, which would have swift, and swiftly fatal, results.

As if by magic the traffic thinned. Between the tall façades of Tshombe's business district, faced with local limestone and glowing almost blue in the sunlight, a BattleMech came striding. It was a *Phoenix Hawk IIc*, the jutting beak shape of its cockpit and the flamboyance of the folded airfoil wings fastened to its back-mounted jump jets marking it unmistakably as the new Falcon mark of the old Steel Viper standby. A Point of elementals in the squat power-armor suits the Inner Sphere forces initially nicknamed "toads" tramped beside its taloned feet.

As they passed, the eighty-ton 'Mech ostentatiously turned its head as if scrutinizing them. Von Texeira felt a certain tightening of his scrotum, knowing that the 'Mech mounted a heavy minigun in its head. It made him laugh aloud.

"I love dealing with the Clans," he declared enthusiastically as BattleMech and retinue clanked past, causing vibrations that could be plainly felt even through the limo's luxurious suspension. "It's like walking in a cage full of wild beasts. Bracing!"

"If you say so," Rorion said sourly.

His master shrugged. "It's an acquired taste."

"Or not," Rorion said. "I grew up hearing stories about *your* exploits growing up."

Von Texeira chuckled again. He glanced back over his shoulder at the rear of the retreating *Phoenix Hawk*.

"I always find those wings absurd. Yet they're nothing compared to the excesses to be found on their shiny new assault-class *Shrikes*. It seems the Falcons have begun going out of their way to make their new-issue 'Mechs look ludicrous." He frowned. "There's something to that, but I can't put a finger on it."

"They're Clanners," his chauffeur said from the front, as if that explained all.

"Ah, but the Clanners seldom do anything without reason. Not necessarily *reasonable* reasons. But reasons nonetheless."

"I take it your lordship had no luck?"

"Again." Von Texeira sighed.

"Small surprise."

The consulate was little help. In von Texeira's experience, which was vast, Inner Sphere consuls to Clan-occupied worlds tended to fall into two categories: stressed to rolling-eyed near madness, like a housecat in a roomful of attack dogs, or into a state of oblivious denial, usually with considerable chemical insulation. The Honorable Ritt Hormauer, the archon's official representative on her former holding of Mkuranga, fell into the latter category. His self-medication of choice was a more-than-acceptable native rum, though, and at least he wasn't selfish about sharing.

"Whom do we ask now?" Rorion asked.

Von Texeira shrugged massively. "Not the Falcons. Such sticklers for rules they are, they might as well be Germans."

"Even though their khan herself requested we send an envoy?"

"Just so."

"Absurd."

"Clan Warriors lack interest in anything that doesn't have to do with breaking things and killing people," the older man said. "You know that."

"Still. They've been administering captive populations and dealing with the Inner Sphere for the better part of a century. You'd think even they would figure out how to do it half right."

"We're from Recife, Rorion. Since when do we expect efficiency?"

"Since we left our homeworld and landed somewhere else in Steinerspace, Margrave?"

"Point taken."

Von Texeira sighed gustily. Then he drew in a deep abdominal breath to soothe himself, momentarily blanking his mind of conscious thought.

His aide left him little time to luxuriate in meditation. "What will *o senhor* do now?" Rorion asked.

Von Texeira glanced out the window. On a broad plaza of faintly pink brick a number of native workers in pale jumpsuits were engaging in group calisthenics under the eye of a minor scientist-caste overseer with a pinched expression and a notecomp. Their motions lacked the customary Clan crispness, not to mention any hint of enthusiasm. Their supervisor would never report their lack of zeal, von Texeira knew: to do so would reflect negatively on her own efficiency rating.

He smiled. The Clanners wore their weaknesses on their sleeves, moreso because few of them would admit their weaknesses existed. They could be almost laughably easy to manipulate. Especially for a manipulator as masterful as Heinz-Otto von Texeira, Lyran merchant prince and chief executive officer (currently on indefinite sabbatical) of Recife Spice and Liquors.

On the other hand, the least misstep in dealing with Clanners meant sudden death. *That* was what made it a game.

"When we get back, have His Excellency's excellent bartender make me up a nice, cold drink," he commanded. "Which I will sip and enjoy while you, as usual, do the hard work."

"Finding a smuggler to take us to Sudeten?"

He leaned forward to clap his driver on the shoulder with a beefy hand. "*Aber natürlich*, Rorion. What else?"

5

"Here's the horsie," Cynthy said, making the small toy rock in her hand across the cracked pale paving stones, "riding to the castle." Burton Bear watched with his bright button eyes, sprawled at his plush-toy ease against the battlement of an actual castle in the afternoon light slanting over the forest-crowded hills outside New London. His mistress wore a blue-and-white dress, with a white bow in her blond hair.

"Why does she do that?" Malvina said. "Clearly, there is no horse. Is she delusional?"

"It is called 'play,' " said Malthus with some asperity.

"So that is what that means," Malvina said. "It appears to give her pleasure."

Frowning, Galaxy Commander Beckett Malthus made himself look away. He was deeply shocked at Malvina's indulgence of the most decadent kind of Spheroid child-worship. That in itself disturbed him: *I hoped I had purged myself of Clan prejudices, through a lifetime of effort.*

Part of being a puppet master, he had long since determined, lay in making sure one's own limbs were devoid of strings.

Galaxy Commander Malvina Hazen stood perched on a crenellation on one leg, her natural one. Her trim body was arched back, her head drawn up and back with her hair falling unbound down her slender neck. With her natural hand she grasped the ankle of her prosthetic leg, which was raised behind her, bent to ninety degrees. The shiny hard blackness of her two prosthetic limbs made a striking contrast to her own white skin, all the more since she was stark naked.

The juxtaposition of white and black, the curvilinear shape his fellow Galaxy commander described against Skye's perpetually cloudy sky, put Bec irresistibly in mind of the *Taijitu*, the symbol of yin and yang so beloved among the Capellans and the Combine. Though he was far from the scholar she was, and that her brother had been, Bec knew it symbolized cosmic balance.

Is it irony? he wondered. *If not, what does she balance against?*

He shook off the thoughts. Such speculations were utterly alien to most Clanners, and strange even for him.

"Really, Malvina," he said, "this is not wise, *quineg*?"

"Wisdom plays even less of a role in my behavior than in that of most Jade Falcons, Beckett Malthus," she said without looking at him. Her eyes were closed.

"I mean displaying yourself so on the rampart."

"By which you mean—?"

"Naked, for one thing."

"Has that ever meant much to a Clanner, *quineg*?"

"Neg," he said, scowling. "It might, however, excite unfortunate passions on the part of the residents of Skye who do harbor nudity taboos."

She opened her mouth.

"Perhaps more important," he said, driving home the point that he was perhaps the one man in human space who dared to interrupt her, "silhouetting yourself against the skyline like this makes you an ideal target to a sniper, your state of dress notwithstanding."

She laughed. If you didn't know her, it sounded carefree, almost girlish.

"In either case," she said, "the response is the same: if the Spheroids act on such foolish impulses, I will teach them a sharp lesson."

Malthus set his heavy face. While Skye's defenders had conceded defeat and requested—and been granted—the right of hegira, or unhindered withdrawal, certain diehards left behind on the planet had not been so willing to admit the obvious. A combination of Seventh Skye Militia laggards and civilians had tried to make a stand in the planetary governor's palace.

A long-range barrage of Arrow IV missiles had rocked the palace, though it did little damage to the palace's thick stressed-cement walls. Then, while rocket-firing Skadi VTOLs provided close air support, Malvina had led an assault in her *Shrike*, "Black Rose," blasting the great gates to smoking ruin with her retrofitted PPCs and kicking them aside. Dismounting in the courtyard she had lead elementals in full battlearmor and conventional infantry in storming the palace, fighting with machine pistol and grenades.

Two dozen survivors had been crucified on great Xs welded from steel girders outside the palace.

That had been her only act of brutality after the conquest of Skye. And even that act, lurid as it might have been, was not truly excessive by the standards of Clan response to defiance, especially after hegira. Indeed, no Clan, or Great House for that matter, was known for its forbearance in the face of an outright challenge to its authority, even the moderately bloodshed-averse Lyrans.

The world's subsequent pacification, and reprisals for resistance, went forward with no more than the customary Clan heavy-handedness. Perhaps, as Malvina had confessed to Star Colonel Noritomo Helmer, she had realized that her brother's approach to conquest and the treatment of conquered peoples was not altogether wrong.

Perhaps.

Malvina released her ankle. Slowly she straightened her leg behind her, extending her arms in front of her for balance. Then she lowered it, bending the knee, bringing it forward. As soon as she could do so she extended the leg again, and raised it, slowly, until her pointed toes aimed directly skyward. It had to be agonizing for her, even after the strengthening resulting from months of the fanatical rehab routine she had imposed upon herself. Yet except for a tightening of the skin around her mouth and eyes, and the beads of sweat appearing at her hairline, she showed no trace of strain. Malthus only saw the signs because he knew to look for them, and looked closely.

She lowered her leg again deliberately. When both feet rested on the stone she hopped down to the terrace and plucked a white linen robe off a nearby crenellation. The child looked up and smiled at her as Malvina wrapped the robe about herself. Malvina smiled back, and the little girl returned to playing with her toys.

Malvina walked toward Malthus, cinching the robe with a belt of the same fabric. The marble flagstones beneath her soles still showed scorch marks from the bombardment. Neglect had allowed aggressive native creeper vines to clamber like a storming party over the battlement; they extended thin tendrils across the pavement, ending in flat five-leaved sprays of dark green that clung to the white stone like drowning men's fingers.

"If you came here to question my judgment," she said, "I doubt it was because of the way I choose to conduct my balancing exercises."

"I did not come to criticize you at all, Malvina," he said. "There are matters I would discuss."

She shrugged. "Discuss them."

He flicked his murky green eyes toward the child. "What I have to say is best said in private, Galaxy Commander."

Malvina glared. "She is a child."

"Little pitchers have big ears, if I recall the Spheroid epigram correctly."

"The child is mine. She stays. Subject closed."

Bec Malthus blew a long sigh out his broad nose. He looked off across the terrace to where a party of locals scrubbed at more blast stains on the paving under the disgruntled eye of a convalescing infantry warrior. Likely they were too far away to hear anything.

"Very well," he said. "Let me ask you something, Malvina: do you expect Khan Jana Pryde ever to send the Jade Falcon touman to exploit our conquests here in the Inner Sphere?"

She looked at him, her pale blue eyes narrowed to slits. "Say on."

"Something has become very clear to me. We succeeded, you, your brother and myself. We won a victory—many victories—worthy not just of inclusion but of many lines in the Clan Jade Falcon Remembrance.

"And yet we are ignored. No more than a few ritual words of congratulations have we had from Khan Jana Pryde since taking Skye. Requests for resupply and reinforcement go essentially unanswered. The dribs and drabs of replacements we receive—well, you have seen them. *Dezgra* MechWarriors. *Solahma*. Malcontents and incompetents who, with pitched battles so rare back in the occupation zone, their commanders have few other means of getting rid of. She sends us *culls*, Malvina!"

Malvina nodded. Her expression had grown relaxed but watchful. "I noticed as much, Bec Malthus."

His slow nod mirrored hers. "I have long resisted the obvious conclusion," he said, his voice rendered grave by the fact that his square chin with its gray beard rested against the gray tunic trimmed with maroon that he wore across his broad chest. "That the khan never *intended* to send the *touman* into the Inner Sphere, regardless of the outcome of our *desant*. Instead it was a way to bleed off pressure—to appease sons and daughters of Turkina who chafed beneath Devlin Stone's enforced peace."

Malvina laughed again. "Do not try to tell me that is all you have concluded," she said. "Come now, admit it: in the eyes of our beloved khan, it is *we* who are the culls. You, me, even my noble brother. Aleks and I posed threats to her, with our *ristar* popularity and impeccably traditionalist credentials. And you"—he stood unmoving as she paced around behind him as if appraising him for purchase—"you were a formerly prized asset whom she had come to regard as a liability. *Quiaff?*"

He turned to face her. His broad, high forehead creased in a frown. *"Aff,"* he said.

Once again I am reminded, he told himself, *under no circumstances to underestimate this creature. Whatever she may be.*

"We could be broken for bloodfoul for this conversation, Beckett Malthus," she said lightly.

The big man rocked back on his heels. "Bloodfoul" was a terrible word. A terrible thing. It sprang from a myth—Malthus was fairly sure it was no more—that during the wars that led to the Exodus scientists had created a terrible pathogen, a retrovirus capable of degrading its victim's very genes. This degeneration was alleged to be both heritable and highly infectious. Whatever the truth, the word had come among the Clans to mean *treason, heresy, blasphemy* rolled into one. It signified beliefs and actions so obscene that they tainted the guilty party's DNA, so unnaturally virulent they could contaminate all those who came in contact with them. The word also meant the perpetrator of such an ultimate crime.

It could, literally, not be spoken lightly by a Clanner.

"I am well aware of the risks," Malthus said at length. He forbore pointing out that those risks underlay his reluctance to speak openly before the Inner Sphere child. The girl, amazingly enough, seemed to have grown quite attached to Malvina. But who knew what she might carelessly babble, to whose ears? Khan Jana Pryde had made the Jade Falcon Watch a reasonably efficient secret police.

He had helped.

"Your caution is well-known," she said softly. He stiffened. "I take it, therefore, that you desire me to derive the only possible conclusion."

"What would that be, Malvina Hazen?"

"It is time that the Eye of the Falcon looked again upon Turkina's eyrie."

He stood, holding a breath half-taken.

"You think the time has come for me to return to Sudeten," she said. Smiling, she reached up and patted his cheek.

"You helped one khan of Clan Jade Falcon to her khanship. Perhaps the time approaches for you to do the same for a second, *quiaff?*"

"I know you, Heinz-Otto von Texeira," she said.

"Quiaff?" he asked. But she did know his full given name.

The long, scarred face laughed silently. *"Aff,"* Master Merchant Senna Rodríguez said. "Most definitely, *aff*. As trading partner and rival. You have quite the reputation, *Markgraf*."

They spoke English. He sat watching her through the smoke-streaked gloom. He kept his face as impassive as years of practice, and a will of endosteel, could make it.

"My man didn't tell you?"

She shook her head. Then she leaned forward with her forearms on the knife-scarred tabletop. "I do not know everything that happens in human space," she said. "Not personally. But in the fullness of time, Clan Sea Fox does."

It was a standard spaceport dive called the German East. Tucked among warehouses in a quick-fab plascrete half cylinder, it vibrated to thunderous harmonics each time a DropShip landed or took off. It was of course gloomy and smoky, otherwise it would have lacked credibility among its clientele, who liked to smoke as much as they liked semi-anonymity. The walls were covered with blurred holopics of nude men, nude women and sporting teams.

Senna drew on her long black cheroot and added her own blue-gray contribution to the pervasive smoke. "The CEO of Recife Spice and Liquors." She pronounced his homeworld's name as a native might, Portuguese-fashion: "Heh-*see*-fee." She raised an eyebrow above a long, slanted blue eye. "You're a long way from the boardroom, Herr Chief Executive."

The contraction didn't surprise him. The Sea Foxes were oddities among the Clans. But they were Clan enough to revel in it rather than try to hide or deny it. Unlike most Clanners, though, they were skilled in dissimulation, a fact he forced himself to keep at the front of his awareness.

He shrugged. "I am on sabbatical," he said, "at the personal request of Archon Melissa herself." It was even true.

"You're the emissary Jana Pryde requested, then."

"Yes. So you *do* know everything."

He laughed to show it was a joke. She smiled. She had a long face, worn and weathered and far from pretty. Yet he, who had seen a great many pretty faces, found it easy to look upon.

"Not quite," she said. "It's no secret that the green bird khan is nervous about the liberties her expeditionary force took with two of the archon's worlds. Especially gassing Chaffee. With The Republic enraged and Clan Wolf poised on the frontier looking for a chance to pounce on their old rivals, the last thing she needs is major retribution from House Steiner. Especially since her little scheme to remove a few painful thorns from her claw may be turning out to have had the effect of transferring them to a more tender portion of her anatomy."

Von Texeira stared at her a moment. Then he put back his great head and laughed. "I grow to like you, Master Merchant."

"That may or may not prove wise," she said. "So the Falcons deny you transport?"

"That, at least, requires no omniscience. I'm here, after all."

"Accommodations in my ship would seem scarcely adequate to a leading merchant prince of the Lyran Commonwealth."

"Luxury liners currently don't travel to the capital of the Jade Falcon Occupation Zone." He smiled and laid his elbows on the table. "You may not believe this, Master Merchant, but this is not the first time I've had to seek . . . alternative means of transport into Clan territory. Although I must admit it is the first time I *didn't* have to worry about evading official notice."

"Indeed. You want a lift to Sudeten?"

"As you say—indeed."

She flipped the silver-blond scalp lock that hung down one side of her otherwise smooth-shaven head. "It'll cost you."

He held up a blunt forefinger. "Please note that while

they do nothing to aid my passage into the Zone, they have not forbidden it. I do carry a safe-passage from the khan herself."

"Which, if you run into adherents of Malvina Hazen's new Mongol philosophy, may or may not be worth a discarded jerky wrapper."

"True enough."

"And, of course," she continued, "Turkina has not gone out of her way to make Sudeten an appealing vacation destination for little Foxes." It was no secret either: the least orthodox of Clans and the most happily fanatical of Clan traditionalists did not make a comfortable combination.

Heinz-Otto von Texeira sighed. As a master negotiator, he knew far too well just what she had him by.

"It'll cost me," he agreed.

Boot heels rapping on floors of dark green marble shined to a mirror finish, Star Colonel Noritomo Helmer held his head high as he strode the halls of the erstwhile planetary governor's palace. *With Malvina Hazen I never know,* he thought with a certain wry amusement, *whether I go to receive accolades, or death.*

MechWarriors wearing holstered sidearms escorted him. He recognized three as among the most fanatic of Malvina's new Mongol adherents. One was a Star captain from her brother Aleks' old Zeta Galaxy, Shar Roshak. He found it disturbing that a Bloodname from Aleksandr Hazen's former command should join openly with Malvina.

They came into an echoing space, with soaring buttresses of white stone dappled in afternoon sunlight filtering down through skylights high overhead. At the far side of the circular floor Malvina stood near the gallery that ran around it, conversing with half a dozen officers. The somber form of Beckett Malthus loomed nearby, a step behind Malvina, as if to impose his presence on the discussion without directly participating.

And there you have the Crow in a nutshell, Noritomo thought. For once Malvina's pet, the orphaned child from the southern half of Skye's lone landmass, was absent. That relieved him. The unnatural quality of the relationship disturbed him in ways even he could not pin to a board.

His escorts swung out to stand arrayed along the gallery to both sides in the same haughty silence in which they had accompanied him. He walked unhesitatingly forward. Malvina spoke in animated fashion, her black hand and her white one cutting the air in fluid but emphatic sweeps. Her listeners leaned toward her, laughing.

It was as if Noritomo's mind sped to outpace the physical world, so that he seemed to move underwater, with the pale light falling on his face as through a pool's surface overhead. He saw more clearly than he could remember seeing in his life, as if truly with a falcon's eyes.

Thoughtfulness was not a virtue Turkina's talons were encouraged to cultivate. Noritomo Helmer understood and even approved of that: he knew his own propensity to think—and second-guess himself—had brought the *desant* and him personally disaster in the Kimball system. Yet even Malvina had acknowledged that his thoughtfulness had proven vital to their victory on Skye. So he reflected now.

The six men and women, MechWarriors, who clustered around Malvina took on a strange aspect, as if they were raptors of a different kind: vultures. *No,* he corrected, *something worse.*

Because animals cannot act with calculated cruelty.

What they showed was not the simple fierce courage of a falcon, joy in the hunt and—yes—the hot blood of the kill. He shared that and was not ashamed: when he had answered Malvina's haughty challenge, before the final attack on Skye, with the simple words "I am Jade Falcon," he had spoken no more or less than the truth.

But these MechWarriors hungered clearly for *pain*. For the terror in their victim's eyes, for the sight of ragged refugees fleeing without hope from horror beyond comprehension. From a desire, not to save the people of the Inner Sphere from themselves, but to feast on their carcasses while they still lived and to savor their screams of agony.

And he realized what he despised, truly despised, about

Galaxy Commander Malvina Hazen and her Mongol doctrine: it was *indulgent*.

Time caught him up. He strode forward again briskly, head high, as befit a Jade Falcon marching to meet Destiny—good or ill.

Malvina smiled at his approach. The others turned lean and eager faces to him. They would welcome him so, he knew, whether or not they meant to rend his flesh like vultures.

"It is good of you to join us, Galaxy Commander," she said.

Now the Star colonel's step faltered. He glanced around. Malvina stood before him like a tiny ice statue; Bec Malthus lurked behind, most of all like a vulture—or a carrion crow. For a wild moment Noritomo Helmer wondered whether Malvina was hallucinating, or greeting the shade of her dead brother—

Malvina's attendants gave yipping laughs, making him think of them momentarily as dogs.

He stopped and looked at the diminutive woman, with her hair cascading about the shoulders of her midnight-black uniform. "Galaxy Commander Malvina Hazen," he said, "I do not understand."

"You are seldom so slow on the uptake, Noritomo. Or, to repeat, Galaxy Commander Helmer."

He stared at her in confusion. His cheeks burned. He could think of nothing to say.

It was Bec Malthus who rescued him—which made him resent the man more somehow. "You have earned promotion, Noritomo Helmer," he said in his deep voice that rolled like surf. "You have proven yours are the steadiest hands in which to entrust the expeditionary force—and by extension, the fate of our crusade."

Noritomo looked at Malvina. He caught himself on the cusp of asking if they were joking.

"What of you?" he asked, his voice rougher than he intended.

"The Falcon has abandoned her boldest fledglings," Malvina said. "Or rather, someone pretending to serve Turkina has. You have seen how we languish here, a lonely salient driven deep into our enemy's side. Yet the promised Jade Falcon *touman* does not come. Instead we are sent culls in numbers insufficient to make good our losses. Someone must now return to the nest and demand accounting."

He stood to attention and waited.

"We go to Sudeten," Malthus said. "Galaxy Commander Hazen and myself."

"I take with me the *Emerald Talon* and a scratch Galaxy," Malvina said, "comprising elements of Delta and Zeta Galaxies and Turkina Keshik. Our equipment, obviously, goes with us."

It was a huge a bite out of his already overstretched resources. He would lose a disproportionate number of his best warriors. But the sting of that loss was soothed, not inconsiderably, by the knowledge that they would also be the worst of Malvina's bloodthirsty fanatics. The more benign vision of Noritomo Helmer—and Malvina's late brother Aleksandr—would prevail in the Falcon's Reach.

For the moment. The obvious question was whether Khan Jana Pryde would confirm such an appointment. But it would show weakness to ask.

"You honor me, Galaxy Commander," he said. He spoke midway between Malvina, the *desant*'s true commander, and Malthus, the titular one.

"Not at all," she said. "You have redeemed your failures, and so proven your worth to the Falcon."

Of course, he thought, *each caress from the velvet glove must be followed by a slap. . . .*

"What are your orders?" he asked a point in space.

Malvina laughed. "Doubtless they will surprise you, Galaxy Commander Noritomo Helmer. They are: *hold*. Hold what the Falcon has seized, consolidate the grasp of Her claws."

"Should a target of opportunity present itself—?"

"Ignore it. I know that every Clansman and woman and machine we have is barely enough to hold our salient. I know that I deprive you of some of our finest steel. To expand our holdings could only weaken our grasp—fatally.

"In fact, should it prove necessary, you may withdraw

from one or more planets we have seized. Anything, so long as you keep a foothold in the Inner Sphere. And above all hold Skye—your life upon that!"

With effort he kept his face impassive. Mad, she was, and he skirted the edge of calling her worse. But she still possessed one of the keenest military minds in Clan Jade Falcon, which meant the human universe. As she had just shown.

"My life upon it," he agreed.

"Very well," Malvina said. "We depart immediately. My new Galaxy already boards shuttles. May Turkina's wings be your shield."

So that is why I've been getting so many reports of activity today, Helmer thought.

Malvina turned and marched out of the echoing rotunda. Her retinue followed like a pack. Last went Beckett Malthus, after one last, hooded look of his eyes, the color of pond water, at the *desant*'s newly anointed commander.

Galaxy Commander Noritomo Helmer stood as if frozen. Not by the task before him, daunting as it was: no man or woman could become and remain a Star colonel in Clan Jade Falcon without welcoming any challenge.

It was the implications of Malvina's act—and Malthus' machinations, for surely he had encouraged her, if not put her up to it—that rooted his feet to the marble. For the two surviving original commanders of the expeditionary force to return to Sudeten, without orders, aboard one of the most fearsome WarShips remaining in human space . . .

It took enormous effort of will to keep his limbs from trembling. He was struck to the soul with the greatest fear he had ever known.

Not for himself.

For Clan Jade Falcon.

He could see only one outcome to Malvina's actions: the unthinkable.

Falcon against Falcon. *A Rending.*

6

Hammarr, Sudeten
Jade Falcon Occupation Zone
12 September 3135

"It would appear, milord," said Rorion from the front passenger seat of the limousine the Lyran Embassy had had waiting for them at Hammarr spaceport, "that someone has given the anthill a mighty kick."

He spoke German out of politeness to the driver, a young redheaded woman in gray Lyran livery.

Outside the long, low-slung ground car's tinted ferroglass windows, people moved not with the briskness one associated with a planet reasonably assimilated to Clan ways, but with a sort of jerky energy, like lizards on a hot day. Not that it was hot: it was seldom hot at this latitude on southern Sudeten, and now it was winter anyway. The sky was like a white sheet hung before a pallid white ghost of a sun, and a half-frozen rain drifted down out of the sky as if diffident about sullying the Falcon capital's streets.

Men and women in the drab laborer jumpsuits dawdled uncharacteristically, heads together in conversation on street corners and in doorways. Nor did the *solahma* enforcers in padded vests and helmets dotting the broad boulevard touch them up to return them to their duties, von

Texeria noticed. They too were busy gossiping amongst themselves.

Hammarr was a city of domes: some flattened on top, some left round, but all built low to the ground and just reeking of structural strength. The sole tall building on the skyline was the Falcon's Perch: residence and command center of the Falcon khan herself, spiking into spires two hundred meters into the thin and chill blue sky, and all of stressed cement reinforced with endosteel and laced with supersized synthetic strands. After being largely leveled during the Falcon arrival the century before, the city had been rebuilt to withstand bombardment.

The streets were broad, the traffic sparse and rigidly controlled. They were as clean, von Texeira thought, as if vacuumed and hand-scrubbed every hour on the hour.

"This city has all the charm of a crematorium," Rorion complained. "It combines all the less delightful characteristics of a factory and a fortress."

"What you'd expect," von Texeira said, in Portuguese this time, "of a world settled by Germans and ruled for eighty years by a Crusader Clan."

"Sim," Rorion agreed.

"But what is all the excitement about?" the merchant prince turned diplomat asked, in German again. "I wouldn't think the serfs were permitted emotion on Sudeten."

"Haven't you heard, Margrave von Texeira?" the driver asked.

"We've heard nothing since entering the system." Through a pirate point, of course, less than a day out from the capital world at a leisurely one-gee accel-decel. Nor had Sudeten orbital control offered more than the conventional challenge to identify themselves as Senna Rodríguez's cargo ship, *Gypsy Tailwind,* approached the planet. The Falcons were not fond of the Sea Foxes but were resigned to their ways, it seemed.

"A battleship has jumped into the system at the zenith point," the driver said, awe evident in her voice. WarShips were rare; a Clan battleship represented the greatest concentration of killing power in history. It was as if a two-

hundred-foot nuclear-powered dinosaur out of a Draconis
Combine tri-vid show were descending on the city. "A
Nightlord. They say it'll shape Sudeten orbit at any
minute!"

Von Texeira felt a sensation in his stomach like a
DropShip on assault descent. "Not—"

"It's the *Emerald Talon*, milord. Word at the embassy is
that both Beckett Malthus and Malvina Hazen are aboard."

Von Texeira brought his ham-sized fist down on the seat
beside him with a sound like a pistol crack. *"Merda!"*

"Lord?" the driver asked in confusion.

"He means *Scheisse*," Rorion translated helpfully.

"Lord Margrave, I am sorry if I spoke out of turn."
Words tumbled from the young driver's mouth. "I know
it's wrong to repeat gossip. I only thought—"

Von Texeira reached forward to give her a reassuring
pat on her right epaulette. "You have served well, dear
child. I wasn't responding to the fact that you spoke, but
to what you said."

"There's something the Sea Foxes didn't know, in any
event," Rorion said in Portuguese. Triumphantly, for he
found the Foxes more than a trifle smug, though much better companions to his tastes (admittedly low) than any
Clanners he had ever met. And he had met more than
a few.

"Or didn't see fit to share with us," his master pointed
out in the same language.

Rorion scowled. "There's that."

If the sterile winter streets of Hammarr buzzed with
muted concern, there was nothing at all muted about the
mood inside the Lyran Commonwealth embassy. The great
stressed-concrete structure, not far from the khan's mid-
town fortress, practically vibrated with a resonance just this
side of outright panic.

Ambassador Graves was a portly man whose head did
not quite measure up to his girth. The face on the front of
that small head, sticking up like a bud from the stand-up
collar of his mauve-and-lavender afternoon diplomatic
dress jacket, was that of a frightened white rabbit.

He stood by the sideboard in his dark-paneled office pouring fluid from a square cut-glass decanter whose facets twinkled in the track lighting. "P-plum brandy?" he asked, pouring about half of it over the exposed white cuff of his shirt. Von Texeira had to look away; the liqueur was bright, deep red. It made the man look as if he had slashed his wrist. "Soothes the nerves wonderfully, I find. You'll not credit this, but it's actually quite good. Jade Falcon merchants make it from fruit grown on land they own. In the equatorial zone, don't you know, where it's warm a good three months a year."

Von Texeira raised a brow. "Summer Home label? I know it well. We import it ourselves. Paying extortionate prices to the Falcon merchants, I might add." It was another testament to the Jade Falcon merchants' status as prophets without honor among their own that of all the Clans only they and, naturally, the Sea Foxes, should be canny enough to produce luxury goods for export to the decadent Inner Sphere.

"Your taste is superb, Excellency," he added. Though it took not so much a refined palate as a pulse to prefer Summer Home brandy to what the Clanners themselves drank. That was suitable only for stripping very old enamel from the bulkheads of scows.

He stepped forward and picked up the glass to spare the man the impossible task of handing it to him. "I thank you, Excellency."

"Proßt," said the ambassador, and dashed his own glass straight down. He managed not to spill a drop.

Inwardly von Texeira sighed. In the best of all possible worlds House Steiner's representative to their powerful potential foe would be a man or woman of indomitable courage and resolve, a lion to their Jade Falcon. That best world, von Texeira always reflected, must lie in some other galaxy, or possibly an alternate universe. In the dimensions he inhabited, a truly forceful representative would inevitably provoke the famous Falcon temper. And be shipped home to the Commonwealth in a cryo-coffin—worst case, delivered by Jade Falcon invasion fleet.

There was a reason Archon Melissa had tapped *him* to

serve as her personal emissary to the khan, knowing as she did his entire résumé.

"I apologize for what you've found yourself dropped into, *Markgraf*," Graves said. "Beastliest time of year on a beastly planet, full of Falcons surly as beasts. And now this beastly mess, to top it all."

"Put your mind at ease, my friend," von Texeira said in his richest, rolling baritone. "I can use a little diversion, now and again." *If only he knew how true that was*, he thought.

"I only hope that we can find ample room for you and your retinue, milord," the ambassador said. "What with the current crisis, the embassy is crowded with Lyran nationals we've gathered in for their protection."

"Splendid," von Texeira said, and meant it. At least the man discharged his duty properly.

"Unthinkable for you and your party to reside outside the walls, of course; it isn't safe. In the mood they're in, these Falcons are capable of anything!"

Timid the man might be, but von Texeira knew he was right about that. The Jade Falcons were volatile at the best of times. They were most definitely *not* safe in the throes of a political crisis that could well turn on the shortest of notice into a bombardment from space.

"No retinue, your Excellency," he said. "Only my man and myself. We take up but little room; his narrowness compensates for my avoirdupois, you see."

Graves blinked his pallid blue boiled-egg eyes. "Heh? Heh? Oh, I see. Your Lordship makes a witticism. Very good! Very good! Facing down all those hostile boardrooms has turned your blood to ice, just as the tri-vids say about you. Superb sangfroid, von Texeira, superb sangfroid!"

He hunched his head further down into the top of the ovoid of his body and blinked at his guest again, near-suspiciously this time. "So small a party, then, for a man of your stature?"

"In my youth I came to appreciate the value of traveling light," he said, with perfect if incomplete truthfulness. "Never fear, my friend: I appreciate the good life as much as any two men, as my girth suggests. But when needs must, even I can tighten the belt."

"Oh. Ha-ha, yes. Very good. Very g-g-*good*. Your reputation as a bon vivant rivals your reputation as a businessman."

"And now," von Texeira said, "if your Excellency will be so kind as to have our slight baggage conveyed to such quarters as you can spare us . . ." *And before you keel over from a heart attack, or we both turn into Davions from all this secondhand French.* "And if I might further impose on you for the loan of a car, I should like to present my credentials to Khan Jana Pryde. She requested an emissary direct from Archon Melissa, don't you know."

Ambassador Graves' lower lip was purple—*Best watch the blood pressure, my man*, thought von Texeira—and moist. It trembled, and he blinked rapidly, as if fighting tears.

"That will require a fast VTOL, milord," he said, "not a car."

"How do you mean, Excellency?"

"An emergency *kurultai* has been called at their Grand Council Hall in anticipation of the arrival of the b-b-b-battleship." He had to pause and shake himself after the exertion of forcing the last word between fear-rubbery lips. "Khan Jana Pryde has already left to preside."

"It's distant?" von Texeira asked. "I'd thought their Grand Council Hall was here in Hammarr."

The man actually smiled: a ghastly affair, showing a plenitude of pink-white gums. "The Falcon's Perch here is of secondary importance. I fear even you, with your well-known wealth of experience with the Clans, underestimates the perversity of the Jade Falcons in their native environment, milord.

"They've built themselves a bloody great new clubhouse three hundred kilometers south of here, perched on a perpetually snow-clad peak in the midst of a howling frozen wilderness!"

"As diversions go, this is right up there with running with scissors and riding a motorcycle in a monsoon," Rorion said. He had to shout to make himself heard over the storm howl and the whine of the contra-rotating fusion-driven rotors bashing the passenger-modified H-8 Warrior through the gale force winds. The environs of the Falcon's great hall were living up amply to the reputation Ambassador Graves had given them.

"Courage, man," von Texeira said, gazing out the ferroglass windows with wholly spurious impassivity at the jagged peaks that surrounded them. *Like the teeth of a giant diamond shark*, he thought. *Very like that.* "I've already had to deal with a bad case of ambassadorial nerves today."

"I don't blame him," Rorion said. "Being constantly surrounded by the damned Falcons is bad enough. To have them like this would put the wind up a stone statue of Aleksandr Kerensky."

"*The Falcon's Eyrie is coming into sight*," the voice of the pilot crackled from the speaker set in the bulkhead separating the cockpit from the passenger compartment. Von Texeira found himself and Rorion pressing their noses to the chill ferroglass like children at a shop window before Christmas. Though as a child he'd only experienced *cold* during a Christmas holiday once, when his mother and father had taken them to Tharkad to meet their distant cousin, the archon.

The Falcon's Eyrie looked as if it had been designed by a madman who combined a love of growing crystals with an obsession for Gothic cathedral architecture from Terra's Middle Ages and Renaissance. It was a collection of square and triangular section spines, sprouting from a common base and soaring skyward. They were made of some pale stone or synthetic or even polished metal; in the doubtful light and through the screen of wind-blasted snow it was impossible to tell. It threw off tantalizing glints of prismatic color in the light of a sun that was barely a patch of relative brightness above the western peaks.

"Impressive," von Texeira said. "I'll give it that."

"If you scaled it down," his aide replied, "it'd make a hell of a tank trap."

"Or, scaled down further, a prickle-burr to place on a teacher's chair." Though a couple of decades separated

them in age, and Lyran social mores separated them further
in status, the two men shared much common ground. Not
least of which was a wide prankish streak.

As the VTOL banked for its approach to a landing pad
marked by bright flashing blue-white beacons, von Texeira
became aware of a rattling around the edges of the window
by his side. Vibration swelled slowly through his bones, his
body, becoming audible at last as a low rolling rumble.

"Thunder?" Rorion said. "In a snowstorm?"

"The primary is a white star. Perhaps its ultraviolet levels
promote lightning."

"At high noon on midsummer's day at the equator, if
the sky by some chance was clear, you could focus the rays
of this distant, dwarfish sun to set fire to a clump of dry
grass," Rorion said. "If you warmed it up a touch first with,
say, a Magna Mk III heavy laser. Do you think such a star
throws off enough high-energy radiation to produce
lightning?"

"Doubtless not. Look up there!"

He pointed excitedly upward. High above in the overcast
a star appeared. Though tiny, it already shone brighter than
Sudeten's sun, and a bluer white. It grew in size and intensity until it could be seen to underlight a swell of
globularity.

"A DropShip!" von Texeira exclaimed.

"Bec de Corbin," Rorion Klimt said. "Beckett Malthus'
personal DropShip. Bet me."

"I don't take sucker bets, Rorion, you know that," his
master said in a tone of mild reproof.

The vast teardrop shape settled down through the clouds
on the far side of the spiny Jade Falcon fortress. A titanic
cloud of steam, now tinged with orange glare, billowed up
to mask it even before the Eyrie intervened.

Von Texeira laughed and shook his great head.

"This Malvina Hazen knows how to make an entrance.
I give her that!"

Inside the Jade Falcons perched on tiers and tiers of seats
arranged around a central hall. With their capes made of
feathers from real jade falcons they had stalked and slain

as one of their warrior rituals, they resembled a flock of surly green-winged birds in the dim afternoon light. Their murmurs had an ominous sound, like heavy rain on the roof in a floodplain.

Over the heads of the assembled warriors the structure soared two hundred meters: a great four-faceted spire. Each facet was made of translucent material, and displayed a stylized, attenuated representation of Turkina, the original jade falcon. Around its base hung banners, some scorched and stained, others pristine: battle honors won by the Clan in its long and tumultuous career.

Into the hall strode Malvina Hazen, her head held high, her unbound almost-white blond hair streaming behind her like a banner that defied her fellow Falcons to capture it. She wore a dress uniform of her own design: midnight black with green and yellow details, and her jade-feather cape flapping about her shoulders. Behind and to her right came Beckett Malthus, in regulation uniform, tall and heavyset and somber, his bearded chin sunken to his chest, his prominent eyebrows furrowed. Both carried their helmets in the crooks of their arms.

A rush of frigid air and the blizzard's bluster accompanied them.

The Grand Hall's round floor was inlaid with the Clan's falcon-and-katana symbol. Across it from the entrance rose a dais draped with the Clan flag. On it stood Khan Jana Pryde in gleaming Falcon dress uniform, with a dramatic helmet like a gold-and-green falcon's head encasing her own. Beside her stood Julia Buhalin, loremaster of the Clan, wearing the green ceremonial robes, trimmed with yellow, of her office.

Khan Jana Pryde watched the two Galaxy commanders striding toward her, a little grateful that the helmet hid her face. She was a tall woman, lean to the point of gauntness, with blond hair darker and more yellow than Malvina's, twisted in a complex braid that hung down her back.

It was you who decided you could dispense with Bec Malthus' cunning, she reminded herself sternly. *Now show that you at least learned something from observing him in action.*

"I welcome two heroes of Clan Jade Falcon back to the

nest of all Turkina's brood," she said. A microphone built into her ceremonial helmet picked up her words, and a system of cunningly placed speakers filled the vastness of the hall with them without creating disturbing echoes or sounding strident. Her words were enough to still the subdued flutter of conversation—which, the khan reflected sourly, reminded her more of pigeons babbling in a cote than of falcons. "You have brought great victory and great glory to Clan Jade Falcon, Galaxy Commander Beckett Malthus and Galaxy Commander Malvina Hazen."

There, she thought. *That'll at least remind the little* surat *of her proper place. And if not her, it will remind the rest of the Clan!* Khan Jana Pryde was notorious for her carelessness with the Clan proscription against speaking in contractions; indeed, she was known to be impatient, at best, with many "sacred" Jade Falcon traditions. She was damned if she'd bother trying to *think* without contractions.

"Your return from the front lines, where foes beset our fellow Falcons on all sides, is nevertheless a considerable surprise to us." *Verging as it does upon desertion in the face of an enemy*. Such an act could be considered dishonorable in the extreme . . . so extreme that instead of a Trial of Grievance against her unruly subordinate, the khan might even call for a Trial of Annihilation. Jana Pryde was tempted to do so just to see the look on Malvina's face.

Softly, softly, she told herself. Malvina had allies in this house. Those tainted with her madness—and others who would not be saddened to see Jana herself plummet from her perch. She schooled herself to keep her voice . . . ceremonial.

"How can I, your khan, serve you?"

Malvina halted far enough from the foot of the dais that she did not have to raise her head much to stare challengingly at her khan.

"You can die!" she cried, her voice ringing up the heights of the hall like a raptor's scream. "I, Galaxy Commander Malvina Hazen, declare you, Jana Pryde, unfit to serve as khan of Clan Jade Falcon. I challenge you to a Trial of Possession for the right to rule!"

7

**The Falcon's Eyrie
Hameward Mountains, Sudeten
Jade Falcon Occupation Zone
12 September 3135**

Silence filled the hall.

"With what do you defend?" Malvina Hazen asked, the question wreathed in echoes.

Heinz-Otto von Texeira and Rorion Klimt lurked in the foyer through which Malthus and Hazen had come into the Great Hall. Not surprisingly, there were no facilities for spectators. Von Texeira was somewhat surprised they had been permitted to penetrate so deep into the Clan holy of holies without challenge. He surmised that, having made it all the way here, the Spheroids were presumed to be under the khan's protection; since affront to them would be in effect a challenge to the khan, the Falcons they encountered did not deign to notice them.

He and his aide looked at each other. "Uh-oh," Rorion mouthed silently.

Silence shattered like ice. The assembled warriors all began to clamor at once. Some roared; some screamed in fury. The noise raked the two outsiders like shards of metal.

Across the floor Khan Jana Pryde seemed to swell with rage.

"My Khan," said Loremaster Julia Buhalin, stepping forward. She was a woman of medium height, with dark brown hair, from which the light through the high windows struck red highlights, cut square across her forehead and falling just below her ears in the back. Her eyes were violet, her skin cinnamon. Unlike Jana Pryde she was statuesque; indeed, Jana suspected her heavy robes of office, like the carefully tailored uniforms she wore on other than ceremonial occasions, concealed a certain softness. Not that it mattered: alone of all members of Clan Jade Falcon the loremaster was immune to challenge. Only a majority of a Clan Grand Council could remove her.

Jana Pryde thumbed a tiny control unit sewn into her tunic that squelched the microphone in her helmet. "I'll kill her," she hissed.

"Wait," the loremaster said. She had broad cheekbones and an expression of determined calm. She was one of the youngest loremasters in a century but had been handpicked by her predecessor, Earl Helmer, who had died suddenly several years before.

"I can't let her think I'm afraid," Jana Pryde said. In her fury she was slinging contractions all over the place.

Since Bec Malthus' exile, Loremaster Buhalin had become the Jade Falcon khan's main confidante and advisor. She had long since grown inured to such sloppy usage despite her role as guardian of Clan orthodoxy.

"Allow me, my Khan," she said. Without awaiting response she glided forward to the front of the dais.

She raised her staff, topped with a perched Turkina carved in jade. The tumult within the hall stilled at once. Despite her relative youth—in the one role in which Clan warrior culture prized age—she commanded great respect. First for the position itself, which, as custodian of the values of Clan Jade Falcon and most of all its holy Remembrance, exalted her in very real ways above the khan herself. And second for her prowess in rising to loremaster status so early in life, since nothing worth having, not even life itself, was easily come by in Clan Jade Falcon.

"What you ask is irregular, Galaxy Commander Malvina Hazen," the loremaster said, her voice amplified to fill the great cold space.

"I ask nothing," Malvina said. "I *challenge*. This has nothing to do with you, Loremaster!"

"This has everything to do with me. I am custodian of Jade Falcon ways. If we throw tradition to the winds—especially in a matter as core as this one—we risk losing our cohesion, our order. Would you render us no better than the downtrodden inhabitants of the Inner Sphere, constantly striving and struggling for political advantage?"

Malvina glared. One of those fierce blue eyes, Jana Pryde knew, was prosthetic. As was a hand and a leg. Although prosthetics were far from uncommon among Clan warriors, there was something about Malvina's choice to refuse regeneration that ran down the khan's spine like an icy trickle of water.

Nonsense, she reproved herself. *I cannot permit the wretched little* surat *to get inside my head.*

Forcing herself back into the objectivity, so difficult for a Falcon decanted and raised, that had played such a major role in her own rapid rise, Jana acknowledged the wisdom of Buhalin's course of action. There was nothing Malvina could say at this point, least of all to the loremaster, without outraging even those among her listeners who might feel drawn to her bloodthirsty doctrines.

"The customary challenge to a ruling khan is the Trial of Position. Why do you offer a Trial of Possession, as if the khanship were a vial of sperm?"

Malvina winced as if slapped. It was all Jana Pryde could do not to grin.

But the renegade recovered quickly enough. "I so challenge precisely because of my concern for the welfare of Clan Jade Falcon," she said. "Merely removing the manifestly unfit Jana Pryde will not suffice. A firm hand must immediately wear the glove on which Turkina's fortunes perch, without an endless string of challenges and Council debates."

Jana Pryde's vision washed out in a wave of red. Her

first impulse was to leap over the dais and land on the interloper like a stooping falcon. The touch of the loremaster's left hand, hidden from view by the podium, stayed her long enough for her self-discipline to reassert itself.

I must keep control, she told herself. *I am Jade Falcon.*

"Your challenge remains unorthodox," Loremaster Buhalin said, "regardless of rationale. Therefore as loremaster I must for the moment take the decision out of the hands of Khan Jana Pryde."

A hissing swelled within the hall like the sound of air escaping from a breached JumpShip hull as a thousand warriors inhaled at once. "I must consult with the Clan Council in private as to the appropriateness of your challenge, Galaxy Commander Malvina Hazen. Only if we deem the challenge permissible will it be presented to Khan Jana Pryde."

Malvina opened her mouth. With perfect timing Julia Buhalin slammed down the metal tip of her staff of office on the polished wooden floor of the dais. Electronically amplified like the contending women's voices, it tolled like a great wooden bell.

"In Turkina's name," Julia Buhalin declaimed, and her own voice rang like bronze, "the loremaster of Clan Jade Falcon has spoken!"

Malvina Hazen's near-white hair swirled like her cape as she turned from the dais. Her face was as frozen as the ice sculpture it resembled.

Rorion Klimt let out a breath in a long voiceless whistle. "That is some woman, my lord."

Heinz-Otto von Texeira probed in his left ear with a great forefinger. "Is it, Rorion? 'Demon from Hell' seems closer to me."

His aide shrugged.

They had reverted to their native Portuguese as a basic security measure. Neither man assumed it provided perfect confidentiality: no khan could survive long without at least fairly competent internal security, provided by either a personal bodyguard or the Watch, especially after the better part of a century's cohabitation with conniving Spheroids had tainted the feral purity of the Clans.

Not wanting for any number of reasons to be any closer than necessary to the furious Galaxy commander when she stormed past, the two faded down a short corridor into an octagonal antechamber. Von Texeira glanced across the smaller but still not insubstantial room.

"Himmelherr Gott!" he exclaimed. "A child!"

It was true: a little girl in a blue-and-white dress was tossing a ball against a whitewashed wall, clapping her hands, then catching it. She was pretty, her blond hair tied in pigtails. She seemed to be singing softly to herself. Over the furious commotion pouring from the main hall von Texeira could make out no words, just a sort of lilting flow. She could not have been more shockingly out of place had she been a four-meter-long Nova Suevian golden *onza* with saber fangs and six legs.

A pair of female warriors wearing sidearms and narrow glares stood guard over her. Several other warriors idling in the antechamber seemed to look everywhere in the room except at the Spheroid child. Their manner reminded von Texeira of a dog which, having two or three times been startled or frightened by something, studiously pretends that thing doesn't exist.

"See the nice new insignia," Rorion murmured. Von Texeira realized that the little girl's two guardians each wore an unfamiliar patch on the right breast of her jumpsuit: a heavily stylized eye, with a stripe descending from it like a falcon's eye-stripe, in brilliant emerald green.

"The Eye of Horus," he murmured. "Apparently what our friend Senna told us was true: our prodigal twins did manage to wangle some rudiments of actual education."

"Appropriate symbol for Malvina," Rorion said. "She and her sibkin were known as the Eyes of the Falcon, *não*?"

"Then Turkina and Malvina have one thing in common," von Texeira said softly as the woman in question and her larger shadow swept by, "in that each has but one eye left."

Six more warriors in gleaming black, green and yellow entered the antechamber to surround the two Galaxy commanders. Three men, three women, two of them elementals, each bore the green falcon-eye symbol that Malvina apparently had taken for her own. From their unit badges von Texeira noted that two came from Malvina's own Gyr-falcon Galaxy, two from her dead brother's Zeta, and two from Beckett Malthus' Turkina Keshik.

"Aren't Turkina Keshik the khan's personal body-guard?" Rorion asked sotto voce.

"So I understood."

Malvina turned aside to approach the little girl. At a word from one of her guardians the child caught up her little ball and turned. Her face lit with delight as she saw Malvina. Still grave as a priest saying Mass, Malvina knelt, gathered the girl into her arms, brushed back a lock of the child's hair with a gauntleted hand—the false one, if von Texeira remembered rightly. Then she turned and swept from the antechamber without another look around.

"You're right, my lord," Rorion said. "That woman is creepy."

Von Texeira fingered his beard. "I wonder," he said, "if Malvina has ever seen an expression like that on the face of anyone looking at her before? It's about the last thing I ever expected to see."

"Let's hope it isn't close to the last thing you do see." His aide looked back into the main hall, from which noise blew out in a continual blast of contention. "And that defines 'hitting the fan.' *Minha nossa*, they sound more like a cageful of angry gibbons than birds of prey, don't they?"

"Try as they might," his master said, "they can't change the fact they're just apes, like the rest of us."

He sighed. "There goes her Khanship and the loremaster," he said as the two women hustled into a dark opening at the dais' rear. "Let's try to find to someone who'll actually look at our credentials before some crazed Clansman decides to vent his spleen on the first lowly Spheroids he sees."

"That *cull*!" Jana Pryde shouted, yanking off her ceremo-nial helmet and flinging it across the room. It bounced. The khan's personal quarters in the great spiny keep were small but appointed quite comfortably, if not luxuriously. Auster-ity for its own sake was one of those Clan traditions with which Jana Pryde had little patience. "I'll take her chal-lenge and burn those mad blue eyes out of her head! That

Shrike of hers must be a limping wreck after all the damage it's taken."

"My Khan," Julia Buhalin said, her voice low and smooth, "do you not believe she has had her Black Rose fully repaired by now? Given the immense amount of *isorla* captured from our enemies on Skye and salvaged from our own machines scrapped in combat, she must have had ample parts available to repair her BattleMech."

Jana Pryde growled low in her throat. "You're right," she said. "Of course." Her Watch spies had kept her apprised of the broad course of events in the *desant*.

She took off her feather cape and flung it over the back of a chair. "So what now?"

"We should consider matters carefully, my Khan. It will do no harm to let Malvina wait."

Jana turned with a slow smile. "No. I suppose it won't."

A tap at the door. The room was an outer one; the translucent ferroglass wall let in the thin gruel of light of the storm and the dying day. Its thickness reduced the wind to a whistle interspersed with booming buffets, just this side of subliminal, and concealed heaters kept the chill at bay.

"Enter," commanded Jana. Only a trusted aide or laborer-class servant would dare trouble her, especially at such a moment as this. Or an assassin—Jana found her gauntleted right hand resting on the well-worn butt of the sidearm laser holstered on her right hip.

I almost hope Malvina's sent murderers after me, she thought. *Time to remind my people I didn't just ride to power on the black-feathered back of Malthus the Crow!*

The door opened. "Excellency," a female servant in a blue-gray and mauve jumpsuit said, keeping her eyes carefully downcast, "there are men from the Inner Sphere to see you. They claim to be personal emissaries of the Archon Melissa Steiner."

"Send them away," Julia Buhalin said. But Jana raised a finger.

"No," she said. "I sent for them. I want to see them. Bring them in."

A pair of young MechWarriors in full battledress and falcon helmets escorted them in. The emissaries were, the khan saw, quite a disparate pair. One was huge, a broad-shouldered, bull-chested man with a frizzy cloud of hair and a gray-dusted black beard framing a broad and jovial dark face. He had a great disgusting belly and limped with the aid of a stout cane. His eyes were a bright astonishing blue. With him came a smaller, slimmer, younger man, about average height for a Spheroid, with lighter skin and dark, dancing eyes. He had about him a slightly vulpine look.

"Khan Jana Pryde," the big man boomed out in English flavored with a Steiner German accent. "It is a great pleasure to meet you. I am Heinz-Otto María Manoel de Soares zu Mannstein, *Markgraf* von Texeira. This is my aide, Rorion Klimt. My Archon, the Duchess of Tharkad, sends us in response to your request, in order that we might restore the peace that has prevailed between our great peoples for decades!"

He turned and deposited the datachip containing their bona fides in the palm of the MechWarrior to his right as if giving the young man a tip. He beamed all over his great bearded face and seemed to Khan Jana Pryde to be enjoying himself hugely. The MechWarrior, who belonged to the Turkina Galaxy Cluster that had taken over for Turkina Keshik when Jana dispatched it to the Inner Sphere with Malthus, looked utterly nonplused.

After a moment he turned and marched up to Khan Jana Pryde, who accepted it with a curt nod. "Dismissed," she said.

The young man stood his ground. His eyes flickered toward the two Inner Sphere men. Jana Pryde's brow hardened, and her green eyes narrowed and went paler in her long, narrow skull. Her bodyguards turned about and all but fled.

As her initial flash of fury faded Jana felt something akin to amusement. *A fat, lame old merchant and a skinny man a head shorter than I, and my warriors act as if they were a pair of real Ghost Bears?* Still, it was the task her guard was set; she must remember not to chastise them for carrying it out in the manner of Clan Jade Falcon. Which was to say, with fanatical zeal.

"I bid you welcome, Margrave, Citizen Klimt. This is Julia Buhalin, our loremaster."

Buhalin's brows were lowered, but she nodded graciously.

"Will you sit?" Jana nodded toward chairs.

The older man nodded gratefully. "Thank you." He sighed as he lowered his bulk gingerly. His aide did not offer to assist him, but did not sit himself until his master was ensconced. "The years and the kilos don't make it so easy on my stump, you know."

She laughed. "You are a most remarkable man, Margrave. Almost as remarkable as the phenomenon of one of the richest men in the Lyran Commonwealth materializing so abruptly in our Eyrie."

"Really, Madame Khan, we had few other options. It was hard enough finding someone in the Eyrie who would read our accreditation. You may imagine what it was like getting here. Which also accounts"—he smiled again and gestured at his aide—"for the sparseness of my retinue."

Her forehead clenched again. "You were hindered?"

" 'Ignored' would be a better word. No one knew what to do about us, so mostly they hoped we would go away." He shrugged. "Eventually we did, so they were wise, *ja*?" He leaned forward with both hands on the crown of his cane. "You know of me then, Excellency?"

"We are civilized here, Margrave. We even received regular Inner Sphere newsfeeds before the hyperpulse generator network went down. You Steiners are our nearest neighbors in the Sphere; you were a prominent media figure."

His eyebrows rose. He seemed pleased. Almost any other Jade Falcon would instantly have passed him off as a mere buffoon, a vain bag of Spheroid wind.

Not Jana Pryde. *I learned from the master*, she acknowledged. *If only he had had the decency to stay exiled!*

As if in response to her thought the exterior wall reverberated to a basso roar. Orange light filled the chamber. A glaring point rose upward, screened by cloud and blowing snow as well as the ferroglass. It brightened, changed color to white and then blue-white before climbing out of sight.

"The Galaxy commanders depart," Buhalin said dryly.

"If she goes anywhere but back to orbit or to the designated cradle at the Hammarr spaceport she will be shot down," Jana Pryde said. "I hope she decides to sightsee."

"You have a WarShip orbiting above your head, Khan Pryde," von Texeira said. "That might be considered a restriction on your scope of action. I confess, I can almost feel its dark mass looming over me as I sit here in your eyrie."

"I have three WarShips orbiting over my head, thank you, Margrave. To answer the *Emerald Talon* I have the *Whirlwind*-class *Jade Tornado*, and *Jade Talon*, an *Aegis*."

"Are not the *Whirlwind*-class destroyers, O Khan?" von Texeira asked blandly. "And is your *Aegis* not a heavy cruiser? And please forgive me if I err, for I am but a civilian and more, a mere merchant, but it seems to me that together they mass about the same as a single *Nightlord*, do they not?"

Julia Buhalin snorted. Jana Pryde regarded the Lyran for a moment with one eyebrow strongly arched. Then she laughed.

"You undoubtedly personify the very class of Spheroid I should most despise," she said. "But your effrontery shows more courage than you may suspect. You are quite right: it would take the *Jade Talon* and *Jade Tornado* together to match the *Emerald Talon*. But don't forget your *Yggdrasil* badly damaged the *Emerald Talon* at Skye—"

"Hardly *my* Yggdrasil, my Khan," von Texeira murmured.

"—and I also have a number of armed DropShips, as well as a great many aerospace fighters on call. Malvina might do substantial damage to Sudeten, but at the cost of her life. And more to the point, her ambitions, don't you think?"

"You are quite correct, Jana Pryde," Buhalin said, a trifle hastily.

"The loremaster speaks truly," von Texeira said. He nodded decisively. "It would appear that you and my sovereign share a problem. Which means that you and I share a problem.

"So how may I help you, Khan Jana Pryde?"

8

The Falcon's Perch
Hammarr, Sudeten
Jade Falcon Occupation Zone
14 September 3135

"**G**alaxy Commander Malvina Hazen," intoned the loremaster of Clan Jade Falcon, "approach the dais."

Her words echoed through a vast circular hall ringed with ranks of seats in which sat Falcon MechWarriors. It lay not within the Eyrie in the desolate Hameward Mountains but rather in the Falcon's Perch, the great structure in the center of Hammarr from which Jade Falcon space was ruled.

It did not escape Malvina that she had been summoned to the political center of Clan Jade Falcon, rather than its heart, to hear her judgment.

The *Bec de Corbin*, Malthus' personal DropShip, had obediently settled in at Hammarr spaceport two days before, a few short minutes after blasting off from the Eyrie. The two Galaxy commanders and their retinues had spent the interval aboard, awaiting the decision of loremaster and Council.

"In the matter of your challenge to a Trial of Possession with Khan Jana Pryde, it is deemed prejudicial to the interests of Clan Jade Falcon, and denied," Loremaster Julia Buhalin said.

Malvina's eyes flashed, but she gave no other sign of reaction. "I challenge Jana Pryde to a Trial of Position then!"

"Denied," Buhalin said.

One can at least say for the Falcons that their proceedings tend to be brief and to the point, reflected Heinz-Otto von Texeira, who sat watching with Rorion from a gallery overlooking the amphitheater. *A short attention span has its advantages.*

"I challenge—" Malvina cried from the floor.

The ferrule of Buhalin's staff slammed down on the word. "Your challenges are improper and disallowed. In matters of this magnitude the interests of Clan Jade Falcon overrule your personal pride and desires."

Malvina's cheeks had slowly reddened throughout the exchange. Now they went dead white. "Hoo," Rorion half whispered. Both Lyrans knew well what that meant: a sudden, massive adrenaline dump within the tiny Mech-Warrior's bloodstream. "She's ready to fight *right now*."

But like a great black raven perched on her shoulder Bec Malthus leaned forward and whispered in her ear. She nodded, abruptly, chin clenched. Color slowly returned to her face.

"All honor to the loremaster and to Clan Jade Falcon," she said. "I obey the Council's decision. I am Jade Falcon!"

The last four words came out as a pealing scream. It was echoed by no small number of the warriors in attendance. A minority, von Texeira could tell. But a distressingly large one.

He looked to Khan Jana Pryde. He was surprised green laser beams didn't spear from her eyes and impale her rival as Malvina spun as if one heel were nailed to the polished marble floor and marched from the chamber. She had not so much as acknowledged the khan's presence since striding in.

He shook his head and shifted his weight, preparatory to leaving. Rorion laid two fingers on his forearm.

"Wait, milord."

Von Texeira raised an eyebrow. "What is it?"

"A feeling," his younger aide admitted, "no more. I smell trouble."

"And I have learned to rely on that nose of yours, my boy," von Texeira said. He grounded his cane again. "We wait. The fleshpots of Hammarr beckon not very loudly at the best of times."

"What now, Galaxy Commander?" It was a lost-child wail from MechWarrior June, one of Malvina's bodyguards who waited outside the Perch, a slender woman with a tattooed face and long black hair.

Malvina looked up. The day was mostly clear, the sky a blue as pale and merciless as Malvina's eyes. She held Cynthy in one arm. The little girl wore a heavy blue coat and white earmuffs against the chill. She clung comfortably to Malvina with her head against the Clanswoman's chest.

"We know *powless*," Malvina said. "For now."

She started down the wide steps of the Falcon's Perch. The air was crisp; the chill suppressed most smells save the dull reek of petroleum fractions burned by internal combustion engines. Across the wide boulevard called Turkina's Path, laborers moved purposefully around a plaza in the white morning light, some engaged in the never-ending chore of sweeping and otherwise keeping the concrete plain spotless, others going from task to task. Her retinue, six warriors and Cynthy's two minders, protectively surrounded her and Beckett Malthus, eyes as keenly alert as their namesakes'.

Nonetheless it was Malvina herself who first saw danger coming.

She turned her head toward four MechWarriors who approached along the street from the right with brightly colored capes flapping from their shoulders. At the same time a similar group moved in along the steps from the left.

"Galaxy Commander Malvina Hazen," said the leading MechWarrior on Malvina's right. He was tall and lean with a scar seaming the left side of his hatchet face and a black

Mohawk waving like a plume. "Your actions have brought disgrace to Clan Jade Falcon. I hereby issue challenge—"

Malvina's right hand whipped up and out to the full reach of her arm. In it she held the laser pistol she wore holstered at her narrow waist. It flashed twice.

The challenger's eyes rolled up to a blue dot in his pale forehead as blackish steam jetted from his ears. His legs folded, and he fell in a heap, shrouded by a black-and-scarlet cloak. The ginger-haired woman who walked to his left also went down, with a hole between eyes bulged from their sockets by fluid and brain matter flash-boiled in the skull behind them.

"Galaxy Commander!" exclaimed MechWarrior Paulus, Malvina's bodyguard nearest her left. "You have violated the rite of challenge!"

"Tactical pincers, you *surat*!" she exclaimed, pivoting left and folding over Cynthy in a crouch. "It's a trap! Fight."

Paulus was staring at her in incomprehension when a burst of submachine-gun fire from Malvina's left cut him down.

Hunched over with the little girl's back propped on her knee, Malvina fired as soon as the front sight of her sidearm bore on the dark face of the woman who had shot her escort; she knew the assassins might wear body-armor vests beneath their jumpsuits that would stop a low-wattage hand laser. Her pistol spat a ruby lance. The target jerked and fell.

Her surviving companions reacted to the danger with Jade Falcon speed and fury not reduced for being belated. Her guards and Cynthy's minders drew sidearms and opened fire. Roaring like a bear, Bec Malthus charged a woman firing an autopistol at Malvina. Malvina felt a tug as a bullet holed her cape. Then the assassin tried to switch aim to the male Galaxy commander.

He hit her in the face with a forearm sweep as he ran past her without slowing. Her neck broke with a sound not much quieter than her firearm's bark.

As Malthus closed with a shorter but sturdily built male MechWarrior, Lon, the male of Malvina's elemental pair, drew his battleknife and threw it at one of the two surviving MechWarriors attacking from the right. It struck hilt first but with enough force to cave in the enemy's ribs; the man went down choking and gagging, his face turning blue. Lon's female counterpart, Cecily, simply picked up the limp corpse of MechWarrior Paulus and hurled him at the last assailant on that side.

Bec Malthus' next opponent tried to tackle his legs from under him. Adroitly the larger Galaxy commander sprawled on him, leaning into the attack and simply pushing his foe aside and past. The MechWarrior's face hit the cement with a crunch and squeal of breaking nose cartilage and splintering teeth. Before he could spring back upright Malthus had drawn his own sidearm and fired a single rapid shot to the back of his tattooed skull. His body convulsed wildly once and then seemed to become half-liquescent and still.

Before Malvina could line up and fire again, her other escorts had blown down the last of the killers approaching from the left.

"Are you all right?" Malvina bent her head to ask her ward. Cynthy's face was pale as Malvina's own, and the hand that clutched her ragged stuffed bear to her chest showed knuckles almost bursting through whitened skin. But she nodded.

Malvina's strong legs, the real and the artificial, propelled her crouching toward the long, low ground car that waited at the curb. "Move!" she shouted to her party. "These stravags are not the last!"

A treetrunk-sized arm enfolded her from the rear. She was scooped up with Cynthy crying out at being crushed against her ribs, then driven forward and down toward the pavement. As she squirmed and screamed with helpless fury, the elemental who had caught her from behind turned so the vast body fell, not upon the diminutive Galaxy commander and the child, but interposed between them and the street.

The ground car exploded with a cataclysmic roar and a red geyser of flame as two heavy short-range missiles slammed into it. The giant encircling Malvina and Cynthy with its arm uttered a soft grunt and then went limp.

A great squat figure landed with a crack of buckling pavement between her and the blazing car. From the discrete headpiece with the typical Falcon beak she recognized modern Clan battlearmor. She snarled and flashed futile beams against its eyeslits from her laser as the figure raised the flamer that made up its right arm.

A dark-clad figure dove from the left, catching the powersuit in a tackle just above the waist. The mass and momentum of elemental Lon, even unarmored, was enough to momentarily tumble the suit's gyros. It fell backward with a crash.

Its rear-mounted impeller-jet snapped it back upright at once. But the gene-enhanced Lon possessed panther reflexes despite his immense size. With a liquid agility his armor-encased counterpart could not match, he flowed around behind onto the suit's shoulders, where the clawed left hand had trouble reaching him. Unable to grip, its talons gouged deep bloody wounds in Lon's thigh as he systematically began unfastening the clasps that held the helmet in place. Once he removed it he could snap the neck of the elemental inside. . . .

Orange flame speared down from the right. Both unprotected elemental and powersuit were instantly engulfed by a roaring inferno. Elemental Lon reared back bellowing in helpless fury as much as unendurable agony as the blazing chemical mixture seared flesh from his bones. He fell thrashing from the back of the battlearmor, whose occupant tried jumping, blazing like a comet, in a desperate attempt to escape the sticky, clinging fuel slowly roasting him alive.

A second Clan powersuit descended from the sky, the bluish-white flames of its jump jets very bright against the white-scrimmed sky. It aimed its flamer toward Malvina. She saw heat shimmer around its huge maw.

A thunderclap splintered the air. White flashes dazzled from the elemental suit's breastplate. It cartwheeled backward in the air, only to be transfixed by a green lance of coherent light. It bellyflopped in the middle of the broad avenue and lay still. A moment later a second burst of autocannon fire raked the flame-wreathed battlearmor, shattering and felling it.

Malvina looked left. At the corner of the plaza a pair of Skadi fast-attack VTOLs hung fifteen meters above the ground. Beneath them a Point of elemental armor bounded forward like fleas. The Eye of Horus glowed green on their breastplates.

A Merlin hover-APC wove past them toward the embattled party with a howl of turbines. Malvina writhed from beneath the quiescent bulk of the elemental who had saved her and Cynthy from the ground car explosion. Even before she saw Lon's doomed attack she knew her rescuer was Cecily: not just from the comparatively slim forearm, twined with the stark tribal-tattoo patterns of enhanced-imaging implants, but from the smell and the general feel of the great lithe-muscled body. Malvina had coupled with both her and Lon; it was her policy with those close to her, to bind them closer.

The exception had always been Bec Malthus. Whatever their relationship was, it did not include sex. Indeed, Malvina's nominal superior and actual mentor never publicly displayed a libido to speak of.

Malvina came to a crouch and held out her arms. She saw the lance-head splinter of hard plastic from the exploded ground car buried deep in the juncture of Cecily's neck and powerful shoulder. Cynthy crawled from beneath her arm, stood and carefully if quickly dusted off her teddy bear. Then she came again into Malvina's arms. Her little face was grave.

In a rising whine of blowers the APC rotated broadside and skidded down the street. Malvina held onto her ward with one arm and her helmet with the other as the vehicle braked fast and dirty by rolling about its long axis to spill a hurricane blast from under its leading-edge skirt. As it settled five meters from Malvina hatches sprang open and five more elemental powersuits sprang out to add their fire to that of their comrades and the Skadis, toward the enemy battlearmor attacking from the east.

"Go!" Malvina commanded, waving her arm. MechWarrior June and one of Cynthy's female nursemaid warriors were also down. The others gaped at her, momentarily dazed by the violent veering of events.

Beckett Malthus moved, clambering rapidly but with a certain dignity into the waiting hovercraft. Malvina's lips stretched in a half grin of approval and half sneer of contempt. *Trust the Crow to see to his self-preservation while others dither*, she thought as she followed with Cynthy.

Inside the APC Malvina quickly strapped the girl into a jumpseat, then took the one beside her at a ferroglass port with a firing slit beneath it.

"Welcome aboard, Galaxy Commanders," a voice said from the intercom. It was the voice of Wyndham. Clan medtech had swiftly healed his femur, broken in the successful duel with Galaxy Commander Tristan Fletcher of Clan Hell's Horses. *"Strap yourselves in. I suspect we are in for a wild ride."*

As Malvina complied orange glare filled the port across from her, lighting the dim passenger compartment with a brief evil glow. She looked out to see the laser-armed Skadi falling into a broken and blazing pile of wreckage in the street. The characteristic unwinding corkscrew trails of gray exhaust smoke left by short-range missiles hung in the air above the pavement.

"BattleMech!" called MechWarrior Theo.

As the 'Mech pounded past at a pavement-shaking pace two disparate figures emerged from the shelter of the Gothic-arched portal of the Falcon's Perch. As they did, the larger released its grip upon the upper arm of the smaller.

"I wondered why no one else was leaving," Rorion Klimt said, watching the *Uller* slam in pursuit of the APC, which appeared to be making for the military spaceport. "Perhaps they were warned." As usual in the JFOZ he spoke Brazilian Portuguese.

He rubbed his biceps and glared reproachfully at his senior. "Did you have to hold on so hard?"

Sometimes even I forget, he thought ruefully, *how much of his decadent softness is an act*. The older man's love of luxury and the high life was certainly no pose. As, among other things, a small army of mistresses not just back on Recife but dotted throughout the Inner Sphere could attest. But just as he showed on this sojourn that he could live without the comforts he so enjoyed, Heinz-Otto von Texeira had just shown again the iron that still underlay his flab.

The older man shrugged. "I wanted to ensure nothing unfortunate came to pass, Rorionzinho," he said mildly.

"I could easily have missed the girl at this range," Rorion hissed. "You know my aim." He was rated a master at combat pistolcraft. Among other things.

"It's not that," von Texeira said. "It's what you'd have *hit*."

Rorion turned his face to the larger, older man with his eyebrows scaling his forehead in outrage. "But that was our chance to take the monster out, this self-named Chingis Khan! Surely you don't play politics now, faced with a threat such as this?"

"The death of Malvina Hazen would be the greatest gift humanity could receive right now," von Texeira said, his voice a quiet rumble over the gradually dwindling thunder of battle. "To have her die at the hand of a Spheroid would be the greatest possible catastrophe."

Rorion stared at him a moment longer. His own face was drained of color and tight as a drumhead. "And to have her killed by a *Lyran* would disrupt certain delicate arrangements the archon has in train, am I right?"

Von Texeira inclined his huge bushy head and said nothing.

"Very well," Rorion said with quiet bitterness. "On your head be it."

"It always is, my boy," said von Texeira gently. "It always is."

9

The Falcon's Perch
Hammarr, Sudeten
Jade Falcon Occupation Zone
14 September 3135

As Malvina's escorts slammed the hatches and hurriedly made them fast, the hovercraft lifted off and began to rotate on its vertical axis for a getaway. Through her viewport the Galaxy commander saw the distinctive low, wide shape of an *Uller* advancing at a prancing trot. As Wyndham turned away from the BattleMech a red light flared from its left arm.

She heard a crack, felt the APC jerk as the beam of the large extended-range laser vaporized a circle of the thin-gauge aligned-crystal steel armor to punch through the flexible skirting beneath. Instantly the timbre of the fans changed as a tornado of air began to bleed out the puncture.

For a moment the injured hovercraft slewed wildly across the street. Even as the green afterimage of the first beam faded from Malvina's vision another laser shot stabbed for them and missed. It sent up a geyser of shattered asphalt. Malvina's blue eyes narrowed as a glowing molten globule struck the ferroglass port right before her face and clung like a wasp.

The *Uller* lurched into a full run, closing for the kill. The surviving Skadi darted past, interposing its horsefly shape between the hovercraft and the 30-ton killing machine. A burst of multiple projectile rounds from the light LB-X autocannon mounted in the BattleMech's right arm shattered its cockpit screen and one ducted rotor, and dropped it to the street, where it *whoomp*ed into yellow flame.

Then Wyndham had control of his damaged machine and was accelerating away from the attacking 'Mech. The hovercraft bucked as if in a spastic gallop, banging its rear skirt armor off the pavement at intervals as air bled out. The fans, driven by the full bore of the turbine engines, reinflated the plenum chamber as soon as its stern touched down, lifting the rear and starting the cycle over.

The hit had erased much or all of the APC's considerable speed advantage over the *Uller*. Another laser beam dazzled a line across the port by Malvina's head as the 'Mech fired and missed high and right.

Malvina might have pressed her face to the ferroglass and possibly have been able to watch their pursuer. She chose not to submit herself to the indignity. *What will happen*, she thought, *will happen*.

She felt calm, although she knew it was a sort of surface effect, bobbing atop a sea of rage that surged and seethed beneath. She glanced at Malthus, seated across the way. His long, saturnine face was impassive. It seemed that he regarded her with a trace more than his usual smugness despite their plight. She burned to ask him how the Mongol force had arrived just in time to rescue them, but the scream of overloaded turbines and the semi-rhythmic banging and screeching of metal on pavement precluded intelligible conversation.

An ear-endangering rattle like hail striking a metal roof announced a glancing hit from shotgun-like LB-X rounds. Malvina was thrown abruptly sideways in her seat as Wyndham broke the APC left as if it were a *Bashkir* with a *Shilone* on its six.

With a clang the hovercraft caromed off a steel light post, which fell across the boxy machine and screeched down its back. Wyndham was already veering right.

Malvina felt her hands ball into fists. Even the prosthetic: it sent feedback directly into the nerves of her arm. Fortunately it also possessed cutouts that would prevent it damaging itself by clenching too tightly.

She fought the desire to strike out against those around her, her surroundings. *They* dared to attack her. To destroy her followers. To endanger her toy.

The latter particularly infuriated her. She did not truly know what she felt for the Inner Sphere child she had adopted. But it was definitely proprietary—and included savage determination to protect the small, strange creature.

Right now she could not.

She looked up to see Malthus' eyes upon her. "*Powless* in all truth," she snarled.

A slam. A grinding roar filled the compartment as the hovercraft scraped along the cement front of a building on the north side of Turkina's Path. Orange sparks streaked past Malvina's port like fireflies on speed. The passenger-compartment deck ran with blood, dark, almost purplish in the light from the viewports. Warrior Sondra, Cynthy's remaining attendant, had not strapped herself down in time. Wyndham's wild maneuvering had tossed her around the cabin and broken her like a doll.

Another screaming careen to the left. Bec Malthus spoke into his personal communicator, calm as if he sat in his study with a goblet of the Lyran brandy that was one of his few vices—which Malvina Hazen knew well he cultivated in part so that he would be *seen* to have vices, and thus seem less threatening to potential rivals and foes. Cynthy sat rigid and white as an alabaster statue, with tears streaming down her face and dripping on her stuffed bear's head. Yet she did not cry out, and Malvina astonished herself by feeling a stab of pride.

Out a left-hand viewport she caught a glimpse of the *Uller* pistoning in pursuit but a hundred meters behind. Wyndham fought his boxy transport hovercraft with immaculate skill. Although his gyrations had killed Sondra, Malvina knew they were all that had kept the rest of them alive.

So far. But the *Uller* slowly gained. It would be only seconds before the BattleMech got close enough to lock its Streak missiles onto the vehicle. Or simply holed the skirt with another lucky laser hit, making its destruction inevitable. *And there might be more assassins*, Malvina thought.

Wyndham banged the craft off another building. Dust knocked loose by multiple impacts filled the interior. The Merlin rattled as if it were coming apart around them. A jet of wind cut at Malvina's face like a cold blowtorch. The APC really *was* breaking up. . . .

As the hovercraft turned to starboard again another giant bipedal shape filled the port behind Malthus. A *Cougar*, its torso rotated right, raced from a side street right ahead of them. Cyan and red light filled the compartment as its weapons spoke in brilliance. Malvina threw an arm around Cynthy—

And saw the green Eye of Horus painted on the interloper.

She looked back the other way. Long-range rockets wracked the *Uller*. By lucky chance—or wizard aim, for Malvina had picked the cream of the battle-seasoned *desant* to return with her to Sudeten—dazzling ruby needles from the *Cougar*'s left arm stitched a line of glowing head-sized craters in the onrushing *Uller*'s frontal armor and slagged a huge hole in its forward viewscreen. A quarter second later the right-arm laser sent a pulse right into the squat forward-thrust "head," filling it with hell-red glare.

Still at a full run the pursuing 'Mech toppled to its right. It slammed against the side of an administrative dome, rolled vertically along the reinforced ferrocrete façade as if pirouetting. Then it sprawled into the street, rolling, bouncing.

By that time the *Cougar* had flashed across the intersection and braked. Straightening, the APC shot right behind its heels with the fallen *Uller* rolling after in a ghastly parody of pursuit. The tumbling wreck slowed and came to a stop on its back, steaming and smoking.

"Galaxy Commanders." Wyndham's voice came over the intercom. It was barely audible above the noise the hover-craft made as it banged its way down the street. A bad fan bearing keened like a lost soul, and the engines sounded as if they were trying to digest a handful of bolts. "We have fighting up ahead. We may have to ditch this bitch and find someplace defensible to hole up."

Even over the awful racket he sounded disgusted; for her part, Malvina was impressed that a former fighter pilot would even form such an alien concept as "holing up."

"Neg," called Bec Malthus. He had a way of filling the compartment with his voice without shouting. "Help is on the way."

Malvina Hazen stared at him. He smiled.

It made her want to smash his face. But she knew she must deny herself that pleasure. She had a terrible feeling Beckett Malthus was just about to prove himself indispensable again.

"Now that's something you don't see every day," Rorion Klimt said.

They stood on the sidewalk in front of the Falcon's Perch. A whole Binary of Jade Falcon security forces had secured the great building and the plaza across the way. A *Spirit* with a ridiculous jut of a lower jaw swelling up from its breastplate stood guard with its handheld Streak SRM quad launcher tilted toward the sky, flanked by a pair of 50-ton Epona hovertanks. Elementals stood spaced widely around the perimeter, while squads of laser-rifle armed infantry trotted this way and that without any obvious purpose. A gang of laborers under the guidance of one white-suited scientist and several technicians examined the scattered wreckage, mechanical and human.

So far no one had spared the pair of outlanders more than a glance. The would-be assassins had obviously been Clan warriors, and not even the most obtuse Falcon could possibly conceive that such men would obey mere Spher-oids, or deign to employ them in their schemes, however mad.

Rorion Klimt did not call his superior's attention to the

hivelike activity in the plaza. Rather he pointed away to the western sky, where a gigantic pear shape hung low above the city. As it approached and grew larger the reflected blue glare of its drive jets clearly illuminated the stylized silhouette of a great black crow, with wings outspread behind and beak thrust pugnaciously forward, painted on the lower curve of the *Overlord-C* DropShip's hull.

"The *Bec de Corbin*," Heinz-Otto von Texeira said. He knew the phrase meant "Crow's Beak" in a dialect of French that had been archaic almost a millenium before Kearny and Fuchida launched humanity into interstellar space. "Beckett Malthus likewise displays a certain flair."

Lightning flashed from the port side of the descending spacecraft. A yellow flame-bloom, bright and low above Hammarr's humped skyline, showed where one of the vessel's heavy particle cannon had struck an attacking helicopter dead-on and exploded it.

"I don't envy any laborers working on rooftops under that beast," his aide said. "Or even in the upper floors. The drives have to be licking the tops of the taller domes."

"The usual fond Clan regard for human life," von Texeira said as the craft stopped and settled.

Then both men ducked reflexively as a sonic boom cracked open the sky above their heads. They looked up to see a pair of heavy *Jagatai* aerospace fighters streaking north. As the Lyrans watched they curved east—away from the now-landed DropShip.

The *Overlord-C* sat amidst a bubbling pool of molten asphalt. Its bulk more than spanned the broad Turkina's Path. On the south side of the boulevard a landing jack had crushed the front of a laborer-caste dormitory.

The fronts of buildings north and south were scorched and glazed from the drives' intolerable heat. It was likely that anyone in the front of the damaged habitation was dead before the vast metal jack crushed the ferrocrete onto them.

If not, the jack had been a crowning mercy.

The Merlin APC's abused engines died as Malvina

Hazen stepped down to the street from the open hatch; their clattering finality suggested "died" was the right diagnosis. A ramp was already descending from the *Bec*'s underhull like the tongue of a great beast.

Shriveled husks lay in charred spots on the pavement: luckless pedestrians caught in the wash of the drive flares. After noting them in a glance Malvina paid no more notice to them than she would so many insects. They were no more to her. She set Cynthy down on the street beside her. The girl's face was unusually pale, but her blue eyes were bright, her cheeks dry.

A squeal of maltreated metal made Malvina turn. The APC driver's hatch was being forced open. Wyndham climbed out to stand unsteadily blinking in the thin but UV-rich light of the morning sun. His face was smudged.

"Wyndham!" Malvina snapped. The erstwhile aerospace pilot snapped to attention. "That was a rough ride you gave us."

"I am prepared to accept all consequences, Galaxy Commander," he said. "I am Jade Falcon."

"Good, Star Captain Wyndham. Turkina has much use for skills such as yours."

The huge amber eyes blinked. "G-galaxy Commander?"

"Do not stutter. An officer of the Jade Falcon *touman* cannot show the slightest hesitancy. And should anyone question your elevation, they shall find themselves in a Circle of Equals with *me*."

The pinched little mouth grew even more pinched. "As my Galaxy Commander orders."

She laughed at his poorly hidden dismay. "If you are still determined to die gloriously, Star Captain," she said, "I assure you that the coming weeks will offer abundant opportunity."

"If you will forgive me, Malvina," Malthus said, coming up beside her, "though *Bec*'s weapons have forced back our assailants, we must make haste. My captain communicates directly with Star Colonel Hastur Chistu." Chistu commanded Turkina Galaxy, which guarded the planet and Khan Jana Pryde.

"Naval Captain Joachim ignores a stream of challenges

from Hammarr traffic control, while simultaneously assuring Chistu that he has no intention of approaching closer to the Falcon's Perch. Jana Pryde broadcasts a message deploring the attack upon our persons."

"What urgency then?"

Malthus smiled thinly above his beard. "I suspect it will not be long before the spaceport tower says something my shipmaster will feel compelled to act upon."

Malvina glared up at him. "I am not yet so far gone in megalomania as to believe I can walk on molten asphalt with impunity, Bec Malthus!"

His answer was a rising gesture of a gauntleted right hand. An open-topped utility hovercraft descended down the ramp toward them, driven by a nervous-looking technician under the eye of a naval warrior.

"Not a conveyance suited to the dignity of the future khan of Clan Jade Falcon, perhaps," Malthus said, "but as is said, when needs must, the Devil drives."

Her eyes drilled into him like lasers a heartbeat longer. Then she laughed.

"You have the gift of making your words speak in several voices at once, Beckett Malthus," she said. "Whether it is a good thing for a son of Turkina to do so remains to be seen."

He genuflected toward her. "As the Chingis Khan says. So long as she moves briskly."

Laughing and shaking back her hair, Malvina reached down toward the even tinier Inner Sphere child. Cynthy solemnly raised a mittened hand. Malvina enfolded it in the gauntlet covering her prosthetic member and led her toward the utility craft as it approached in a miniature whirlwind.

Even as acceleration pressed Malvina into a blast couch on the bridge of the DropShip ascending toward *Emerald Talon* in orbit, her mood flashed over again.

"What happened down there, Malthus?" she raged.

"Certain warriors allowed their emotions to be so affected by your words and actions," her nominal superior said blandly, "that they acted in a deplorably irresponsible manner. Their codices are being examined and the qualities of their genetic lines scrutinized for defects. If one believes what Jana Pryde currently broadcasts to all Sudeten."

"I mean, why did our forces arrive so conveniently to rescue us?" Once aboard, Malvina had stooped to kiss Cynthy's cheek and sent her off with a pair of techs to be strapped down in her quarters for takeoff. The wounded, including the newly minted and still sullen Star Captain Wyndham, had been dispatched to sick bay.

"Is my khan dissatisfied at being rescued?" Malthus murmured.

"Answer, damn you! Do not press me now, Beckett Malthus."

"As the Chingis Khan commands. If I may incur the risk of boasting—"

The mask of rage overlaying Malvina's white features softened into a mean little smile. "A self-effacing Falcon warrior is a contradiction in terms. Spit it out, Bec Malthus."

"—I possess some small knowledge of our Jade Falcon character. I deemed it likely that an attempt would be made upon our lives today when we appeared at the Falcon's Perch, irrespective of the Council's judgment concerning your challenge, and for that matter with or without . . . shall we say, *encouragement* from a lofty perch?"

"You expected treachery? That filthy *surat* Jana!" Malvina shook her head. "I should simply have shot her where she sat, and damn the consequences."

"The consequences," Malthus said with quiet emphasis somehow clearly audible above the muted thunder of the drives, "would have been futility. Clan Jade Falcon would never acknowledge as khan one who acted so dishonorably. Indeed, were they to do so, it is not inconceivable the other Clans might call a Trial of Annihilation against us. Many Clans seethe with jealousy of the Falcon; it would not be the first time the Wolves have played upon the fact.

"Besides, I do not believe the khan stands behind the attack on us. For her to order such a thing, or even be seen to countenance it, would risk tearing the Clan apart. Much as she surely hates you now, she is utterly devoted to Turkina and Clan Jade Falcon, in her way. As I know well."

"Whose side are you on?" Malvina flared.

"The Falcon's," the big man said imperturbably. "More proximately, I am now committed entirely to yours, willynilly. You must surely see that Khan Jana Pryde cannot but view my actions as being of a parcel with yours. I am no less renegade in her eyes now, regardless."

Malvina sat back with a strange little V-shaped smile on her lips. "Yes," she said. "I rather suppose you are. And whatever connivances you had in mind before, you are mine now, Bec Malthus."

If she sought to distress him she failed—visibly, at least. He inclined his head. "As you say, my Khan," he replied.

"You keep calling me that."

He inclined his head to the side. "Am I mistaken, then, as to your intent, Malvina Hazen? Do you intend to flee into exile? The Periphery perhaps?"

"You know that before I do that," Malvina said, "I will die. But not alone. Not by any means."

Malthus turned his head forward again. Acceleration pressed the flesh of his face toward his ears like grayish putty. "Then you must declare yourself Khan of Clan Jade Falcon," he said, "and make it stick."

In the studio attached to her quarters within the Falcon's Perch, in which she privately indulged her vice of puttering at handicrafts—what the decadent Spheroids called *hobbies*—Khan Jana Pryde stood gazing out a high narrow window at the sky. A white overcast had covered it, as if to hide from her sight the heavens that sheltered her enemy.

In the present emergency she might have repaired to the Clan Jade Falcon command center buried many stories underground. She chose not to hide from her enemies. At least, not until they moved openly against her.

"Khan Jana Pryde," a wall communicator said. *"The* Emerald Talon *has just requested clearance to depart orbit for the zenith jump point."*

"Now is your last chance to stop the *stravag*, Jana," said

Loremaster Julia Buhalin. Like her khan she stood, with her staff of office somewhat grandiosely in hand.

Jana turned with a questioning lift of her eyebrow. "You would try to stop a *Nightlord*?"

"We have WarShips," the loremaster said. "The *Talon* is still operating at less than maximum capacity, *quineg*? She was badly hurt in the fight for Skye by the Inner Sphere battleship *Yggdrasil*."

"Ah, yes," Jana said. "The Lyran WarShip." She frowned thoughtfully for a moment, then shook her head.

"I have no desire to see a space battle in orbit above the capital world of the occupation zone," she said, "nor to see Hammarr become a new Turtle Bay."

"My Khan," Buhalin said, her face set in earnest lines, "if you let that Hazen miscarriage escape it will mean a Rending."

Jana drew in a deep breath, let it out in a sigh. The words *civil war* were too obscene to pass her loremaster's chaste Clan lips. She had little taste or patience for euphemism herself. But she must indulge her staunchest ally at such a time.

"How well I know that, Julia. Yet my responsibility is to Turkina and my people. If a Rending must afflict our Clan, let it do so elsewhere than above Clan Jade Falcon's beating heart!"

"*Khan*—" the communicator prodded, with hesitation obvious in the young male voice.

"Grant permission to *my* WarShip *Emerald Talon* to depart Sudeten system," Jana said.

Buhalin's face tensed. "Yes, Julia," Jana said. "On my head be it. I am khan. And no matter what that twisted little freak believes, I am Jade Falcon!" She practically roared the last words.

Her loremaster bowed. "You are Jade Falcon, my Khan."

Jana Pryde drew a deep, shuddering breath. She sighed.

"Your assistance has been invaluable to me, Julia," she said. "Your advice has helped me steer our Clan through crises before. You will not take it as an affront to your considerable abilities, nor to your unmatched service to khan and Clan, if I now feel I must seek certain specialized assistance."

Buhalin looked up past lowered brows. "My Khan?"

"Security desk," Jana told her communicator. In a moment a female duty officer answered. "Somewhere in proximity to the Falcon's Perch you will find the two emissaries from the Lyran archon. Bring them to me."

She listened a moment. "No," she said. "They are not prisoners. Do not construe that to mean they have a choice, however."

She looked back and smiled into her friend's expression of shock and nascent outrage. "I need cunning and skill in treachery now, Julia Buhalin. For along with Malvina Hazen, I go up against Beckett Malthus. And to your credit, you are no Crow."

Wordlessly the loremaster bowed again.

"And where better to turn for devious counsel," Jana Pryde went on with feral smile, "than to a Steiner? *Especially* a Steiner merchant prince."

10

The Casts
Hammarr Commercial Spaceport, Sudeten
Jade Falcon Occupation Zone
17 September 3135

"Bargained well and done," von Texeira said blandly, extending a broad pink palm to his factotum. Scowling and griping, Rorion dug in a pocket and dropped five gold coins onto it.

It was night in The Casts, the outlanders' quarter: the inevitable stews of shops, warehouses, dingy flats and spacers' taverns that had sprung up like fungus around the fringes of Hammarr's commercial spaceport. Inside the crowded canteen they could have heard a hand-grenade pin drop.

The tuft of hair atop the rangy Sea Fox woman's head dipped like a cockatiel's crest as she nodded acknowledgment of her foe's tap out. The resemblance was unusually close because she had dyed the scalp lock white and yellow, apparently in anticipation of a festive night out. She released the arm she held captive—gently, von Texeira noted—and sat up.

"Wise choice," she said, leaning down to pat the cheek of the youthful Falcon MechWarrior she had just defeated.

"You fought well. Get your friends to help you put the joint back. You'll be fit in a few days."

She stood up, dusting her palms against each other. Then she walked toward the edge of the cleared circle of floor, already beginning to fill as the bar's clientele, with the show over, began to mill. By chance, or so it seemed, she came almost directly toward von Texeira and Rorion.

Her eyes found von Texeira. The diplomat was not exactly inconspicuous in most crowds, and fat people were no common sight on any core Clan planet. Her brows rose questioningly.

His own deep blue eyes went wide.

Senna Rodríguez ducked down and right. The heavy metal chair the defeated Jade Falcon had swung one-handed at the back of her narrow, crested skull grazed her shoulder and struck the cement floor with a ringing clatter.

Senna kept spinning, right into her attacker. A two-edged fighting dagger had appeared in her right hand, blade tapering downward from her fist. Whirling behind the off-balance MechWarrior she struck him in the right kidney. Not once but half a dozen times, too fast for the eye to follow, reminding Heinz-Otto of an industrial sewing machine as much as anything.

Dropping his failed makeshift bludgeon the Falcon arched up and back, his face a mask of agony. Veins and tendons stood out like cables from his neck. A strained, keening whistle emerged from his wide-open mouth. It changed to a gurgle as Senna slashed him across the throat, stepping deftly back to avoid the blood that hosed from severed arteries as he fell.

"No second chances," she told the crowd. "That's the kind of woman I am." She plucked a stray napkin off the floor, wiped the blood from her dagger, made the weapon disappear.

"Buy a girl a drink?" she asked von Texeira with a half smile, wiping red droplets from her face with another napkin she snagged from a table in passing. The three men who sat at the table, outland spacers by their dress and somewhat soft appearance, said nothing.

"He can afford to," said Rorion sourly.

"Hush," von Texeira said. "It was my intention even before your most remarkable display." He gestured to a vacant chair. She sat, crossing long legs. She seemed restless.

"Of what? Utter incompetence?" The Sea Fox shook her head. "I'd break a 'prentice to laborer for such misjudgment."

"What do you mean?" asked Rorion thunderstruck. "It was brilliant."

She looked at him with her brow furrowed. "What do *you* mean? Bad business all around."

"To kill a full-fledged Falcon MechWarrior? If you'll refrain from killing *me* for disagreeing with you, that is a most impressive feat."

The noise was coming back as the mostly-offworlder crowd returned to the serious business of drinking by the strands of multicolored lights strung along the bar and ceiling in a failed attempt to alleviate pervasive drabness. Someone started another mad electronic song skirling from the player.

Senna gave Rorion a grin rather more lupine than vulpine. "I try not to kill men who make an effort to charm me. You'd have definite potential, if I went for glib. Sadly, you're a touch too callow."

Rorion sat back trying not to look outraged. Von Texeira tried to suppress a laugh. He wondered when was the last time his aide—whose feats as a lady-killer nearly matched the legend in his own mind—had heard himself described by a woman he'd just complimented as *callow*.

"I meant, it was *bad business*. What kind of practice is it to kill a potential customer?"

Von Texeira noticed that the body of Senna's foe had quietly disappeared. He heard the incident being discussed in hushed tones, but the talk concerned the remarkable prowess a despised Sea Fox, Bloodnamed or not, had shown. The killing itself was a commonplace; it might not have been the tavern's first that night. Life was valued differently in Clan space than in even the most desperate *favelas* of Recife, von Texeira knew from weary experience.

"What an amateur mistake," Senna said in disgust. "I

misjudged him. I forgot that while these Birds possess all the physical courage in the universe, they're scarcely aware the moral brand exists."

"How could you know he'd dishonor himself after a challenge?" Rorion asked.

She laughed shortly. "Dishonor? A Falcon Court of Honor would have cleared him in an eyeblink, certainly. Any warrior Clan would do the same. There's no dishonor in stamping on a *stravag* like me."

Rorion blinked and pulled his head back, astonished to hear a Bloodname bearer, no matter of which Clan, refer to herself by the most viciously derogatory term for *freebirth*.

"So why have you come here, your Merchant Highness? A taste for these surroundings?" She waved a hand around at the dark and humid bar, which was beginning to return to normal. "Or perhaps you didn't get enough of my sparkling company?"

"Do not undervalue your charm, dear lady."

Her laugh was harsh as a vulture's call. "You try to flatter me? I am Clan."

"I do not flatter," he said, a trifle sternly. "But despite the genuine merits of your conversation, I have more specific ends in mind."

"You've no doubt heard by now," Rorion said as a dour waiter plunked down a tray of three glass mugs filled with pale and slightly murky local beer, "of this morning's amateurish attempt on the lives of Malvina Hazen and Bec Malthus."

"Amateurish?" Senna asked with a lift of her eyebrows.

Von Texeira looked to his subordinate. "It failed," the younger man said with a shrug.

"If you'll pardon my saying so," von Texeira said, "it's the Clan proclivity for trying to drive a tack with an assisted-inertia sledgehammer. Hopeless."

"What would, say, a Lyran CEO have done?"

"Not resorted to assassination, one hopes. Still: only luck can prevent a sufficiently resourceful and determined individual from getting within range of his target with a scoped rifle," von Texeira said. "Should the rifle be powerful enough, the target can even be killed with a reasonable chance of the assassin escaping. The flip of a coin, in any event."

"As you say, that is not the Clan way. Not even of Clan Sea Fox. Too distant and impersonal a kind of murder. Though I daresay we Foxes would make a better job of it."

She rocked back in her seat and looked at them beneath lowered brows. "A succinct appraisal, anyway. Is this standard operating procedure for Lyran diplomats, then?"

"Let us just say," von Texeira said, "that any negotiator's hand is strengthened by an appreciation of the realities of the way the world works."

She shrugged. "I've noticed the same thing, myself," she said, drawing abstruse patterns with her finger in the water condensed on the scarred tabletop. "So. You need an adviser on high-energy Clan politics, *quiaff*?"

"You are most perceptive."

"I was waiting. What kind of interstellar trader would I be if I didn't know babes in the woods when I saw them?"

Rorion looked sour and took a drink of his beer as if biting it off. "We are not so cherry in dealing with the Clans as you seem to think," he said.

Senna leaned forward and smiled a slow smile. "But never so close to the center, I wager," she said. "And never for such high stakes."

"Is it good business to make fun of your customers, then?" von Texeira asked. His eyes twinkled—but the question still rang with challenge.

"Sea Fox or no, I'm still Clan. A little arrogance goes with the territory." She slouched back and sipped from her mug. Her long turquoise eyes held von Texeira closely. "Anyway, we have a seller's market here, *quiaff*?"

Von Texeira slammed a palm down on the table and laughed. He did not laugh quietly; he never did. He believed anything worth doing was worth overdoing. Heads turned to stare. But briefly.

"Aff," he said.

"It'll cost you," she said.

They dickered for a time. Rorion amused himself sitting back with a half smile, walking a Steiner gold piece over his knuckles, making it appear and disappear. Around them conversation ebbed and flowed; they were basically ignored. Even in Clanspace a spaceport dive was pretty much a spaceport dive.

At length Senna leaned back and favored the two men with a lopsided smile. "You do not disappoint, Heinz-Otto von Texeira. You may have inherited your position, but you hold it with considerable skill."

A shadow seemed to cross his face. "I have increased my family's wealth," he said with simple pride. "I note also that, whatever the nature of your Clan's Trial of Bloodright, you have well earned your Bloodname."

"I did," she said. Her gaze flicked toward Rorion, who gave her back a hooded smile. "And remind me never to play cards with your man."

Von Texeira laughed. "A wise course even if he doesn't cheat."

"You offer an attractive bargain," the Clanswoman said. "But what if your archon decides you've exceeded your discretion?"

"Her Grace the Duchess of Tharkad has extended me considerable latitude for this assignment. And I doubt strongly you can find anything prejudicial to the interests of either the Commonwealth or House Steiner in the offer I've made. If anything, expanding trade with Clan Sea Fox will likely benefit us, especially in such uncertain times.

"But should my archon decide to disavow my agreements with you, in whole or in part, you have my word that Recife Spice and Liquors and *a família* von Texeira zu Mannstein stand ready to make good on them."

"Are you not maybe relying a little too much on still having your job when you get home? Out of sight, out of mind, or some people say. Heads of states have been deposed in their absence. I suspect the same fate has befallen corporate heads, a time or two."

"This week," agreed von Texeira. He leaned forward and held up a finger.

"Now. Whatever anyone else within the family may think—and I grant you, some of them are certainly thinking hard along the very lines you have suggested—the real head of our family has given her blessing to this undertaking and will permit no moves against me in my absence. I speak of Mamãe Luci, our matriarch."

Rorion hoisted his half-empty mug. "And a fearful old gargoyle she is," he said, and drained the dregs. Then he grimaced. "These damned Falcons could be more subtle in their recycling of this stuff. At least filter it a time or two before pouring it back in the bottle!"

Senna's scrutiny never left von Texeira's face. "Are you that sure? Your Victor Steiner-Davion could give you testimony about the keeping of faith within powerful Inner Sphere families."

"Indeed," von Texeira said with a nod. "And with the greatest respect for my distant, and ever so venerable, cousin, for all his vast experience I submit that even he has very little to teach a man of my home province of Nova Suevia about full-contact familial politics."

The master merchant rubbed her chin. Then she nodded and tossed back the last of her own beer.

"Very well," she said, setting the mug down with a clack. "Bargained well and done!"

11

Jade Falcon Naval Reserve WarShip Emerald Talon
Orbiting Graus
Jade Falcon Occupation Zone
19 September 3135

"**M**y intentions?" Malvina Hazen flared her voice to seeming fury while showing a feral grin to Beckett Malthus, who stood upon the WarShip's flying bridge with her in the bright yellow shine of Graus dayside. "My intentions are my own, Star Colonel Watrous. Must I then challenge you for my right, as a Galaxy commander of the Jade Falcon *touman*, to make planetfall upon one of Turkina's worlds?"

Silent naval crew and technicians bent to their consoles. Dressed in shorts and a short-sleeved shirt, her hair carefully arranged in pigtails by the laborer attendants Malvina had now assigned to her, Cynthy stood with nose and one hand pressed against a port. Burton Bear dangled from the other.

There was actually a stammer in the voice that emerged from the speakers. *"Ah—of course not, Galaxy Commander Hazen,"* the planetary governor said. *"It is merely that we received no advance warning of your arrival. It is most irregular for a vessel of the size and nature of the* Emerald Talon *to shape orbit without notice."*

Or what little notice the planet's administrators—and putative defenders—would have gotten when the million-plus metric ton WarShip had popped into existence from a pirate point scarcely eighteen hours out at standard one-gee thrust like a smuggler or a Sea Fox.

Malvina wore a midnight-black jumpsuit that clung to her trim form. Her pale skin and hair looked ghostly in the planet shine. She walked to stand beside her ward and stroke her hair. The little girl looked up at her, smiled, then returned her attention to the commanding spectacle of an entire world spread out before her wondering eyes.

From a corner of her real eye Malvina saw Malthus' long, heavy face momentarily stiffen into greater-than-usual impassivity. She laughed silently at his priggish disapproval. *I keep the child and see her cared for and schooled in accordance with Inner Sphere customs, in part from plain curiosity, in part because it gives me pleasure—and altogether because I can.*

"I await, Star Colonel Watrous," she said aloud. Watrous, she knew, was, like Malthus, old for a warrior. The fertile world was something of a breadbasket for the Jade Falcon empire. Recent industrialization, including commissioning of a BattleMech factory, had enhanced its strategic value. Even among the Falcons, the governor of such a world must be a more capable administrator than fighter, even if extensively advised by a cadre of scientists, as was indeed the case. Like a naval admiral, therefore, he tended to be immune, by custom and force of Khan Jana Pryde's titanium will, from challenge by inferiors. Only if he displeased his khan by no longer being able to discharge his duties—meaning, to meet quotas—would he face a trial.

As a warrior in name only he was naturally despised by his nominal peers. Despite his indispensable service to Turkina, the Star colonel bore no Bloodname, and never would.

"A-await what, Galaxy Commander Hazen?"

"Either landing clearance," she said sweetly, "or a declaration of the forces with which you intend to defend the planet."

"I—we would not dream of resisting your landing, Galaxy

Commander," Watrous said. *"We are all Jade Falcon, after all. I shall instruct New Paris traffic control to transmit permissions and landing paths to your DropShip pilots immediately."* The colossal WarShip, of course, was not streamlined for atmospheric insertion, nor could her whale bulk survive the forces involved, much less grounding on a surface under about a standard gee. The *Nightlords* were creatures of deep space, like all WarShips.

"Hazen out," Malvina snapped, cutting off Watrous, who seemed to be drawing breath to say more.

Anger flared within her. She withdrew her hand from the child's head, turned and paced toward the center of the bridge. "The spineless fool!" she said. "I should order Binetti to part his hair with a naval PPC. If not scour New Paris from the face of Albion." Albion, in the northern hemisphere, was Graus' main and most populated continent.

Malthus arched a brow. "It would be most inadvisable."

"Why? Damn you, tell me why." Anger filled her now; it prickled her skin, and itched like a rash at the interfaces between her prosthetic arm and leg and the natural stumps, and deep within the socket of her synthetic eye.

"For one thing," Malthus said, "it would obviate much of our reason for coming to Graus by damaging the key industrial center. Please recall that, thanks to Countess Tara Campbell's destruction of the Cyclops, Incorporated, facility on Skye, we have been unable to make full repairs of our 'Mechs and vehicles, despite the amount of *isorla* we took."

"I know that as well as you do," Malvina said. Her own *Shrike*, the Black Rose, remained but marginally operable from the brutal battering it had taken in the fight for the Prefecture IX capital world. "What else?"

"The power this vessel gives us is immense, but tenuous as mist," he intoned. His manner only infuriated her more. He was something else rare among Jade Falcons: pompous. Worse, he knew she could not stand it. "Despite the damage *Yggdrasil* did, her weapons remain capable of easily ravaging planetary defenses—and the cities they defend.

Let us once use that power for such a purpose, though"—
he snapped blunt fingers—"and it will vanish."

"Why should that be, Beckett Malthus?"

"Should we employ your Mongol doctrine of terror for
strategy's sake against our fellow Clansmen and women,"
he said, "every Jade Falcon alive will turn her or his hand
against us. That will be the end of us. And your ambitions.
The *Emerald Talon*'s armament gives us no more than the
common hostage-taker's advantage: if the hostage is actually killed, the advantage not only vaporizes but turns to
lethal liability. Such threats become worse than useless
once carried out."

Malvina's shoulders and full breasts rose and fell in an
angry sigh. "So you have told me, many times. And once
again, I see the force in your arguments. The time has not
yet come to let Jade Falcon feel the lash."

She walked back to the great ferroglass viewport and
stretched out her hand with her fingers curved like a raptor's talons.

"Yet."

Her fingertips touched the insulated glass. "But when
that time comes, they *will* learn what terror means. As
Chingis Khan, I swear it."

Belching fire like a legendary dragon, the *Bec de Corbin*
descended toward the New Paris spaceport. While it sat
well distant from the city center, port and shuttle having
after all been built by the prudent Steiners long ago, the
landing field was surrounded not just by warehouses and
workshops but immense blocks of worker housing. The Falcon found it efficient to keep them near their jobs. Should
a landing go awry or a DropShip's fusion bottle lose
containment—there were more workers where those came
from. Such was the Clan way.

Above *Bec* two white contrails spiraled lazily downward,
tipped by starlike drive flares: a pair of small *Broadsword*-
class DropShips, streamlined for atmospheric maneuvering
and capable of horizontal landings, either rolling on
wheeled gear or dropping straight down on ventral jets.

Then the sky split with a tremendous crack as a pair of assault-class *Scytha* fighters, extravagantly winged and canarded and bristling with lasers, whipped at hypersonic speed over the city at less than a thousand meters. They flew so fast that their leading surfaces glowed bright yellow from air compression, and they drew glowing lines of ionization far behind their wide-flaming drives. For kilometers to either side windows shattered; the shock wave tumbled pedestrians directly under their flight path off their feet.

Malvina Hazen marked Graus for her own. Were the New Parisians wise, they would feel nothing but gratitude that she settled for doing it this way.

What Star Colonel Watrous, watching from an observation deck of his spaceport command center, thought of the display, his aides wisely forbore to ask.

Even as the *Bec de Corbin* settled toward the four jaws of the landing cradle, great ports yawned open in her fat flanks. Fast Skadi attack VTOLs swarmed out, followed by a pair of lumbering Cardinal transports. Then came a full Star of elementals, using their jump jets to fly well clear of the drive flames before rotating and using them to brake their descent. Last a mixed Star of light and medium 'Mechs jumped out: two *Koshi*, an *Eyrie*, a *Gyrfalcon* and a *Shadow Hawk IIc*. As they struck the pavement they spread out as if securing a hostile perimeter.

Braked by retro-rockets, the two aerodyne DropShips separated, curveting down to land flanking BattleMech Fabrication Unit #1 and its neighbor, an electronics plant that made control and sensor components for the giant striding war machines as well as conventional vehicles and even aircraft.

With a roar and a rush *Bec*'s vast pear shape settled into the cradle's welcoming embrace. The drive flame went out. Its howl was replaced by almost musical groaning and ringing as metal cooled and stresses eased.

A ramp descended to the scorched and scarred pavement beyond the scarp of the blast pit, whose internal walls glowed yellow from fusion heat. Through the fumarole shimmer strode a mighty figure: a 95-ton *Shrike* on great clawed feet. Despite the battle damage clearly visible beneath fresh paint it moved with an imperiousness unusual even for one of the most potent ground-borne killing machines ever constructed, its beaked head held at a haughty angle. Upon its right thigh-plate glistened a black rose, on the left a stylized jade-green eye with human shape and a falcon's vertical stripe. Over the covers of the long-range missile launchers in its breastplate were painted two staring blue eyes: the Eyes of the Falcon, as Malvina and her brother had once been called. Her *desant* had taken them as its unofficial badge during the Skye campaign; now Malvina, having adopted the Horus eye as the symbol of her Mongol faction, used them to denote veterans of that struggle.

She intended to attract many more followers to her cause. Despite her precipitous withdrawal from Sudeten she had brought some away with her.

The BattleMech stepped onto the paved soil of Graus and paused. From behind its back slowly unfolded a pair of great jagged wings, painted gold and buff on the undersides like the plumage of an adult Jade Falcon.

Watching the display, Star Colonel Watrous scratched his beard with fingers long grown unused to the joystick of a BattleMech cockpit, and fretted. Scientist aides, quietly respectful in white but visibly agitated beneath their studied caste calm, brought whispered word that mixed forces of 'Mechs, vehicles and infantry had occupied the two large factory complexes on the landing field's far side. His frown etched itself deeper and deeper into his spare sundarkened face.

It was all correct, if unusual. Malvina Hazen was a *ristar*, a famous champion of Clan Jade Falcon. More to the point, she and Beckett Malthus were both Galaxy commanders, superior to Watrous, and Bloodnamed into the *batchall*. If they cared to assume control of Graus with its forests and fields, not to mention its BattleMech plant, that was their right.

The newcomers showed no hostility toward the locals they encountered, whether Clan warriors or labor-class menials. But to Watrous' mind the crisp, efficient brutality of their actions had the character of armed invasion. If not a rape.

A chill passed through his wiry frame. Not for himself; soft he might have become, and maybe he had always been more bureaucrat than a razor-edged claw of Turkina. But he had been raised to live for glorious self-sacrifice to Clan and Falcon. Rather he feared for the world he administered with all the zeal and precision of a Clan warrior, if none of the glory.

Beyond that, he feared for Clan Jade Falcon itself.

═══ 12 ═══

The Falcon's Perch
Hammarr, Sudeten
Jade Falcon Occupation Zone
30 September 3135

"**M**obilize the entire Jade Falcon *touman* immediately, my Khan," said Heinz-Otto von Texeira, his deep voice smoothly matter-of-fact, as though he discussed the morning stock prices from the Lyran Grand Bourse on Tharkad. "Crush Malvina and her brood of vipers on Graus, where they are concentrated and near to hand."

She rules as khan the world on which I find myself, he thought. *Ergo: my Khan. Child's play, as rationalizations go. I can explain away* much *worse before my morning coffee.*

Khan Jana Pryde stared at him through narrowed green eyes. "Advice most forceful from a Lyran businessman."

Hands braced on the silver ram's head of his cane, he tried to ease himself in the none-too-comfortable chair in the khan's surprisingly small, Spartan office. "I may not be a warrior, Excellency, but I must admit to not being a total stranger to combat. In the days of my youth, joyfully misspent as it was, great profit often occasioned great peril. More pertinently: as you perceive, I am a man keenly attuned to the bottom line. Here is yours: act decisively, over-whelmingly even, before the opportunity passes."

Julia Buhalin scowled. "That means embroiling the Clan in a Rending."

Von Texeira glanced at her. He was well practiced enough that it took no effort to hide his irritation at her interjection. It took slightly more to hide his amusement at the euphemism.

The fact that they were women gave him no difficulty taking her, or her khan, or that she-devil Malvina for that matter, with utmost seriousness, even though on the surface Recife society was male-dominated. He had grown up in utter terror of his own clan's matriarch, the fearsome Mamãe Luci, a wizened ebony effigy with a cotton-top like a tamarin, already octogenarian when he was born, even though he was fully as tall as she when he was eight years old. Granted, he'd sprung up quick. . . .

Now Mamãe Luci was over a hundred and thirty and, if anything, more formidable than half a century before. Age seemed to just concentrate her, make her even harder and more obdurate. Nor were the other women of his *família* in any sense weak, including his adored older sister, Annal-ise, as fair and golden-blond as he was dark (no uncommon thing in Recife families), a MechWarrior who had died fighting in the LCAF when he was fifteen, or his own dear wife, Irmagilda, true daughter of the San Luca clan of fierce reputation. Even his own daughters had grit enough to defy his wishes.

One of the reasons I consented to this Himmelsfahrtkom-mando, he thought, *if not the most pressing.*

"What do you think you have on your hands now?" he asked the khan. "You know Malvina Hazen's out of control—out of your control, certainly, maybe out of Bec Malthus'. Even her own, so far as we know. If she hasn't declared herself khan yet, it's but a matter of time."

Pryde frowned. Her eyes slid to Buhalin. The loremaster looked troubled.

"He has the right of that," she said.

"Malvina Hazen is a brilliant commander," von Texeira said. "You knew that when you appointed her to command a Galaxy in your *desant*. I suspect you were also well aware that she's a total monster—by your standards at least as much as ours. What she did to Chaffee was as repugnant to Clan Jade Falcon tradition as to Inner Sphere mores. If you do not crush her promptly the consequences will be disastrous."

The khan showed him a lopsided smile. "You show great solicitude for the welfare of Clan Jade Falcon," she said, "especially given the attack on Porrima and the seizure of Chaffee."

She has bits of brass, I give her that, von Texeira thought. "The archon's response to those attacks is her purview and not mine; I reiterate her express desire to restore and maintain peace between our realms."

Uncharacteristically, his smile was strained. "As for my personal concern, let me say it is first and foremost for *all* humanity, where Malvina Hazen is concerned. I honestly believe her to be the greatest threat to arise in my lifetime."

In the silence the chime from the office communicator rang startlingly loud. Frowning, Jana Pryde said, "Speak."

"My Khan," a female voice said. *"A Falcon merchant JumpShip has arrived at the zenith point from the Graus system. Her commander says she has an urgent transmission for you."*

"Of what nature?"

"She declines to specify, other than that she believes it must be seen by your eyes only."

Julia Buhalin rose to her feet. She cast a meaningful glance at von Texeira, who stayed with his broad butt planted in his chair and a smile of bovine placidity on his face. The loremaster cleared her throat.

A Jade Falcon hinting? he thought. *Truly, will wonders never cease?*

A slow, sly smile spread across Jana Pryde's thin lips. She shook her head slightly. Buhalin looked outraged but said nothing. "One moment, then," the khan said to the communicator. "At my command, feed the transmission through to me."

Von Texeira raised an eyebrow. Jana Pryde picked up a

small control wand from her near-empty desktop. A touch brought the lights low and closed shutters over the narrow arched windows. A second touch made her desk unfold like a plastic and metal flower. In a few soundless moments it had become a small holostage.

"Fox gimmickry," Jana Pryde said, smiling openly. "The *stravags* are cunning, one must give them that. And they have their uses."

Buhalin's smooth brow hardened slightly. Here at least was a Falcon undercurrent von Texeria could sense. For all its warrior fanaticism Clan Jade Falcon boasted the most astute and successful merchant caste of any Clan—save Clan Sea Fox. To be outdone by their despised commercial rivals tasted bitter on Falcon tongues.

But nothing to what now literally unfolded before them.

Clad in her midnight-black dress uniform, with its token emerald trim, the jade feathers of her cape scintillating in spotlight beams that converged upon her like lasers, Galaxy Commander Malvina Hazen stood straight as a blade and ominous as a black flame behind a podium draped with the banner of Clan Jade Falcon. The three-dimensional image's focus was tight; von Texeira felt more than saw a sense of space around her, a vast hall filled with barely pent Falcon emotions and anticipation.

And, falconlike, Malvina stooped straightaway for her prey: *"By her cowardly behavior in failing to send the* touman *of Clan Jade Falcon to exploit the victories of the* desant, *for which so many brave warriors gave their lives, and her appeasing of the Inner Sphere by refusing to carry the great Crusade of Kerensky into the heart of The Republic, the woman Jana—so-called Pryde, so-called khan—has shown herself craven and bloodfoul. I name her unfit to bear the Pryde Bloodname. I name her unfit to be khan of Clan Jade Falcon!"*

Instead of bursting with raucous screams, if nothing else at Malvina's effrontery at uttering the unspeakable, the unseen audience's silence deepened, perceptibly across astronomical-units of transmission that strewed little pops and flickers of solar wind–induced static through the projection. Von Texeira felt his nape hairs rise. *For the first time*

I begin to feel *the hold Malvina has upon her Mongol faithful,* he thought.

"*As of this day, in Turkina's name, I declare this Jana deposed. As she has refused to meet my challenge, I claim the right of forfeit. From this day hence, I, Malvina Hazen, am lawful khan of Clan Jade Falcon.*"

A moment's more silence. Von Texeira felt himself actually squirming in his chair.

A thousand voices screamed as one: "*Hail Khan Malvina Hazen! Hail Khan Malvina Hazen!*"

The cry changed, with an abruptness that seemed rehearsed, although given the fractious Falcon temperament, that struck von Texeira as vanishingly unlikely. Without faltering the chant became: "*Hail to the Chingis Khan! Hail Malvina Hazen, Chingis Khan!*"

Hail to the Emperor of All Mankind.

"She saw me off in such fury, she was frozen white," von Texeira said, accepting a mug of steaming coffee from a hand nearly as dark as his own. A single orange cord encircled the bony wrist. "As if she had got herself marooned in that God-forgotten waste where the Falcon improvidently keeps her Eyrie. Yet still she equivocates!"

"Your heart, Margrave," said Rorion, genuinely concerned.

"Bah." He thumped his chest with his free hand. "In here beats the heart of a lion. A *pissed-off* lion!"

Petah traded glances and grins with his equally tall and skeletal twin and fellow bondsman, Nestah. The extravagantly dreadlocked pair, who hailed from some unlikely Periphery planet, were Clan Sea Fox factors for Sudeten. Their bondholder was none other than Master Merchant Senna Rodríguez.

Heinz-Otto von Texeira and Rorion Klimt found themselves seated on a couch in the house the pair leased in The Casts outside Hammarr proper, where the blast of departing DropShip drives shook the walls at unpredictable intervals. The dwelling they themselves had been assigned stood only a few blocks' walk away through a bright and almost warm morning—for spring, such as it was, advanced

upon the capital like a timid army, two days after Malvina's
long-range bombshell exploded in Khan Jana Pryde's office.

The twin bondsmen murmured oddly accented excuses
and withdrew to the rear of the house, from which emerged
a low thudding of rhythmic bass-heavy music.

"I believe you had a question for me, gentlemen."

The master merchant herself sprawled among some
brightly printed cushions piled against a whitewashed wall.
Though von Texeira could see she had never been pretty,
even before years and hard usage had left their marks, for
the first time he became aware that she was nevertheless a
striking woman, with long strong legs and full breasts that
seemed impatient at being constrained by the white silk
shirt whose tails she had tied up above her muscle-ridged
belly. A white scar crossed her stomach at a transverse
angle. Her manner suggested a great cat in repose.

Von Texeira and his aide had been surprised at how
ready Senna was to remain on the surface to play consul-
tant for them. Granted, her fees were good—*extortionate*
might not be too strong a word. But the Sea Foxes were
notorious for their preference to live out their lives in orbit,
in their cargo ships or vast agglomerate habitats called
ArcShips, making only brief forays planetside. Obviously
Senna Rodríguez did not: although rangy, she was simply
too well muscled and sleek to have spent all her time in
orbit, catching exercise on gravity decks and special
mechanical-resistance machines. Even though orthodox Sea
Foxes kept themselves fit with typical Clan single-
mindedness, they almost always had a spindly, almost ethe-
real look to them. Senna was as substantial as the cement
wall surrounding her little villa.

"Yes," Rorion said. "Why is Jana Pryde so reluctant to
pull the wings off Malvina?"

Senna cocked a brow at von Texeira. "I notice your aide
does a lot of talking for you, Margrave."

"He seeks to save me the effort. Part of his job, after
all."

She laughed.

"We have been together many years," von Texeira said.

"It breeds a certain familiarity." He glanced at his aide. "No doubt overmuch."

"Your caste system." She sipped her own brew. "Now, if you care to hear the answer you paid for: like all human groupings Clan Jade Falcon has factions. Jana Pryde must contend with two of consequences. Naturally, they hate each other passionately. They require constant refereeing, not just in Council but the streets of Hammarr, or they will deplete the warrior ranks with incessant duels. Basically, one faction is fanatically traditionalist, while the other seeks to accommodate the modern—some might say the *real*—world to some slight degree. Both are rabid Crusaders, screeching ultra-conservatives by outside standards. And you can't call any Falcon *moderate*."

"So what we have," Rorion suggested, "are the raving fascist zanies versus the totally psychotic."

Senna nodded. "And there you have it. The psychotics, as you put it, the extreme traditionalists, are popularly called the Slips. The merely raving are Jesses."

" 'Slips'?" asked von Texeira. " 'Jesses'?"

"Falconry terminology. Part of Clan Jade Falcon's current revival of Crusader zeal manifests as a fascination for the ancient lore of falconry. Back to the roots, as it were. *Jesses* are restraints, bands which bind falconer wrist to falcon leg. To *slip* is to loose a bird at prey. Basically, the names reflect the urgency with which the factions seek to prosecute the Crusade: the Jesses wish to gather strength and knowledge, while the Slips want to fall on the Inner Sphere straightaway and rend it like a rabbit."

"Delightful," said Rorion. "So the Slips support Malvina?"

"If you know everything, what do you need me for? Your mind is obviously too full to hold more information."

"Whereas my mind," said von Texeira, "is empty as a Falcon's soul. Please say on."

Senna laughed uproariously. "You are an amusing old scoundrel, Heinz-Otto von Texeira. Does playing the fool actually work in Lyran boardrooms?"

He shrugged. "I find that ego drives us all to believe that which best pleases us."

She chuckled and shook her head. "I would pay a great fee to watch you in action . . . to business. Khan Jana Pryde initially dispatched the *desant* to appease the Slips. But now they are outraged by Malvina's flaunting of custom. Her very unorthodoxy appeals to the Jesses. But they are appalled by her taste for atrocity."

"But if both factions oppose Malvina—"

"Both find fault with her. Both also are drawn to her. The Jesses are keen to strike at her, while ironically the Slips, self-proclaimed fire-eaters that they are, drag their feet. At the moment.

"But there's the key: *at the moment*. Falcon moods change like the wind. Jana Pryde might act to accommodate one faction, only to find it has changed its mind and both factions are aligned against her."

"The Falcons are fighters, though," Rorion said. "Will they really play politics in the face of a threat like Malvina?"

"Do not underestimate the power of denial," Senna said. "In their ways both factions hope that if they hunker down long enough this will all blow over. Malvina will come to her senses—or be killed by one of her uncontrollably vicious acolytes. The latter, you must admit, is at least feasible."

"If unlikely," von Texeira said.

"How can they be so blind?" asked Rorion. "I wouldn't have ever thought to accuse the Falcons of giddy optimism before."

"Not that," she said, "but fear of the alternative."

"Fear?" Rorion scoffed. "Clan Jade Falcon?"

"Again I call your attention to the difference between physical courage, which Falcons possess to a ludicrous degree, and moral courage. The real danger Malvina poses is civil war."

"Which the Falcons fear above all things," von Texeira said. "Enough that they won't even say the words."

"Which the *Clans* fear above all things," Senna agreed.

Rorion leaned back and put his arm up on the back of the couch. "Why, exactly? I mean, I know General Kerensky founded the Clans out of disgust over all the strife that was tearing up the Inner Sphere. But why this deep dread? It's not as if the Clans fear much."

"More than you might think," Senna said, with a taut little smile. She sipped from her mug of the eye-popping local schnapps. "It isn't just because of the Founder. What I am about to tell you no other Clanner will speak of, not even another Sea Fox. I ask you as a professional courtesy not to let slip where you heard it; my honor and my status are . . . peculiar, even in my Clan and Aimag, but they are not armor-plated. And I am attached to them, in my way."

Rorion raised his charcoal-smudge eyebrows and sat forward. The blandly cheerful expression on von Texeira's face didn't change.

"During the Jihad a great war broke out among the Clans of the homeworlds," Senna said. "Over points of philosophy you would find either utterly opaque or utterly ridiculous, if not both. Unless that's just me. But the outcome was anything but trivial: a Trial of Reaving, of Annihilation and of Absorption all rolled into one, on a Clan-wide scale.

"The destruction was cataclysmic. Untold Bloodnamed were Reaved. No fewer than five entire Clans were obliterated."

"Deus meu," Rorion breathed.

"If we had not had decades to recover, not even I would tell you this," Senna said. "Despite my quirks, I am Sea Fox, I am Clan."

"Our intelligence services have gleaned a certain knowledge of these events," rumbled von Texeira, from deeper in his chest than usual. *More than a little*, he thought. At the very least he was certain that would come as no surprise to Senna. But he didn't say it. As she was Clan despite her idiosyncrasies, he was LIC in spite of his.

"The real reason few Clanners would speak of these events to Spheroids," Senna said, "is embarrassment. We like to lord it over you soft, undisciplined denizens of the Sphere, with your disorderly ways. It pains us to admit we fell into a conflict as self-destructive and pointless as any succession battle within a Great House. But the reason we fear civil war, and call it by euphemisms like the Falcons' 'Rending' when we speak of it at all, is that it might draw other Clans into a second War of Reaving. Which could spell the end of our Clan. And maybe of the *Clans*."

Von Texeira closed his bearded lips upon an *amen*. He liked this wild and peculiar Sea Fox merchant. He sensed that she liked him. But if he hinted just how minuscule a tragedy he thought it would be for all the Clans to simply go away . . . even the bonds of profitable transaction might strain.

"So it's in almost everyone's interests to prefer to believe that all of this is no more than Malvina Hazen's impetuousness: the high spirits expected of a Falcon *ristar*. The situation might simply resolve itself. *If* they do not honor it by calling it rebellion—or worse, a Rending."

"Even now that Malvina has declared herself khan?" Rorion asked.

Senna nodded. "Oh, yes. Extravagant pronouncements and grandiose gestures are not exactly alien to the Falcons, you know. And even now, if Malvina were to see reason and submit herself to Khan Jana Pryde's will, Jana would have to accept. Nor could she make the *surkai*, the punishment exacted for disobedience, too severe. Not just to appease the conservatives, but for the unity of the Clan. Do you see?"

Von Texeira sighed. "So Khan Jana Pryde finds herself in a cleft stick."

"But I thought her power base lay among the moderates—the Jesses rather," Rorion said.

Senna dipped her head to one side. "So it does. Yet she must maintain balance—to keep the peace, as well as her position."

"And then," von Texeira said, "there is her new advisor, Julia Buhalin."

Senna's smile was slow and sly. "I thought her newest advisor was a certain Lyran merchant, whose seemingly soft exterior conceals a mind as sharp as one of Turkina's claws."

"You flatter me, Master Merchant."

She laughed. But it held an edge like glass. "I have said before: I do not flatter. I might be selective as to what truths I tell. But flattery is a lie. And a Sea Fox merchant does not lie."

"How about bending the truth?" Rorion asked brightly.

"Hush," Senna said. "The loremaster must be a politician in a way—as must anyone who holds high rank in any large organization. But her position does not require her to build coalitions or accommodate shades of opinion. She is a Slip as rabid as any."

"I suspected as much," von Texeira said.

"She actively hates the Jesses. Almost as much as she despises the coterie of high-ranked scientists and technicians who really run Sudeten and the *touman*—and by extension, Clan Jade Falcon."

To Rorion's look of outright disbelief she said, "You don't think warriors would stoop to such mundane tasks as administering an army, or an empire, do you? But leave it. Julia Buhalin is intelligent and formidable. And she hates readily and well. You would do well to be wary of her, Merchant Prince."

"I have . . . experience of women with strong wills and—shall we say, tempestuous natures," he said.

"Really?" Senna asked archly.

He chuckled. "And speaking of strong-willed women—you strike me as most unorthodox, if you will forgive my saying so, dear lady—"

"There's a lady present?"

"—even for a Sea Fox. I did not believe any Clan encouraged quite such a degree of individualism."

"Delta Aimag of Alpha Khanate is known for going its own way among Foxes," she said. "I am known for going my own way in the Aimag. In a way, my behavior can be rationalized as simply taking our group traits to their logical extreme. The real reason I am tolerated is that Clan Sea Fox identifies honor with the bottom line. I deliver results."

"Profits," said von Texeira.

"Among others."

"And of course you fight like a devil," murmured Rorion.

"My Clansfolk have not found challenging me a profitable pastime, *aff.*"

She stretched. Von Texeira tried not to stare at her chest. *Lecherous fool! And what could such a one—a Clanswoman, however unusual her outlook—see in such a fat, old cripple?*

"I trust you will excuse me," Senna said, rising. "You pay handsomely for my advice—but I have other interests to attend to while I'm on Sudeten."

"Of course," von Texeira said.

But as he rose with the aid of his cane and a certain amount of puffing, he tried not to wonder too hard what those interests might be. Clan Sea Fox drew little distinction between commerce and war, he knew—and its relations with Clan Jade Falcon were as tangled as they were unfriendly. He had a high estimate of her ability, or he never would have hired her: despite openly flaunting orthodoxy, she had attained an advanced age for a Clanswoman as well as a Bloodname. But it made him uneasy to have to rely on her not to make some mistake that might bring the wrath of an already roused Turkina slashing down on Rorion and himself.

The lengths I go to, to put off facing my dilemma, he thought. *Ah, well: it's not as if anyone leaves this world alive.*

13

"**M**y Khan," a voice called from behind.

Walking with Cynthy holding onto her hand among machines the size and general shape of hover-APCs, which hummed industrial as within them multiple-axis machine tools robotically milled BattleMech drive-train parts to comply with three-dimensional drawings, Malvina stopped and turned. Pacing on her other side with a glum expression, Bec Malthus mirrored her. A young male warrior strode quickly after them across the machine shop's cement floor.

After finally wresting Graus from the Lyran Commonwealth, Clan Jade Falcon had brought strategic industry to what once was an altogether bucolic world. They built a complex of factories next to New Paris spaceport, including one producing vehicles and IndustrialMechs. Though pacifists, the agrarian communalists who inhabited the world assimilated quickly and well into Clan culture—as docile laborers. Their original back-to-nature bias long forgotten, since laborers knew only what their masters taught them, the Graussians had adjusted quickly to the occupiers' new industrialization program.

Offworld visitors marked down the somewhat excessive size of the 'Mech-works' computer-controlled manufacturing centers and assembly bays to a known Jade Falcon tendency to overbuild, arising from their usual grandiosity of self-regard, as well as the fact that the Falcons were neither the most precise nor subtle engineers among Kerensky's heirs.

The factory began producing ever-expanding numbers of military vehicles after the disappearance of Devlin Stone became known in the JFOZ. When the HPG net collapsed, only the most besotted enthusiasts for The Republic could have been surprised when the factory switched almost literally overnight to building full-on BattleMechs. Production had not reached high enough levels to benefit Beckett Malthus and the sibkin Hazen when the *desant* was launched into the Inner Sphere. But the bipedal land dreadnoughts were walking off the lines at regular intervals now.

Today Malvina Hazen toured the industrial complex preparatory to taking possession of her *Shrike*, whose repairs had just been completed in the BattleMech assembly facility.

"What is it?" she asked the warrior. He was clearly a messenger. Malvina refused to carry a communicator or allow her immediate retinue to do so.

The young Falcon saluted the two Galaxy commanders with a certain awe. Or perhaps it was reluctance to share his news: "Khan Malvina Hazen, we have just received word that the Alessio Five laborers dormitory has mutinied."

Malvina looked blue laser death at Malthus. "You advised me to leave Watrous in his post!"

His answering look was bland. "Should he prove malleable enough to accede to a *fait accompli*. As he did. You need Graus, my Khan, and you need its production as unimpaired as possible. Which meant interrupting as few routines as possible."

"But now the fool's very softness threatens to interrupt it."

Malthus inclined his great head. "I presume the Khan shall now show the iron fist?" One of her first deeds to gain renown—and notoriety—was putting down a laborer revolt. That won her the sobriquet *Butcher of Wotan*.

Indeed, quelling this revolt with Mongol savagery would win Malvina support in the Council. If the Clans dreaded one thing more than a Rending, it was an uprising by the lower classes.

"No." She smiled sweetly. "*You* will. See to it. And *I* shall see to Watrous after reclaiming the Black Rose."

He pressed his palms together before his chest. "My Khan commands," he said, and departed, with the aide trotting at his heels like an uncertain dog.

Malvina scowled after his broad retreating back. The plant technicians, in rose and lavender jumpsuits, all stood by trying to look exceptionally obedient.

"Take me to the Vehicle Assembly Building," she commanded. "I wish to test the repairs done to my machine."

Her tone did not suggest a happy fate in store for the Fab's staff should she not be fully satisfied with their work.

"Initiate test sequence," Malvina Hazen said, fastening her safety harness. She was dressed in the usual neurohelmet and Clan cooling-mesh bodysuit, with an additional cooling vest over it. Around her, lights began to flicker on and off in the *Shrike*'s narrow cockpit as the computer queried its various systems, both software and hardware, and recorded and analyzed the responses. When she had brought up the fusion bottle moments before, the 'Mech had performed a power-on test; Malvina wanted to confirm its systems were truly nominal.

For the same reason she had spent half an hour doing a personal walk-around inspection of the refurbished war colossus, trailing a small constellation of nervous technicians. Many Clan warriors, especially Jade Falcon, disdained such activity as beneath them: ensuring their 'Mechs functioned properly was the province of lowly techs.

Like her brother Aleks, Malvina had always regarded such attitudes as both stupid and lazy. The BattleMech was the MechWarrior's soul. Her life, her codex and the honor of her Clan depended on its being in the best condition possible—and when unrepaired battle damage limited the 'Mech's performance, she had to know exactly how so as to compensate in battle. Although his manner was always gentler than Malvina's—gentler than any lesser Jade Falcon warrior could afford—Aleksandr Hazen had been no less ruthless than his sister in stamping on that particular caste affectation in his commands.

From thirteen meters up Malvina watched through the viewscreen as a pair of female laborers stolidly swung a jump rope for Cynthy to skip through at one side of the VAB floor. As usual, Malvina's ward clutched her floppy stuffed toy to her breast. The girl's small face was solemn, although her motions were lively and deft.

Malthus, of course, would disapprove.

Perhaps his unspoken criticism is right, Malvina thought. *Perhaps she does soften me, my Cynthy. For now there is a human creature I do not hate. And whom I will protect when I drown this foul race, and at last myself, in blood and fire.*

She alone shall I never harm.

Klaxons blared from Black Rose's internal speakers. *"Galaxy Commander Hazen! Alfa Star-Six!"* the warrior commanding her personal-security detachment cried from the radio. *"We are under attack by unknown—"*

A crash of static, followed by a loud white-noise hum.

Alfa Six's brace of elementals and fifteen hoverbike-mounted infantry were meant mainly to prevent ad hoc assassination attempts like the one on Sudeten. For more serious assaults the light force could expect little more than to serve as a tripwire. Basically, die noisily. *As indeed they most likely have,* Malvina thought.

The speaker noise was louder than a simple carrier. And her sensors showed nothing unusual. Even through the VAB's stressed-ferrocrete walls her BattleMech's suite should detect some sign of any attacking force more substantial than a pure conventional infantry Star. *The stravags use electronic countermeasures,* she thought. They also actively jammed her comms.

"Omega Galaxy, this is Galaxy Commander Malvina

Hazen." She used the general frequency circuit for the Galaxy she had chosen from the warriors who accompanied her and Malthus back to the JFOZ. A light mobile unit could blanket her receivers with static; they could hardly keep her 'Mech's fusion engine from driving a signal *out*. "All Omega units, go to Code Black. Condition Black."

Code Black meant *war*. Not imminent. Now.

Power cables parted and fell like severed snakes, bleeding sparks, as Malvina walked her *Shrike* out of the repair bay without the nicety of disconnecting. Ten meters away the two laborer women stopped to gape at the metal behemoth that had broken its shackles to take a clanking step toward them. They dropped the rope and fled.

Cynthy turned and looked up at the 'Mech's beaked head.

"Stay still, Cynthy," Malvina commanded over her loudspeaker. "I will not hurt you."

The girl nodded, pigtails bobbing. She stood unflinching as the metal monster crouched before her.

Malvina reached for her with the *Shrike*'s left hand. Its three-digit claw could crush a ground car. Without the most perfect control those curved steel talons would pinch the Inner Sphere child in half.

Malvina Hazen had such control. The great claws enfolded Cynthy. Had she been an egg her shell would not have cracked.

The girl laughed as the BattleMech straightened, lifting her high off the cement floor with its color-coded lines and geometric patterns. *Perhaps we occasionally underestimate these people,* Malvina thought.

With a hiss of entering air the cockpit side hatch opened. Without prompting the tiny girl clambered out of the colossal fist and into the BattleMech's head.

"Sit behind me," Malvina instructed. The girl nodded. The jumpseat behind the command couch would have been cramped even for diminutive Malvina Hazen. Her ward fit it quite well. She quickly figured out how to secure its five-point safety harness, which was designed simply for speedy operation.

Once the child was buckled in Malvina turned around and put her from her mind. Now she would live or die with Malvina. And the White Virgin *always* liked her chances.

Warnings lit Malvina's heads-up display red. Alarms trilled. Either the enemy's ECM malfunctioned or, more likely, its coverage was insufficiently wide to mask all the attacking units. Her sensors detected the electromagnetic signature of a long-range missile launcher rack warming up some three hundred meters west-southwest: basically ahead and to the left of where she stood inside the great doors of the VAB. The display tagged it in pink as a Bellona medium hovertank. The light hue indicated the battle computer's lack of confidence in its identification; the color showed her computer had no doubt it was a threat.

Neither did Malvina. She knew at once what was to come. She smiled. *Such a plan I myself might have conceived.*

As alarms crescendoed and warning lights strobed frenetically to indicate imminent launch, she clutched in the gyros. Black Rose toppled forward. Using the impetus of gravity Malvina hurled its ninety-five tons into a hammering run with its talons digging deep in the cement.

Though the *Shrike* was not the slowest of the monstrous assault-class BattleMechs, there was no such thing as a truly *fast* one. Malvina's risky maneuver started it at unexpected speed. Sitting behind her head, Cynthy watched raptly as the massive steel doors filled the viewscreen.

The doors exploded as thirty LRMs smashed into them.

Malvina screamed in something like exaltation as gray clouds rolled toward them. Dust and smoke enveloped them. The BattleMech's mighty frame rang and rocked as shards of steel and chunks of concrete cascaded over it.

They were through, into the afternoon sun. Malvina put the 'Mech's right foot down hard, knee actuator locked, pivoted right and ran northwest.

The second volley of twenty-five missiles, fired on a flat trajectory, passed right behind the lumbering assault 'Mech. Some slammed against the sagging outer wall of the VAB. Most streaked straight through the hole of the doors, striking the bay where Black Rose had stood. Had Malvina not reacted as she did they would have shattered her massively armored 'Mech. At the least it would have been badly damaged, and Malvina herself stunned, allowing her attackers to finish her quickly.

And Cynthy. Her rage was ice and fire.

The Vehicle Assembly Building's west end gave onto a vast paved vehicle yard—what in the decadent Inner Sphere would have been called a "parking lot." Beyond it an old sunken railroad line crossed at a transverse angle from northeast to southwest; beyond that rose small but steep hills, well forested by broad-leaved trees.

Malvina's HUD clearly showed four major threats now: the Bellona and three BattleMechs approaching from the west. She could see them herself: a tall *Thor* with a barrel-shaped LRM launcher on its left shoulder, rising over the trees just south of the peak of the tallest hill; two smaller 'Mechs advancing through the woods to its left and right.

Elementals leapt at the *Shrike* like jet-assisted fleas. *I'm facing a mixed Star,* Malvina guessed, as she caught one in mid-leap with her claw. The battlearmor waved frantically to bring its right-arm flamer to bear on Malvina's cockpit as she brought it close up.

If it is just a Star, she thought, *I have them where I want them.* The motion of the battlearmor's limbs grew more frenzied as the metal casing buckled under the relentless pressure of her claw. Cracks appeared, the viscous black of harjel sealant scarcely diluted by thinner red fluid streaming from them.

With a final pressure on the grip controller she squeezed the suit and occupant in half and let the pieces fall.

Its fellow elementals she ignored, though at least two struck her legs like wasps, clinging and trying to sting. Thudding at a run across the cement expanse she swung her targeting pip onto the *Thor*—the most dangerous opponent in view—and loosed ten long-range missiles at it.

Rocking back as explosions flashed across its breastplate, the *Thor* fired its particle-projector cannon at Malvina. The discharge passed behind her, raising the hair on her neck. Blue-green and red lasers stabbed for her, gouging glowing streaks in the pavement. Hits sang off her armor; she didn't need to check her damage displays to know they were glancing blows. Taken aback by their quarry's dramatic countermove the killers fired wide, if not wildly.

Extended garrison duty had made Graus' defenders soft. She was surprised they found the courage to rebel. *I should have purged them,* she thought, *for incompetence if not doubtful allegiance.*

Chain-link fencing, an ancient yet widely used technology, was surprisingly resilient. The perimeter fence around the VAB yard parted like rotten twine before Black Rose's legs.

A *Spirit* emerged from the trees on the foreslope. It aimed the weapon held in its right hand at Malvina. Four short-range missiles snaked out to slam full into the *Shrike*'s torso, homing on a Streak laser-paint. The massive BattleMech rocked, faltered, ran on, driven as much by sheer inertia as piloting skill on Malvina's part. Without conscious attention she registered from her damage display that most of the blasts' energy had been spent tearing huge chunks from the armor plate beneath her LRM racks. Electronics and hydraulics had taken damage, but nothing that wasn't covered by backups.

She laid her crosshairs on the light 'Mech's jut-jawed head and fired alternate bursts from the twin PPCs in her left arm. Both lightning-like blasts struck their target in geysers of white and yellow coruscation. The *Spirit* fell heavily on its back.

Multiple projectiles from the *Thor*'s LB-X autocannon rattled against her left arm but did not penetrate the armor. An elemental's arm-mounted flamer sprayed her right lower leg with clinging fluid fire, undoubtedly bubbling off the Horus eye insignia so recently repainted there.

Malvina frowned. *I have to change the odds, and quickly.* A wireframe drawing in her display showed that while she had hurt the *Spirit,* neither machine nor pilot was out of the fight. The two particle beam hits right in the cockpit area had startled a relatively green MechWarrior into yanking back the controls and overbalancing her biped machine, with a little assist from the jet-recoil effect of several hun-

dred kilograms of armor erupting in the form of superheated vapor and embers.

Malvina took a slight hop without using her jump jets
and landed in the railroad cut. Once she ran her eye over
any terrain she had an accomplished stage performer's
exact feel for where every feature was. It *was* her stage,
the battlefield, after all. The cut was deep, masking her
machine almost to the hip actuators.

It was also not empty.

14

BattleMech Fabrication Unit #1
Outside New Paris, Graus
Jade Falcon Occupation Zone
17 October 3135

No trains had run the track for years. But an Epona pursuit tank, the final element of the attacking Star, crept along it blowing a whirlwind of dead leaves and twigs from beneath its armored skirts. When the *Shrike* jolted down mere meters in front of it the whirlwind became a tornado as the pilot jammed full power to the lift fans.

The tank's four medium lasers pulsed green energy into the lower torso and legs of Malvina's 'Mech as the top turret swung desperately around to bring its Streak quad-launcher to bear. The tank rose two meters into the air. At fifty tons the Epona was at the upper limit of hovercraft weight. It could not raise itself as high as a much lighter *Scimitar*—or escape the cut.

The *Shrike* leaned forward. Its two shoulder-mounted medium lasers speared down. Both penetrated the boxy launcher. Yellow flame jetted from the holes as the propellant for one missile blew. Then the other three rockets exploded, shredding the launcher and sending bits of burning propellant, burning blue-white like magnesium, spiraling away drawing yellowish smoke corkscrews behind.

A devil's tympani erupted in Black Rose's cockpit as a multiple salvo of long-range missiles slammed home on its left shoulder and head and both banks of the railway cut. Malvina ignored the impacts. She raised her 'Mech's right foot. As the Epona's four lasers futilely raked the thighs and groin of the *Shrike*, making molten armor bleed down its legs in glowing yellow streams, she slammed the claw down on the ruined SRM launcher.

The Epona was over half the weight of Malvina's BattleMech, but it was never designed to absorb abuse of that sort. The twin-level turret pancaked and was crushed down into the body of the tank. Despite screaming lift fans the *Shrike*'s weight drove the hovertank down until its chassis cracked with a noise like a Gauss shot hitting its target.

By instinct Malvina crouched the Black Rose. A PPC bolt from the *Thor* crackled overhead. She straightened and returned a volley of missiles.

Her four missile-firing opponents dumped salvos on her as fast as the automatic feeders could reload their racks. Long-range missiles fell all around the *Shrike*, exploding on the bank, inside the cut, knocking divots from the machine's tough ferro-fibrous armor, making a tremendous clamor more like continuous fireworks than anything else. The bombardment raised a perfect storm of smoke and dust and debris. . . .

Perfect for Malvina. Thick clouds dense with thrown-up dust and hot gases from dozens of warheads exploding partially masked her 'Mech from infrared as well as visual observation and interfered with targeting radar, already questionable with the Rose in effect buried hip-deep in the planet. Lasers in several colors and the sporadic blue-white flash of a PPC strobed through the cloud. Most missed the big 'Mech.

But like a person standing behind a loose-woven curtain Malvina could see out, and target, rather well.

Black Rose shivered and rang. She was taking a lot of hits. But a 95-ton killing machine could absorb horrendous punishment, and the LRMs' individual warheads were small. Yet soon, Malvina knew, the sheer *concentration* of firepower directed against her would result in a telling hit. If her 'Mech was immobilized, or sent to redline shutdown of her fusion engine by soaring heat, it would mean the end of Malvina. And, more importantly, her dream.

The third attacking 'Mech, a *Cougar*, had come down out of the trees and strode out onto the apron, angling for a better shot at the *Shrike*. The *Spirit* struggled to get to its feet. Malvina targeted its right knee and hosed it with a PPC.

In a shower of red sparks the actuator fused. The *Spirit* promptly collapsed onto its back once more, unable to rise.

From the corner of her eye she saw an elemental leaping like a flea at her from her left. A volley from its own side raised earth fountains around it; an accidental hit ruptured the one-shot launcher on its right shoulder, tumbling its gyros and knocking it off the thrust-columns of its jump jets. The squat power suit fell from view and did not reappear.

Why did they send battlearmor in the first place? Malvina wondered. The elementals had proven utterly ineffectual, five one-ton powersuits against ninety-five tons of BattleMech. Another 'Mech or even a single tank could have given her attackers the edge.

She guessed the elemental Point had been deployed to dispatch her in the cockpit of her disabled BattleMech had the initial sneak attack succeeded, or hunt her down and kill her should she somehow get clear of a stricken Rose. The Graus rebels displayed about the mix of Jade Falcon arrogance and near-superstitious dread of a fearsome *ristar* that Malvina, scarcely less cynical in her assessment of her Clansfolk than Bec Malthus, would expect from second-line garrison troopers.

But they were persistent. And they still had her outnumbered and sorely outgunned. A multiple-projectile blast from the *Thor*'s autocannon hammered into the *Shrike*'s beak and viewscreen with a horrifying noise. Another salvo of rockets smashed up and down the whole front of the 'Mech. Cynthy pressed her hands over her ears.

Malvina let go the control stick with her left hand to touch the girl once, briefly. Then she resumed her grip. Through swirling smoke and dust she targeted the 70-ton enemy 'Mech in an icy fury. With red and yellow indicators flaring all over her damage display she launched the *Shrike* in a jump.

A PPC blast from the *Thor* ripped the air beneath the jumping BattleMech's talons. Malvina held her machine steady against the turbulence, as she did when another autocannon blast pounded up the front torso. Her own heat had actually dropped.

About half her left-side missile racks showed red for nonfunctional. She had lost both torso-mounted lasers. She triggered off what LRMs she could into the *Thor*. Then, descending, she aimed a bolt from one of her own PPCs into the enemy machine's cockpit.

Melted armor cascaded down the *Thor*'s front torso in yellow streams. As Malvina landed on the hillside thirty meters from the *Thor*, its PPC hit Black Rose in the left breast. The BattleMech rocked back as missile tubes exploded. Its shoulder actuator locked. Malvina could only aim her PPCs by swiveling and tilting the *Shrike*'s torso.

Despite secondary explosions ripping through the *Shrike*'s body Malvina launched the machine in a low leap. At its apex she unfolded its great metal wings. The *Thor* ducked, its pilot anticipating a death-from-above attempt to smash its cockpit with the assault 'Mech's massive feet.

Instead Malvina skimmed over the enemy machine to land heavily right behind it. The *Thor* tried desperately to turn its torso to fire at her. Too late: Malvina's right claw locked into the barrel-shaped missile launcher on its shoulder. Heavy-gauge metal crumpled in its three-taloned grip. Holding the top of the enemy machine well above its center of gravity Malvina merely walked the greater mass of her *Shrike* a few paces down the backslope, shouldering trees aside.

The *Thor* driver was helpless to prevent his machine from overbalancing and toppling backward to land with a bone-crunching impact. Letting go of the ruined launcher, Malvina turned, brought the muzzles of both particle-projector cannon to within two meters of the fallen Battle-Mech's viewscreen and fired.

Her cockpit instantly became an oven. But the *Thor* cockpit became Hell. All within was instantaneously vaporized or slagged—almost incidentally including the slight organic mass of the pilot.

The *Shrike* rocked. The *Cougar* raced widdershins across the paved vehicle yard, the large pulse lasers in its arms stitching the left side of the Rose. From Malvina's right the Bellona's big laser hacked at the armor of arm and side like a great red sword, leaving gaping, glowing wounds. Had her attackers coordinated their efforts this well from the outset, she would be dead now. As it was . . .

The bars displaying the crucial heat levels of chassis and engine fell quickly, though Malvina sweated freely through her cooling mesh and the sweat ran in tickling rivulets down her face. Cynthy sat huddled in the seat behind Malvina and watched out the viewscreen. Though her tiny frame shook, the Spheroid child made no sound.

Malvina led the darting *Cougar*, aiming a pitiful four-rocket salvo to land in front of it. As she anticipated, the inexperienced MechWarrior shied from the blasts and jets of gray-white cement dust in his face. When the 'Mech paused to change direction she hit it with a blast from one arm-mounted PPC, then the other.

The 35-ton 'Mech staggered as hundreds of kilograms of armor, myomer pseudomuscle and endosteel skeleton sublimated away. With deadly accuracy Malvina punched a third particle beam into the left side of the *Cougar*'s torso, firing the millisecond her heat levels dropped enough that a shot would not drive her to shutdown. She felt herself baking, smelled burning hair.

Another PPC blast struck home in whitish vapor and yellow sparks. Orange flame vomited out. Though the light BattleMech had fired most of its rocket reloads, the probing lightning-like beams had found the ammo storage and detonated what remained.

The *Cougar*'s large-laser left arm went spinning away, trailing smoke and gobbets of glowing metal. Desperately its pilot tried to pivot the unbalanced machine, turn its torn-open left side away from its relentless foe. Instead Malvina stabbed in a final blast of high-energy particles, closely followed by a hissing missile volley.

"Hide your eyes!" Malvina shouted to her ward. The girl did, covering her head in arms reddened as if from sunburn.

The *Cougar* toppled away from the Rose. As it did, the containment on its fusion engine failed. Malvina averted her own eyes as a white flash devoured the 'Mech's left side and cockpit. A moment later the truncated mess, steaming and smoking, bounced off the pavement with a clang.

The Bellona charged close. Its missile stores depleted by mostly ineffectual volleys, its commander had worked behind the *Shrike* while Malvina was preoccupied with the last BattleMech, engaging with its two bow-mounted flamers as well as its large laser. It was a bold and cunning stroke: the tanker knew Malvina was crowding the redline with frequent pulses from the heat-hogging particle gun. He hoped to drive her over the redline.

The *Cougar* destroyed, the Black Rose now turned to face the 45-ton tank. It veered to Malvina's left. She raked the hurtling vehicle with LRMs and a particle discharge. The beam ripped open the skirt, dropping the tank's snout to the ground. It slid along the pavement raising a bow wave of sparks until Malvina leaned down and punched through the cockpit with her BattleMech's fist.

She straightened her *Shrike* and looked around. No other enemies presented themselves in the immediate area. But contrails twined the blue sky, suggesting aerospace fighters overhead. The *Cougar*'s ECM suite had failed but the radio-frequency jamming had not. Mass detectors picked up movement to the east, approaching through the BattleMech factory complex. *I must assume them hostile.*

She spoke to Cynthy. "Are you all right?" she asked. Her voice was cracked, her tongue swollen. It was still burning hot inside the cockpit, though she only now grew aware of it again.

Cynthy reached forward and touched her head in answer. Malvina smiled.

It turned to a twist of rage as she checked the damage

display. Her newly repaired *Shrike* had incurred terrible damage, worse than what had just been so laboriously made right. Aside from losing her lasers and most of her LRMs and literally tons of armor, and having one shoulder locked, the right leg's myomer pseudomuscle was damaged so badly the 'Mech could only limp at no greater than half its normal speed. Which was none too swift to start with.

Yet I live, she thought with the bright hot joy of a bird of prey, *and my enemies are dead*. A sense of invincible purpose filled her. Thrilled her.

They cannot stand against me! They cannot deny my destiny!

"Hazen," a voice said suddenly in her ears. It was a familiar voice, and not one she expected to hear, driven through the white-noise jamming by a fusion generator far more powerful than her own. "*Galaxy Commander Beckett Malthus aboard* Bec de Corbin *calling Galaxy Commander Malvina Hazen. Malvina, answer!*"

"Hazen here," she replied on the same wavelength. Between her own fusion powerplant and the DropShip's huge receiving antenna array she had no doubt of being heard. "What is it, Malthus? What occurs?"

"*Treachery. Rebellion.*"

"I knew that."

"*Not all, Malvina. A JumpShip out of Blair Atholl has emerged from a LaGrange point near the planet's second moon. The entire Vau Galaxy is inbound on DropShips. They are less than an hour out. Already their fighters enter the atmosphere. Had Watrous' fools not been so fearful of you, and thus impatient to kill you, the blows would have struck us as one. We would surely have been overwhelmed.*"

"Have they challenged?"

"*Galaxy Commander Erik Chistu broadcast a* batchall *for a Trial of Annihilation. He intends to exterminate you and all who follow you.*"

"They dare not presume so much! They *dare not!*"

"*They dare presume plenty, my Khan. Our WarShip orbits at the system's far end. Eight days away at standard thrust. And they come in unanswerable force.*"

Malvina laughed. "Then we must prepare a mordant answer."

"No, Malvina. We must leave. The laborer rebellion was no ruse: Watrous himself raised the lower castes against us as renegades and bloodfoul. Not even your genius can prevail: our enemies far outnumber us. And they are Falcons. We must withdraw while we can bring away most of our assets."

"Flee before these fools?" Malvina screamed.

"Yes. Flee. Now, for they will grant no hegira. Or your dream dies here on Graus. We must go someplace we can gather our forces to strike back."

For a moment she sat, glaring unfocusedly at the skies, breathing hard through flared nostrils.

"I come for you," Malthus said. *"At least another Binary advances to attack you. Enemy VTOLs are on their way from south of the city, and already our fighters engage advance* Peregrine *aerospace assets as well as local craft."*

A white flare and pillar of white smoke appeared above the tree-clad hilltop that masked the landing pit from Malvina's view. As *Bec de Corbin* hove into sight, rockets flashed off against its armor-plated hull. Heavy autocannon roared reply. A tilt-rotor Skadi fell to the landing field in a ball of orange flame.

Warning tones sang shrill in her ears. Her computer threat assessment had identified the leading attackers. At least four more BattleMechs approached, including a 65-ton *Rifleman IIc*. Given Black Rose's brutalized condition, she could never match them.

The *Bec de Corbin* swept low above the vehicle yard. A hatch yawned black and wide to receive her.

Uttering a final falcon scream of defiance, Malvina jumped. Her BattleMech rose ungainly into the sky on sputtering jets of flame. The waiting hatchway swallowed it up and closed behind it.

As an aerial battle broke out all around, the DropShip lit its three great primary drives and, ascending rapidly through a scrim of smoke, left the world of Graus behind.

15

"**I** should have brought the *Talon* back to Graus and laid waste that rookery of bloodfouls. *And* the damned Peregrines!"

"If you devastate the Jade Falcon Occupation Zone world by world, Malvina," Beckett Malthus murmured in a deep and honeyed voice, "what will you rule?"

As she spun, blue eyes mad-hot, he went on: "More to the point, without all the resources you can lay hands upon, how will you ever extend your rule over the other Clans, not to mention the teeming trillions of the Inner Sphere? Even you must have a power base; even you cannot conquer single-handed—my Khan."

"Damn you, Beckett Malthus!"

"Should the archaic superstitions retained by many in the Inner Sphere possess some validity," he said, undeterred, "doubtless it is already accomplished. Nonetheless I am yours to command, O Chingis Khan."

At that she could only laugh.

Before them rotated a tawny ball. They stood on the

darkened bridge, surrounded by low-murmuring crew, as the *Emerald Talon* approached orbit around the red-giant sun Antares' lone habitable world. It had declared for Malvina when she assumed the khanship.

"We do not lack wholly for resources even now," Malvina said. "Dompaire has declared for me."

"And Antares remains subordinate to you," Malthus said smoothly, "or so they say, with the *Emerald Talon* approaching like a killer comet. Yet neither planet felt inspired to send actual reinforcements to Graus, *quineg*?"

"*Neg*," Malvina said.

"Our defeat there shows that the weight of Jade Falcon opinion lies against us. Ours is a conservative people. We have started a civil war. That is an intrinsically unpopular course."

She turned sharply toward him. He steeled himself to weather the onslaught—especially since he had used the forbidden phrase. Instead she asked levelly, "Do you think we have lost, then?"

"If I did I would have advised you to order Star Admiral Binetti to take us outside the occupation zone," Malthus said. "Possibly into the Periphery. We have not lost. Yet. But our next moves will determine whether we can win."

Malvina looked at him a moment longer. Then she smiled a strange smile. She walked to the ferroglass viewport and pressed her nose against it. She reminded Malthus uncomfortably of the Inner Sphere child she unaccountably continued to carry along with her.

"Our next movement must be something bold," she said almost breathlessly. "Is that what you tell to me, Beckett Malthus?"

Despite alarm rising within him, Malthus said, "It is, my Khan."

She let herself lie almost sprawled against the great viewport, that artifact of arrogant power. Then she rolled to put her back against the ferroglass.

"Then bold shall I make it."

"Impossible." Khan Jana Pryde fetched the wooden frame a mighty kick. It flew across her crafts studio in the

Falcon's Perch and shattered against a ferrocrete wall. "Not even that little *stravag* would do such a thing."

Heinz-Otto von Texeira stood leaning on his cane with an eyebrow upraised. "It would appear that she has, my Khan," he said equably.

"We have her," Loremaster Julia Buhalin said smugly. "Surely Clan opinion will turn upon her now."

"Undoubtedly you are wise, Loremaster," von Texeira said. She gave him a furious violet gaze. She wasn't buying it. He didn't sigh, but he wanted to. *I hate it when I make beautiful women angry at me*, he thought. *That's one reason I agreed to leave home.* "Forgive me, a poor foreigner far less steeped in your Clan's noble traditions. I thought that up until very recently freebirths of appropriate heritage were permitted to test for full warrior status within Clan Jade Falcon."

Jana Pryde had walked to the wall and picked up a splintered piece of what had been a wooden loom. A swatch of loosely linked yarn in several drab colors dangled from it. She regarded the wreckage with a certain gloomy satisfaction, then let it drop.

"You are correct, Margrave," she said. "I proscribed the practice. I did it primarily to appease our more conservative Clansfolk." This with a narrowed eye cast in Buhalin's direction. "And also because we found ourselves with too many warriors and too little war. It is a volatile combination."

"Whereas Malvina has need of nothing so much as warriors," he said. "Which explains why she chooses to appeal to young candidates fresh out of the sibkos who have yet to pass their Blooding and become true warriors. And more than that, please correct me if I misperceive."

"She permits those who failed their first Trial of Position to try again," Jana Pryde said grimly. "Our Clan rulership has grown soft and corrupt, she says—meaning me, of course—and therefore the entire system has become perverted. The little witch goes so far as to suggest that the trials themselves may have been compromised!"

"So she offers all a chance to redeem themselves," von Texeira said. "By battle, of course. I understand there is some precedent among the Clans, in isolated units or even Clans whose warrior ranks have been over-thinned by battle loss."

"There is," Jana Pryde said grimly.

"Chalcas," said Buhalin. It sounded like a curse. From the lips of a Clan loremaster, von Texeira knew, it was—perhaps the direst imaginable, except for *coward.* Which no one not madder than Malvina Hazen herself would ever accuse Malvina of being. "In this case it is *chalcas.*"

Von Texeira beamed at her as if she had just invented reading. "Precisely, Loremaster!" he exclaimed. "Not that I presume to compare my poor comprehension of Clan ways to your peerless own. It seems to me you have hit upon a perfect means of turning Malvina's tricks against her. Khan Jana can now appeal to your Jesses as well as your, ah, Slips, to lay aside their differences until the war is over. For all the lip service Malvina pays traditional Falcon values, she commits *chalcas.* Or acts which can be seen that way, certainly. Even your Jess faction loudly deplores *chalcas,* does it not?"

"Loudly," Jana Pryde said dryly.

Von Texeira held up his palms. "And so: Malvina presents you, Khan Jana Pryde, with a golden opportunity to lead a glorious Slip–Jess coalition to fight evil *chalcas.* Yes?"

The khan laughed silently. "Cynical yet succinct," she said. "Spoken like a true Lyran merchant."

Von Texeira performed a mock bow. "I thank you, Khan Jana."

"A strong khan has no need of coalitions and backroom dealings!" Buhalin flared.

"With all respect, Loremaster," von Texeira said, "is your Remembrance so selective?"

Jana Pryde could not restrain a snort of laughter. "Close. Not quite."

Buhalin pressed her full lips to a line. Her glare suggested he was not making her like him any better. "I should better have said, for a strong khan to use such means is not the Falcon Way."

It was Jana Pryde's turn to narrow her eyes. "Do you suggest that I am not a strong khan?"

"*Neg*, my Khan! Rather, I say it is a . . . a perversion of Turkina's Way and of your destiny that you should be *required* to adopt such expedients. And I perceive this situation offers us opportunity not to coddle the factions but to put an end to their machinations for good and all."

Jana Pryde brushed a lock of hair that had wandered loose from her taut ponytail off her forehead. "You interest me strangely, Julia," she said. "Go on."

The loremaster leaned forward, eyes aglow with passion. Von Texeira willed himself to look away from the front of her green robe, which tended to hang open, revealing interesting depths. He was of course a man of Recife, and though he got on in years and weight, a viper's cold blood did not yet flow through his veins. But he was also on service to his archon. To get caught ogling the cleavage of the loremaster of Clan Jade Falcon, however impressive . . . inconceivable.

"You have no need of these Jesses anymore, my Khan," Buhalin said. "You may openly side with those who espouse the truest and purest virtues of Turkina. The Jesses must go along or be seen for what they are: weak-willed Wardens willing to countenance even challenge to our sacred caste system!"

Jana Pryde stood with her arms crossed tightly beneath her breasts and her chin down on her clavicle. Her narrow green eyes flicked from her loremaster to her ad hoc advisor from the Inner Sphere.

"The loremaster's suggestions do credit to her zeal," von Texeira said, thinking, *If not to her bloody bedamned sense.* "And is it not likely that in the extremity of a Rending, the khan has need of all the most eager support she can get? Will not the Jesses' enthusiastic support serve the Falcon better than the consent of grudging silence?"

"Our guest appears sincere in his desire to assist us in these matters," Buhalin said. "Since the interests of his people seem to run along the same lines as ours in this instance, I feel inclined to trust him—so long as they continue to do so. But not even a Lyran is infallible. Need I remind my Khan that the Margrave suggested you mobilize the entire *touman* to crush Malvina Hazen? And did not the Vau Galaxy of Galaxy Commander Erik Chistu, deployed on his own initiative, suffice to drive her in disarray from Graus?"

"To be sure," von Texeira said, trying to keep his smile from looking too impaled. "It did not, however, suffice to put an end to Malvina herself."

"True," Jana Pryde said. "Too damned true." She was looking very sour now. Buhalin had outmaneuvered herself by bringing up Chistu's failure to kill or capture the unspeakable Malvina or even her current, and Jana Pryde's quondam, gray eminence.

And there's something else here, von Texeria thought, *something I can't quite see.*

Jana rose from her chair, stalked across the chamber. She shied slightly like a startled horse when her foot bumped a chunk of what had recently been the loom's framework. With a silent snarl she kicked it. It split in two.

She smiled. "You know, you Spheroids are onto something with these hobbies of yours," she said. "They can be most wonderfully relaxing."

16

Ground-car-sized muzzle flame ripped the orange twilight from a parking structure a block ahead. Twenty-centimeter autocannon shells slammed against the left side and arm of Malvina Hazen's borrowed *Thor*. Concussion started the heavy BattleMech falling to its right.

With consummate skill, and with alarms going off all around her, the diminutive MechWarrior got her machine's right knee beneath her, plunging a meter deep into the pavement but preventing the 'Mech from sprawling helplessly across the broad roadway. The covers blew off the CASE in her left arm as the ammunition for her own autocannon exploded. Despite the cellular storage system venting the force of the blast away from both the BattleMech's torso and structural components of the arm, the heavy shells had fatally weakened it. The arm containing the LB 10-X sheared away just below the shoulder actuator and crashed to the street.

From her cockpit on the *Thor*'s right shoulder she fired back with the right-hand particle-projector cannon. A seven-meter oval segment of cement wall near the parking garage's ground-floor entrance exploded outward into dust and sparks and smoke. Malvina smiled. *The crew must think I am even more inept than they are, to miss them so badly.*

The burst had come from the *fourth* floor; no mistaking that, the way yellow muzzle flare had billowed into the early-evening gloom like dragon's breath. Her battle computer was repeating the obvious: she had been ambushed by an SM1 tank destroyer. There weren't many other platforms in the JFOZ that could carry a weapon as potent as its monstrous autocannon into such a constricted space. She was lucky. Had the gunner kept his nerve long enough to hold fire until she was even with the garage he could have blasted the BattleMech's cockpit point-blank.

The Jade Falcon defenders of Zoetermeer were few and second-line. There wasn't much here for them *to* defend.

She fired her LRMs and hit the jump jets. The *Thor* rose off the street at a crazy angle. A doubled rate-of-fire burst of twenty-centimeter shells shattered the whole width of the street where she had rested an eyeblink before. The tank destroyer crew was cagey enough to fire from some distance inside the building; structural steel had prevented her sensors from picking it up, and she still could see no more of it than the flickering tip of the cannon flame.

It made no difference. Her fifteen-rocket volley snaked into the huge opening Malvina's PPC had blasted in the front of the building. They took out three concrete support columns and weakened the floor overhead. With a grinding crunch of fracturing cement and squeal of failing rebar the ceiling buckled and dropped.

The rest of the structure promptly pancaked on top of it, leaving the parking structure collapsed in the center like a failed cake.

As Malvina fought the seventy airborne tons of BattleMech under control, the red symbol for the enemy SM1 winked out on her threat display. An instant later blinding white shafts of light stabbed out through the rubble as the hovertank's fusion bottle let go.

She was already looking for more targets as the 'Mech touched lightly down. *Solahma* infantry with laser rifles moved past her in quick fire-and-move pulses along the building fronts to either side, eager to win distinction and a chance to gain—or regain—full warrior-caste status. Elementals leapfrogged along the rooftops to either side of the street on pencils of blue fire.

The *Thor* rocked forward into a deliberate walk toward the center of the town of Hohenzollern. Past the hollowed-out parking structure the road crested a hill. At the top Malvina saw a flurry of activity and explosions beyond. The SM1 crew had been professional enough to permit her scouts, a Point of hoverbike infantry with the rather nominal support of a 20-ton Asshur hovercraft, to pass unmolested. They may or may not have known its pilot was the terrible White Virgin, Malvina Hazen, but the Mongol raiding force's largest BattleMech was clearly a target worth blowing their cover for.

Or maybe they *had* known, and that had made them shoot too soon. The notion amused her.

A black smoke ball rushed upward from the hill's far side. It told her before the disappearance of the green symbol from her heads-up, and the radio calls from her hoverbikes, that the scout hovercraft was destroyed. She stepped to the right side of the street, halted the *Thor*, and radioed an order to the ungainly vehicle waddling down the cracked pavement behind her.

The BattleMech rocked to a mighty wind of passage as the JESII strategic missile carrier lit off its whole awe-inspiring barrage of a hundred long-range missiles. The setting sun turned the twisting smoke trails to blood and fire, appropriately enough.

Malvina had brought no Arrow IV–capable machines in the DropShip she had landed in the wasteland (which was pretty much all Zoetermeer had to offer) a few kilometers outside the city. She wanted to test the abilities of the green *solahma* and fledgling troops she had brought along, not smash defenders from a distance. She did, however, want to allow her infantry a chance to show their artillery-observation skills, and the JES crew to test its ability to deliver called fire. As it had to do, since its Artemis IV fire-control system was of no use firing indirectly.

She had in all a Nova: a mixed Star of two BattleMechs,

hers and a *Gyrfalcon*, and six vehicles, including the missile launcher and the now-defunct Asshur, and an infantry Star with two Points of elementals, a Point of hoverbike riders, and two Points of standard foot-sloggers. No more than an augmented Trinary, commanded by a superannuated Star captain named Dougray, defended the world. Which meant Hohenzollern, since there was nothing else worth fighting over.

For her part Malvina was confident she could conquer the place with a single mixed Star. But she wanted to blood as many of her untried replacements and would-be warriors as possible—with a victory to cut the bitter taste of Graus. So she had not taken her invasion force down to cutdown.

Secondary explosions lit the slate-colored sky behind the hill like sheet lightning. From the triumphant cries of her scouts the barrage, plunging down onto relatively vulnerable top armor, had just flatlined the heavy hitter among the Zoetermeer garrison's vehicles, a 60-ton Oro heavy tank. She frowned, but briefly. *I must teach sharp lessons regarding radio discipline.*

Still, she was not altogether displeased. She liked the flash-and-dash her un-Blooded fledglings of the hoverbike unit displayed. They had the collective sense of a grunt-level laborer's shovel, but she did not think that all bad either. After all the bitter contention with her military-genius brother during the Skye campaign she leaned toward the conclusion that more than one truly capable, let alone *imaginative*, mind per military formation was superfluous. If not actively detrimental.

An elemental standing atop a four-story warehouse—the tallest building in the vicinity, since she imploded the old parking garage—radioed warning that a trio of BattleMechs, an *Uller*, a *Koshi* and a *Hunchback IIc*, approached from the town center.

She smiled as she set her *Thor* moving again. She commanded vehicles and infantry to hold position. Mech-Warrior Zed in the *Gyrfalcon* she ordered to follow her in echelon left, one block over.

"Star Captain Dougray comes out to play," she told him. "We do not want to disappoint him."

*   *   *

"I understand"—*snip*—"that Galaxy Commander Erik Chistu stepped on it in a major way by trying to drop a Trial of Annihilation on Malvina Hazen."

Spring had apparently come to Hammarr, meaning snow hadn't fallen for two days and wide patches of dry ground actually showed through. It was still abysmally cold by Heinz-Otto von Texeira's standards; he and Rorion were bundled in their winter coats.

"How so?" Rorion asked. He had his hands thrust deep in his pockets.

Master Merchant Senna Rodríguez, on the other hand, was dressed in khaki shorts and a dark short-sleeved shirt, on her knees in the front garden of her factors' house pruning some thorny bush which had begun to bud out in purple and green.

She chuckled. "In his boneheaded zeal Chistu called a Trial of Annihilation against everybody who *followed* Malvina. If he wins, not only must all the warriors with her be executed, but every single warrior in any younger sibkos that carry blood from any of those warriors must be culled as well. Clan Wolf could never dream of gutting the Jade Falcon *touman* so completely at a stroke."

"Good point," said Rorion.

"So we may assume Khan Jana sent a rocket to her errant Galaxy commander," von Texeira said.

"Aff," Senna said. "Look for a notice that he has formally amended his challenge to a Trial of Abjuration."

"A Clansman admit he was wrong?" asked Rorion.

She shrugged. "Happens. Even Jade Falcons sometimes have to accommodate reality. A century ago, a half-century even, perhaps it went differently. But now is now."

Von Texeira chuckled. "Do I detect a note of Sea Fox philosophy?"

Her smile was even more lopsided than usual. "This Sea Fox's philosophy, in any event."

Von Texeira jutted out his bearded chin and frowned thoughtfully. "I find myself short on insight," he said. "Khan Jana Pryde consults me regularly. But I find her hard to read as a glacier."

"That's why you hired me." *Snip*.

"What insight can you give me, then, Master Merchant? How can I persuade her to mobilize the Jade Falcon *touman*?"

For a moment Senna concentrated on her work. "In ways she's in a worse dilemma than before," she said at length.

"How can that be?" Rorion asked. "The loyalists won a pretty substantial victory on Graus, chasing Malvina and Malthus off with barely a fight."

She raised and eyebrow and grinned at him. "Ah, but therein lies the problem, *quineg*? Yours is one way of looking at it. But I can guarantee you Jana Pryde is digesting the lining of her own stomach even as we speak because Erik Chistu let the renegade Galaxy commanders get away."

"In other words," von Texeira said, "a two-fold screw up."

"Which will be entered into the Remembrance as a glorious victory," Senna said. "Or not, if Malvina wins. In fact Jana Pryde has more excuses now for *not* acting: after Malvina's humiliation on Graus, the argument will go, surely she will see the error of her ways and seek to make her peace with the Falcon."

"Do you think that'll happen?" Rorion asked.

When she had finished laughing Senna dabbed at her eyes with the back of a gloved hand. "I needed that, Rorion. That was good." She gave him a flatiron look. "What do *you* think? That Malvina has suddenly gone sane?"

Rorion made a face. "Not my best thought, I admit."

"For your sake I hope so."

"All that aside," von Texeira said, "which way do you think the khan will jump this time?"

"Who left first, you or the loremaster?"

He sighed. "If there is a practicable way for an *Auslander* to get the last word with the khan, I confess I lack the wit to see it."

"Me neither. Buhalin will outsmart herself again, as usual. She's not stupid, mind; but she has less sense than is usual even for a Falcon."

"I gathered as much. What can I do?"

She rose and dusted off her kneepads. "In answer to the question you're actually asking, keep using that silver tongue and everything in your Lyran merchant prince bag of tricks to try and get Jana Pryde to see sense," she said.

She stripped off her gloves and mopped her forehead with a tissue from her pocket. "What you really need to be told is: tread warily. You are babes in the woods still. I cannot always be about to protect you."

"We can handle ourselves better than you give us credit for," Rorion said sullenly.

"I am not talking about fighting, Rorion. I suspect either of you is capable of handing a Falcon warrior a lethal surprise. No, don't interrupt—I know no secrets, but neither am I blind. The *Markgraf* does not carry himself like a man as innocent of combat as he claims to be."

"Me? Innocent?" Von Texeira made large eyes.

She ignored him. "But you cannot fight them all, any more than Khan Jana Pryde can. And understand this: even the simplest Clan warrior is adept at twisting our stringent codes of honor to her own designs. We start learning the justifications in the sibko. So while our ways offer you certain protections, you cannot afford to rely on them."

"Meaning—" von Texeira said.

"When the chips are down," she said, "trust no high-caste Clanner. She can turn on you with no warning you can possibly hope to perceive."

"My Khan," said Naval Captain Louisa.

Standing on the bridge in the centerline of the *Tramp*-class JumpShip *Brightness Reef*, commandeered by virtue of the injured *Emerald Talon*'s still-awesome array of naval weaponry at the Graus zenith jump point, Malvina looked away from the holographic display. It showed nothing interesting, anyway: space around the Antares jump point through which they had just emerged, meaning just stars and a pair of JumpShips the ship's battle computer tagged as hers. She knew. "Yes, Naval Captain?"

The JFNR officer hesitated. "Antares traffic control reports there is a WarShip orbiting the planet." Another

pause as Malvina's natural eyebrow, the reconstructed one
having not yet reacquired the knack, shot up.

"It is the *Bucephalus*, Khan Malvina."

"Again? What do those imbecile Horses want this time?
To fight a Trial of Refusal for the right to use contractions?"

"Antares Control says Galaxy Commander Manas Amirault has landed his entire Galaxy on the Westmacott Plain.
He—he desires parlay with you, he says."

"And Galaxy Commander Beckett Malthus permitted
the landing?"

Naval Captain Louisa stiffened. Antares Traffic Control
was not going to presume to account for a Galaxy commander's decisions to a mere JumpShip commander. "The
Westmacott Plain does lie on the planet's far side from
Alba, my Khan," she said.

Malvina nodded acknowledgment. The red giant's solitary world was not vastly more desirable than Zoetermeer,
which she had just added to her collection—it was still too
pitiful even for her to think of as an empire. The only asset
of real value was an ancient Star League base buried beneath the capital city, Alba, which the ever-brusque Khan
Elias Crichell had bombed off the face of the planet with
his aerospace fighters during the first invasion. Anything of
use in the base had of course long been looted and hauled
off to Sudeten.

"Another *ristar*, *quiaff*?" Malvina said, her mood veering. "Hell's Horses will run out if they keep sending them
against me."

"As my Khan says."

Malvina pondered. The Zoetermeer venture had been an
overwhelming success, as far as it went. For four dead and
a handful of wounded, all expected to return to full duty
in no more than a couple of weeks, she had gained three
BattleMechs in reparable condition, several vehicles, some
Mongol-convert warriors, and a drab little planet now garri-
soned by a Star of *solahma* infantry that she did not care
if she ever got back.

Star Captain Dougray, the world's ruler and defender,

had fought bravely if not well. To the death, as befit a Jade Falcon. Malvina had, as a matter of unwonted compassion, settled that matter of honor by firing the *Thor*'s PPC directly into the cockpit of his *Hunchback*, which she had toppled by fusing its left hip-actuator, so as to spare him the temptation to disgraceful surrender.

His other two MechWarriors had capitulated after getting knocked around by the two much larger invader Battle-Mechs enough to satisfy honor. Malvina had accepted their oaths readily enough, though she suspected the whole Zoetermeer garrison would have followed Devlin Stone come back from Hell had he offered them a way off the miserable dust ball. They had about as much promise as one might expect, but her need for warm bodies for her own brand of Crusade overrode pickiness.

She raised her eyes to the shipmaster's. "Order my DropShip prepared. Tell the crew to make ready for two-gee acceleration. I don't want to give this Manas Amirault a millisecond longer to get wild Horseman notions than I absolutely must. Founder knows what mischief brought him here."

She wondered briefly how her ward Cynthy would bear the discomfort. It hardly mattered; she was young and resilient, and twenty-odd hours at two standard gravities would do no lasting harm. *At least I save her the hell Aleks and I had to endure!* she thought, and felt her cheeks flush with rage at the memory.

Calm, she told herself. *Master yourself. Only thus will you master the cosmos. And win your revenge.*

══ 17 ══

"**D**rive," she said.

"As the Galaxy Commander commands," a sullen voice said through her headset. From another she might have taken offense, with lethal result to the speaker.

But this was Wyndham being Wyndham. Truth to tell, she found his surliness and utter lack of awe refreshing. It bespoke the very core of reckless Falcon courage, though in unconventional wise.

With the vast metal pear of the *Bec de Corbin* looming behind, the Scimitar II hovertank lifted from the sand in a rising whine of turbines and slid forward. Malvina rode half out of the turret with her commander's seat cranked up as far as it would go. She wore goggles to keep sand from her eyes—it was especially distracting when it got in between her prosthetic eyeball and the soft tissue that lined the socket. Her hair blew free in a brisk breeze. To the northeast, left and ahead of her, hung the red ball of Antares, disproportionately huge in the mauve morning sky.

Before her a long, low ridge rose like a sea wave from the pale orange sand of the Westmacott Plain on the southern landmass: shale plates from the bed of an ocean long dried, fractured and thrust upward by tectonic shifting. Beyond its saw teeth waited the Hell's Horses DropShips.

On a cushion of air the Scimitar slid up the slope and through a notch between edgy slabs.

"Horses?" Wyndham said. "Sod me for a *stravag*."

"Unlikely in the extreme, Star Captain," Malvina Hazen replied.

She took in the scene in an instant: three DropShips, with what looked like a small city of tents sprouted around them like Cubist mushrooms. Ranks of vehicles sat parked or moved slowly. Behind them stood BattleMechs, fewer than would have been seen in a Jade Falcon cantonment even before the current crash rearmament sparked by the collapse of Devlin Stone's long-resented peace. Groups of human figures, tiny with distance, moved with purposes not immediately obvious even to Malvina's keen eyes. And between camp and ridge, four horses carried three riders straight toward the hovertank.

Wyndham had braked the tank the instant he spotted the Horse encampment, leaving his light vehicle hull-down behind the ridgetop. It hovered in the midst of a small artificial cyclone.

"Forward," Malvina commanded, "slowly."

Even over the engine, the fans, and the wash of dust and dried vegetation from below she heard her driver grumble. But he tilted the fans and the craft slid over and down the foreslope as ordered.

A quarter kilometer away the four big animals stopped and stood awaiting them with the wind spinning dust around their fetlocks. "Ground us a hundred meters off," she said. "Leave the fans spun up to minimum rotations but feathered."

"Galaxy Commander—" Wyndham began, outraged. In an emergency, boosting the skirts high enough out of the soft sand for the tank to become mobile again would burn precious milliseconds.

"I have no wish to sandblast the Galaxy commander and his pets," Malvina said. "Inadvertently, at any rate."

She lifted binoculars to scrutinize the middle rider. "Hmm," she said. "This one and I are going to be *friends*."

"They are armed," Wyndham said.

It was true. The Horsemen wore tan tunics and trousers, trimmed in darker brown, boots to the knee. By their legs stubby wicked-looking weapons Malvina took for laser carbines nestled in buckskin scabbards. Above one or the other shoulder of each rider jutted the hilt of a curved-blade sword.

"So am I," she said carelessly. Her laser pistol and knuckle-duster battleknife counterbalanced each other at either hip.

The Scimitar grounded with a thump that jarred Malvina's tailbone. She laughed. Her driver *could* have landed like a feather. *Wyndham is always Wyndham*, she thought. It amused her greatly.

She started to peel off the goggles. On second thought she left them on, pushed up onto her ice-blond hair, in case dust blew up. Fortitude was one thing, but the Eyes of the Falcon could hardly stay keen when blinking away high-velocity pink grit. *And what have I to prove about fortitude?*

She dropped to the ground. Glancing back at Star Captain Wyndham she saw the expected scowl pinched into his small features. She tossed him a cheery smile and walked toward the waiting Hell's Horses. Her step was jaunty in her khaki and green tanker battledress.

The Hell's Horses awaiting her had brown skins, through varying measures of genes and sun exposure. One man had blond hair; the woman and the second—or, rather, unmistakably the *first*—man had hair as black as space. They were wiry-lean even by the standards of Clan warriors. Their horses looked wiry too, and on the small side, but Malvina was hardly a judge of the beasts.

As she approached, alone, head up and hands empty, the foremost rider covered his right fist with a long slender left hand before the breast of his tunic and bowed. "Welcome to the camp of the Fire Horse Galaxy," he said, "and salutations, Khan Malvina Hazen."

She looked into his eyes—and stopped. They were brown,

but to say they were simply *brown* was like saying the sea was green: too simple, too shallow. Like the sea they were deep and varied. They closed straightaway above her head.

For a moment they stood and sat, eyes locked, as a sensation flowed between them as of recognition between those long parted.

She did not allow her surprise to register on her face. "I thank you, Galaxy Commander Manas Amirault," she said with the same smile she wore before, but a bit breathlessly. "Welcome to my planet."

He laughed. His teeth were white and even in his long tanned-leather face. Of course the genes for degenerative conditions such as tooth decay had been ruthlessly weeded out of the Clan gene pool centuries before.

"You have no guards?" he asked. "Not even spies in the hills?"

"None," Malvina said. "Friend or foe, few would name Clan Hell's Horses other than honorable. You bade me come to parlay. I place myself readily in your hands, Galaxy Commander."

He raised a black brow at this. Malvina felt a quickening of her already lively interest. He had at least some grasp of wordplay. It was more than she could say for many of her fellow Falcons.

"Fairly said, Galaxy Commander. Most fairly. Will you now ride the conveyance we have brought for you"—he waved a brown hand at the horse—"or would you prefer I summon a more conventional vehicle?"

"I will ride."

He raised a brow. "And do you know how to ride, if I may ask?"

She strode to the creature, put a hand to the front of its saddle and vaulted aboard. The small, tan animal with the black tail and mane back-stepped a pace and bobbed its head, eyes rolling. "I do now."

"What is your intent on coming to Antares, Galaxy Commander Amirault?" Malvina asked, as they began to ride a wide circuit of the camp. "Will you challenge me for

Possession of the Mongol doctrine, as your predecessor did?"

He laughed. He was a handsome devil to whom laughter seemed to come as naturally as riding one of these confounded uncomfortable quadrupeds. She found wherever she looked across the bleak pink landscape her eyes slid ever back to him. When they did, his eyes were always on her.

"I fear Tristan Fletcher had but small comprehension of what you mean by 'Mongol doctrine,'" he said. "He was more passionate than perceptive, in his way. He was a fine warrior and a good companion; I thank you for giving him an honorable death."

"It seemed the least I could do."

"We harbor proprietary feelings toward the ancient Mongols," Manas said. His two companions, both Star colonels, rode a few meters behind him and Malvina chattering to one another amiably as a pair of songbirds. Around them undulated thorn vines, the color of bleached bones, two-meter spikes thrusting from spiraled ground-hugging stems. "The Founder in his wisdom modeled much of our society after them, borrowing many terms such as *khan* and *touman*. But the Mongols were one thing first and foremost: horsemen and women.

"Alone among the Clans do we *truly* emulate those ancient horse-borne steppe nomads. We reflect it in our councils and in our tactics, although of course in battle we ride metallic steeds powered by internal combustion or fusion, not grass and grain. But we still ride horses from earliest crèche days, to keep vital our traditions and sense of history."

"Most Clansfolk have little regard for history," Malvina said, "except for their own, and that solely in the form of the Remembrance."

He nodded. "But you were different, Malvina Hazen. You and your brother Aleksandr Hazen."

She looked at him, genuinely surprised at the usage. It was an archaism, connoting ancient family ties that Clan culture and even reproduction had been designed to supersede. It was the way Aleks and Malvina had referred, illic-itly, to themselves.

"We studied history outside of Clan Jade Falcon's in order to better serve the Falcon," she said.

He nodded. "We in Clan Hell's Horses are well aware. Your fame is wide, Malvina Hazen."

Her answer was a smile.

"As to what we intend," he said, "we would join our efforts to yours."

"Meaning?" she asked. The motion of the horse beneath her was alien but not disquieting. She became aware of certain unusual muscular discomforts, however.

"In the Draconis Combine, sword-smiths still practice the ancient Japanese art," Manas Amirault said, half-cryptically. "Although modern alloys have long superseded the neces-sity, they make sword blades by beating together layers of hard but brittle steel with a softer but very durable steel. In this way they forge blades of a sharpness and toughness it took centuries for science to equal."

"Indeed." Malvina might have shown impatience with another for speaking so elliptically. But she did not feel it. The Fire Horse Galaxy commander was young, handsome, and while relaxed by Jade Falcon standards, projected mas-culine confidence and strength. She found him most intriguing—on a number of levels.

"Just so might your ways and ours blend together to forge a blade to carry the Clan Crusade to victory through-out settled space," he said, "and usher in the golden age which Kerensky intended for all humankind."

She looked at him. "You say—"

His teeth were very white in his dark-tanned face. "I and my Fire Horses will submit ourselves to you as Chingis Khan, to launch a great Crusade."

"What says your own khan about this?"

"As Galaxy commander I am allowed a great deal of leeway and initiative," her escort said. "As perhaps you gathered from the actions of my predecessor. I act not as representative of Clan Hell's Horses but of my Galaxy alone. At the same time, let us say that my Blood-kinsman, our khan, knows what I intend, and does not disapprove."

She cocked a brow at him. "In other words, he waits to see whether I stand or fall before he links Clan Hell's Horses' star to mine?"

He laughed. "Of course," he said. "Do things go differently in Clan Jade Falcon?"

"The Clans were created to put an end to such political maneuvering," she said with apparent severity. Seeing his expression grow guarded, she laughed. "But in truth—of course not. Nor is it Jana Pryde's fault alone, by any means. We Clanners, it would seem, are no more inferior to our Spheroid cousins in the skill of rationalization than in most things.

"Now," she said, nodding toward the horse's head bobbing before her saddlebow, "how fast will these things truly go?"

"Indeed you Falcons are adaptable," said Star Colonel Amalie with a laugh. "For ones accustomed to soaring through the air, you take readily to riding an earthbound beast." Her companion, Star Colonel Telford, joined in the laughter.

Malvina showed her a little tight smile. Internally she cursed Manas Amirault and his whole Clan as the party completed its circuit of the far-flung Hell's Horses encampment.

She was no stranger to pain. Every day since the disaster of the first assault on Skye, she had lived with brutal agony. She refused any medications to ease the torment, except what was absolutely necessary to snatch at least a few hours' uneasy sleep a night. And every day before that she had known pain, too, though not always of the body. . . .

But now she experienced pangs of a nature she'd never encountered before. Specifically, it seemed as if the saddle between her hindquarters and the horse was lined with razors.

She had to admit she could detect no mockery in the voices or mannerisms of the Horse warriors. Either they were so used to the saddle they had no clue what she went through, or they intended to haze the Hazen. In which case she apparently passed the test.

Because it was part of shared Clan lore, Malvina knew how the Hell's Horses came by their totem beast. The hell's horse was no natural, if alien, animal. Rather, a uniquely misfired attempt to gene-engineer terrestrial horses to survive upon the Clan's harsh homeworld had spawned it.

The magnificence and ferocity of hell's horses had obviously impressed their creators enough to take them for their namesakes. Still, the Clan eagerly began raising their beloved true horses as soon as they had conquered other planets where they might thrive *without being* turned into savage flesh-eating mutants.

It still amazed Malvina that the Horsemen would take the damned things on military expeditions, though. She didn't know whether to admire their audacity or laugh aloud at their folly. She did wonder fleetingly what they did with the horses during high-gee maneuvers.

Manas Amirault rode silently by her side. She was aware from time to time of appraising glances he cast her way—or admiring ones. Mostly he was content to let his subordinates banter, which they did with a careless ease Malvina was altogether unaccustomed to among the testy Jade Falcons.

"What do you think of our horses, Khan Malvina?" he asked as they came round to complete the circle at the gates through the wire tangles that surrounded the cantonment.

"They seem fragile to me," she said. "Not robust designs at all."

He tipped his head back and laughed. His long black hair streamed like a horse's tail from his shaven-sided skull down his wedge-shaped back. "Most perceptive. Most folk unfamiliar with them find their bulk and strength intimidating. Yet they can be surprisingly delicate. They can also be surprisingly durable—in both cases like humans."

As they turned in toward the gates Malvina realized for the first time that what she had earlier taken for some kind of infantry maneuver drill was in fact a game played by two sides kicking a ball toward nets at either end of a cleared field perhaps a hundred meters long. From differences in the participants' garb she realized with a shock one group consisted of warriors while the others could only be members of the technician caste.

"What is this?" she asked.

"Football," said Telford. He made a face. "I fear the techs are getting the better of us again."

She raised a brow and looked at Manas. He seemed blithely unaware of the *chalcas* implicit in allowing mere technicians to compete with warriors. Much less so blithely to admit to being bested by them!

The gate guards saluted and dragged the obstacles out of the way with snorting diesel donkeys. At the sound the other horses bounced their heads and danced; not for the first time Malvina suspected her own mount was unusually docile, perhaps narcotized.

Anger flashed through her: *How dare they patronize me!* And yet she knew it would not enhance her dignity as a Clan Galaxy commander, far less a khan, to have the wretched beast run away with her or pitch her off into a serpent thorn.

They rode through the gates, past the playing field, where the contestants stopped to watch. As they rode in among the ranks of parked vehicles and BattleMechs Malvina saw something that astonished her far more than the mixed-caste game.

"Are those warriors I see helping technicians perform maintenance tasks?" she asked.

Manas looked at her with what seemed honest surprise. "Of course."

Malvina felt compressed upon herself as she rode. She felt disoriented. She and her brother had both been compelled to fight Trials of Refusal for ordering warriors of their own commands merely to do walk-arounds of their 'Mechs before missions.

This, though, struck her as the most obscene thing she had ever seen. *Deliciously* obscene.

For just that reason she found outrage transmuting to intrigue.

"You are surprised," the Star colonel said gravely. "Ahh.

I forget, though I have studied the ways of other Clans. You Falcons practice teamwork, but grudgingly: it goes against your fiercely individualistic grain.

"We Hell's Horses *prize* teamwork. Not simply among warriors but between castes as well. All serve the Clan in their ways; none can function without the others. Our castes remain distinct, the authority of warriors is respected. Yet we have no fear of cooperation."

As a good Jade Falcon—especially one who had displayed her fanatic traditionalism like bright post-molt plumage throughout her career—Malvina Hazen might have been expected to flash over into *yarak*, the raptor's eagerness to *hunt*, at the imputation her Clan feared to have its warriors work alongside lesser castes. Even though it was quite manifestly true. Truth was a feeble thing in the face of Clan honor and tradition—and no mitigation of *chalcas*.

But Malvina seldom did the expected. Her breath caught in her throat. But not in fury.

"Among Hell's Horses," Manas told her loftily, "the warrior is a servant, not a master of the people."

It was magnificent and absurd, as specious as the concept of noblesse oblige on medieval Terra, which she and her beloved sibkin Aleksandr had read of so avidly in crèche days. Notwithstanding, the awareness of *possibilities* burst inside her like a bomb.

I can use such attitudes, she exulted. *Without, of course, losing sight of the fact that that in all cases, I am not servant, but master.*

And laughing aloud she rode in among the yurts of Clan Hell's Horses.

Near Alba, Antares
Jade Falcon Occupation Zone
8 December 3135

In the darkness, a sea of wavering torchlight, yellow and amber.

After Alba's near-destruction by Khan Elias Crichell's aerospace fighters, the Jade Falcon occupiers had rebuilt the capital, such as it was, in a haphazard, expedient way. In its seeming randomness it resembled a shantytown, perhaps most of all because of the rude spacers' quarters that grew up like fungal forests around nearly every DropShip port in known space. Except that its structures were much more durable and blast-resistant: even in their temporary nesting sites, the Falcons built to last. And defend.

The one real exception, the single carefully planned element about which all the scattershot construction grew, was a vast paved plaza a kilometer on each side. Like all totalitarian cultures from the mists of pre-Kearny–Fuchida time, the Clans felt a need for grand spaces in which to exalt power itself in shared rituals of worship.

Here in scratch-rebuilt Alba the message ran: *We care little for comfort and convenience. But we are here to stay, and our true mark is this shrine to the glory of Turkina.*

A statue of the eponymous jade falcon rose from the center of the ferrocrete lake in green translucent stone thirty meters high, wings outspread as if in stoop, clutching a katana in her claws. Now two throngs surrounded it, torches held high, divided in two by canals of darkness.

Scaffolding stood beside Turkina's likeness. Huge banners of the Hell's Horses and Jade Falcons hung side by side, illuminated by floodlights. Giant bonfires blazed to either side, like pyres for an order now ending.

On a platform in front of the Clan banners stood three figures clad in white. Beckett Malthus wore long robes not unlike his customary garb. Before him stood Malvina Hazen and Manas Amirault side by side, dressed in identical tunics and trousers of white whipcord. The contrast was startling: Malvina tiny against the Horses' *ristar*, who stood not much shy of two meters tall. But it would have taken a uniquely *suicidal* wit to comment on the potential comedy of the picture they made.

Nothing was further than humor from the minds of the Falcons and Horses assembled beneath a star-shot sky. They stood with faces and bodies molded into forms of solemn, even worshipful attention. Yet electricity seemed to charge the air like the muzzle of a particle cannon the microsecond before discharge.

All castes stood assembled there in separate ranks: laborers, technicians, scientists, warriors. Though such commingling was common in Clan Hell's Horses, it was the first time, perhaps, in the history of the Falcon. It would not be the only such first.

The two young Galaxy commanders stepped forward. "Hail, Hell's Horses!" cried Malvina. Her voice was amplified by a concealed microphone and discreetly placed but very powerful speakers to fill the whole crystal dome of night. In response, the Horsemen and -women whinnied their nasal battle cries.

"Hail, Jade Falcons!" Manas' baritone pealed like a great bronze bell. Fierce Falcon cries skirled skyward.

Malvina said: "I am Hell's Horses." Her Clansfolk assembled echoed her words.

Manas said, "I am Jade Falcon." The Horses repeated the phrase.

Then both, in unison: "We are the Clans."

They paused to allow their followers to repeat their words, as they did after every clause of the great oath they swore.

"This fire we kindle	*"Our blood is yours.*
"To set the Universe ablaze.	*"Blood of Kerensky*
"This we pledge:	*"Holy Blood*
"We join together	*"Shall flow together*
"In a Golden Ordun	*"A rising tide*
"Courage to courage	*"In sacred Crusade*
"Destiny to destiny.	*"To drown our foes in a*
"Your strength is our strength.	*crimson flood!"*

Both commanders flung their arms high. Their followers joined them in a wordless scream of exaltation and naked lust for blood and victory. Overhead the stars quivered in the shimmer of the world's thin atmosphere.

The screams died away as Malvina stepped back. She mounted a low dais set several paces behind. Beckett Malthus stepped to the fore.

In stifled silence he and Manas turned to face the diminutive woman whose blond hair swirled in the slight breeze like a battle flag about her shoulders. They knelt. Manas Amirault looked serene. Malthus' spade-bearded face seemed drawn extra-taut across its lantern-jawed skull, as by turnbuckles. His robes hung with unaccustomed looseness from his powerful frame. In the past few months, much of the excess bulk built up through prolonged fondness for decadent Spheroid cuisine had melted from his powerful frame.

Speaking together, the two proud Galaxy commanders pledged their undying fealty to Malvina Hazen as Chingis Khan of all men, emperor.

The cry went up from thousands of throats, from the lowest laborer to the haughtiest MechWarrior, starting low, but rising like a triumphant tide: "Chingis Khan. Chingis Khan.

"Chingis Khan!"

After Malvina's initial meeting with Amirault, the Hell's Horses had packed up and loaded back into their DropShips, to relocate on a plain a kilometer or two east of Alba. In the field the Horses dwelt in power yurts: smallish internal-combustion lorries that when parked, unfolded into tents. Although Clan Hell's Horses emphasized friendly coopera-tion among castes, it did not by any means erase the lines of demarcation. Yurts were allocated on the basis of rank: MechWarriors, tankers, and elementals customarily two to a tent. High-ranked scientists lodged three to a yurt. Infan-try and *solahma*, as well as technicians and more modest scientists, four. And so on, down to larger fixed-bed trucks that blossomed into barracks housing ten laborers each.

On her earlier trip Malvina could not help noticing, with unexpressed amusement, that the power yurts were indis-tinguishable from a certain class of what frivolous and luxury-obsessed denizens of the Inner Sphere would call *RVs*.

Such humorous comparisons were the furthest thing from Malvina's mind when, sometime after midnight, clad in a simple white silk gown, she let herself into Manas Amira-ult's power yurt. As Galaxy commander he rated one to himself. Around her the Horses cantonment buzzed and flashed with activity: the voices of warriors and technicians and laborers working together in heretic harmony to ser-vice their war machines; music, bubbling quicksteps and plangent ballads; the whine of sono-wrenches; showers of sparks from plasma cutters and welders. She smelled the tangs of hot metal and ozone. Like her Falcons in and around Alba, the Horsemen worked watch-on-watch to hone the edge of their battle force: on the heels of the night's oath-ceremony had come the word that the enemy had entered Antares system at zenith and nadir jump points almost simultaneously. They now drove toward the world at full two-gees acceleration. They would arrive in five and a half standard days.

*   *   *

Long-range observation revealed they carried a number of DropShips sufficient to transport upward of two full Galaxies. In addition they brought a WarShip, the *Aegis*-class heavy cruiser *Jade Talon*. They emerged at the zenith point, where Binetti's battleship lurked to seize passing traffic as well as defend against attack. Although the *Emerald Talon* remained far more powerful than the much smaller newcomer, much of the severe damage it had been done by the Lyran battleship *Yggdrasil* remained unrepaired and irreparable shy of a protracted refit at an orbital shipyard. To directly contest the smaller vessel would risk further diminution of the *Talon*'s battle-readiness, or even its total loss.

But it was not the Chingis Khan's intent to resolve this battle either in or from space. Her Golden Ordun would meet the Falcons on the pink dust plains beneath Antares. Accordingly, she ordered Star Admiral Binetti to withdraw in-system ahead of the invaders, harrying with fighters and using his still-formidable armament only to preserve his command from harm.

It went against the crusty old space dog's nature to run in such a way. But he had accepted Malvina Hazen's mastery, and his sense of duty was too great to issue a Refusal despite his personal feelings, or even military judgment. He carried out his orders with the precision and fury expected of a Jade Falcon naval officer.

The only communication had been a terse holovid from the invasion force's leader, Galaxy Commander Erik Chistu, demanding of all bloodtrue Jade Falcons in-system that they should immediately deliver the heads of the traitorous renegades Malvina Hazen and Beckett Malthus (attached to still-living bodies, strictly optional) or face outlawry after a Trial of Abjuration. He uttered no challenge. Just the naked demand to submit.

In return Malvina recorded and beamcast back her invitation to the invaders to swear allegiance to her new Golden Ordun. She challenged Chistu himself to a one-on-one Trial of Possession for his war fleet.

No answer came back. That was as Malvina anticipated.

When Erik Chistu delivered his response, it would come in the form of hot steel, high explosives and ravening energy beams.

As would Malvina's rebuttal.

"Enter," a deep voice came from within the yurt.

Malvina parted the heavy fabric hanging and stepped up a short perforated-metal stair to the platform inside. It was dark, lit by low amber lamps placed on short-legged tables. The sleeping platform was lined with cushions, furs and silks. Tapestries hung from the walls, laser-printed with scenes of Hell's Horses victories.

In their midst stood Manas Amirault, to his bare shins in cushions, wearing a short dark robe of some lightweight material.

His teeth shone bright in his dark face when he smiled. "I bid you welcome, my Khan."

"Here," she said, "we are not Galaxy commander and khan. Here we are Manas and Malvina."

She let slip her own robe. Beneath it she was nude. Her natural alabaster skin made a strange contrast, a curious *Taijitu*, black yin, white yang, with her opposed artificial limbs of shiny obsidian.

"Do my deformities displease my *ristar*?" she asked in a level voice.

"I see no deformities," he said. "Only marks of courage and indomitable will."

"And what will I see beneath your robe?"

He held his arms out to his sides. His smile widened to a grin. "Look for yourself, and judge."

"Judge you I most certainly shall," she murmured. She glided forward, managing by dint of extraordinary control of her body—not bettered by any Spheroid gymnast or dancer despite her prosthetics—not to waddle and wallow through the thick, resilient bedding. She undid the belt and unfolded the wings of the light garment down his muscle-roped arms.

As expected, his torso was spare as desert land, ridged with muscle. Pale scars ran across it like rills and gullies.

A puckered pink crater the width of a fist and depth of a finger's breadth dented his ribcage beneath his right nipple.

"You too bear the marks of valor," she said.

She embraced him then, the cheek with the scar pressed to the depression in his chest. His arms went around her whiteness like dark metal bands. He felt hot to her skin. She felt cool to his.

For a moment they gripped each other fiercely. She tipped her head back, eyes half closing, lips parting. Their mouths met and melded in a kiss. His eagerness burned like metal heated by a cutting torch between her breasts.

Then breaking free, she slid down him with agonizing deliberation, hands flowing cool down his sides as she folded to her knees, to begin her own private ritual of sealing his fate to hers.

$$=== \mathbf{19} ===$$

Alba, Antares
Jade Falcon Occupation Zone
14 December 3135

Screaming like their namesakes amplified ten millionfold, Jade Falcon aerospace fighters attacked into the vast, bloated crimson face of Antares rising.

Galaxy Commander Erik Chistu may have been a student of history, recalling in his tactics how Crichell served the Lyran defenders during the glorious Return. More likely, since he had seldom impressed anyone as particularly thoughtful, or overly attentive to recitations of the Remembrance (indeed, his eyelids had been observed to droop during lengthier passages), he simply hoped to smash the bloodfouls in their dens.

His surprise seemed complete. Only a few laser beams, ill-armed missile volleys and bursts of autocannon fire greeted his craft as they seeded the town with bombs and rockets. Fire, smoke and ruin blossomed rapidly in their wakes.

The shock wave of their hypersonic passage, less than five hundred meters above ground, only added to the destruction. Even the great statue of Turkina toppled in the middle of its great cement square. Though they had been ordered to avoid hitting it, the dynamic overpressure of multiple blasts and passage had done the trick.

Since the first rude combat jets screamed into the skies of Terra, *fast movers* had always been notoriously bad at spotting targets on the ground, or even engaging them at speed—if they happened to be smaller than, say, a town, or at least an armored column caught in the open. These craft of Chistu's, his *Sholagar*s and *Vandal*s, rode fusion flames to velocities far higher than any mere jets could attain. So they curved around, taking kilometers to do it, for a second pass without observing anything of note below them. Nor did they on the third pass, nor the fourth, as their beams and projectiles raked the ruins. By the last turn they were mainly stirring dust and broken chunks of masonry.

Chistu ordered them to attack at speed because *Emerald Talon* had taken station in geosynchronous orbit directly above Alba. Whether the great WarShip intended to participate in the coming battle against Khan Jana Pryde's invading forces he had no inkling. It clearly meant to prevent *them* from bombarding the defenders from orbit, and it succeeded. If the *Talon* tried to use her naval weapons when Chistu's ground forces struck he would defy the spirit if not the letter of his khan's orders and risk his own valuable WarShip, as well as DropShips and fighters, to drive away the wounded giant. Short of that, he took no chances with his bombing and strafing runs.

He landed his DropShips west of the smoking waste his aerospace crews had made of Alba. While other fighters with full magazines engaged renegades in combat high overhead, drawing twisting contrails in the violet morning sky until they could no more be traced than a full bowl of spaghetti, he unloaded his 'Mechs and vehicles and VTOLs and arrayed them in the order he desired on the pink hardpan.

Then, preceded by Stars of hoverbikes, scout cars and ducted-fan Skadi aircraft, the avengers of Clan Jade Falcon's established order advanced.

They met . . . nothing.

*   *   *

A frown compressed Galaxy Commander Erik Chistu's already compact and generally pugnacious features as his *Night Gyr* stalked through the husks of Alba. Controlled through the neurohelmet clamped over his shock of stiff brick-colored hair, the 75-ton metal monster waded easily through grayish-pink dust that had drifted in places to the height of a man, compounded of the world's friable soil and cement powdered by the merciless aerial bombardment.

It had savagely provoked him already. While little but dust-covered mounds and broken shells remained of the Falcon-built settlement, they and the deep dust slumping to cover all the streets had proven to be almost impassable barriers for his track-laying vehicles. They were forced to wing out north and south of the ruins, become mere reserves backing his BattleMechs, elementals and infantry clinging to the backs of hovertanks or riding in ground-effect APCs as they cleared the town.

But the town, it appeared, was already clear. He hadn't seen so much as a dead laborer in the debris as he advanced, flanked by his command Star. *What is mad Malvina up to*? he wondered.

Out of respect for the Hazen Bloodname he refused to append it to her, even in his mind. It was a good thing she was so famously the last of her sibko left alive. Malvina had been Decanted of a tainted batch: she was truly bloodfoul. Certainly every microliter of that particular sibling cohort's genetic material must be poured down the drain.

But that was not his concern. Crushing this . . . it was more than rebellion. It was a sacrilege against Turkina and the Falcon Way. Crushing this abomination, and incidentally avenging his own long-distance humiliation by his Khan, *was* his concern.

He entered the central square. Perhaps a quarter of Alba's total area, even its cement, blast-heaved and crazed, was drifted with dust like gritty snow. He averted his maroon eyes from the statue of Turkina, overturned and shattered by his bombs, his rockets. *Another crime to add to Malvina's codex,* he told himself savagely.

"Galaxy Commander," a voice said in his skull. *"Tango Rider Two."* It was the recon Star of hoverbikes, supported by Nacons and elementals, scouting the devastation in advance of his main force. *"We take fire from the rubble on the eastern outskirts."*

"Flush them and crush them, Tango Rider Two. We advance to support."

At last! he thrilled. *The stravags dare to bite back.* He kicked in his four powerful jump jets. His form-fitting seat pressed his back and tailbone. The heavy 'Mech, with its dome head hunched down between huge shoulder-actuator armatures, took off in a long leap and whirl of dust.

As it reached the apex of its long, low trajectory, Skadi VTOLs, summoned as if by his will, prowled past on down-blasts of their great shrouded fans. They raked the half-intact buildings from which enemy fire came with lasers and rockets. Chistu smiled as his threat-assessment display blanked out the symbols representing first one, then two knots of resistance, identified as enemy infantry supported by a few elementals. He was not vain enough to feel anger at being cheated of first blood. Not *quite.* And anyway he presumed that honor had gone to his aerospace fighters when they pounded Alba to shards and powder. But his heart sang with joy that the infection raging within the blood and body of his beloved Clan was at last being expunged. Even one cell at a time.

Alba rested on a low plateau surrounded by rolling plain, irregularly twined with giant serpentine whitethorn and dotted with clumps of dark blue brush with tough swordlike leaves. From below the far western lip of the plateau now sprouted a hundred white tendrils, like plant stalks growing in fast motion.

"Long-range missiles!" Chistu called out on Vau Galaxy's general frequency. "Evade, counterattack, destroy!"

The *Night Gyr* slammed down in the middle of a street, its jarring impact scarcely cushioned by a meter of dust. Held in place by the five-point harness clamped over his sternum, Chistu instantly crouched the huge, blocky machine and launched it in another leap. The hot lust to be *at* his foes, tearing out their throats and tasting their tainted blood, overpowered concerns of heat management. Besides, he had yet to fire his weapons.

That changed as his BattleMech descended into the very fringe of the rubbled town. As Arrow IV missiles streaked overhead, from behind him a half dozen conventional infantry in green-and-black Falcon battledress bolted from a small ruined structure to his left.

Striding his BattleMech forward, he swiveled its torso to bear on them. Green beams lanced from the *Night Gyr's* torso and head. Where the medium-laser spears touched running soldiers, the enemy simply vanished into puffs of black greasy smoke and pink-tinged steam. Transmitted by audio pickups, the last shrieks of air superheated by the beams, bursting from their lungs out through their mouths, sang like the calls of dying prey-birds in his ears. Those sounds of final agony made him hard within the tight white trunks of his MechWarrior suit.

Reports of enemy forces sighted swamped the death cries as the last fleeing bloodfoul was vaporized. Chistu turned forward again with his heads-up display lighting with threat reports processed through the 'Mech's battle computer. Apparently, his enemy had abandoned the town to await his assault concealed by the escarpment and by arroyos and folds of the land beyond. With the ferric mass of the immense Star League base buried beneath the plateau to mask their magnetic signatures, and proper orbital surveillance forestalled by the Sword of Damocles presence of *Emerald Talon* overhead, simple drapings of camouflage netting had sufficed to hide the renegade army from detection by *Peregrine* fighters as they flashed overhead in their ground-attack runs.

Now Mongol VTOLs appeared over the far horizon, rapidly growing larger in Chistu's viewscreen. Most of his aerospace fighters had returned to base well in the rear, or to DropShips in their own geosynchronous orbits with the planet's bulk between them and the dark metal cloud that was the enemy's mighty WarShip, to replenish their munitions. Those still on station reported the arrival of enemy fighters at high altitude, evidently forming a giant combat air patrol to interdict further aerospace attack. Glancing briefly up he saw contrails twine like yarn high above; a small white flash turned into a small white puff as a fighter was exploded by a foe's weapons.

The battle for Antares, and the heart and soul of Clan Jade Falcon, would be fought and won on the plains west of ruined Alba. Erik Chistu smiled.

That was just the way he wanted it.

Leave the pilots to their games, he thought, *and let Jade Falcon MechWarriors do the real fighting. Just as it should be.*

He ordered a general advance. His heat levels already settled back to nominal, he led his forces on a pounding charge from the rubble.

The enemy vehicles did not close with his units. Rather they swept at top speed back and forth before Chistu's onrushing tanks and BattleMechs, drawing rooster tails of pink dust behind them and raking the invaders with their weapons. To his right his saw a little Fox armored hovercar take a head-on hit from a hypervelocity ferro-nickel Gauss slug. The twenty-ton mass leapt straight up in the air before the inertia of its two-hundred-kilometer-per-hour-plus speed flipped it forward to bounce across the plain, coming apart in chunks and finally vanishing entirely into a yellow smear of burning fuel.

"Galaxy Commander," one of his own scout units reported, "many enemy vehicles display the insignia of Clan Hell's Horses."

"What?" In his surprise he almost faltered his 'Mech's forward stride.

A Scimitar II darted at him from ahead to his right. Unwisely, for by attacking straight-on its pilot threw away most of the advantages of his high rate of speed and solved most of Chistu's targeting problem for him. Splendidly proficient at MechWarrior skills Chistu found it crèche-play to line up the sights of the Ultra autocannon in his 'Mech's right arm. Almost contemptuously he fired a normal-rate burst. A one-hundred-millimeter shell smashed the hovertank's left SRM rack. Another smashed through the armor of its right bow, tearing open the skirt.

Bleeding air, the 35-ton craft dropped its prow into the sand. A normal driver might well have lost control at such breakneck speed. But this pilot was a master. He—or she—managed to keep the craft under control, even as it fishtailed madly, plowing up a great surge of earth that must have almost obscured the view from the cockpit.

Bleeding smoke from its destroyed double-rocket rack, the hovertank turned away. Erik Chistu was amazed to see the unmistakable flaming horse-head badge painted on its hull. The news of Hell's Horses involvement had slipped from his awareness; he had a mind poorly suited to hold more than one thought at a time.

Before he could finish his prey a spread of short-range missiles slammed into it, ripping open its whole port side. A moment later the strobe of a medium pulse laser probed through the great rent in the Scimitar's armor. Flame vomited reply.

As the hovertank began to roll to its right the cockpit canopy popped open. A figure clambered out, a long brown tail of hair streaming behind its head. Chistu just had time to register the khaki-clad form as female. Then the driver was thrown free as the doomed Scimitar struck a boulder and bounced in the air. She fell ahead and to the right of her tumbling craft. A moment later it landed on its back on top of her and skidded forward thirty meters, striking sparks from rocks in passing, before coming to rest and being engulfed in orange flame and black smoke.

"Hell's Horses!" Chistu exclaimed, as if discovering the fact for the first time.

He opened his general freq. "All who fight alongside our enemy are our enemies. They are no less befoulers of our true Clan blood! Crush all without mercy!"

Rockets exploded all around Chistu's BattleMech as he continued to advance. Beams slashed past and overhead, or gashed glowing-glass gouges in sand. He absently registered the sledgehammer bangs of long-range missiles striking his armor; the relatively light warheads had small effect. His electronics sizzled and squealed and the hair rose on his nape as a particle beam kissed the upper curve of his left shoulder-housing. It glowed momentarily yellow, cooling at once to cherry red, but the glancing strike did no real damage.

Wrecked vehicles blazed to both sides. Most bore the Horses badge or the green Horus-eye of the Falcon *stravags*, he saw with satisfaction. Even as he took a quick look around the developing battlefield he saw a renegade *Fire Falcon*'s pointed snout unfold and the ejector seat jet clear with the MechWarrior as the 25-ton BattleMech's mutant-chick profile was torn apart by its short-range missile magazines exploding. As the bloodfoul's chute deployed, Chistu exulted to see laser beams stabbing for it from all directions. Steam puffed as two converged briefly on it. When the smoldering figure dropped to the dust several hundred meters south of the *Night Gyr*, Chistu saw his infantry drop from the two-gun turret of a huge, eight-wheeled D1 Schmitt heavy tank and run forward to make sure of the deviate with their laser rifles.

But the enemy's slashing attacks took a toll of their own. A Vau *Eyrie* bounced past Chistu's 'Mech at its peculiar prancing gait, firing a spread of advanced tactical missiles at a target Chistu couldn't see. A streak-guided SRM swarm rained down from its left, shattering its hip-actuator. Its wingtip hit the ground and flipped the 35-ton machine onto its front, crushing its beaklike cockpit into the hardpan.

Movement snapped Chistu's gaze to his left. A *Hellhound* attacked. The two blue eyes denoting Malvina's personal retinue of fanatics, the self-proclaimed Eyes of the Falcon who had accompanied her back from Skye, glared insanely from the front slopes of its chest armor against an unmistakable Jade Falcon camo pattern in locally appropriate shades of pink and gray. A green Horus eye was painted on one concave shin shield, the Falcon ensign on the other. Chistu gritted his teeth to see Turkina's likeness so defiled.

Ruby light stuttered from the large pulse laser clutched in the *Hellhound*'s right hand. Fired at a dead run over broken ground, the burst missed Chistu's *Night Gyr*. This was no slash-and-dash caracole; ignoring the 25-ton weight disparity in their 'Mechs as single-mindedly as he did the massive spread of Arrow IV missiles exploding in a curtain of red dust and rocks not fifty yards behind his running BattleMech, the renegade Falcon steered straight toward Erik Chistu.

"If you want death, defiler, I am happy to oblige!" he snarled. He tipped his 75-ton machine into the controlled fall of a tailbone-slamming full-speed dash at his foe.

A green flash filled the cockpit. Although the viewscreen scattered enough of the high-energy coherent light to prevent the Galaxy commander's being blinded, Chistu blinked momentarily at huge magenta blobs of afterimage. A medium laser, fired from well beyond effective range, had illuminated his cockpit dead-on.

He allowed himself a glimpse past his rapidly closing foe. Far beyond the *Hellhound* a *Dasher* light BattleMech raced from left to right. It was painted shiny black with blazes of brilliant orange trim. It was clearly a Hell's Horses machine. Although both Malvina Hazen and Beckett Malthus painted their own machines black, flouting camouflage, this was no Jade Falcon aesthetic.

He fired one of the PPCs tandem-mounted in his 'Mech's left arm. The pseudo-lightning struck an arc-welder spray of sparks from the *Hellhound*'s left thigh-plate. It left a glowing-edged wound through which the pulsing of the myomer muscle driving the limb was clearly visible.

Recklessly the *Hellhound* came on. Its big pulse laser stitched the *Night Gyr*'s chest, making molten armor flow like incandescent blood.

Chistu slowed to a walk. *Why add to my heat by running when the bastard comes to me?* he thought, not even aware of using a Spheroid epithet. He blasted the oncoming BattleMech with both his PPCs, spiking his thermal load near redline.

The *Hellhound*'s upper chest erupted in smoke and white embers and secondary static discharges. The heavy machine reeled and actually paused from the jet-recoil effect of a ton of armor sublimating away as vapor in an instant. Then it came on, blasting its foe with the two medium lasers mounted on its torso.

Right below them a hole gaped in the armor. As his heat

indicator eased down Chistu fired a normal-cycle burst from his autocannon into the breach. He shouted triumphantly as the smaller machine staggered, almost lost balance.

Chistu triggered a single PPC and charged. This time the bolt blasted away the twin lasers' lower housing, causing the emplacement to collapse in on itself, sparking. Chistu fired his three medium lasers. The beams deeply scored the scarred and scorched armor.

The *Hellhound* slammed four short-range rockets from its two double racks into the *Night Gyr*'s torso, putting its left-side medium laser out of action. The others continued to flash, softening the *Hellhound*'s left-hand chest armor and making it sag. A double-rate Ultra-autocannon burst punched through the now-plastic plate.

The stored Streak SRMs exploded. Sheets of yellow flame spurted from shoulder and waist as the CASE system's armor lid blasted free, venting most of the blast and superheated gas out the 'Mech's back.

As Chistu's thermal gauges redlined, the two machines collided. Just before impact he turned his torso counterclockwise to slam the lesser BattleMech with the big humped armor housing that shielded his shoulder-actuator. Momentum told. The 50-ton machine fell with almost balletic slowness to the ground. It struck with an impact that Chistu felt in his tailbone with an almost sexual thrill.

Raising a huge foot he smashed it down on the cockpit of the supine BattleMech. Once, twice, three times. As he would stamp upon a noxious insect in the latrines at night.

Another green flash. Sparks fountained from his left shoulder. He looked up from savaging his fallen prey to see that same black-and-orange *Dasher*, racing left to right beyond the swirling dogfight on the plain. He fired a PPC. But the *Dasher* was among the fastest of all BattleMechs. Despite superb marksmanship he missed.

Frustrated anger overrode the triumph and vindication he got from stamping the life from a monstrous bloodfoul. But then his ears rang with multiple falcon screams of triumph.

"Galaxy Commander! The surat *flee!"*

20

Galaxy Commander Erik Chistu gazed around the battle-field.

It was true. Past the forest of smoke pillars that marked the pyres of machines and men, the enemy vehicles had broken off and begun to stream away across the undulant pink hills.

Not all of them: six BattleMechs, a *Loki* and a mix of medium and light machines, all showing renegade Jade Falcon insignia, stood their ground and fought as Chistu's Peregrines surrounded them. And more: Chistu saw an *Uller*, its left shoulder a sparking stub, charge directly at the *Vulture* piloted by his aide, Star Captain Djala Helmer.

Helmer slammed it with a volley of LRMs and a flickering coruscation of all four arm-mounted pulse lasers. Bleeding smoke and pale flames and vaporized armor plate, the light BattleMech continued its attack. Other weapons reached to slash at it now, from tanks and other Battle-Mechs. The *Uller* pitched forward, cartwheeled once, then rolled over and over to settle in a cloud of dust and smoke almost at the *Vulture*'s two-taloned feet.

The other bloodfoul 'Mechs had been surrounded now. Elementals swarmed over two of them. They were quickly pulled down, in a fashion suggesting more a pack of wild dogs than solitary birds of prey.

Erik Chistu nodded in grim satisfaction. The *stravag* deserved no better. They had sacrificed all consideration of honor when they rose illegally and in violation of tradition against their rightful khan. Now they were out-caste: lower even than the laborers who cleaned the sewage-treatment vats.

Already the pursuit had begun. His Peregrines' blood was up; vehicles and BattleMechs rushed in pursuit of the fleeing foes.

Reports streamed to him in voice and data. The battle was huge. His attached Vau Galaxy, augmented to almost twice normal strength, was engaged along its entire front. From monitoring battle reports Chistu's operations officers, following two kilometers behind his main force in their Tribune headquarters vehicle, told him almost a full-complement Galaxy had faced him.

Now it ran from his warriors like so many cowardly Spheroids.

"All *Peregrine* forces," he broadcast, "this is Galaxy Commander Erik Chistu. Pursue and destroy the enemy wherever they run, wherever they hide. Strike with the fury of Turkina Herself, and leave none alive!"

"They follow in hot pursuit," Manas Amirault reported, *"already strung out over half the distance between where we clashed and your position."* Malvina could imagine his slashing, thrilling grin.

But at once his tone turned serious: *"Your folk suffered heavy casualties. Many refused to heed the plan, but threw themselves in the teeth of our enemies."*

Waiting in the cockpit of her mostly-patched Black Rose, screened behind low hills the color of dried blood, Malvina frowned. But she did not allow herself the luxury of fury.

It was not wholly unexpected, Falcons being Falcons. They preferred to break rather than bend; to flee before an enemy, even their very own kin, grated against their every nerve. Perhaps *especially* to flee their own Clansfolk.

But: "They gave a good account of themselves, I trust?" she asked.

"They died like Clan. So have many invaders."

"Excellent." That would stoke the heat of the invaders' rage to white inferno. What judgment and discretion they had—hardly measurable at the best of times—had certainly evanesced like snow kissed by a heavy laser.

And if the surat *I sent with Manas will not follow orders, my orders,* she thought, *what real loss are they?*

Blazing like a meteor it fell, at meteoritic speed. A yellow streak, slanted just off true vertical, struck the valley floor half a kilometer east-southeast of Erik Chistu's trotting *Night Gyr.* His battle computer barely had time to register it as a 35-ton *Sholagar* fighter—one of his own, captured from House Kurita more than eighty years before, kept in Jade Falcon garrison service since.

By almost mathematically impossible bad luck the yellow fireball dead-centered a Kelswa heavy tank. It and the five battlearmored elementals riding its back simply vanished in a funnel-shaped geyser of dirt and smoke. All that remained was a smoking crater.

For all their vaunted adherence to scientific principles the Clans harbored mystic streaks. The Falcons, for once, were about the middle of the pack: less prone to superstition than the Nova Cats, not so scoffingly skeptical as the Sea Foxes. Had the Galaxy commander been of even average Jade Falcon superstitiousness he might have taken the strike as a peculiarly ill omen.

But Erik Chistu was that rarity: a stolid Falcon. Outsiders widely perceived Turkina's volatile sons and daughters as possessing vastly more imagination than sense. Chistu harbored little of either. The eradication of some of his best assets in an eyeblink only poured coal on the low fires of his anger—which burned most of the time, in the midst of battle or not.

His glacial rise to high rank—for he was the opposite of a *ristar*—had been driven by a sullen, stubborn tenacity more appropriate to a Ghost Bear than a Falcon. It was widely whispered that his genotype in fact contained substantial DNA from a *giftake* from a mighty Bear warrior killed in a raid into the JFOZ.

One thing Chistu did not do was attempt to impose his impassivity upon the high-strung raptors under his command. They had the taste of blood and raced after the routed foe as fast as they could. It had cost his outsized Galaxy whatever cohesion it possessed. But even if *zellbrigen* and single combat were relics of the glorious past, few Clans concerned themselves overmuch with tight formation discipline—and Clan Jade Falcon less than most.

Besides, the fight was won. He knew. All his warriors knew. What remained was the joyous chore of slaughter.

He might still have taken warning when a cloud of enemy VTOLs suddenly rose up from behind the line of hills that marched across the eastern horizon and swarmed out of the vast swollen crimson face of rising Antares to meet his own aircraft. But he *knew* the rebels were defeated. This could only be a desperate attempt to cover the flight of their ground forces, presumably back to their DropShips and hoped-for escape from this planet and, of course, bloody vengeance. It would be his great pleasure to crush those hopes as he had crushed the bones of the *Hellhound* MechWarrior.

Galaxy Commander Erik Chistu had in the course of a long and reasonably illustrious career been wrong before. It was a major reason his un-Falconlike habit of grinding persistence had served him so well. He would not, however, often be wrong again.

When the first fast scout vehicles and *Dasher*s of the pursuing Vau Galaxy crested the first line of the Rakusian Hills and found themselves confronted not by the rear armor of fleeing hovercraft and tanks, but a phalanx of big BattleMechs and AFVs, they thought no more of it than the fact that their own air cover had been abruptly peeled away, left behind in a twisting dogfight with enemy VTOLs.

They were victorious; they had broken their enemy like whipped curs. So they simply charged, brave green-and-black pennons whipping from their antennas.

Awaiting them, Galaxy Commander Malvina Hazen ordered the countercharge as if singing a victory hymn.

The fast *Peregrine* light BattleMechs and vehicles were crushed beneath a metal tsunami of rebel medium, heavy, and assault tanks and BattleMechs. Unlike Clan warriors of yore the neo-Mongols did not scruple to combine fire. Rather they did whatever they could to destroy their enemies as expeditiously as possible, ganging up, ramming, literally rolling over their lighter foes. They screamed their glee as they slew. Then the heavy-metal tide rolled on.

The Rakusian Hills were redder than the surrounding soil because of massive iron-ore concentrations in their rocks. Though they lay conveniently near Alba, the deposits had been little exploited, either by the Lyrans or their Jade Falcon successors. When the Star League founders built the subterranean base, they preferred to use asteroid metal, founded and forged in orbit with optimal efficiency. Antares' vaguely habitable world didn't actually *make* anything; little reason existed to hold it, save for the vague prestige and the fact that it was, after all, an inhabited world in space conquered by Jade Falcon. Once Turkina's talons closed on something, She did not like to let go.

For the Golden Ordun it was, literally, simply, a place to *stand*.

With hematite veins fouling the *Peregrines'* magnetic anomaly detectors, and adequate overhead surveillance denied them, it was easy for Malvina and Manas to hide their heavy hitters. And wait for the *mangudai* to bring their enemy, disorganized and hopelessly scattered, to them.

To die.

The majority of his lighter, faster machines were already smoldering derelicts when the onrushing battle line collided with the leading ranks of Chistu's heavies. These had not dispersed as widely as the lightweights, simply by virtue of being slower. At the rebels' sudden onslaught they began to clump, the front runners slowing, the rear catching up.

Somewhere in the furthest recess of his mind his subconscious dinned warning of impending disaster. But Erik Chistu was Jade Falcon. He knew one way: all-out attack. He would live and die by that.

And so he did.

Even before her transformation into . . . whatever it was she had become, and was becoming . . . Malvina never shared the doctrinaire Clan distaste for tactics, especially traps and ruses. *Winning* served the Falcon best; in this she and her beloved sibkin Aleks had always been in perfect agreement. At least until her notion of the means of winning expanded to encompass mass terror as a tactic . . .

Mad as she knew herself, defiantly, to be, she was still a supremely capable commander as well as an unmatched MechWarrior. The military expert part of her mind knew too well that for all the proficiency of the battle-hardened veterans she had brought back with her from the Inner Sphere, warrior for warrior she enjoyed no superiority over Chistu.

Nor had she any advantage in battle machines. Despite getting chased off Graus, her Mongol Omega Galaxy had experienced few materiel losses. They actually got away with more than they arrived with, for they had already appropriated not just fresh-built BattleMechs and vehicles but a huge stock of replacement parts, already loaded into their DropShips for future conquest, when the balloon went up.

Although she looked terrible, even Black Rose had mostly been repaired in transit to Antares and then while Malvina went raiding in a borrowed *Thor*. Her torso-mounted LRM launchers' magazine-feed system had resisted repair, so that for today's battle Malvina had only the single ten-rocket volley loaded up in her Longbow tubes. She was content to rely upon her pair of torso-mounted extended-range medium lasers, her ER-PPCs and her marksmanship, augmented by her targeting computer. Between those things and an intuitive feel for *heat* that enabled her to put out every joule of destructive energy her ride was capable of without driving the reactor to safety shutdown, Malvina felt as arrogantly self-assured as usual.

But the invaders outnumbered her by a small margin, even counting the Fire Horse Galaxy. Erik Chistu, she knew, had his force bulked out with inferior *solahma*, second-line and garrison troops. But then, so did she. And her Falcons and Manas Amirault's Horses had gotten no time to practice fighting as any kind of cohesive unit.

So she must cheat. Not only was Manas Amirault fine with that, he *suggested* it. He and Bec Malthus, trickster to the core . . .

And so *bad war* began.

While neither side made any pretense to challenge or *zellbrigen*, once Falcon locked on Falcon neither turned away, however outnumbered, whatever befell them. Mech-Warriors slugging it talon to talon died oblivious when other BattleMechs came up behind to incinerate their cockpits at touch range. Their minds held but one thought-sequence: Find enemy. Engage enemy. *Destroy* enemy.

The blood-madness of hate seized even the infantry. The Falcon khan's warriors and the Mongols killed each other rifle to rifle, knife to knife, bludgeoned each other with rocks when batteries drained and battleblades broke. Screaming Falcons armored in no more than camo battledress attacked elemental battlearmor with bare hands. Sometimes in such numbers that they managed to rip open the suits' closures and slay the giants within with hands and teeth despite horrific losses.

Personal survival never entered the equation. No more than mercy did.

Malvina strode and slew through maelstroms of dust and smoke though her *Shrike* streamed molten armor like blood from a score of wounds. She rode down a *Spirit* that was hobbled by a laser-fused knee-actuator and trampled chest and cockpit of the light BattleMech into crumpled ruin without glancing down as she lashed a distant *Thor* with alternate lightnings from her PPCs.

The red sun had risen fully now. It was a drawn-out process. Antares was a cool star, and the zone capable of sustaining life hugged its scarlet-flaming skirts. Now hanging like a runaway planet about to fall, it would have

caused vertigo and apprehension among the newcomers—
it always did—had they not had eyes and minds fixed firmly
upon butchery. Antares seemed to fill the sky, so great it
almost showed its globularity. Nor was it bright enough to
dazzle: human eyes, unprotected, could gaze full at the
giant, see world-storms warring their way across it.

Now Antares seemed to laugh like a monstrous idiot face
at the doings below. With evil joy: for its fire was blood's
own color.

Many acts of great courage played out beneath the gloating sun. And cowardice too. But no glory would be gained
in these hills soaked in blood scarcely darker than their
rocks and soil. For the first time in the Clan's collective
memory Falcon fought Falcon in a battle as immense as
any in the Remembrance.

But they were still Falcon killing Falcon. Now that tactics
and even skill was largely abandoned, mere numbers ruled.
Galaxy Commander Erik Chistu had more big 'Mechs and
vehicles than Malvina. So the tide slowly turned against the
warriors of the Chingis Khan.

But if the Eyes of the Falcon and even their commander
had lost themselves in happy murder, in blood-drinking ecstasy that welcomed death if it came with beak and claws
at an enemy's throat, *tactics* had not been altogether
given over.

The Hell's Horses' Mongol doctrine (as opposed to Malvina's calculated use of atrocity) tended to exclude the middle. Fire Horse Galaxy, having come into existence since
the Jihad, particularly reflected that. They possessed few
infantry, even elementals, except for garrison troops, nor
many medium-weight vehicles or 'Mechs. Rather the pre-
ponderance of their forces comprised the very fastest and
most agile machines: hovercraft, VTOLs, super-speedy light
'Mechs like the *Dasher* Amirault had used to open the
battle. All built around a core of behemoths intended to
deliver the killing blow.

Outdistancing their pursuit with practiced ease—for unlike
most Clans, Hell's Horses *did* drill for mass maneuvers—
Galaxy Commander Manas Amirault had led his well-

bloodied but largely intact *mangudai* back behind the sheltering hills. Unlike the Falcons, who had proven so resistant to the *turning and running* part of the plan, they had suffered light losses, but their munitions, fuel and pilots were completely exhausted. They needed time to rest and recharge.

But the plan gave them such time. Leaving them to recover, Manas transferred to a waiting *Masakari*. In the 85-ton BattleMech he led the *tulughma*, the standard sweep of Hell's Horses heavy and assault machines, moving wide to strike at the rear of the *Peregrines*, who were utterly engrossed in trying to destroy the hated heretic rebels.

With a grinding shriek, three meters of the end of the *Shrike*'s right wing gave way and broke loose. The stub glowed red where a laser had cut through it.

Malvina slammed her *Shrike*'s right elbow into a *Thor*'s front viewscreen. The heavy 'Mech reeled back. It raised its right arm as if to fire; disoriented, its MechWarrior had forgotten its PPC was gone, torn away by a burst of heavy autocannon shells from a D1 Schmitt tank.

Malvina fired both her own PPCs into the torso of a smoke-wreathed *Loki* approaching from her left. Ignoring an Oro heavy tank smashing autocannon and laser fire into its legs from less than a hundred meters behind, the *Loki* fired back its own particle projector. For a moment three strands of twisting artificial lightning linked the two huge machines, lighting their fronts blue as liquefied armor splashed away and clouds of white vapor enveloped them. Then the 65-ton 'Mech went dead as its reactor scrammed in redline shutdown.

The *Thor*'s autocannon raked Malvina's left side. As damage warnings sang in her ears she put the targeting computer's pipper onto the enemy machine's cockpit. Her elbow had holed and cracked the ferroglass screen. She shot a single PPC bolt into it. Yellow flame jetted from the pillbox-like cockpit. The great machine toppled forward to the ground.

The Black Rose rocked forward as two more PPC bolts

slammed into its back: an invader *Puma* attacked from the rear. The *Shrike*'s cockpit filled with terrible metallic screaming as the entire left wing, weakened, tore free and fell away of its own weight.

Malvina tried to turn to confront the lesser BattleMech, but her machine responded slowly. Her damage display indicated serious short-circuiting in the controls for the *Shrike*'s leg-actuators. Multiply redundant backup buses had been knocked out by the pummeling Black Rose had absorbed.

Malvina uttered a falcon scream of frustration. *It cannot happen that I be defeated by a machine massing hardly more than a third of mine!* But the *Puma*'s only weaponry, a pair of particle cannon, gave it terrific striking power for a 35-ton machine. If the bigger BattleMech could not maneuver fast enough to bring its own battery to bear . . .

The *Puma* reeled as a pair of particle beams struck its right side. An autocannon burst sparked across it, blowing chunks of armor from its shoulder-housing and the crab-like carapace.

The blocky bulk of a *Masakari* closed with the *Puma* at a full run. It was painted gleaming black, with a stylized Hell's Horses head snorting flame from its nostrils painted across its head and back. The *Puma* fired both PPCs at Malvina again, risking redline in a frenzy of desire to take down its great enemy. Red lights flared on Malvina's damage display as all armor was sliced from her right hip as if by a great plasma cutter.

A volley of LRMs struck the light 'Mech full in the side. It staggered. Then the *Masakari* halted its headlong charge to loose a terrifying blast of all four PPCs against armor cratered by the missiles. The *Puma*'s right arm flew away as its carapace was ripped open. At nearly a hundred kilometers per hour it stumbled as control systems slagged.

The 35-ton BattleMech lost balance and began to fall to its left as momentum drove it on. Warnings lit up Malvina's threat display as its magnetohydrodynamic fusion engine's containment field generators failed. Autopolarization darkened Malvina's viewscreen as sun-bright light flashed from the 'Mech's violated side. Its neck severed by superhot plasma, the *Puma*'s jutting head fell off as the 'Mech tumbled across the ground.

"Why did you have to destroy it?" Malvina flared over her private channel to the Hell's Horses commander. "We need all the machines we can get!"

The black-and-orange *Masakari* raised its right arm in salute. Heat shimmered upward from the muzzles of its particle guns.

"You are welcome," said Galaxy Commander Manas Amirault. Despite their generally easygoing ways, the Horses were utterly scrupulous about avoiding the use of contractions.

Malvina Hazen saw the threat before her battle computer, still well taxed by the fight surging all around, picked it out. She raised her left arm to bear on the *Masakari* fifty meters away. Twin lightnings leapt from the PPCs.

Both struck the cockpit of a Donar attack helo diving on the unsuspecting Horseman from behind. The hawk-nosed Peregrine Galaxy VTOL simply vanished into a yellow fireball that struck the pink dirt so close that blazing fuel splashed up the back of Amirault's BattleMech.

"You're welcome," Malvina said.

All around Vau Galaxy VTOLs had broken off dogfighting to fall upon the Mongol ground forces. Malvina soon saw the reason.

Though a few isolated machines stood and fought, the Peregrine vehicles and BattleMechs had broken. They streamed away from her and her ally, fleeing toward ships waiting beyond the rubble of distant Alba.

The Battle of the Rakusian Hills had ended in one of the greatest victories in the glorious history of Clan Jade Falcon.

And its greatest defeat.

Camp of the Golden Ordun
Near the Rakusian Hills, Antares
Jade Falcon Occupation Zone
14 December 3135

"**M**y Khan," said Beckett Malthus over Malvina's left shoulder, "this assault was extremely well coordinated. It was likely engineered by Jana Pryde herself. She does possess a marked degree of executive ability." He sounded almost proud of his former master and protégée.

The self-proclaimed khan of Clan Jade Falcon, and all humanity, sat in a dim-lit pavilion upon a camp chair turned by silks and cushions into a field-expedient throne. Gazing at the assembled senior commanders from her Galaxy and Manas Amirault's, their faces quietly exultant in the golden glow of lamps turned low, she idly stroked the unbound yellow hair of her ward, Cynthy. It rested on the sheer, pale-green silk robe covering Malvina's left thigh.

Hell's Horses, Malvina thought, *do these things in better style than we.*

"You sound almost proud of your former master and protégée," she said. Malthus stiffened. She uttered a low, husky laugh. "She does not fight herself, though, does she? But sends her attack dog Erik Chistu in her stead."

"She awaits you, O my Khan," her gray eminence said, "on Sudeten."

"Where I shall not disappoint her," Malvina said softly.

Cynthy turned to look at her. Malvina smiled at the child. The little girl smiled shyly back.

I will allow nothing to spoil this moment, Malvina told herself sternly. *Least of all thought of that unworthy creature who calls herself khan of Clan Jade Falcon.*

With both DropShip flotillas grounded side by side a few klicks east of the dragon's spine of the Rakusian Hills, the victorious Mongol Galaxies made a sea of raucous celebration beneath the obsidian dome of night. At the center of all the light and joyous noise, hard by the landing jacks of the great DropShip *Bec de Corbin*, Manas Amirault had decreed this pavilion for the Great Khan.

Malvina had earlier appeared on the *Bec*'s ramp in the B-sun glare of spotlights to accept the plaudits of the mob of Horses and Falcons, screaming the chant, "Chingis Khan! Chingis Khan!" until their throats were as raw as if they were back in their BattleMechs in the brutal heat and infiltrating dust of the day's great battle.

She had also accepted the submission of more than two hundred surrendered Peregrine and Vau warriors and numerous auxiliaries. Ever mercurial, she greeted them with smiling benevolence, having gotten past the shrieking fit she had thrown in Black Rose's steaming-hot cockpit that afternoon, when Galaxy Commander Beckett Malthus' voice, powered by his DropShip's fusion generators, reached out across the wreckage-dotted plain to offer amnesty to all warriors who would acknowledge Malvina Hazen as rightful khan of Clan Jade Falcon and swear fealty to her.

Manas Amirault had spoken quickly to soothe her from his *Masakari*. She barely restrained an impulse to blast him with an alpha strike. But the fury squall passed quickly, and in its wake Malvina's matchless military mind reasserted itself.

Her Mongol cause needed all the fighters she could get,

the more skilled the better. She was not naïve enough to believe this crushing victory would completely implode opposition within Clan Jade Falcon. Rather it would *polarize*: even as it energized her true believers and swung sympathizers to open allegiance, it crystallized her enemies' determination. Likely it would bring Jana Pryde more converts than she lost through defection; Falcons were nothing if not stiff-necked and contrary. For all the Clan ethos of success worship, many of Turkina's spawn would see Malvina's victory over her own as supreme *dezgra*.

Playing on that very success worship, allowing the disgraced losers to redeem themselves by binding themselves to the victors, was an inspired means of expanding her force. As for their pledging allegiance to Malvina as Chingis Khan—

That last was an innovation, all out of synch with the Clan way. On this great and terrible day on which all things were turned upside down, if not smashed to pieces, such a sea change could pass with small remark.

The thoughtful frown that had replaced Malvina's twisted scowl of fury smoothed into a smile. *And so a new and different thing comes into the circumscribed world of the Clans*, she thought, sitting in the furnace heat of her cockpit with sweat streaming down her face, her pale naked skin and hard black plastic.

Once again the wisdom of Bec Malthus is proved. And so, of course, was his danger to his present khan.

Seeing their fellow warriors overwhelmed on the surface, the invading VTOL pilots had ceased aerial combat to dive to help them in a wholly un-Falconlike act. That lay behind the Donar's death stoop on Manas' *Masakari*, so rudely interrupted by Malvina's PPCs. It was a gallant gesture. Perhaps the day's only one.

It was also suicidal. With the land battle whirling at daggers-drawn, aircraft had little chance to fire for fear of hitting their own. Meanwhile Malvina's and Manas' VTOLs, which had begun losing to superior numbers, were allowed to devote full attention to shooting down the distracted invaders. They themselves were never meant to play a significant ground-attack role. Loadouts one-sidedly weighted for air combat reflected the fact.

The Vau flyers' heroic efforts to succor their ground-bound Clansfolk got them wiped out even more comprehensively.

Most of the fleeing ground forces accepted Malthus' offer. The rest were hunted down by Mongol VTOLs and light mechanized forces fully recovered from baiting Chistu's augmented Galaxy into its fatal charge. Only a handful of survivors reached the ruins their own side had made of Alba.

But they found only temporary shelter, not escape. So stunned by their impossible defeat were the surviving invaders that Star Captain Manfredo Mattlov, Malvina's senior surviving elemental, led Horse and Falcon elementals riding Cardinal transport VTOLs in a lightning raid that seized an enemy DropShip, the *Union-C*-class *Emerald Egg*, sitting on its jacks. The spaceship's armament exacted a brutal toll, including all but one of the escort VTOLs, but it was as nothing compared to such a prize.

A second Peregrine Galaxy DropShip, fleeing, was shot down a hundred kilometers west of Alba by Malvina's aerospace fighters. It crashed with the loss of all aboard, but from such a low altitude that it might well be salvageable. Even if it proved not to be, the wreck was still a treasure trove if scrapped for parts.

The other enemy DropShips had escaped to space. As many as could docked with the WarShip *Jade Talon*, which then risked jumping out via pirate point rather than contest the victorious Mongols and their still formidable WarShip. Bec Malthus suggested the cruiser's commander, Star Admiral Edwina von Jankmon, had acted on sealed orders from Khan Jana Pryde to *sauve qui peut*, using the charge stored in the ship's lithium-fusion batteries to jump back to Graus.

Mongol DropShips pursued the remaining Jana Pryde faction ships toward their JumpShips waiting at the zenith point. They could not catch them, but did ensure they kept heading the right direction.

*   *   *

As for Galaxy Commander Erik Chistu, Manas Amirault and Malvina Hazen vied for the honor of slaying him. But it was not to be.

Finding himself left quite alone by an eddy of the brutal battle, Erik Chistu had done the thing he knew best how to do: doggedly advance, seek out foes, smash them. Then move on and repeat the cycle. He did not concede defeat. He did not concede the *possibility*.

But a Kelswa heavy tank rolled from the mouth of an arroyo not fifty meters to his left. With brilliant aim, or luck, both ferro-nickel projectiles spat from its paired Gauss rifles struck his *Night Gyr* in the hips, penetrating and jamming both leg-actuators.

Though anchored immovably, Chistu twisted the big 'Mech's torso and blasted his assailant with as much of his battery as remained after he had fought and disabled two heavy BattleMechs: one Falcon bloodfoul, one interloping Horse. Two medium pulse lasers, a heavy Ultra autocannon restricted to normal-cycle firing by damage to its regulator chip and a lone PPC lashed the rebel tank. As enemy BattleMechs closed in like jackals from every side, Chistu burst the barrel of the Kelswa's starboard gun and smashed the right side of its forward set of tracks.

Grinding his powerful jaw in fury he continued to punish the tank as it tried to back out of harm's way, until a violent explosion ripped the turret apart. Then, his cockpit like a furnace and redline warnings shrilling in his ears, he turned his weapons toward the nearest attacking 'Mech, a Falcon *Shadow Hawk IIc*.

The battering his *Night Gyr* had received had disabled many of its sensors. Otherwise Chistu's battle computer would have warned him that Horsemen in Sylph powersuits had infiltrated to the feet of his immobile 'Mech and begun to scale its gouged and pitted flanks.

His first warning came when a servo-powered claw began pounding on the left side of his viewscreen. He raised his 'Mech's arm so that the glowing hot muzzle of his remaining functional particle cannon touched one of the armor suit's feet. With a sizzle it welded in place. He discharged the weapon, filling the cockpit with hideous glare and vaporizing the rear half of suit and occupant.

The viewscreen's other side burst inward like hail, as ferroglass sugared rather than rake its occupant with sharper-than-razor shrapnel. Roaring in fury, Galaxy Commander Erik Chistu turned, clawing for his autopistol.

The peculiar hard-edged brilliance of coherent ruby light filled his cockpit, his eyes, his skull, his being—and was the last thing he knew.

Having accepted the adulation of her Mongol commanders, Malvina sat in a sort of warm haze inside her pavilion. She had ordered Cynthy choppered to her from the *Bec de Corbin*, where she waited out the battle under the care of scientist- and technician-caste minders. Now the girl half sat, half sprawled against Malvina's leg with her teddy bear dangling from one hand. Her blue eyes gazed calmly at the warriors assembled in the tent—taking all in, while giving back nothing.

If the Falcons had been scandalized at Malvina's indulgence of a Spheroid child, they had long ago learned to show no sign of it in range of Malvina's lethal temper. The Horses seemed if anything to find it charming, and openly discussed the possibility of acquiring Inner Sphere children of their own as pets. Now, after today's monumental victory, she could literally do no wrong in the eyes of any in the Golden Ordun.

Armored elementals thrust into the tent two dozen men and women. Many wore nothing more than trunks and cooling vests over the meshwork bodysuits of Clan Mech-Warriors. Others wore torn and scorched tanker battledress. Tattoos marked them as Jade Falcon warriors—if their hauteur, furious even in captivity, did not sufficiently identify them.

A braid of three colored strands encircled each captive's wrist: a bondcord, indicating the Clan, unit and warrior who had compelled their surrender. Not surprisingly, most cords showed Hell's Horses black and orange.

The bonded prisoners constituted but a small portion of the tremendous *isorla* that had fallen to the victors that day. Horrendous as the destruction of humans and machines had been, seldom was a BattleMech damaged so badly it could not be rebuilt and brought back to service, and almost never beyond being salvageable for precious parts. Vehicles were more fragile, but still had high recovery rates. Malvina had to acknowledge another benefit of Malthus' amnesty: those who took it brought over their equipment in at least workable condition.

But while the fate of captured machines and scrap was not controversial, the human bounties might well be.

With the captives came a few Mongol Falcons and Horsemen who had taken captives that day. "Is everyone here who claims a bonded captive?" Malvina asked.

Her new aide, Star Captain Timon—her most recent aide, Star Captain Felice, having died in her *Eyrie* today (Malvina went through aides at a prodigal clip)—moved through the crowd asking quiet questions. Malvina slumped on her throne smiling vaguely. Fatigue had begun to set in.

The bondholders identified themselves. "Step forward," Malvina ordered. The Horses obeyed without so much as a glance for confirmation at their own Galaxy commander, Malvina was gratified to see. *After today, they too are mine*.

She patted Cynthy's head with a certain emphasis. Obediently the child slid off her and sat back on her heels, always watching silently and solemnly with her great blue eyes. Malvina stood.

"It is my wish to offer these bondsmen and women full freedom and status as warriors," she declared, "on condition they swear allegiance to our Golden Ordun, and to myself as Khan of Clan Jade Falcon and Chingis Khan. Do any challenge my wishes, *quineg*?"

"Neg!" the Horses bondholders shouted at once. It was just the kind of romantic gesture she had quickly come to realize appealed to their nomad-warrior mind-set. After all, these captives had not given up even when all was lost: they had been forcibly subdued, only consenting to take the bondcord after being vanquished individually.

The five Falcons who had taken captives—one, the newly promoted female commander of the Second Falcon Jaegers Cluster, had two—exchanged uneasy looks. Malvina's request violated both custom and their own prerogative.

Bondsmen served at the pleasure of their captors, who snipped the cords one strand at a time in recognition for meritorious service, granting freedom only when, and if, the final cord was severed. Yet Bec Malthus had taught Malvina much of the nature of her Clansfolk. She perceived in her warriors severe discomfort at their unprecedented position of holding *Falcons* as bonded chattel.

Dampening any potential challenge to a Trial of Refusal was the fact that none had ever faced Malvina in single combat and survived. Save only Aleks—and if any of these *stravags* thought themselves equal to *him*, she would exult in teaching them just how wrong they were.

"Neg," all five Falcons answered at last.

"You choose well," she said. "You may sever the cords."

Drawing belt knives, the bondholders complied. The captives swore the required oaths and were welcomed by their new sisters and brothers with back-pounding embraces and sharp raptor cries.

"But what of the prisoners who refuse to submit?" asked Timon, almost managing to sound unrehearsed. Malvina doubted any Falcon but herself and Malthus would know—and Bec Malthus himself had coached the earnest young man with the carefully waxed crest of blond hair.

"Bring them before the khan," Malthus declared in his deepest, most doomful tones.

These were a few more than the bonded captives, bitter-enders taken alive by one means or another. More than half bore bandaged wounds; seven were brought in on litters, incapable of walking on their own.

Senior among them was Star Captain Djala Helmer, Chistu's own aide-de-camp and ranking survivor of the day's massacre. She glared at Malvina with unmasked hatred in her dark eyes. She could do no more: the Gauss slug that had shattered her *Vulture*'s cockpit had broken her spine. Straps held her to a gurney, an electro-nerve block fixed to the nape of her neck rendered her incapable of sensation and completely immobilized her, to prevent her further injuring herself. Like all Hell's Horses captives, her wounds had been treated as assiduously as if she were a Horsewoman herself.

All the holdouts had been captured by the Horses. Malvina's Falcons had killed all the wounded they could reach, even after Malthus called amnesty. As had their foes.

"Do you submit to Malvina Hazen, rightful Khan of Clan Jade Falcon?" Beckett Malthus asked.

Djala Helmer's eyes blazed. She spat at Malvina. Fortunately for all concerned, the glob fell a meter short of the toes of Malvina's bare feet. Fortunately for all concerned, Bec Malthus had accurately calculated in advance how far a well motivated Falcon warrior could spit.

Manas Amirault stepped up to plead mercy for fellow warriors who had conducted themselves in such a way as to bring no shame upon themselves, their genetic line or their Clan. He had given, extempore, the same speech that afternoon in Bec Malthus' mobile HQ after another patented Malvina screaming tantrum had cleared the Tribune of staff.

Though perhaps not her match in intelligence, even Malvina appreciated Amirault was a wonderfully smooth talker. Eloquence was much admired and cultivated in Clan Hell's Horses. Unlike Clan Jade Falcon, where speeches longer than a paragraph, other than the Remembrance, tended to be interrupted by sudden violence.

Malvina made a great show of resistance. Then Beckett Malthus spoke, no less compellingly than the Horseman *ristar*. He omitted what he had said that afternoon, with just the three of them present, about the mighty cargo of demoralizing shame the captives would carry back with them to Jana Pryde. His logic—this time—was every bit as leaky as the enthusiastic Manas Amirault's. But that was Bec Malthus' art.

When he wound up, the Falcons cried louder than the Horses for clemency to the men and women they had so desperately tried to murder that afternoon, with only a bit of flagrant shilling by Timon and a small clique picked from Malvina's most fanatic disciples. Subtlety was not just wasted on Jade Falcons, it was seldom noticed at all.

"You have spoken, my glorious warriors," Malvina declared. "Because of the honor you have brought our united Clans this day, I can only accede."

She looked at the captives. They stood or lay glaring unrepentantly at her. *They long to tear my throat out with their teeth*, she thought. The realization made her giddy, so that she must struggle to keep from spoiling the whole well-crafted moment by laughing aloud. Never before, perhaps, had she so fully *felt* her power.

"Hear my judgment: you will be placed upon a fast shuttle and delivered under truce to your JumpShip waiting at the zenith point, thence to be taken where her master chooses."

That had been settled by sunset with the naval colonel commanding the Peregrine vessel. Senior naval commanders tended to be far more reflective than Falcon warriors of other branches, but if anything less perceptive of nuance. The Sudeten-faction shipmaster had immediately agreed to receive the prisoners and allow the Mongol craft and crew that delivered them to return in-system unharmed.

Still unspeaking, the captives were hustled out to a Cardinal VTOL waiting to carry them to the shuttle.

"My Falcons, my Horses," Malvina said, "Mongols all. I salute you for your victory."

It was the signal for Timon and her command staff to usher out the officers. Malvina bent and helped Cynthy to her feet. The little girl threw her arms around the woman's neck and kissed her scarred cheek. Malvina handed her to her attendants, and Cynthy was taken off to bed.

The Chingis Khan was left with her chief advisor and chief ally, alone in the pavilion. "You have served me well too, Bec Malthus," she said. "Most well."

With a sardonic half smile, he bowed.

"You may leave us," she said.

"As my Khan wishes," he said. He turned and glided out without seeming to move his feet beneath the hem of his robes.

Malvina turned to Manas Amirault. Her robe fell open. Beneath it she was nude.

She reached out and took his strong, scarred hand and placed it on a pink-tipped breast. "Come," she said in a low voice. "It is time for *our* celebration."

22

"**M**y Khan, we cannot abandon the occupation zone!" Loremaster Julia Buhalin almost wailed.

"With all respect, Loremaster," Heinz-Otto von Texeira said with his customary smiling blandness, "no such thing need occur. The more worlds Malvina's Mongols seize, the more they must deplete scant resources to keep them. Popular as the Mongol doctrine has become, the overwhelming majority continues to reject it as destructive to your great Clan. The renegades face incessant, disruptive guerrilla warfare."

Such as we face on planets that have declared for us, he did not say. He had almost grown inured to thinking of Jade Falcons as *we*.

The far-off primary sprayed blue-tinged morning light through a narrow arch of window into Jana Pryde's office in the Falcon's Perch high above Hammarr. Von Texeira took advantage of his prosthetic leg, and the fact that little was expected of Spheroids but weakness, to sit with his hands folded on the crown of his stout black cane. Julia Buhalin stood by the door, wearing emerald and cream robes suitable to an important member of the Falcon warrior caste, clutching her staff of office. Jana Pryde herself stalked back and forth before the window, like a secretary bird on the veldt of Afrika, the little-settled eastern continent of Recife, her stern but handsome features a battleground between the pale hair yanked taut in a ponytail behind and the scowl that sought to pull them forward. She wore a white jumpsuit, its crisp bright purity broken only by the requisite badges of Clan, caste and unit.

Despite the situation's deep gravity, a restless and unruly part of von Texeira's mind could not help wondering at the Clan obsession with jumpsuits. Especially Clanswomen. *Are they gene-designed so they only have to pee once a day?*

"Moreover," he went on, "Malvina has experienced dedicated guerrilla resistance firsthand, in the zone she conquered within The Republic. Even on those worlds where she unleashed her frightful Mongol doctrine"—diplomatically he refrained from speaking the name *Chaffee*—"the occupiers face relentless rebel attack. No degree of counterstrike or reprisal has sufficed to still these insurgencies. Surely no one believes that Jade Falcons have less fighting spirit than denizens of the Inner Sphere?"

No longer are the people of the Inner Sphere content casually to accede to changes of rule, as they did during the heyday of Great House rivalries, he thought, not without triumph. *The Inner Sphere rejects the Clans and their unnatural system. We have learned at last that we cannot acquiesce without losing first our identities, and then our humanity.*

He was in unusually sour mood, so much so that it was hard to plaster over with his practiced demeanor of good spirits. He had fought with his aide (and bodyguard, and other things as well). That grieved him, for it had gone far beyond the chaffing that passed semi-constantly between them, to the perplexity of outsiders.

Yet it was far from the most grievous thing he had experienced today.

Khan Jana Pryde had assigned the Lyran diplomats a ground car and driver, the former armed and armored mostly out of habit, the latter a sullen female *solahma* garrison trooper. Von Texeira knew enough of Clan ways to be wary of her: such persons generally thought of little but securing honorable death in battle. If battle were denied them, it might, it always seemed to him, occur to them to find some way at least to avoid the crowning *dezgra* of death in bed. In this context the words *vehicular suicide* sprang irresistibly to mind.

Apparently they or similar terms had sprung into the khan's mind. Her minions had quite obviously instructed the driver that should any mishap befall her passengers, her gene-stock, already called into question by her failure to maintain front-line warrior status, would be poured straightaway down the drain.

Accordingly, whenever she took them anywhere she drove in precisely the manner of von Texeira's eighty-five-year-old maiden aunt Dona Tilda, half-blind but refusing regeneration or even correction, at a stately twenty kilometers an hour. At least there was nothing wrong with the Falcon's eyesight, garrison soldier or not: she did not bounce the sedan off the odd wall or imperil inattentive pedestrians the way Aunt Tilda did.

So von Texeira and Rorion tended to walk when time allowed. The exercise did neither of them harm. The fact that walking any distance shot pain up von Texeira's stub of thighbone, through his hips, up his back and down his arm, did not deter him. He had lived with those pains for years, and long ago resolved they would never get the better of him.

This afternoon on their way to the Perch they passed an open field near a clot of drab structures, not readily distinguishable from the rest, which must have housed a crèche. The sky was even more crowded with cloud than usual, the color of the sidewalk, hanging low over the heads of the two outlanders as they walked along with their breath emerging in visible puffs.

A crowd of warrior-caste children had gathered in the midst of the field, otherwise bare but for dried and colorless scraps of ground cover. A pair of minders in pastel-green jumpsuits and technician-caste badges stood disinterestedly by.

The children laughed and called out in piping imitations of the bird-of-prey war cries affected by their elders. All except one. That one—male or female, von Texeira couldn't tell—screamed in authentic agony and terror as several sibkin joyously kicked and stomped on it.

"What in Hell's name is going on?" Rorion demanded, his handsome face gone pale in outrage.

"What does it look like, Rorion?"

The attacked child's cries grew more desperate, gasping. Squaring his shoulders, Rorion began to march into the field.

Von Texeira grabbed his arm. Rorion spun back around, dark eyes wide. For a moment he tensed as if about to try to break the grip. Then he visibly decided against it. Wisely—and not just because of respective rank.

"Wait. There's more at stake here than your preferences."

"My *preferences*? This is brutal murder! Of a child!"

"Yes. How many children—how many *Lyran* children—will die if we throw away whatever tenuous influence we have here?"

"*Iemanjá*, it's Christmas Eve!"

His master continued to stare at him with expressionless blue eyes.

Rorion's slender frame swelled as he drew in a deep breath. Then it deflated. He tried to turn.

Von Texeira let him go.

As they walked away the younger man asked, "Why do we help these monsters?"

"You were ready to help one of them."

"A child, Margrave! A *child*."

Von Texeira's great shoulders lifted and dropped the straps of his black greatcoat in a sigh. "Yes. We help monsters because we must. It is the best way to serve our archon."

Rorion shook his head. His face was pinched, bloodless, almost purple around mouth and eyes, from more than chill. "Always this duty to the archon. Is there nothing else?"

"After the service you gave Duchess Melissa, you can ask that?"

"After my service I have earned the right to ask! Following orders I murdered and tortured and terrorized, for the greater glory of House Steiner. Have I not earned my humanity back? Haven't *you*?"

Von Texeira stopped and spun to face him. Fury knotted his big face. His nostrils flared like a bull's. But in a single breath the air and tension flowed out of him. His shoulders fell. His jowls sagged. He looked old and his skin was touched with ash.

"I will serve my archon as I swore long ago," he said sadly. "But in this matter I fear what I really fight for is the future, not just of the Commonwealth, but of the entire human race. I pray daily to *Espírito Santo* that those interests never conflict."

Rorion looked up into his elder's indigo eyes for a long moment. The breath puffed out of him, and with it the fight, as von Texeira's anger had fled a moment before. He seemed to melt from the older man's grasp as he turned to walk on.

"I feel soiled," he said as his superior joined him.

Von Texeira walked with head down and hands in pockets. The sounds had dwindled behind them to the point he could pretend to hear them no more. "Surely that's no new sensation for you. Any more than for me."

Rorion's mouth compressed to a line. He wagged his head like some kind of confused herd beast.

"What is worst," he said, "other than hearing those screams in my dreams the rest of my life, is that this horror awakens in me a sense of sympathy for Malvina Hazen." He looked up at his senior with stricken eyes. "What she had to go through, she and her brother, to make her what she is. Can you imagine feeling sympathy for such a monster?"

Von Texeira laid a hand on his shoulder. "Very well, boy," he said, "very well.

"And is that not what keeps us distinct from monsters, despite our sins?"

*   *   *

"None but a fool would say any in the Inner Sphere has more heart than Turkina's brood," Buhalin said hotly.

Von Texeira smiled hugely and nodded energetically. "Spot-on, Excellency! So we can hardly doubt, can we, that true Falcons will continue to fight Malvina or her fanatics and make their lives miserable on whatever worlds they take. Naturally there can be no question of abandoning the occupation zone. But I say it is impossible to do so, so long as some hold faith with Turkina."

"They do!"

Jana Pryde leaned back against the sill. "Your enthusiasm is laudable, Julia. Based on what my Watch tells me, it is well-founded enough."

Von Texeira smiled. *Time to press the advantage.* He leaned forward keenly.

"Malvina has keen strategic insight; and if not her, Galaxy Commander Beckett Malthus. One of them unquestionably will perceive that spreading the chaos of irresoluble warfare can only invite Turkina's enemies to launch a finishing stroke at her. Already you have Clan Hell's Horses involved, although Khan Gottfried Amirault blandly insists his Bloodname kinsman acts on his own initiative, without official sanction. How long will the Wolf hold back from rending the Falcon, when such a wonderful opportunity presents itself?"

Buhalin's handsome olive face drained of color. Khan Jana Pryde's resembled a statue's. Von Texeira was reminded that behind the Falcon khan's façade of flamboyant emotionalism coiled a calculating, highly capable brain. The khan said nothing.

Taking as his principle *qui tacit consentire*, von Texeira plowed on. "Surely Malvina has seen by now that not even she can hope to conquer Clan Jade Falcon piecemeal. Indeed, is it not fair to say, O Khan, that Clan Jade Falcon can *never* be conquered—only destroyed?"

Pryde went white at that. Her eyes flamed. Mouth compressed to a lipless slit, she nodded once, briskly.

"Only one way presents itself for Malvina Hazen to win: she must invade Sudeten system with all the force she can muster. Whether you face her 'Mech to 'Mech or army to army, she will force you to a de facto trial for the khanship. If she wins, will not the overwhelming majority of Clan Jade Falcon grab at the chance to end the dangerous disruption and fall back upon the custom of honoring the verdict of trial by battle?"

He turned to Julia Buhalin and performed a half bow. "In this matter I defer to the far superior wisdom of the loremaster. Is it so?"

"It is," she said. From the spark in her eyes he could see she wished him, in the colorful English expression he had heard as a young man adventuring in a rustic region of Prefecture IX, "in hell with his back broke." Yet he would do all he could to win her over, even at this late date.

He turned back to Pryde, who stood by the arched window with harsh sunlight rendering her visage almost skull-like. "I submit that our only chance to save Clan Jade Falcon from the chaotic insanity of Malvina Hazen and her Mongols is to muster the entire *touman* here at Sudeten. Any lesser measure can result only in disaster."

For a moment she gazed out over Hammarr's buildings. Then she nodded once, like an ax descending.

"I shall give the orders at once," she said hoarsely. "You have the right of it, merchant. That witch Malvina has but one goal. And when she comes to grasp it I shall crush her like the stinking *surat* she is!"

23

The greatest Jade Falcon disaster since Tukayyid sparked a wildfire that raged rapidly throughout the JFOZ. Open war between Khan Jana Pryde's adherents and Mongols broke out on half a dozen worlds. Perceived foes of the dominant faction were arrested or simply attacked in overwhelming numbers and murdered without quarter. Clan traditions of honor, fraying steadily since initial contact with the treacherous and unpredictable denizens of the Inner Sphere, were on some planets shredded completely in the claws of the Rending.

The conflagration quickly blew back in the faces of Malvina and her Golden Ordun. On only a quarter of occupation zone worlds did her adherents prevail. In most cases they found themselves beset by pro–Jana Pryde guerrillas—a form of warfare that ironically proved well suited to the Jade Falcon mind-set, with its love of savage slashing attacks.

Not only warriors opposed the Mongols. On Botany Bay

a conspiracy of senior scientists and technicians introduced an aerosol nerve agent into a meeting of the revolutionary Council. Pro–Jana Pryde warriors quickly overpowered the surviving Mongols. Convicted quickly in show trials, they were declared *dezgra* and publicly executed. Holovids of the proceedings were quickly dispatched throughout the JFOZ.

Camped out in the steppe east of the Rakusian Hills on joint maneuvers with the Fire Horse Galaxy, Malvina reacted to the holovid with a shrieking tantrum that gave everyone within a thirty-meter radius of her mobile yurt someplace else to go in a hurry. Even Beckett Malthus, who had weathered many of her eruptions, bowed and withdrew with all deliberate speed as she frothed threats to purge her own technician and scientist castes.

The only soul with courage to remain was Galaxy Commander Manas Amirault. His response to her outburst was to seize her, kiss her deeply and begin tearing her uniform off.

A normal woman of the day might well have resented such treatment. But this was Malvina, in whom homicidal frenzy and erotic passion were separated by the thinnest of membranes. Manas was rewarded by a ride wild even for a Horseman.

Later, as her Hell's Horses playpartner nursed a collection of bruises, bites and gouges that made it hard for an outsider to tell whether he had made love or experienced an assault with intent to kill, Malvina watched a *second* set of holovids from Botany Bay. These showed how, outraged by the unforgivable *chalcas* the lower-caste conspirators had perpetrated against the renegade warriors, the resurgent Jana Pryde–faction warriors rounded them all up, under the guise of rewarding them, and put them to death as well. Then, driven by fear or bloodlust or both, they proceeded to totally exterminate the planet's scientist and technician populations.

That give Malvina pause—then kicked her brilliant and twisted mind into overdrive.

"So this is how Jana's lackeys serve those who serve

them," said Malvina to Manas. He sat beside her on a rumpled pile of cushions, predictably shocked speechless by the pro–Jana Pryde warriors' cruel perfidy.

She stretched, catlike, and smiled. *If I needed anything to cement him and his Horses more tightly to me*, she thought, *this holovid provides it.*

Aloud she said, "If *chalcas* is what they fear so much, then *chalcas* shall I give them!"

"Malvina Hazen is losing," said the small, wiry man perched none too comfortably on the sofa of Nestah and Petah's house in The Casts outside Hammarr. Trader Wingo seemed perpetually nervous planetside, hands twisting, features pinched and cold-looking under a skullcap of space-black hair. But he called his cargo ship the *Dreaming Butterfly*, an allusion that surprised and delighted von Texeira. "None can stand against her in the field. But too many Falcons feel she has gone too far."

Sunset slowly darkened the room. Von Texeira thought he better saw how Senna turned the profit that brought her not just tolerance but a Bloodname. Wingo no doubt used diffidence as a mask to gain advantage, but it was obvious enough to put a canny trading opponent on guard. Whereas a Spheroid could relax with the uncommonly accessible Senna Rodríguez, laugh and joke and drink the night away. And in the morning sign on the dotted line.

Was that why you *made her such liberal terms?* asked that trickster voice from the back of his great skull. He had freely spent his sovereign's money, though Archon Melissa, God guard her and send her strength, like any good Steiner, threw *pfennige* around as if they were WarShip hatch covers and made generous concessions on behalf of Recife Spice and Liquors. While his bone of calculation, supercooled as a New Avalon Institute of Science supercomputer, told him those bargains were good for country and company and *a família*, he knew he might have cut closer. But, in truth, he liked Senna, Clan or not. *She* is *a boon companion.*

Or do you just grow susceptible to feminine wiles in your dotage, old man? the voice persisted. Von Texeira snorted into his cup of Rasalhaguian *akvavit* brought along as house gift by Wingo. After Recife's lithe-limbed beauties, his fire-haired wife and his mistress, the *gaucha* Margrete, how far could he be led astray by a rangy Clanswoman whose face had never threatened to make her a tri-vid star before it acquired its broken nose and overlay of scars? *Still*, another part of him thought, *if no beauty, she is all woman. . . .*

"You must forgive my *patrão*," Rorion said solicitously. "He's getting on in years, and when he stays up drinking after his bedtime shows a regrettable tendency to drift away."

"I'm alert enough to cuff your empty head, cub," the larger man growled.

He wasn't really angry. This was just a game they had played for a very long time. Wingo cast an uneasy look at Senna. Her lanky frame shook to unvoiced laughter. Her fellow trader relaxed a screw-turn or two.

"At least Jana Pryde has opened her eyes," Senna said, reclining at her full impressive length on a couch. Von Texeira could not decide if she truly reminded him of some sybaritic ancient queen at a banquet. "The Buhalin's fit to be tied. You should have heard her screeching at the *kurultai* when the khan proposed rallying the *touman* on Sudeten."

Coughing violently, Rorion jackknifed in his chair, as if the schnapps were too strong for him. "You bugged the *Eyrie*?"

"Not at all," Senna Rodríguez said blandly. "Khan Jana's security forces did. Very well, I might add."

"And you sold them the devices?" Rorion asked.

"Oh, no. That would be obvious, would it not? We developed the technology and sold *that* to them. They make their own."

"We like to keep abreast of things," Wingo said. "Especially where Clan Jade Falcon is concerned."

Von Texeira roared with laughter. "Master Merchant, you are a marvel!"

She smiled lopsidedly. Her long turquoise eyes seemed to watch him closely. "Perhaps. But I had nothing to do with it."

"I insist."

"You are the customer," she said, shrugging. "Don't let it make you think you're always right, though. I am still Clan."

"And myself a Spheroid," von Texeira said, "howbeit a somewhat oblate one."

Senna laughed uproariously. Wingo sat with both hands on his drink, blinking at her in the gloom as if afraid she might jump on him and bite him.

"Unlike our Falcon cousins, bless their simple black souls," she said, eyeing him obliquely, "we Foxes make it a practice not to judge contents by their packaging."

A couple of hours, and bottles, later, Trader Wingo excused himself, pleading press of business. Von Texeira suspected he was mainly eager to get back to his shuttle and back to orbit. These Sea Foxes never seemed anything but ill at ease with the feel of real dirt beneath their feet.

Except Senna, of course.

Having risen to see him off, von Texeira thought to make his own excuses once Senna had come back in after accompanying her peer out onto the porch. He swayed slightly. *Is it accumulated fatigue and stress*, he wondered, *or am I so old I can no longer hold my* cachaça?

Senna returned, closing the door behind her. "We have enjoyed your hospitality, Master Merchant," von Texeira began. But Rorion, himself a bit unsteady, settled his weight suddenly forward in a pugnacious pose.

"Why do you help us?" he demanded.

Senna regarded him coolly. "For pay, of course."

"Why do you help us?" he asked again.

To ask the same question twice of a Bloodnamed Clanswoman was to invite sudden death. Senna Rodríguez's scarred face showed no flicker of emotion.

"To pluck some pinions from the Falcon's wing," she said.

Rorion's eyes had retreated in their sockets; his face was sallow, but his cheeks flushed as from some Recife jungle fever. "Why do you really help us?"

"Rorion," von Texeira said softly.

But Senna smiled slowly. "We are the most adaptable of

Clans, you know," she said. Rorion pulled his head back on his neck as if the seeming non sequitur was a slap. "We changed our name twice, and so our nature. Other Clans think us fickle and weak.

"But in truth we know how to *adapt*. So we—some of us—or is it only I?—study the Inner Sphere and its ways not just to learn how to better it in negotiations or battle but to blend its best with ours. Because we must. Or the consequences are unthinkable.

"Kerensky did many things well. But in the long term his vision was flawed. Fatally flawed."

Rorion's brows had started to clench again. Now his eyes widened in surprise. It was as if his grandmother had spat at an image of the Blessed Virgin.

In Clan eyes, Senna had spoken pure heresy.

"Malvina Hazen, you see, is not a freak," Senna said. "No aberration. She is the only logical culmination of Clan genetics and culture. Wherever Kerensky meant to steer his children, *she* is the polestar toward which our course is truly shaped. Should she fall short of her terrible ends, there will only rise another, and another. Like her but even more capable. Until . . ."

She stopped. In amazement von Texeira realized she was choked with emotion.

"The Founder sought to bring an end to the endless strife and discord, the corruption and the wars they engendered— the billionfold suffering and death. But what he has *done* is to raise up ultimate evil. An exterminating angel."

"Abaddon," von Texeira whispered. His aide crossed himself.

"To you, stopping Malvina is a goal in itself, Merchant Prince," said Senna. "To me it is a step—a crucial step, but only one—in a longer journey. That is why I walk the path I do. It is a wayward path, even in the eyes of my own notoriously nonconformist Clan. And yet I will find a way to drag them after me. Because I must. For Clan Sea Fox, for all the Clans, and for all humankind."

She looked down at the red tile floor, then shook her head so her crest of hair waved like a frond. "Perhaps I am no less mad than Malvina Hazen." She shrugged—then raised her head to gaze at them with haughty eye and smiling lips.

"But what of that? I am Sea Fox. I too am Clan!"

A moment passed in silence. Von Texeira stepped forward, extending his right hand. Senna gripped his forearm, and he hers. An instant later Rorion stepped up and caught the Clanswoman's left hand the same way.

"If there is one thing a *Recifeiro* understands," von Texeira said, "it is a hopeless romantic gesture. We are with you, Master Merchant."

It was a young Falcon warrior who brought the news: a freebirth half-breed from Dompaire who won his right to Trial of Position in the blood-soaked Rakusian Hills. He rode a hoverbike wildly through the night.

Cynthy's small hand warm and dry in hers, Malvina Hazen walked through a forest of aligned-crystal steel. The legs of parked Jade Falcon BattleMechs rose like dark rectilinear trunks about them. Above they bloomed into a mad topiary of shapes against the starry sky of Antares.

They walked alone, no guards shadowing them. When she wished solitude, solitude she would have. And if she chose to share her private moments with a pampered Inner Sphere child—she was Chingis Khan.

If my command can burn a world, surely I can walk alone with this child if I choose.

"Why do I keep you?" she asked the girl. Cynthy looked up at her, her blue eyes wide and nothing of apprehension showing on her open young face. Her teddy bear dangled limply over her other arm, which she held crooked against the front of her blue-and-white dress.

"Destiny drives me," Malvina said. "Destiny and dreams . . . bad dreams. My destiny is nightmare; I have known it since the crèche, although I did not consciously realize it until recently."

She looked down again. Attentive to her actions, Cynthy met her gaze. "Is that love I see in those clear blue eyes? Trust? We are not supposed to know these things."

Malvina reached down and stroked the backs of two fingers down the girl's soft, round cheek. "Nor how I feel when I do this. Could this be tenderness?" She shook her head in wonder.

She understood her feelings poorly. They were not sexual. There was seldom anything *tender* about Jade Falcon sex anyway, least of all Malvina Hazen's. *Touch* was intended to arouse or wound—if not both.

What I feel for the child is akin to what I felt for my brother, Malvina thought. She struggled to understand—for what she did not understand, she could not control. And what she did not control might control her.

"I think," she said at length, "that at the last that I would have someone in all the universe to mourn me.

"When I have won, and the last stinking, puling remnant of humankind is extirpated, I shall take my ship and drive at full acceleration into the heart of a sun. And you shall remain alone. Khan of the galaxy. And you, dear one, shall have the choice: shall you start it over again, this stumbling human race? Or rule alone in perfect stillness and solitude, until the night closes over you as well? Choose well, my child.

"Choose well."

A snarl of engines, a rising mosquito-whine of fans. Ahead at the end of the avenue of walking war machines a hoverbike rounded into view in a coil of dust. Its goggled rider accelerated directly toward the pair.

Fury went nova inside Malvina. "I ordained that no one trouble us!" she snarled. Her free hand dropped to the butt of her laser pistol.

She felt a touch on the back of her hand. She looked down. Cynthy had pressed her fingertips into Malvina's hand as if to restrain her. Astonished, she forbore from drawing and burning down the messenger.

Instead she stooped, hugged the girl fiercely, kissed her cheek. "They are wrong, my darling, who say you are not brave as any Jade Falcon tiercel," she said, hot tears running inexplicably down her cheeks.

She rose with Cynthy on her arm to await the rider, whose life the girl had won.

The new-fledged Falcon curveted his machine to a stop, careful that the braking blast did not scour Malvina and her pet with sand.

He snapped his salute with a gloved hand. "My Khan," he said, "a JumpShip has just emerged in-system. It beam-cast news Star Captain Timon thought you should hear at once."

"Say it, then."

Her scar darkened as he did. In response, she told him to take out his hand communicator and transmit a certain word. Clearly puzzled but eager to justify his new status in his supreme khan's eyes, he obeyed.

Somewhere in the night a siren began to wind. Lights awoke in the neighboring camps of the Falcons and the Horses. As the hoverbike rider watched in gape-mouthed astonishment, a DropShip rose from the plain a kilometer to the north on a three-lobed pillar of blue flame. Another followed, and another. Engine noises roared from the plain like surf as vehicles carried MechWarriors and techs to the silently waiting battle machines. Vast mechanical creaking and clanking sounded as 'Mechs, already piloted, strode toward DropShips waiting to lift them to orbit.

Malvina began to laugh. The courier stared at her in confusion.

"See, my darling?" Malvina said to her ward. "We have a sign! Destiny, that foul reeking *surat*, has made Her choice. Clan Jade Falcon's oldest and bitterest foes have opened the door for me. To victory!

"The Golden Ordun marches. And that march shall not end until all humanity drowns in a sea of blood and fire!"

Malvina's face was turned toward the heavens now, where the sparks of aerospace fighters spiraled upwards like fireflies, drawing faintly luminous trails of ionized air behind, to rendezvous with carrier craft in orbit. So she did not see a single tear well from the lower lid of Cynthy's blue eye, and roll slowly down her cheek, to drip into the sand at her feet.

24

"**I** cannot believe that you have done this thing!" said Beckett Malthus, storming up to Malvina Hazen as she stood gazing through the glass of the gallery overlooking the battleship's immense hangar deck. He scarcely remembered to add, "my Khan."

She tipped her head sideways and gave him that maddening insouciant smile of hers. "Believe it, Galaxy Commander."

"At least you might have told me in advance."

He was scared. It was not even so much *what* she had done that frightened him, although that threatened to rock the whole of Kerensky's legacy to its bedrock. Nor even that she had hidden her actions from him, sending emissaries to spread the word throughout the JFOZ, but not openly decreeing it on her headquarters planet until her army spaced and began its drive toward Antares' jump point. What made his joints tremble like an aging Spheroid's was that she had conceived and taken such an action entirely on her own.

It was bitter medicine for one whose entire existence had long depended upon the indispensability of his counsel to the powerful.

Khan Jana Pryde had exiled him in the guise of promotion, in implicit expectation that he, like his potentially turbulent young *ristar* subcommanders, should fail gloriously and die. *How might* Malvina *dispose of one whose usefulness has passed?* The thought would make shudder a bronze statue of Elizabeth Hazen herself, semi-mythical Founder of Clan Jade Falcon and owner of the original flesh-and-feather Turkina.

"Truth?" she asked him, lips smiling, her eyes laughing with malice. "I wanted to delay the moment at which I must hear you squall like a Capellan fishwife whose market stall has been upset."

The deadliness of such an insult to a Falcon warrior caused barely a tick of his pulse. What made him feel as if his substance fell away behind the slab façade of his face was the careless way she displayed her own certainty that he would not challenge her.

She reached up to pat his bearded cheek, which he knew to be ashen despite his iron self-control, as if he were a child she wished to comfort, like her unnatural pet Cynthy. "Poor, dear Malthus! Forgive me. The weakness was mine in wishing to avoid a scolding."

He shook his head. She was surely dead to all shame. *But then*, he thought, mastering his roil of emotions once more, *we knew that already, quiaff?*

"But to grant the lesser castes the right to trial for warrior rank?" he almost stammered. "Even mere *laborers*? Unthinkable!"

"But the Clans have adopted not just freebirths but Spheroids in the past," Malvina said. "They have no caste at all."

"But these were warriors, in fact, who won the right with deeds."

"And so shall those who win the chance at a Trial of Position," she said. "And they will fight like Jade Falcons in fact for the merest chance of such advancement."

She regarded him through eyes half-lidded. Lazy-looking.

Malthus' blood ran chill as the metal of a ship's hull in space. He could not yet let go.

"But it will topple our society from its very foundations!"

Her smile, her eyes, were mad as wasps. "Precisely as I intend, Bec Malthus. Precisely as I intend!"

Head sunk into the fur-lined collar of his greatcoat and bitterest funk, Heinz-Otto von Texeira walked beneath the streetlights of Hammarr with his hands thrust deep in his pockets and the taste of ashes on his tongue.

I have doubly failed, he thought. *First, I have conceived no resolution to the dilemma that drove me from my family. And now* this.

He had spoken quite briskly to Rorion. He might say the boy got above himself—that his own leniency with his aide's willful ways and especially his unruly tongue, only encouraged excess. But that was all *merda*: he was being pissy, and he knew it. Decades of professional observation of the human beast in its illimitably varied habitats and behaviors had taught him that this was the very crowning characteristic of pissiness: being too pissy to make the effort to *get over* being pissy.

So marinating in—whatever—he stalked alone through The Casts' nighttime streets. Rorion had been particularly alarmed for his safety: the news had acted upon the Falcons, already on their mettle from too-close concentration and the imminence of war, like a stick whacking a hornets' nest. A fat Spheroid out wandering alone, a merchant at that, might invite deadly assault.

Let them come, he thought savagely. *Any less than an elemental in full battlearmor shall have a nasty surprise themselves.* For he was not *merely* a fat Spheroid merchant. Nor even merely a merchant prince.

If he was no longer the perfect killing machine he had been, just out of adolescence, when he served as one of the archon's own terrorists in Loki, he had lost few of his skills. And gained much knowledge.

But no Falcon obliged him by stooping on what seemed a helpless boar, only to unleash a megasaur. Instead von Texeira was walking in the dark of a broken streetlamp half a block from the Sea Fox factors' house when a new sun flared in the sky above.

He stopped. It was a small sun, although not that much smaller in apparent size than Sudeten's bitter primary at noon. It lacked but the star's eye-searing intensity.

It did not fail to sear his soul, that flame of distant fusion drives, joined now by one, two, three, a constellation of other drive flares. The JFNR Grand Fleet, assembled for the decisive contest with Malvina, broke orbit for the zenith jump point.

With the monster herself almost certainly on her way, they abandoned Sudeten. On Khan Jana Pryde's orders. He raised his fists and raged against heaven.

The fit passed. He lowered his fists. His throat was raw. He actually felt better, and the greater fool for doing so.

Mãe do Deus, he thought, *pray for us*.

He heard a strange high skirling sound. For a moment he froze, blood colder than the night air. *What creature is this?*

Then he recognized *melody*, mad, undisciplined, yet played with unmistakable skill upon a violin. It came from the direction of Senna Rodríguez's house.

He walked on. As he approached, the source of the sound localized itself to the walled garden behind the bunkerlike dwelling. He reached the wooden gate, its paint, gray in the light of the stars and the dwindling fusion-drives, blistered and peeling from the merciless daytime sun.

He hesitated. The music soared and dipped and drove in his ears. If his intrusion was resented, or even mistaken, it could cost him dearly. He raised a heavy fist, pounded against the gate. Then he tugged the latch and let himself inside.

In the midst of winter-bare furrows stood a strange figure: tall and gaunt in white, playing a violin tucked beneath its chin. As he entered the garden it turned.

The tune died on a last defiant scream of strings. Then Senna the master merchant lowered the instrument from beneath her chin. Her eyes were fixed upon him.

"I didn't know you played the violin," he said.

"I am a woman of surprises."

"You have heard." It was no question.

"That Clan Wolf has mysteriously pulled back from its border with the JFOZ?" she asked. "Or that Loremaster Julia Buhalin persuaded Khan Jana Pryde that Malvina must certainly make peace now, in the wake of this ominous move by the Falcon's great enemy, freeing the khan to send her war fleet to the Wolf frontier?"

He could only shake his head. In his mind he saw again the gloating in Loremaster Julia Buhalin's violet eyes as Khan Jana Pryde gave the fatal order. Shutting his eyes as tightly as he could only squeezed tears out to roll into his beard.

"You could have done no more," she said gently. "And since you could not prevail, no one could."

He spread his hands beside him toward the ground, half-frozen by a resurgence of bitter winter.

"What are you doing?" he asked. His voice croaked as if he had wandered a desert for days.

She laughed. "I play a dirge for Clan Jade Falcon and the universe we have known," she said. "The Falcons are an evil lot, by and large. But they are nothing to the wrath to come."

She let bow and instrument fall to her sides. Her white robe fell open. She wore nothing beneath it.

"I have awaited you, Merchant Prince," she said. "Come inside."

Clad in form-fitting dark uniforms, two dozen people worked in the vast warehouse bordering the Allison City spaceport on Porrima, running final checks on weapons and highly specialized equipment spread out on metal tables. There was none of the chattering and grab-assing customary among those preparing for imminent action, especially in the somewhat casual Lyran Commonwealth Armed Forces.

But then, these men and women were not LCAF.

Most knew each other, having undergone a grueling and not infrequently lethal training program together, or through refresher and skill-updating courses during infrequent stand-downs from action. Yet each operator seemed to work in isolation. Notwithstanding the real camaraderie of their unique *Brüderschaft*, brutal training and even more brutal experience had conditioned them to avoid unnecessary contact, to slide away from attention and never, ever, to look squarely at their targets, lest poorly understood but well-documented "sixth senses" alert the prey.

Hauptmann Kommandant Balto Jäger stood with his hands behind his tapered lower back, gazing down through the window of the small office perched at catwalk level high above the stained cement floor. He was a tall man, his bearing reminiscent of an early stint in the LCAF. He wore LCAF battledress as elementary cover. His hair was a steel brush, his face darkened and seamed and scarred by dozens of suns and hundreds of battles. The black ceramic disk covering his right eye gave his stern face a terrifying aspect. Or so he sometimes heard the typing pool whisper.

Spotlights clamped to the steel tracery speared down like blue-white laser beams. The space above, between the catwalk and the stressed-ferrocrete structure's high, rounded roof, was dark as the belly of space itself. It might as well be an open invitation to black-clad intruders to spy on the proceedings, relying on the operators' night vision being totally disrupted by the glare.

Jäger wished they would. He was himself drawn taut as a bowstring, yet he, unlike his operators, would find no release in action. He would only learn outcomes later— months later, indeed, unless the insertion of one or more Loki agents went disastrously wrong. *Then* he'd learn all too quickly.

It would be gratifying for his site security team, with their bunker-buster Zeus rifles and starlight scopes, to blast a few ninja-clad DEST off the I beams. It was also unlikely. Even the SAFE agents who had swarmed to Porrima in the wake of the devastating Jade Falcon raid had been trolled in by a mole hunters sweep weeks before.

He cleared his throat. "It is trite to say so," he said aloud, "but I wish I was going along."

He looked back at his aide, who stood half-bent over a computer display projected above the desk in the darkened office.

"You too, Erich?"

"Nein," said the young man without looking up. He likewise wore LCAF camos, with a first leutnant's bars on the shoulders. "I am just as happy to be convalescing for this one, *Herr Hauptmann Kommandant.*"

"The Falcons are a handful, I admit," Jäger said. "Still, where's your sense of adventure, boy?"

"I am still waiting for it to be fully regenerated along with my leg," the leutnant said, slapping his thigh. "And was it not you who said there are old Lokis, and bold Lokis, but no old, bold Lokis?"

"One says so many things," Jäger said, gazing through the glass again.

"In any event," the younger man said, "another adventure will doubtless come along soon enough. Perhaps a nice holiday jaunt into the FWL."

The corner of Jäger's mouth twitched. They weren't supposed to know anything, of course, since even a Loki operator could in time be compelled to speak if she fell into enemy hands. But everyone in the LCAF and House Steiner's intelligence apparatus knew perfectly well a major strike was being prepared against the Mareks. It was a sign of how seriously the archon took the dangers posed by this Falcon renegade and her bloodthirsty fanatic followers that they diverted the resources to launch this substantial probe into the JFOZ. That, and to draw attention from the preparations along the southern border . . .

A reconnaissance in force and a retaliation for the Porrima raid and the rape of Chaffee, the simultaneous strike against five Falcon-held worlds would also serve to cover the insertion of Loki teams to do what they did best: sow terror and confusion over the coming months.

"Hauptmann Kommandant?"

Arching a brow in surprise, Jäger turned back. It was rare to hear hesitation in his hotspur aide's young voice.

"Na ja, Erich?"

"What about the archon's special emissary to Sudeten? The *Markgraf* von Texeira zu Mannstein?"

Jäger's forehead furrowed and his jaw jutted. "What of him?"

"Won't things go hard for him when word of these raids reaches the khan?"

"He knew the risks when he undertook the mission." The *Hauptmann Kommandant*'s voice had taken on something of the nature of ball bearings in a grinder.

"But I have seen the files. He was one of us once, *nicht wahr*? And that aide of his, as well, Rorion Klimt—I took a close-combat class from him once, on Donegal. He fights most brilliantly."

Jäger spun back to face the window so his aide would not see the anger suffuse his features. "He was, yes. Von Texeira. But some of us old boys have reason to believe that after he retired back to his whores and his boardrooms, he chose to join Heimdall."

Erich stiffened. Heimdall was the secret watchdog society formed as a check on Loki's recurring tendencies to apply its brutal methods to citizens of the Lyran Commonwealth itself. It was almost as old as the terror branch itself. Some members had long been rumored to be former Loki operators. It made them extremely effective. It also earned them undying hatred from certain conservative elements within Loki.

"We have been watching him secretly in hopes he might lead us to a much larger school of Heimdall fish." Jäger shrugged. "He has yet to do so. He's cagey as the Devil himself. But we still think he betrayed his comrades. So screw him."

He uttered a metallic chuckle. "And I've no doubt the damned Falcons will do just that."

25

The Casts
Near Hammarr Commercial Spaceport, Sudeten
Jade Falcon Occupation Zone
9 March 3136

She lay with the sinuous pale extent of her angled across rumpled indigo sheets, propped on her elbows. A cigarette trailed lazy blue smoke between the fingers of her right hand. Her slanted blue eyes were half-lidded.

He trailed stubby fingertips down her back. Her skin was surprisingly silky. The muscles beneath were firm. "You spend a great deal of time planetside."

She snorted smoke. "You expect me to be a spindle, like so many of us Foxes? They spend too much time in space. How can you trade a world unless you spend time with your feet on its soil, feeling its wind in your face, its sounds in your ears? How can you bargain properly with people if you don't spend hours watching them, getting drunk with them, above all listening to them?"

The bedroom was small, cozy, warm with hidden heaters and with the heat of recent exertion. A squat-bellied lamp glowed low beneath a metal shade pierced in indecipherable geometric designs. A hint of incense hung in the air.

"Too many of my fellows are content to hide in their

own holds, trusting to the awesome Clan reputation to overawe the locals, and leave the doing of real business to the factors." A throaty laugh. "Why should I complain? That's why I have my Bloodname."

He raised a brow. "You must fight many trials."

"Not all my body modifications come courtesy of lucky Spheroids—although Periphery pirates and outcaste Clan bandits have contributed their share, I'll allow."

"I've seen you fight. You are a formidable grappler."

"It comes in handy. You know Clanners don't fear death. But humiliate them by making them tap out . . ."

She shrugged. "And thank you. That is high praise, coming from you."

"What do you mean?"

"You hold a fifth *dan* in Brazilian jujitsu from the hand of Rianna Gracie-Goldschmitt herself, *quiaff*?"

He sat bolt upright. The movement reminded him uncomfortably of a Recife mammoth seal surfacing. "How do you know a thing like that?"

"Your public relations department," she said. "You must recall the Lyran press made much of it. I told you, we follow your Inner Sphere media. At least, those of us who like to turn a profit do."

He shook his head. She was full of surprises, this one. He eased himself back down and regarded her.

Even the dim bedroom light did little to soften her face, though age had hardly affected her, he thought. But the years had been hard ones.

From his reclining position von Texeira took note of the tattoo on the generous upper swell of her right breast: a sea fox caught in the jaws of a diamond shark.

"Why that tattoo?" he asked, voice slightly husky.

She shrugged. It made her breasts do interesting things. The sea fox seemed to struggle in its slayers' jaws.

"To remind me of the struggle within us all," she said, leaning over to stub out her cigarette in a pewter mug on the floor.

Or is it to remind others of the fact? he wondered. *Specifically, lovers.*

"Why me?" he asked.

She laid her cheek on his wiry-haired flesh-and-blood thigh and gazed at him.

"We Clanners admire skill," she said. "You have displayed extraordinary ability in a range of endeavors particularly esteemed by the Sea Fox."

He felt a twinge. *How much does this woman* really *know about me?* he wondered.

"Then, too, I find you personally interesting. Fascinating, you might say. I have followed your career for years. And then, of course, you make me laugh."

"I find that's one of the most reliable routes to a woman's heart," he said. "But I don't flatter myself that I'm an Adonis. I'm middle-aged and overweight—or old and fat, depending on how honest I'm being with myself. And I thought you Clanners worshipped physical perfection."

"You should also know we Sea Foxes have our own perceptions by now," she said. "My Aimag in particular is known for its eccentricities. Which is why it accepted me— a freebirth."

He blinked. "You?" Although the most cosmopolitan of Clans—maybe the only Clan to whom the word even applied—the Sea Foxes struck him as likely to be most insular in their breeding practices, given their preference for spending their lives aboard ship.

Her face tightened. "I'm sorry," he said quickly. "I know—belatedly—how that question must sound to Clan ears. But I'm a Spheroid, as well as a good Catholic." *Who's long overdue for confession*, he thought, *though this sin is the least of reasons*. "I'm certainly not going to think less of you for not having been poured out of a beaker."

She shook her head. He thought he actually saw her eyes glisten with a tear. *Only a trick of the light*, he told himself.

"It is strange," Senna said, "to find such vulnerabilities in myself at such a time."

"It's a somewhat vulnerable kind of time," von Texeira said.

She raised her head, rolled her body so that she lay propped on an elbow with her cheek in her palm. Shadows molded her heavy breasts.

"I've told you something intimate about myself, Heinz-Otto," she said. "Now tell me: why are you really here?"

He drew in a breath—and let it slide forth in a sigh. "You mean, aside from duty to my archon and my people."

She nodded.

"It's my family," he said.

"As in your tyrannical grandmother?"

"She's the least of my worries right now." Senna cocked a skeptical eyebrow. "Well, of course she worries me. The bloody woman terrifies me. Always has. But I have more pressing concerns."

"Your wife does not understand you, perhaps?"

He laughed. "Dona Irmagilda understands me all too well. Lately she and my mistress, Margrete, have become thick as thieves. Which poses its own problems. Margrete is the volatile one; she's a *gaucha*, a cattle herder from the high plains. Dona Irmagilda is more prone to slow boils. Yes, they do bedevil me, I won't deny it."

"But they are not the reason you accepted such a hare-brained mission?"

He sighed again. "Your assessment parallels my own. Well, I did hire you for your discernation. No, the real problem concerns my son, Emilião. The eldest of our three children."

He laced his fingers behind his head and gazed up sightlessly at the ceiling. "He is a good boy. Really he is. I love him very much."

"Yet he disappoints you?"

"No! I mean, not exactly. You see, he's a very talented lad. An actor. He has made a start at a splendid career in tri-vid."

"Is acting not a useful skill for a merchant?"

"Ah, but he has the business head of an actor. He's got no gift for trade at all. And he hates it."

"I begin to see the problem. Still, what of your two daughters?"

"Benigna, the elder, weeps a great deal. She has already entered a convent. My youngest child, Imaculada, long ago fled to Tharkad, where she took a doctorate in sociology and professes undying disdain for wealth and religion alike."

"So you've run out of heirs. What about some likely lieutenant? Or even taking on an apprentice?"

"Therein lies the scorpion in the bedclothes. My lady wife is ambitious. Specifically, on behalf of her eldest, Emilião. She feels the tri-vids are unworthy of him. Or at least of our two great families, the von Texeiras and her people, the San Luca clan. She insists that he should succeed me. She feels he and I are being selfish in seeking to avoid that."

"That's what propelled you into the middle of the Jade Falcon Occupation Zone?"

He shrugged. "It may seem trivial to an outsider. Perhaps it is. Even most of my fellow Lyrans would find it somewhat so, I suspect. But we Recifeiros take family seriously. And neither Irmagilda nor her atrocious kinsfolk are under any circumstances to be taken *lightly*."

"And looming over all is your grandmother."

"Mamãe Luci," he said. "Although 'loom' isn't perhaps the word I'd choose. She's tiny. Formidable. But tiny."

He scoured his palms in his frizzy coarse hair. "The time impends when I must begin grooming my successor. No candidate in view is acceptable. And so I seek shelter here, amidst mere physical danger."

Senna shook her head and laughed low. "Knowing you is never dull, Margrave."

She rolled over to lie on his legs, breasts flattened on his thighs. Her hands did intriguing things. "Have some respect for age, woman!" he gasped.

"I let you rest this long, *quineg*."

"Is it not beautiful, Bec Malthus?"

The space within *Emerald Talon*'s colossal hull had been filled with stores now consumed. Now Malvina Hazen floated naked near the focus of an array of UV-rich spotlights and water misters that had been made fast to the bulkheads. She tended with surprising care to her latest fancy.

Sourly Galaxy Commander Beckett Malthus watched her from the resilient synthetic covered runway where his gripshoes held him firmly in place.

"It disturbs me, Malvina," he said. "I find it unnatural."

It resembled a frozen explosion, a ball of twisty dark vines spiked with long black thorns and pallid leaves with dark suggestive veins. Its outer surface was covered with dozens of roses, each gleaming, each the color of deep space. Only one black rose, the largest, had a straight stem; the others were curved and twisted.

While her fleet recharged at reconquered Graus she had received it from, of all people, her coregn back in the Falcon's Reach in the occupied Republic, provisional Galaxy Commander Noritomo Helmer.

"They breed true," she said, carefully trimming bits of dead growth away from the tangled branches with pinches of her white flesh-and-blood fingers. "They were created over decades by careful culling and hybridization by inhabitants of the Crespo Major space habitat in the Kimball system asteroid belt. No genegineering involved. Isn't that fascinating?"

"They are still not natural."

Her laugh was musical malice. "What about us Clanners is natural? Our very conception, if you can call it that, our gestation and birth are exemplars of the artificial."

As she spoke she rotated in midair to face him. He saw a drop of blood on the ball of her thumb, the red shocking, the only hint of true color in the black-and-white chamber—for he was well aware his own drab presence brought color nowhere. His khan looked at it curiously, smiled, licked the blood away with her small pink tongue.

He repressed a shudder.

"We are created in such a way as to eliminate the vagaries of natural reproduction," he said, annoyed at himself for sounding pedantic and twice as annoyed at her for forcing him off-balance so that his usual graphite-smooth glibness deserted him. "Yet we are also taught to appreciate nature and live harmoniously with it."

"I had this conversation with my brother, I believe—the last friendly encounter we had. It was on the gallery overlooking the shuttle deck of this very ship, before the first assault on Skye."

And not long thereafter you were trying your best to kill

Aleksandr in a Trial of Refusal, he recalled. He forbore to mention the irony of her calling Aleks "brother." Which to his mind was the most unnatural thing of all.

"Will there be no end of your taking on pets, Malvina?" he asked.

She glared at him, eyes sapphire lasers, her hair a nimbus of pale fury. "Do you dare to question my taking Cynthy to my side?"

Not anymore, he thought, controlling with effort the twitch that wanted to pluck at one corner of his wide mouth.

"By no means, Malvina Hazen. With your—sponsorship— of the girl, you have taken upon yourself what you clearly regard as grave responsibilities."

He reflected briefly how odd it was for Clanners to be discussing a concept like *responsibility*. He doubted the word had actually existed in the Clan lexicon before contact with, and contamination by, the Inner Sphere.

But we are the oddest of Clanners, he thought. *Or are we? Might we be the two divergent paths down which the Clans inevitably evolve—one toward accepting Spheroid self-interest and duplicity, the other embracing the pure hot madness of total destruction for its own sake?* The thought chilled him like a kiss of liquid nitrogen.

She was watching him closely. Ever mercurial, her expression had flowed from rage into knowing amusement.

With scarcely a pause he continued, "It concerns me that you risk adding too much to your already overwhelming burdens of command."

"As for my pretties," she said, turning to run her fingers around the swelling bloom of the one straight-stemmed black rose as if tracing the curve of a sex partner's breast, "I have a use for them in mind. And as for you—"

She laughed again. The sound made him wonder if some decadent Spheroid culture, within the Capellan Confederacy perhaps, made use of small silver bells in its funerary practices.

"Your usefulness to me consists in smoothing my road to my Destiny. Let *me* worry about how I travel it."

=== 26 ===

The Falcon's Reach
Colquhon Mountains, Chaffee
Jade Falcon Occupation Zone
22 March 3136

Flame jetted from a dozen ruptures in the *Centurion*'s chest armor. White smoke gushed out to envelope the 'Mech as it tipped ponderously backward. Conifers splintered behind it. Just downslope of it two tanks and a hover APC burned on a narrow road that wound its way along the face of the hill, sending pillars of black smoke up into the blue horsetail-flecked sky.

Ignoring Lyran infantry flushed like quail from around the stricken BattleMech's feet, Star Colonel Folke Jorgensen already had his 'Mech in motion, turning away in search of fresh targets. In these mountains, veined with hematite deposits not rich enough to justify exploitation to support the world's nonexistent industry but ample to scramble magnetic detection, he would get little warning.

Ever systematic, the Steiners had swept his surveillance satellites from orbit before their DropShip descended into an enormous circular depression, caldera of an ancient volcano, in the Colquhon range. Their aerospace fighters fought off Jorgensen's pitiful contingent, preventing decent observation. Making use of local woodsmen as guides they marched in company strength on Chaffee's capital McCauliffe via a path—barely a game track—of which the Falcon occupiers were utterly unaware. Only a chance observation by a scouting Donar, quickly shot down by marauder VTOLs, had alerted Jorgensen to the route the raiders took.

The local ferromagnetism also meant the Lyrans had no advance warning their secret route had been compromised until the Ghost Bear *abtakha* and his Star hit them in the flank, strung out along a narrow trail between steep peaks with slopes crowded in tall, great-boled trees. Trees too huge to be bulled out of the way by the heaviest 'Mech or battle tank . . .

The *Centurion*'s MechWarrior punched out as his machine fell. The blue-and-white chute deployed above trees on a ridge across the declivity.

"That one is my bond," Jorgensen radioed his elementals. "Capture alive if possible." The Lyran had showed courage, if more promise than actual skill as a Battle-Mech pilot.

From a ridgetop to his left a salvo of long-range missiles lanced toward him, their smoke trails feathered by the stiff breeze that blew up the valley. He backed his machine a handful of meters, allowing some of those monster trees to absorb the missiles.

As rockets gouged three-meter splinters from trunks thick as a man was tall, leaving bleached-white wounds, he caught a Bellona in his crosshairs. Like the *Centurion,* it had turned to face the Jade Falcon attackers, its large laser and long-range missile rack providing covering fire for the withdrawal of the ambushed raiders.

They make a nuisance raid, the dour former Ghost Bear thought. They were clearly making a stab at the McCauliffe spaceport, the only target of any military value in the area—if not on Chaffee.

Not for the first time he damned Malvina Hazen.

His 50-ton *Black Hawk* had the Jade Falcon insignia painted on the right side of its fuselage-like torso and, defiantly, a photonegative Ghost Bear badge on the left. But the 'Mech showed no blue Eyes of the Falcon, nor green Horus eye, nor yet whatever symbol the madwoman might have taken for this new rebel alliance with Hell's Horses. Nor would it ever while Folke Jorgensen drew breath.

It was the very BattleMech Aleksandr Hazen had captured along with Jorgensen himself in a border skirmish six years before.

Jorgensen was the senior of officers remaining from Aleks' Zeta Galaxy. Ironically, the now battle-hardened *Turkina's Beak* formed the bulk of the forces Malvina and Bec Malthus had left behind to garrison their salient thrust like a spear deep into the side of the Inner Sphere. Noritomo Helmer, who now led the *desant*, came from Malvina's own Gyrfalcons—but close exposure to his superior's methods had driven him into deep sympathy with her sibkin's more humane approach to conquest. Knowing that Jorgensen shared his belief, Helmer had set the erstwhile Ghost Bear to command the force holding the world that had suffered most from Malvina's Mongol notions.

Volatilized steel wisped from the Bellona tank's front glacis beneath the retina-searing ruby lash of the *Black Hawk*'s large lasers. The hovercraft tried desperately to back up the slope, its fans raising billows of dust and dried brush around it. A burst of one-hundred-millimeter autocannon fire struck it from Jorgensen's left, cracking its already-scorched canopy.

The Steiners were shrewd to weight their forces to fast-moving 'Mechs and hovercraft, he thought with his customary calm. *Or would have been had we not caught them still in the mountains.*

Out of the Trinary of full warriors, augmented by odd lots of *solahma* replacements, he had been given to defend Chaffee, Jorgensen had three other BattleMechs and six elementals with him. Another 'Mech was on its way. Several vehicles, including a Cardinal full of conventional infantry, had joined the fight.

His vehicles dueled with the Steiner tanks and 'Mechs while the infantry skirmished forward under cover of their fire, supported by his leaping elementals in their powered suits, to root out the Lyran foot soldiers gone to ground. He was glad he kept most of his regulars in McCauliffe, partly to respond in force to threats—and partly to keep them from being picked off in the constant erosive ambushes and attacks the Chaffee woodsmen waged against the occupiers.

Chaffee had no strategic value. The main reason it had survived centuries of war almost unscathed was that it wasn't *worth* anything. Its sole industry of size had been tourism: wealthy Spheroids who paid stiff fees to hunt the planet's intractable wildlife. The collapse of the hyperpulse generator net had put an end to that.

The only reason Clan Jade Falcon held onto Chaffee was that the *desant* could not afford to relinquish a single world of the tiny foothold it had clawed out of the Inner Sphere.

More LRMs cracked off against the giant trees. It was a serious barrage: a storm of dead needles fell on his *Black Hawk* like dried rain, dislodged from branches mounting a hundred meters into the sky. Jorgensen's battle computer had tagged the distant shooter as a *Catapult*. The 65-ton BattleMech was slow for this lightning raid. Doubtless the Lyrans intended it to hang on the edge of the spaceport, giving long-range support from its big missile racks and light but far-reaching autocannon, while the faster machines raced about releasing hell and havoc. Meanwhile, once roads were left behind, in mountains such as these any BattleMech, no matter how ponderous, moved faster than any conventional vehicle, wheeled, tracked or even hovercraft.

A thin-lipped smile spread across the Star colonel's long, pale, ascetic's face, barely dewed with sweat. *As the Lyrans discover anew, now that we have caught them.*

Across the valley the Bellona had stalled. It had apparently backed into a granite outcrop concealed by dense brush. Its pilot directed the full thrust of its fusion-driven fans downward, attempting to lift the 45-ton machine over the obstacle by brute force. He was having little luck.

Folke Jorgensen's heat remained well within limits. He speared the trapped tank again and again with both lasers. The trees shook and his cockpit rang with the thunder of yet another long-range missile barrage. It was as if the distant *Catapult* sought to cut down a tree on top of him. Should one of the forest giants fall on the *Black Hawk* it would break its back like a lapdog's. But good luck to the Steiner if he thought his rockets equal to the task in the time he had remaining—

The *Bellona* exploded as its missile magazine went up.

Star Colonel Folke Jorgensen had been among those in the abandoned expeditionary force who argued that not just Chaffee but the whole salient should be abandoned as untenable. Better to withdraw voluntarily and with honor than be driven back when The Republic, with glacial slowness but also glacial inexorability, mounted its inevitable counterattack in overwhelming force. No price, the malcontents said, was worth paying to keep a handful of trophies for a bloodfoul's shelf.

Noritomo Helmer refused. Notwithstanding her crimes— or the way she repeatedly humiliated him (and Jorgensen suspected that leaving him in command of the rump occupation was the greatest insult of all)—Malvina Hazen was his rightful superior when she gave him his orders. Duty to Turkina demanded obedience.

So far none of those favoring return to the occupation zone had challenged Helmer. They knew they needed every Jade Falcon they had. They respected Helmer for his courage, not least in standing up to Malvina. And news of Malvina's latest madness had weakened Helmer's resolve.

But the Steiners were attacking *now*. Need and honor alike required Folke Jorgensen to go out and fight them.

Ignoring the *Catapult*'s weight advantage, and the fact that it seriously outgunned his *Black Hawk* at long range, Jorgensen charged forward out of cover of the woods. A final volley of thirty LRMs crashed down behind him. With an almost human groan and a crack loud enough to be heard above the cacophony of battle, the tree that had stood directly between him and the Lyran BattleMech gave way and fell. Had he stayed, it would have crushed his machine.

Dust geysers and glowing gobbets of earth flash-fused to molten glass spurted from the ridgetop as he returned fire with the two large lasers mounted along the BattleMech's fuselage. His threat display told him the Steiner was trying to lock him up with his Artemis IV fire-control system. He wanted to make it as hard as possible for the enemy MechWarrior to succeed.

To preserve heat he fired no more laser bolts but raced the big machine full tilt down the mountain in what was as much a barely controlled fall as a run. The impacts of its big three-lobed feet jarred through his tailbone and clashed his jaws together. He put his 'Mech's right foot on a hump-back boulder in his path and used the thrusting power of that leg's myomer pseudomuscle to help launch his machine in a jump across the narrow valley.

On the far side several more wrecks blazed, including a *Pack Hunter* with its right arm and torso-mounted particle cannon torn away and its cockpit a flame-spewing crater. The other Steiner machines vanished over the ridgeline as comrades laid down covering fire. In his HUD Folke Jorgensen saw the green ticks of his own machines surge forward, following his lead.

A bold and dashing Jade Falcon MechWarrior might have jumped straight up at the *Catapult*, to negate its tremendous range advantage by coming to grips. At close range the *Black Hawk*'s Streak missiles and hands would give it all the edge over the armless support BattleMech, heavier though it was. But a bold 'Mech jock would also have been painted against the sky by the *Catapult*'s FCS and blasted off its jump jet drive columns to crash to ruin in the boulder-lined streambed below.

Instead, Jorgensen took a short, fast, flat-trajectory jump straight across to the opposite slope. He hit the ground running. The ridge's mass now masked him from the Lyran's potent long-range battery.

The *Black Hawk* rocked as a heavy short-range missile fired from a man-portable launcher slammed against his right torso, just forward of the 'Mech's massive coaxially mounted shoulder and hip joints. Red lights flashed on his heads-up display: his right-side laser's primary control circuit was gone. He ignored both the shot—that was what redundancy was for, and a green light told him a secondary circuit had kicked in—and the grounded infantryman who launched it. With his battle-hardened elementals to back them, he trusted even the green *solahma* foot soldiers' fire-and-moving-forward to police up stranded enemy infantry.

In his three-sixty view strip he saw one of his battlesuited giants flipped over in midair by a burst from the *Catapult's* twenty-millimeter gun. It dropped straight down into the trickle of stream. As he charged upslope with what in any 'Mech-driver less supremely proficient would be mad recklessness, Jorgensen registered from his eye's corner that elemental Dot's tag now flashed yellow. She was no doubt out of the fight, thoroughly stunned and probably sporting broken bones, but telemetry showed she still lived. *A good thing, for I can spare no frontline warriors . . .*

These Steiners were unusually good, he noted. As the *Black Hawk* pounded upslope, swerving around a house-sized jut of grey stone, he wondered, *Can they possibly think of retaking Chaffee, instead of hitting and running?*

No, he decided. They surely had spies slipping in- and out-system to inform them of Jade Falcon strength on Chaffee. The Steiners were too keenly aware of the bottom line to dream of trying to overcome his garrison, small as it was, with a single DropShip-load of attackers.

As he neared the ridge-crest he angled left toward where the *Catapult* had been firing from, to muddy its targeting solution. His *Black Hawk* topped the slope at a dead run, over sixty kilometers per hour even uphill, so fast it actually flew several meters into the air.

As the Star colonel half anticipated, the enemy Mech-Warrior had been shrewd enough to displace the instant the Falcon machine was out of sight. The *Catapult* backed down the backslope, almost into the forest fifty meters away. Most of its comrades were already lost among the giant trees.

As soon as the *Black Hawk* hit ground Jorgensen turned and accelerated it straight for the enemy BattleMech. The *Catapult* lashed him with autocannon, the shells bursting in white flashes on his joint-housings and cockpit. A lucky hit starred the front screen ferroglass, but the shells were too small to seriously damage his armor in the brief time he gave his foe. The Lyran 'Mech panic-fired both fifteen-rocket shoulder racks. A couple of missiles hit noisily but to no effect.

Then he was upon his foe. Without hesitation he powered his lighter 'Mech into the heavier. Still desperately backing downhill the *Catapult* was instantly overbalanced, although the impact crushed Jorgensen's right-hand laser to uselessness. Jorgensen seized the teetering *Catapult*'s left leg and the snout of its pointed fuselage with his *Black Hawk*'s massive hands. Steel buckled in their crushing grasp. He heaved.

The *Catapult* fell over backward. It hit so hard it bounced. The shock actually lifted his own 50-ton 'Mech perceptibly off the ground.

He had lost his grip when his enemy went over. Now he stepped up and canted his fuselage down to close his 'Mech's right hand over the fallen machine's cockpit. "Yield," he said, keying his radio to a general frequency he knew the LCAF used.

"I yield," a feminine voice replied at once. You could always count on a Steiner for that: no futile shows of resistance.

Behind him his Cardinal hover transport prowled over the ridgeline drawing a vortex of dust behind it. It reported scooping up two Points of his foot. He ordered the *solahma* to debark and secure the surrendered MechWarrior as he straightened to seek more foes.

None remained in sight. His threat display showed intermittent flickers of red for briefly confirmed enemy units and yellows for probables as the Steiners retreated through the forest. Green indicators showed his other BattleMechs and vehicles coming up with him.

Star Colonel Folke Jorgensen could not but take a Ghost Bear warrior's grim satisfaction in victory. Yet its savor was tainted by the sheer pointlessness of the action. And by the malign implicit presence of Malvina Hazen.

A siren crowed. His HUD highlighted in red what his eyes showed as a tiny silver speck high and to his right. As his eyes flicked that way it grew winged and double-lobed: a 65-ton *Ironsides* aerospace fighter. It flashed before him not two hundred meters over the ridgeline. The shock wave of its supersonic passage rocked his BattleMech back on its rear toes and filled his cockpit with thunder as it climbed away to the west.

The message was unmistakable. A rapidly summoned readout on his HUD showed that neither the Steiner fighters nor his own pathetically outnumbered aerospace contingent had done the other much harm. The invaders had not pressed their edge overhead—but they had it.

The *Ironsides* had flown by much too fast for a firing pass. *This* time. Star Colonel Folke Jorgensen knew full well if he pursued the withdrawing raiders Lyran fighters would smash his ground units.

It was a simple decision. Jorgensen's unremitting Ghost Bear tenacity latched itself not to a foe that had already conceded defeat but onto his overriding mission—unwelcome and strategically ludicrous as it was—of holding Chaffee at all costs. He respected Noritomo Helmer too much to imagine the Galaxy commander would send so much as a box of replacement bolts to keep useless Chaffee, hard-pressed as he was to hold more valuable conquests.

"Pursue the Lyrans at walking pace," he ordered. His fighters understood *walking pace* for a BattleMech. "Keep them moving in the right direction."

It was but a token to keep wily merchants playing warriors honest.

He raised his face to the sky. High up on his viewscreen a dark spot appeared, blotting out the tiny blue disk of Chaffee's primary in an artificial eclipse: to look at it directly for even a fraction of a second meant temporary blindness. To its right a red reticule indicated the Lyran fighter, its small size indicating the rapidly diminishing threat status his battle computer assigned it.

"Bargained well and done," he murmured. He set his *Black Hawk* walking deliberately after the pilot's ground-bound comrades.

27

Harz Mountains, Sudeten
Jade Falcon Occupation Zone
3 April 3136

Khan Jana Pryde was hunting snowstalker in the Harz Mountains, a hundred kilometers southeast of Hammarr, when she got the word.

The day crackled cold. Ice weighed down the branches of the bushes where she sheltered. Crouched haunch-deep in snow, she had stalked to within fifteen meters of the sinuous five-meter-long predator and taken aim with her single-shot fourteen-millimeter handgun when the communicator tingled at her belt. She knew at once what it signified.

But she failed to react. Instead she continued to take up slack on the trigger.

Unaware that it was itself prey, the six-legged monster continued its own stalk of a trio of great curl-horned herbivores with long knotted hair feeding upon the blue-leaved nettle bushes. Its rank smell filled the khan's nostrils and sinus cavities and made her eyes water. She was joined to it in the timeless space of *the hunt*. Her mind was focused, compartmentalized; the communicator's insistent buzzing belonged to another dimension. Another *self*.

When the handgun fired it took the snowstalker by surprise, as she intended. It bucked and rose. The creature spun. The khan had already seen the spot dark against the snowstalker's white-and-blue streaked flank. For a moment the creature glared at her with eyes purple beneath protective juts of bone. It gathered itself to leap.

Khan Jana Pryde straightened and stood composed. *If I have missed my mark*, she thought, *then let it take me now and be done.*

Instead the ferocious light fled the violet eyes. They glazed. The creature slumped abruptly into the snow as the heart-shot took effect.

The khan sighed. She broke the action of her hunting handgun, slid in a fresh thumb-sized cartridge, holstered the piece. Then she removed the communicator from her belt and opened the channel.

It was time to return to the world of time and space. And the reality in which she, too, was now prey.

"Speak," she said.

The person at the other end did. Jana Pryde listened. Then she gave crisp orders.

Putting the comm unit away, she drew a deep breath. Cold seared her lungs like fire. *Will I feel its sting again?* she wondered.

She turned toward the east. While her security detail keep its distance when she hunted—at least she could *pretend* she preyed alone—a fast Skadi VTOL waited in a clearing a handful of kilometers away. It would arrive in seconds.

And then the fight for Sudeten, and the heart and soul of Clan Jade Falcon, would commence.

"Was ist los?" asked Heinz-Otto von Texeira, raising his chins from the black fur collar of his greatcoat: *What's going on?*

"Sirens," said Rorion Klimt, who walked beside him through The Casts in a heavy padded jacket. His own younger face, normally classically handsome, was creased like a worried hound's.

The wailing rose and fell, a lost winding sound with a bit

of grind, like a self-aware robot lamenting its discovery that it lacked a soul. *My, but my mind runs along morbid tracks today*, the acting diplomat thought as he gazed at a speaker horn set atop a hundred-meter tower.

Where he and his aide stood, the road sloped fairly steeply before them, down into a district of workshops and distribution centers. To their left stood a dispensary of some sort, shuttered at this hour. To the right the slope from the crest lay bare but for a few silvery tufts of dead vegetation poking through lumpy two-day-old snow.

"But what can it mean?" Rorion asked.

They were not long in finding out. When the siren had wound on for a whole minute a voice crackled suddenly from speakers somewhere nearby. Metallic, masculine. It struck von Texeira's ears as dispassionate, yet ringing with that certain superciliousness he had come to associate with senior members of Sudeten's scientist caste, who Senna said did the real work of running the world—and the Clan.

"This is a Class One Emergency," it declared. As it repeated, von Texeira heard echoes from all around: apparently speakers blanketed the city. "Return at once to assigned mustering points in dormitories and workstations for a televised announcement." It began to cycle through its litany, interspersed with wailing from the giant horns.

"We should perhaps wend our own way home," said von Texeira.

Their domicile had its own holovid stage. Clan Jade Falcon actually ran a broadcast system. It offered four channels: for the laborer masses, exhortations and simple melodramas on the virtue of patient service; technical education and military dramas for technicians; advanced education, scientific news and impenetrable science fiction for the scientists; and for the warriors, lurid adventure yarns, for the most part incredibly cheesy thirty-year-old Liao and Kurita costume melodramas with plenty of wire-work swordplay. The crèches, von Texeira and Rorion understood, had their own internal systems, combining music, pedagogy and cultural indoctrination as part of the Clan's program of relentlessly meddling in every aspect of its members' existence.

"Why hurry?" asked Rorion sharply.

Von Texeira set his jaw and scowled at him. *Do I permit overmuch familiarity? Still, I don't know what I'd do without him. I depend upon the boy. And he seldom lets me down.*

"We know the only thing it can be," the younger man persisted. "Malvina and her demon hordes have arrived."

As if in confirmation, thunder rolled across the city, blotting out for a moment the public-announcement honk and squawk and drone. Both men turned to see a blue flame rising from the spaceport, east of them by seven kilometers of snow-covered heath. Atop it perched a great globular shape, swathed in wisps and veils of cloud. The DropShip climbed into clouds which hid all but the three-lobed artificial star of its drives.

"And there goes our esteemed khan," von Texeira said conversationally. "Not to mention our closest thing to an ear at court."

Rorion crossed himself. "It is true, then," he said, and moistened his lips with a near-colorless tongue. "May God have mercy on our souls."

Von Texeira crossed himself as well. "We can hope, certainly," he said. He turned and set his bulk in painful motion toward their house, the better part of a kilometer away. His prosthetic ground and gouged at the stump of his leg even more cruelly than usual; he put it down to chill.

"You are my designated coregn," the face said from the flat projection. Scan lines tracked across it and white static fuzzed at the edges. The passage of the khan's DropShip *Falcon's Egg* through the planet's atmosphere interfered with bandwidth-heavy audiovisual communication. But this was no matter to wait even for the ship to reach orbit. *"You command Sudeten until my return. In the event I do not—"*

She paused. Standing in the darkened Falcon's Perch communications center, Julia Buhalin, loremaster of Clan Jade Falcon, could see fatigue stamped deeply in the face of her khan despite the doubtful reception. Yet she also thought to see *relief*.

Mad Malvina, Beckett Malthus, their renegades and their Hell's Horses allies had emerged into Sudeten system.

Characteristically reckless, Malvina had jumped her whole force in via a pirate point just over thirty-one hours from Sudeten at one-gee acceleration. Though formidable, as any force boasting two WarShips must be, it could not hope to match the strength of Khan Jana Pryde's grand fleet, even though her WarShips were individually much smaller than the *Emerald Talon*.

Khan Jana Pryde's armada, however, led by the destroyer *Jade Tornado*, was at the wrong end of a four-plus-day transit to the zenith point for its departure to the Clan Wolf occupation zone. Even at two-gee acceleration, which would significantly impair even tough Falcon warrior capabilities, they could not return in time to prevent Mongol malice from striking Sudeten with full force. So Khan Jana Pryde flew to her flagship, the *Aegis*-class heavy cruiser *Jade Talon*, to lead her sorely outnumbered remaining forces in an attempt to delay the invaders until the grand fleet could return and crush them.

Julia Buhalin blamed the Steiner emissary for the disaster. *How could even Falcons properly foresee, with his lies and sophistries beclouding our eyes?*

"—in the event I do not return," Khan Jana Pryde continued at last, "*you will serve as provisional khan until a* kurultai *can be convened to . . . see to the matter of succession.*"

Julia Buhalin saluted, then bowed in deep submission and respect. "It shall be as you command, my Khan," she said. "I shall well keep your Clan until you return."

But even as her head bowed her violet eyes gleamed. *Indeed, I shall do more than keep it, great Khan,* she thought, as Jana Pryde concluded the transmission and the projection evaporated. *I shall undertake the housecleaning you, with your need to balance forces, never could.*

"And when you resume your rightful place," she said aloud, "you shall lead a stronger and more unified Clan Jade Falcon than has been known for years. This I pledge, my Khan!"

Technicians at work in the red-lit cavern glanced up fearfully at the tone of her voice. Then they looked hurriedly back to their instruments.

*   *   *

"—do our duty and remain at the tasks assigned us by our Clan," said the tall woman in the black-and-green Jade Falcon battledress. A beaked falcon helmet constrained her flowing pale hair. A cape of brilliant jade falcon feathers draped her shoulders. *"The* stravags *must and* shall *fail in their challenge to our sacred Crusade and our very way of life. . . ."*

Back in their small, stumpy house in The Casts, the tri-vid had turned itself on. Khan Jana Pryde herself orated from the corner, a meter and a half high. Apparently that was a built-in function of all sets on Sudeten, so that no Falcon of any caste might miss an important Official Pronouncement. It gave von Texeira a slightly creepy sensation, fluttering in his stomach and tightening between his shoulder blades.

But why, he asked himself sternly, *since we've assumed all along the place was bugged?*

"Shut that damned noise off," he ordered peevishly as he went to the communicator on its table by the couch.

Rorion reached inside his coat. His hard brown hand came out with an autopistol. It barked once, eardrum-threateningly loud in the room's cement confines. Glass shattered; the holographic image vanished in a final fairy-dust spiral of colored motes.

To his master's glare the younger man returned a shrug. "I doubt we're getting our damage deposit back anyway."

"Come on, pick up," von Texeira murmured as the communicator rang Senna's personal code.

"You hate it when people say that to you," Rorion said, slipping a fresh magazine into the butt of his handgun and pocketing the old, now short one round. He made the weapon vanish again.

"Pick up, pick up," von Texeira said.

"Perhaps you should play the message we have waiting, lord," Rorion said mildly.

With a last annoyed grunt deep in the thickness of his throat von Texeira aborted the call and hit the playback button. The dark, dreadlock-framed features of one of Senna's bonded factors appeared above the set. He looked somewhat haunted, his skin touched with gray; to his aggravation, von Texeira still couldn't tell if it was Nestah or Petah.

"Ye best be makin' scarce from y'house," he said in his weird English patois. "Dread times may be come fe—"

Chocolate eyes sidled rapidly sidewise. The image flicked off.

"Rorion," von Texeira called, "we'd better get our things—"

Rorion was already emerging from the back of the house with their two light travel bags slung from his shoulder. From their Loki service, separated though it was by more than a decade, both men had long been imbued with the principle *Rely upon nothing beyond your own skin—and if it drops in the pot, thank the good Lord if you get away with that intact.* As a matter of convenience they traveled light and kept such things as they did not need on their persons stowed for instant flight.

"You were saying?" the younger man asked.

"Nada interessante," von Texeira said. "We must get to Senna's house. Her bondsman looked scared. I can't raise her. Something may have happened."

"Can't she take care of herself?"

"Perhaps," von Texeira said. "But with Khan Jana gone and Malvina on her way with a bone in her nose, who will take care of *us*?"

"Point taken, milord," Rorion said.

28

Star Colonel Han Crichell, tall, dark and hatchet-faced, stood glaring haughtily across the cement hangar floor at the party of warriors marching toward him. Beside him the splayed steel talons of his *Gyrfalcon* seemed to grip the stained cement.

The five warriors wore green armbands. They stopped several meters away. Two fanned out to each side, hands on their holstered sidearms. The central warrior, with an emerald-green cape hung from the shoulders of his orange-and-yellow jumpsuit, put his hands on his narrow hips and met the Star colonel eye to eye.

"Star Colonel Han Crichell?"

"Do your eyes fail you, Star Captain Bodhi? You know me well enough."

He certainly knew Bodhi. The man was a very vocal member of the Slips in Council, a noted lapdog for faction chief Star Colonel Maurai Roshak. Only the traditional disapproval of challenges in Council, backed by a set of exceedingly humiliating guidelines for *surkai* drawn up by Beckett Malthus, had kept him from a dozen duels over his sneering manner.

Unlike Crichell, who sported a full if somewhat unruly head of raven's-wing hair, Bodhi's head was shaved to a central crest of hair dyed pink and yellow. The stooping-Turkina badge of Clan Jade Falcon was tattooed on one side, the glaring yellow-eyed jade falcon head symbol of the traditionalist faction on the other.

"Star Colonel Han Crichell," he said again, not bothering to keep contempt from his voice and scarred lips, "you are to accompany me to a place of confinement."

"On whose authority?"

"On the authority of Loremaster Julia Buhalin, acting in the name of Khan Jana Pryde."

Crichell arched a brow. "So that is how the land lies. And if I refuse?"

Bodhi showed his perfect teeth. "Then we shoot you down like the *surat* you are and drag your corpse to the Falcon's Perch by the heels." He and his four companions drew their sidearms.

A roaring shattered the air. It went on and on, accompanied by a huge flame flickering from up and to Han Crichell's left.

The Star colonel could actually see his enemies' clothing, and Star Captain Bodhi's lean features, distorted by the potent blast from the minigun not five meters away, firing from the right arm of a parked *Koshi*. Then the five were washed away by the stream of heavy-jacketed bullets, to lie shattered, torn and sodden on the pavement to Han Crichell's right.

The gunfire ceased. The echoes chased each other around the vast hangar like giant bats, dwindling with agonizing slowness into a silence that seemed itself to ring. Or perhaps that was just the Star colonel's ears.

The *Koshi*'s cockpit side hatch opened. His aide-de-camp, MechWarrior Jeni, stuck her head out. Her fresh feminine features were flushed with passion, her green eyes bright.

"So far has the honor of Clan Jade Falcon fallen," she said. "And these *stravags* claim to be the true guardians our tradition!"

"You were right," Crichell said without looking away from the pile of steaming, maroon cloth, all that remained of arrogant Star Captain Bodhi. "I did not imagine Julia Buhalin could act so rashly. She shows herself to be as mad as Malvina."

He shook his head. "Our course is clear," he said. "We must act swiftly to defeat her insanity before facing the insanity of the Mongols.

"To think such a day could ever dawn over Turkina's own nest!"

It was not only members of the "moderate" Jess faction that Julia Buhalin sent security teams, augmented by trusted Slip warriors, to arrest. She also availed herself of the opportunity to troll in certain ranking scientists and technicians who, in her opinion, exercised altogether too much power over Clan affairs. Using the emergency as a pretext to humble the lower castes was to her mind among the greatest services she could render Turkina and her khan.

Having just received disturbing news from the Lyran Commonwealth border, she dealt also with a certain other annoyance.

Julia Buhalin was constitutionally incapable of truly comprehending Malvina Hazen's most recent proclamations. Otherwise she would never have acceded to the exalted rank of loremaster. It did not occur to her that, by arresting the very scientists and technicians who actually ran Clan Jade Falcon, she might be removing the cooling rods that regulated a potentially disastrous reaction.

She was not history's first politician to be ignorant of the law of unintended consequences.

"Now that's a sight I never thought I'd see," Rorion Klimt said.

Grimacing and puffing from the brisk walk to Senna's house, von Texeira asked, "What's that?"

A street declined to their left, in the direction of the commercial spaceport around which The Casts had sprung up. Although non-Clan offworlders (and of course the Sea Foxes, whom the Falcons only grudgingly considered Clanners) were largely shunted into the quarter, they weren't the only ones to work here. A laborer gang in brown shopworker jumpsuits had gathered in the street at the foot of the hill. They actually appeared to be arguing with a tall man with a crest of green-dyed hair, dressed in green and canary yellow with a scarlet cape flapping in the icy breeze, who could be nothing but a MechWarrior.

"Astonishing," von Texeira said. His big round face creased in a scowl of perplexity and concern. Street demonstrations were no uncommon sight on Recife, unusual for the free but Teutonically order-minded Commonwealth. *But on a Clan world? And the occupation zone capital, at that?*

"Talking back to a MechWarrior like that is pretty bold," Rorion said. "To understate the obvious."

To show just how understated, the MechWarrior reached abruptly to his belt. His hand came up. Ruby light flashed three times. Three laborers fell. One thrashed and howled. The other two just lay smoldering in the trampled slush.

Some laborers from a nearby warehouse, broad-framed in pink jumpsuits and some nearly tall as elementals, had joined the dispute. One of these now snatched up a bright blue plastic drum which, if full, must have weighed forty kilos, swung it over her head, and threw it at the MechWarrior. Still clutching his laser pistol, the warrior flung up both arms. He managed to fend the barrel from his head. But its mass staggered him, and even upward of a hundred meters away the two Lyrans winced, a beat later, to hear the crack of a forearm snapping.

Before he could recover, a shop worker stepped up behind him and swung a meter-long tool two-handed at his skull. It struck with a noise like an ax hitting damp wood.

The warrior went to one knee. With an inarticulate cry of fury, the laborers surged forward. The warrior quickly vanished beneath a seethe of bodies and fists and heavy work boots.

"Perhaps justice of a sort for that scene we witnessed yesterday, Rorion," von Texeira said.

"So social revolution comes at last to the Falcon heartland," Rorion said, "courtesy of Malvina Hazen, the arch-reactionary."

"Let's hope her evil burns out here and goes no further," his master said.

Down the hill the laborers, now calling out in hoarse triumph, seemed to be engaged in some sort of tug of war.

"Come," von Texeira said. "We'd best get to Senna's as quickly as possible. The laborers may have half a millennium's resentment built up against their overlords, but they regard *us* as no better than rats. I suspect the streets won't be healthy for outlanders.

"And besides, I don't really think we need to see any more here, do we, my boy?"

"Certo," the younger man said, reseating his pack and hurrying on.

In space ahead new stars appeared. Others faded, vanished.

Standing beside Malvina Hazen on the *Bucephalus*'s observation deck, Cynthy clapped small hands together. "Pretty," she said.

Beckett Malthus felt his gorge rise. The word was the first he had heard the Inner Sphere child speak. And what she called *pretty* was Jade Falcon Clansmen and women dying in their aerospace fighters.

Killed by their fellow Jade Falcons. *What have I done?*

The cold calculator in his mind—the part which, ultimately, had always ruled him—said, *What seemed best at the time, always. And whatever you have done, can even a mind as devious as yours conceive a way to* undo *it?*

Galaxy Commander Manas Amirault stood on Malvina's other side, smiling slackly as a Spheroid at a sporting event. Then again, Bec Malthus reflected, they weren't *his* Clansfolk killing each other out there. Or mostly not: his own aerospace forces swarmed in a protective globe around his WarShip, following the wounded *Emerald Talon* toward Sudeten.

"Great Khan," a Horsewoman naval aide murmured respectfully to Malvina, "the Falcon Star admiral wishes to speak to you."

"Send," she said. A holographic stage rose from the floor of the ferroglass-fronted observation chamber, which was lit only by the lights of stars—and battle.

Dolphus Binetti's gray visage seemed sunken behind his helmet visor. He and his bridge crew wore pressure suits so that a hull breach would not incapacitate them all at a stroke.

"*Jade Talon approaches, my Khan*," he said. His image flickered with transients, yellow and white scanlines and sparkles, from the energies unleashed by the fighter battle and the battleship's defensive batteries. The energies about to be released would dwarf them. "*She will come within primary-weapon engagement range within three hundred seconds.*"

"You have my complete trust, Star Admiral," Malvina said. "Fight as you choose."

"*Galaxy Commander Malvina Hazen,*" he said with painful correctness, "*duty compels me to confess your faith might prove misplaced. As you are well aware my ship remains grievously damaged from her engagement at Skye. Though I pledge to you the utmost efforts of myself and my crew, my abilities may not suffice to defeat an undamaged WarShip, smaller though she is, in company of so many fighters and DropShips.*"

"You will do what you must, Star Admiral Dolphus Binetti," Malvina said. "You are Jade Falcon."

A pause, crackling with static. "*I am Jade Falcon.*"

"Then engage the *stravags*, and destroy!"

The house looked peaceful and oddly homelike under its blanket of snow. Its mounded shape, harsh ferrocrete outlines softened by the blanketing snow, might have been a natural feature. "Reminds me of a hobbit hole," von Texeira said with a certain satisfaction.

"What's that?" his aide asked. The younger man looked briskly around, black eyes bright. The hand inside his jacket pocket, von Texeira knew, clutched his handgun.

"From a book I loved as a child," the Margrave said.

Rorion bent his sleek head toward the city. "That low intermittent rumble is gunfire from street battles, milord," he said. "The invaders aren't even here yet. Now may be a poor time for reminiscence."

"Impertinent as usual," von Texeira said. He sighed heavily. "Also, as usual, correct."

"I live to serve, *mestre*."

"My large left buttock. Although you do serve me well, my boy. Well, let us proceed and find out what Petah and Nestah find so momentous but cannot share over the phone."

As they approached the dwelling a horrific crack struck their ears like an ax. Both men hit the slush-wet pavement. Glass exploded from the windows of a panel van parked a few meters down the street.

"What in hell's name was that?" shouted Rorion. He had his gun out and lay prone, looking wildly around for enemies. His voice was scarcely audible above the ringing in von Texeira's ears.

The older man pointed off toward a bright blue spark moving low above the center of Hammarr. Green beams snapped toward it, leaving streaks of afterimage pulsing magenta on his retinas.

"*Now* the invaders are here. Malvina announces her presence in advance."

"Will they bomb, do you think?"

Several kilometers to their left a series of flashes lit the sky, silhouetting structures humped on a hilltop. Brown smoke boiled upward, quickly turning black. A rippling crack hit their ears several heartbeats later.

"You needed to ask?"

"Wonderful," Rorion said.

"Look on the bright side," said von Texeira, picking himself up gingerly. "If only all our questions could be answered so quickly!"

He dusted at the fronts of his pants legs. "Let's see what our Sea Fox friends have to tell us."

The gate into the front court, surrounded by a low wall

stuccoed a strange dark-mauve color, stood ajar. Rorion frowned. Von Texeira gimped to the door.

"Open," he said softly.

"I don't like this."

Fusion jets and the drum thunder of more bombs growled in the distance. "We face a menu of unpalatable dishes," von Texeira said. He pushed inside.

He stepped quickly inside and to his right, exiting the notorious "fatal funnel" in which an enemy waiting in ambush could easily target him. Rorion followed his handgun through a beat later. He shifted left.

Von Texeira blinked. The only illumination was cloudy daylight filtered through half-closed blinds. After the greater brightness of outdoors it took his eyes a moment to adjust.

Enough to see the dark shape sprawled between the low table and the sofa.

29

The Casts
Hammarr Commercial Spaceport, Sudeten
Jade Falcon Occupation Zone
3 April 3136

"**D**ead," said Rorion, crouched by the fallen man's lolling head. "Neck's broken. It's Nestah."

"How can you tell?"

"Can't you?"

Before von Texeira could respond a noise from behind made him turn. A gigantic ginger-haired face leered into his. The doorway behind had filled with an elemental, bent over like a fairy-tale giant entering a cottage.

To avoid being knocked down, von Texeira sidestepped further away from the door. A tall, slender youth emerged from the house's rear: a Jade Falcon MechWarrior by the badges on his yellow-tan jumpsuit, with a needler in his hand. Another elemental, female and entirely shaven-headed, came in after, likewise bent over to clear the door from the hallway. In the main room she could just stand full upright with her shaven pate almost touching the ceiling.

"You outlanders must have thought yourselves quite clever," the MechWarrior said with a sneer. "Have you been sending back messages to your friends so that they might attack Sudeten, too?"

"Sudeten?" asked von Texeira.

"Too?" said Rorion.

"We have learned of your treacherous Lyran raids along the frontier," the female elemental said. Her voice rasped, suggesting a serious blow to the throat at some point in her young life.

Von Texeira stared at her. His big broad shoulders rose and fell in a profound sigh.

"Fuck *us*," he said.

"They have," Rorion said cheerfully. "Just like the good old days, *não*?"

"There were never any good old days in Loki," said von Texeira.

The MechWarrior drew his head back on a slender neck. "You admit to being terrorists?" he said, sounding half eager and half astonished. He had a fine, thrusting bone structure and slanted lavender eyes that made him appear almost elfin.

We never encountered nonhuman intelligent life, von Texeira thought incongruously, *so we've gone and made ourselves aliens.*

"Retired," Rorion said.

"What does it matter?" von Texeira said. "Julia Buhalin sent you to kill us anyway, *quineg*?"

The elemental who loomed to von Texeira's left like the proverbial elephant in the parlor laughed like a boulder rolling down a chute. *"Neg,"* he said. "She wants you questioned and given public trial. *Then* executed."

"Following the forms," the MechWarrior said, smiling unpleasantly, "just as your Devlin Stone would have wanted."

"He was never our Devlin Stone," Rorion Klimt said. He shot the MechWarrior through the chest twice, firing from inside his coat and blowing the pocket into a smoking lint cloud.

Roaring wordlessly, the male elemental reached for von Texeira. The diplomat turned to face him, apparently overbalanced and fell onto his broad posterior on the throw rug.

The woman lunged at Rorion. She was wiry for an elemental and moved much faster than he anticipated. She swept up the end table, upsetting the lamp to shatter on the floor, and flung it at him. Struggling to extract his handgun from his ruined pocket he had to let go to ward off the piece of furniture.

Grinning, her compatriot advanced on the fallen *Markgraf*. "Fat, clumsy cripple," he said. "You make it too easy."

Von Texeira clutched his right hip. He raised his false right leg straight out with his heel toward the vast face. He clenched his lower belly muscles in a certain way.

His shoe heel exploded. The elemental's face seemed to implode, crumpling around the dense column of double-ought buckshot fired from the single-shot twelve-gauge shotgun built into von Texeira's prosthetic leg.

"Depends on your definition of 'easy,'" the margrave muttered through ringing echoes, wincing at the pain the recoil shot up his stump. He had to roll to the side to avoid being pinned to the floor by the giant's inert bulk.

Half-crouched, arms outspread, Rorion faced the female elemental. She was seventy centimeters taller than he, and her own arms, likewise spread, seemed to span the room. The shotgun's bang drew her gaze aside.

Rorion moved. Not left or right; instead he threw himself forward and down, into a handstand right in front of her. Her eyes went wide.

She started to smile. Rorion's right boot slammed into her mouth. Her head rocked back. She leaned farther back as he spun on his hands to deliver a second capoeira kick that broke her nose and sent blood cascading down her upper lip.

She screamed in rage and fell backward, unbalanced more by sheer surprise than pain or the force of the blows. She landed sitting. Rorion flipped himself the rest of the way over and landed astride her lap. He slammed his open palms together on the sides of her head, breaking her right eardrum. She screamed again, lashing out half-blind. He ducked the strike, scrambled behind her and up onto her shoulders like a monkey. Wrapping his arms about her head like steel bands he drove his weight sideways with all the strength in his legs.

Her neck broke with a noise like a cannon.

Rorion sprang clear as she collapsed. He looked to his boss. The older man had pulled himself up to a sitting position against one wall and sat clutching his own holdout pistol in one vast paw.

"Well done, lad," von Texeira said.

Abstractedly Rorion nodded. He finished extracting his Taurus autopistol from his blown-open jacket pocket. Holding the weapon in both hands he quickly checked the other rooms of the small house.

"I found Petah in the second bedroom," he reported, returning. "He was dead too. Shot—looks like he put up a fight."

The older man crossed himself. Rorion put his autopistol in his intact pocket.

"So Archon Melissa crossed us up," he said bitterly.

"Someone did," von Texeira agreed. "But after all, we always knew we were expendable, didn't we? It's not as if things have changed from the old days."

"We both know the real reason for the raids, don't we?" Rorion asked.

They spoke Portuguese, which Senna had confirmed few Jade Falcons understood. Nevertheless, von Texeira held up a stubby finger as he nodded, warning his aide to say no more. *They may have planted bugs after murdering the Sea Fox factors*, he thought.

"I wonder where Senna is," he said.

"Well away from here." Rorion searched the room rapidly and methodically. Not from any real expectation of finding anything, von Texeira knew, but from habit. Instilled by long training—and hard experience.

"Ah, well." Von Texeira sighed volcanically. Setting his cane, he began to struggle upright. "She always told us not to rely upon her—"

The house shook around them. Dust fell from the ceiling.

In a bound Rorion was beside the older man, reaching down to grasp him under the arms. A monstrous thud resounded. The floor jumped in response.

"Come on, old man," Rorion shouted. "Get up! We have to—"

The roof fell on them.

"Chingis Khan," the Horsewoman said, "Star Admiral Dolphus Binetti reports that he has lost most systems in the *Emerald Talon*. He strives to recover at least maneuver control."

Beckett Malthus marked how the warrior aide addressed Malvina directly without looking at her own nominal superior, though Galaxy Commander Manas Amirault stood directly at Malvina's side. Amirault apparently did not notice. Between Malvina and the space battle unfolding before their eyes, he was thoroughly entranced.

"But they have dealt their opponent deadly blows," Malvina said. She actually clapped her hands in delight, seeming as young as the girl who still stood by her side, speechless again, the teddy bear dangling from one pale arm.

"We have received independent communications from the *Emerald Talon*," the Hell's Horses aide went on. "A missile penetrated the combat information center. Star Admiral Dolphus Binetti has suffered severe injury. It seems he refuses treatment."

"Ahh," said Malthus. It was almost a sigh.

Around them holoprojections showed images of the action, computer-assembled from a range of sensor inputs and enhanced into video that lagged imperceptibly behind the actual events. Even seen unassisted through the great ferroglass viewports, the battle had been breathtaking in its chaotic fury.

Ravaged by the *Emerald Talon*'s terrible broadside the *Jade Talon* drifted, a dark mass, her main drives cold. A greatly diminished swarm of Sudeten fighters orbited her like fireflies. But the mighty battleship now drifted as well, hundreds of meters of its length masked by clouds of condensate, lit only by pale flames fed by oxygen leaks, and here and there a lamp's icy gleam. Had it not been for a scatter of radio transmissions, she could have been a ghost ship.

The naval aide, one ear encased by a comm-button, cocked her dark-blond head suddenly to that side. Hell's Horses naval personnel tended to wear short full-head cuts, rather than the flamboyant ponytails and scalp locks their ground warriors favored. The rare Horse elementals, male and female alike, wore buzz cuts.

She spoke softly to Amirault. He pulled a mouth, nodded, then grinned at Malvina.

"A call for you, O Khan," he said.

Malthus opened his mouth to caution his protégée. "Put her on," Malvina Hazen said.

Khan Jana Pryde's face appeared in projection to port of the central viewport. It was sallow; the skin seemed to sag on the angular scaffolding of her cheekbones. An angry red weal streaked her right cheek, and something black was smeared above her left eyebrow.

"What do you wish of me, Jana Pryde?" Malvina asked.

The head raised. The skin seemed to tighten on her face, and her slanted green eyes flared.

"You have not yet won," she said.

"True enough," Malvina said with a careless gesture. "But every second that we speak brings me closer to victory."

"Perhaps," Jana Pryde said. *"But this much is certain: every second—every death, every fighting machine disabled or destroyed—weakens Clan Jade Falcon. At a moment of great uncertainty, and perhaps grave threats to our Bloodlines."*

She shook her head, weary, slow. *"I believed that you would give up your rebellion once word came of the Wolf withdrawal. Believed that you, with your vaunted strategic vision, would understand both the crisis and the opportunity it posed for Clan Jade Falcon."*

"I might observe that the Wolf's mysterious actions make it more imperative than ever to have a firm hand in control of the Falcon's destiny," Malvina said. "But if we debate politics, I prefer to let my warriors do it for me. They appear to argue most persuasively."

Jana Pryde glowered. *"Already* Emerald Talon, *pride of our fleet, floats helplessly, a crippled husk. My flagship is seriously damaged, as your sensors no doubt show. But despite your intact outlander WarShip, you will not quickly overcome Sudeten's defenses. And when my Grand Fleet arrives—"*

"I trust you reach for a point?" Malvina said. "By the time your fleet returns, the *Bucephalus* can make green glass craters of Sudeten and the Falcon's Eyrie as well."

"You wouldn't!"

Khan Jana Pryde had always been careless about contractions, Malthus thought with a bit of pedagogic twinge. But that was one thing Malvina would not criticize her for. Perhaps the only one.

"Don't talk nonsense," the tiny woman with the white-blond hair said, as if to emphasize Malthus' unspoken thought. "You know of what I am capable."

For a moment the two women looked death at one another. Had thousands of kilometers not separated them, Malthus had no doubt they would leap at each other's throats. He noticed how Cynthy's hand had gone white where it gripped Malvina's, how the tiny chubby fingers dug in.

Jana Pryde sighed. *"I do. I cannot comprehend your madness—let it go."*

She shook back strands of straw-colored hair that had escaped her ponytail and drifted across her high forehead. "You challenged me to a Trial of Possession for Clan Jade Falcon. I now accept that challenge. I will fight you, one on one. The loser's forces will swear uncompromised obedience to the victor. The war must end here and now!"

"That challenge has rather passed its due date," said Malthus, pleased at being able to use a Spheroid metaphor—and far more pleased at getting to sneer at his former protégée who had cast him aside.

"I accept," Malvina said. "We shall fight in BattleMechs. The Circle of Honor: outboard the *Emerald Talon*. The time: two hours."

"Done," Jana Pryde said. The screen went blank.

Beckett Malthus shouted in outrage. "You cannot do this! I—"

Malvina turned, stepped close, slapped him sharply cross

one bearded cheek. She was a very strong woman, for all that she must stand tiptoe to reach him. The blow stung.

Malthus' cloudy green eyes slowly blinked, once, twice. They stung as well.

He felt wide eyes upon him, was aware of mouths gaping in slack faces. His vision had contracted to a tunnel. No graver insult could be offered a Clansman. Indeed, he could not recall ever hearing of anyone slapping a Clan warrior—much less living to tell of it. It cried out for a challenge.

He said nothing. Did nothing. Not even reach to touch his face.

"Never," Malvina said, practically hissing anger. "Never tell me what I can and cannot do. I am Chingis Khan!"

She swept a glare about the chamber like a large laser. "None of you! I am Emperor of All. You have acknowledged me, and now we crush all before us!"

Cowed by her stellar-furnace fury, the Hell's Horses aide dropped to one knee and bowed a submissive head. Beckett Malthus was next, thanking Turkina he did not have to go first. One by one the technicians left their stations to turn and kneel before the khan.

Smiling slightly, Galaxy Commander Manas Amirault was last to kneel and lower his head. Only Malvina remained standing. And the tiny child who clung stubbornly to her hand, but who did not cry, and whose face showed no fear.

Malvina stepped forward to stroke the shaven side of Manas' head. Then she turned to approach Malthus. He steeled himself, but felt a hand catch him gently beneath his beard, raise him up with insistent gentle pressure.

Malvina beamed at him as if he had done her a marvelous favor. "There, now, Bec Malthus," she said. "No long faces. Don't you see? Our enemy has delivered victory into our hands."

She turned to take in the others with her declaration: "Into our hands! The *surat* Jana was right, I'll give her that: every death diminishes the strength we must have for the Great Crusade to come. Every death but hers!"

"Excellency," Malthus said, finishing the somewhat laborious process of getting all the way back to his feet: he was heavier than a Clan warrior customarily got, as well as older, and thanks to accumulated stress and damage his knees were not all they once had been. "You take much for granted."

She faced him with a look of surprise that her blue eyes mocked, laughing. "You do not think I intend to *lose*, do you?"

"Jana Pryde is a most formidable MechWarrior," he said. He deliberately omitted the honorific to which Jana Pryde was, if only pro forma, still entitled. "She has the strength of desperation to aid her."

"I am no weakling as a MechWarrior. And I have my Destiny to aid me."

Malthus bowed. "As you say, my Khan."

But as his gaze broke from hers he wondered: *Does arrogance rule her now? That can be fatal, faced with the warrior I know Jana Pryde to be.*

Fleetingly he wondered what he would say to Khan Jana Pryde should she prevail. And smiled.

Judging by our intelligence reports from Sudeten, he thought, *she would appear in need of an advisor.*

30

"**S**ave yourself, boy!" commanded von Texeira as Rorion tugged his arm. "Go!"

Rorion Klimt ignored him.

"As your overlord I command you: leave me!"

"La, la, la-la, la," Rorion grunted in time to his pulls. "I'm not *listening*."

A curved section of cement ceiling had landed on von Texeira, pinning him from the hips down. Miraculously, nothing seemed broken, for he felt no stabbing pain. *Or perhaps my spine is gone in the lumbar region, and with it feeling. . . .*

Von Texeira could sense what Rorion clearly ignored: the nearness of the giant metal foot that had come down through the rear of the house. A huge shape loomed against the painfully blue sky. *Maybe he thinks he has no chance*, he thought.

A brilliant blue-green flash filled von Texeira's eyes, momentarily washing away his vision. A tremendous crack stabbed his eardrums. He closed sightless eyes and commended his soul to God.

. . . He became aware of a strange floating lightness in his lower body. Icy air laved his face. He was being carried, impossibly, on Rorion's back. He remembered, vaguely, that lasers had a way of shattering cement with special vehemence—and realized his prosthetic leg must somehow have propped up the fallen cement slab, prevented it from crushing his hips or good leg.

It did not explain why they had yet to be killed by the BattleMech that had crushed the house.

A rough purplish blur in front of his eyes unfocused by shock became the stuccoed front wall of the courtyard. Then he was falling as his aide dumped him unceremoniously over.

He struck the sidewalk heavily. Now pain came in force: it seemed as if red-heated spikes were hammered into his real thighbone, his hip, his belly.

Lying on his back he blinked at the sky and groaned. Getting dropped onto cement from a meter and a half in the air had done his internal injuries no good. But the calculating part of his brain that had kept him calm in angry boardrooms—and alive under fire—for more than three decades had kicked in. *The boy has in mind keeping me alive* long enough *for internal injuries to kill me*, he realized.

It was a daunting task. He heard Rorion shout, trying to attract the MechWarrior's attention. A big laser crack again. A section of wall seven meters from him burst outward to a spasm of cyan light.

Over the top of the low wall he saw the distinctive flat-headed shape of a *Dasher*. It was the smallest possible BattleMech, a mere twenty tons, one not commonly favored by Clan Jade Falcon. It might as well have been a hundred-ton *Atlas*, though, pitted against Rorion and his handgun.

Von Texeira's aide had dodged behind the parked van. He popped out now, fired three quick shots at the *Dasher*'s viewscreen. In response a short-range missile spurted from the launcher in the 'Mech's right arm. Rorion dove away as the truck rode upward on a blast that turned to a pillar of orange flame as the fuel tank blew. The van tipped to the side and fell in the midst of the street with a terrific bang and spraying of glass, like something from a Davion spy-action holovid.

Von Texeira shouted, "No!" But Rorion seemed unhurt, rolling purposefully toward an intact section of the wall around the courtyard, nothing daunted in his hopeless battle with the 'Mech.

The BattleMech stepped forward, birdlike, the left arm with its twin medium lasers poised. The *Dasher*'s small but potent battery could have simply vaporized the minor obstruction posed by the cement and stucco wall. But the Falcon MechWarrior seemed content to play with his prey.

Heinz-Otto von Texeira gritted his teeth in helpless frustration. Dragging himself to a half-sitting position, propped against the wall, he found his own sidearm and drew it. *If this is how it ends, on this cold and heartless world surrounded by our enemies and forsaken by our friends*, he thought, *then let me die fighting, not lying helpless as a side of beef.*

The *Dasher* approached the section of wall behind which Rorion crouched. It raised one foot, painted to resemble a raptor's claw, preparing to bring it down on its unseen but trapped quarry.

Green light flared. Von Texeira winced as refracted spears of coherent light seared his eyes. A blue light flashed, then green again.

The *Dasher*'s rear erupted as the plates blew off the CASE-equipped ammo stowage for its short-range missile racks. It swayed forward, driven by the vented force of ongoing explosions of propellant and warheads. As it began to fall onto the pinned-down Rorion, a steel hand seized it by the housing of its right shoulder-actuator. It was yanked backward to land with the SRMs still cooking off inside.

A small humanoid BattleMech with a curious up-jutting head painted to resemble a jade falcon stood behind the *Dasher* where it lay half in the wreckage of the Sea Fox factors' house with flames booming out around it. Von Texeira recognized a *Piranha*. It pointed its two arms at the fallen 'Mech's viewscreen and loosed green bolts from medium lasers.

Von Texeira ducked his head to prevent himself from being blinded. The lasers cracked three times. Then silence hit like a slap.

"Rorion!" called von Texeira. He coughed on dust and smoke. Spears seemed to pierce his belly. "How are you, boy?"

"Alive," called back a voice as husky as his own. "And astonished by the fact."

"Margrave, Rorion," a voice boomed from the victorious BattleMech, *"quit screwing around and come out. We don't have much time before more of these Slip half-wits turn up looking for you."*

Heinz-Otto von Texeira stared in amazement at his aide, who lay supine in the gutter with his jacket up over his head.

It was the voice of Master Merchant Senna Rodríguez.

In space the vessels flared and died silently. Their occupants' cries, if any, went unheard.

Malvina Hazen smiled through her pressure suit's faceplate at the combat still flaring all around her Black Rose as it hung seemingly suspended a hundred meters above the husk of the *Emerald Talon.* Jana Pryde had asked for a cease-fire during their trial. Malvina refused. While in strategic terms she was as eager to conserve the fighting resources of Clan Jade Falcon as was the pretender who still styled herself khan, she felt only bleak amusement at each brief nova that marked the death of a MechWarrior or shipman or aerospace pilot. They were all *things* to her, their deaths no more than the crisping and smoking of ants beneath the rays of a summer sun focused through a child's magnifying glass.

Although *Jade Talon* had limped off at a tangent, unwilling to risk confronting the untouched *Bucephalus,* the fighting still raged unabated around the drifting battleship. The Circle of Equals was a hundred-kilometer exclusion zone, a sphere marked out by transponder beacons, centered on the *Talon*'s midpoint. By space-war referents, the duel took place in the thick of battle.

The voice of Galaxy Commander Beckett Malthus droned

in Malvina's ears. As senior officer present, he presided over the trial. *That must rankle Jana Pryde*, she thought. It, too, amused her.

A small red sun appeared between the opponents, separated by the length of the great WarShip. Malvina's heart jumped in happy anticipation. The flare was the signal to commence.

She flew her *Shrike* forward at full thrust of its jump impellers. Both Black Rose and Jana Pryde's *Turkina*, "Greenfeather," came jump-capable, a rarity among top-end assault BattleMechs. For the space trial, an unusual affair for BattleMechs, each was equipped with strap-on tanks of water to be lased into plasma for reaction mass.

The *Turkina*'s jets were a white spark. It moved to Malvina's right and grew, meaning its pilot angled toward her on an oblique approach. She maintained an altitude of about fifty meters above the hull.

The WarShip formed a unique battlefield. Its vast cigar shape was ravaged by beam and blast; white vapors still pooled in craters and drifted off it in feathering wisps. Horrific bombardment had sculpted the hull into almost a sort of strange cityscape, with towers, racks, gantries and buckled plates protruding. They created terrain for the duelists to fight in.

As did the very space around. A space battle generally entailed both sides matching vectors fairly closely. They then could rip and tear at each other continuously, fighter packs whirling in dogfights, instead of exchanging brief furious fire as fleets flashed past one another at cometary closing speeds, followed by hours or days of deceleration, then speeding toward each other again. Accordingly, much wreckage, almost-whole fighters and the odd gutted DropShip, followed the same orbital trajectory through Sudeten system as *Emerald Talon* herself.

Malvina adjusted course to fly directly toward the point for which her foe made, as if they followed two legs of an angle to its apex. Despite Malvina's targeting computer, the *Turkina* had the better of her at range. The *Turkina*'s two left-arm LB 5-X autocannon had a slight edge in reach over the particle projectors that were Black Rose's main punch, even at extended range. Greenfeather carried twin PPCs as well, and its shoulders mounted LRM launchers that threw three times the projectiles Malvina's Longbow 10-rack did.

At closer quarters, the medium lasers on either side of the *Shrike*'s thrust-beaked head evened the odds somewhat, though Jana Pryde's firepower was nothing diminished. The *Shrike* had superior jump jets and surface speed. The double-capacity heat sinks with which Malvina made up the substantial difference in mass and bulk between her PPCs and the hundred-millimeter autocannon and ammo stores they replaced had done much to overcome the significant disparity in heat the two weapons systems generated. Jana Pryde's 'Mech had double heat sinks as well—and the fifty-millimeter autocannon gave off little heat, whereas Malvina's medium lasers ran relatively hot. Despite the *Turkina*'s larger battery, Malvina would have to watch her thermal gauges more closely than did Jana Pryde.

Dancing light announced that Jana Pryde had opened the engagement with her autocannon. The *Turkina* changed course to head straight for Malvina's *Shrike*.

Black Rose carried the better armor, ferro-fibrous as opposed to conventional aligned-crystal steel. But it was only at grips where the *Shrike* enjoyed a clear offensive advantage: its great three-fingered claw, able to shear or crumple even a *Turkina*'s thick plate.

Malvina's heart sang and her blood crackled like current as she flew to met her foe. In a meeting of 'Mechs of identical displacement, advantage went to the superior Mech-Warrior. She had no doubt it was she.

She fired a particle cannon, intending to see if the blue-white lance, lacking lightning-like ionization effects outside a planet's atmosphere, might make her opponent flinch. Her heat gauge spiked but promptly dropped. In vacuum, heat radiated more rapidly unless the sun shone directly on them. And they commenced their battle on *Emerald Talon*'s "night" side.

Jana Pryde fired again as she closed. A fifty-millimeter shell burst against the right side of Black Rose's chest. Without conscious thought Malvina worked her jump jet throttles, adjusting thrust to keep her machine's vast mass upright in relation to the ship—mainly out of habit, since it mattered little enough outside a gravity well. The hit did little more than blister the paint around her rocket ports.

With a flick of downthrust she grounded her 'Mech on the artificial asteroid. A shiver ran through its endosteel skeleton and her tailbone as the talons touched the metal hull. Magnetized pads affixed to the BattleMech's feet gripped like a spacer's ship slippers.

Although she had practiced little space combat in her 'Mech, her landing was immaculate.

Jana Pryde's 'Mech grew as it flew toward her. Malvina laid her crosshairs on the *Turkina*'s flattened-egg snout, assisted at this long range by her targeting computer. She fired. Yellow sparks arced and metal flash-heated to plasma flew from right beneath her enemy's cockpit.

31

Jade Falcon Naval Reserve WarShip **Emerald Talon**
Approaching Sudeten Orbit
Jade Falcon Occupation Zone
3 April 3136

If the current khan of Clan Jade Falcon flinched from the wash of blinding light and heat into her cockpit, she showed no sign. She instantly fired back one of her own arm-mounted PPCs, following it with another autocannon burst. The particle beam struck the *Shrike*'s left breastplate where it flared winglike in front of the left shoulder housing. Sparks streaked from Malvina's machine; the plate's tip glowed white. Heavy cannon shells pounded the big Battle-Mech's torso.

The *Turkina*'s upward-pointing jets pushed her down to the hull. Malvina had already jumped again, in low skimming flight toward a hundred-meter length of deck plate upheaved twenty meters by colossal internal overpressure. She had thoroughly studied holos of the battleship's damage as *Bec de Corbin* carried her, along with its master Malthus, Galaxy Commander Manas Amirault, and her ward Cynthy, toward the chosen Circle. She knew of the artificial ridge's presence—as well as what lay beyond.

Jump jets raised her "up" and over the rearing steel slab

as missiles slammed into it, white flashes dancing in her wake. At once she applied downthrust. The ninety-five-ton mass of Black Rose plummeted into a great jagged-toothed pit.

Inside, a hangar deck had been ruptured by the terrific barrage that had buckled the hull. Its cavernous expanse was eerily lit by floods. Chunks of debris drifted among yawning silent bays. Some were the limp forms of technicians. An unlucky few had been caught without pressure suits when the great ship-killing missiles had struck an expanse of hull weakened by naval PPCs.

A man floated past Malvina's cockpit as she descended, eyes bulging from his face, bloodred from ruptured capillaries. The skin and even the tongue protruding in final surprise were mottled green and black as fluids gradually escaped the cell. In time, vacuum's relentless pull would draw all water from the corpse, leaving it a desiccated husk like a spider-sucked fly, its jumpsuit and tough sack of skin collapsed inward.

The Rose's legs flexed as her talons hit the deck. A corner of Malvina's mouth twisted as she turned and jetted toward a great stanchion standing like a rib inside a whale's carcass. *Unless I misjudge*, she thought, *Aleksandr and I had our last face-to-face meeting on that observation deck there.*

The ferroglass pane between bay and gallery remained intact. Whether pressure remained on the far side she could not tell. For a flash she entertained a vision of the ghostly figures of herself and her brother up there, watching this duel for the fate of Clan Jade Falcon.

It amused her to know he would not be rooting for her.

Overhead, the hole in the hull was an irregular pool of blackness, in which floated stars. Jets flamed across the black lake. Jana Pryde had cannily circled the hole and entered on the far side. With all weapons blazing.

Crouched in what Malvina had expected to be cover as well as concealment, Black Rose rocked to hammer blows from autocannon and rockets. Bathed in PPC-hellglare as a ton of armor flashed into plasma and recoil effect tipped the huge machine sideways, Malvina launched a volley of

LRMs and sprang right for her foe. She gambled everything on getting to grips before the *Turkina*'s tremendous firepower disabled her 'Mech.

But Jana Pryde's nerve broke first. Or her shrewd tactical mind reckoned her range too short to be sure of stopping the Black Rose before its terrible claw tore her BattleMech open. The *Turkina*'s jump jets flamed, momentarily washing out the yellow blaze of floodlights. Greenfeather broke to its right, turning on its vertical axis to flee down the great cavern of the hangar deck.

Malvina screamed her frustration. She had fired one of her PPCs, smearing a glowing streak across the upper surface of the *Turkina*'s egglike fuselage. Between its discharge and the heat dumped into her *Shrike* by Jana Pryde's particle cannon, thermal levels had shot perilously near redline. She could not jump again immediately or even risk a chasing shot. Instead, with sweat pouring down face and flanks in the furnace of her cockpit, she must settle for rocking the BattleMech into a walk, its feet clinging magnetically to the deckplate at every step.

Unlike her *Shrike,* the *Turkina* could flip its arms to fire backward. This Jana Pryde did, raking Malvina with autocannon fire. Red warnings gleamed in Malvina's HUD. Fifty-millimeter shells had taken out a pair of launch tubes on her right side. In the wireframe damage display her 'Mech's whole front seemed to glow amber. Already she could take little more punishment before starting to lose systems wholesale.

Instead of accelerating, she fired a PPC as soon as she dared. It tore open the flex housing of the *Turkina*'s right elbow joint in a rooster tail of orange sparks, exposing myomer pseudomuscles bunching and relaxing on endosteel armatures.

A moment to bleed heat. Then Malvina accelerated to a run. The *Turkina* grounded briefly as Malvina swerved around a small shuttlecraft still in its berth. Both 'Mechs fired PPCs, missed.

Before Greenfeather the hangar deck's rear bulkhead loomed like a dully gleaming cliff of steel. A 'Mech-sized gangway leading aft to a machine shop opened in its base.

Malvina knew the shop had been blasted open to space as well. She ground her teeth. *She must not escape!*

The *Turkina* leapt again. A PPC beam brushed the *Shrike*'s left flank. Electronics screamed.

Malvina jumped, throttled her main forward-thrust jets to full. A spread of rockets sparkled off all over the *Turkina*'s back. Using her targeting computer, she thrust twin green-laser spears into the rear housing of the left-shoulder LRM rack. Molten metal splashed away.

Expecting her opponent to bolt down the tunnel, Malvina ceased firing. She left her throttles wide open, preventing her heat gauge from dropping. *I've got you now,* she thought, unconsciously flexing the clawed right hand of her 'Mech.

When she overtook her prey, heat would not matter.

But instead of diving into blackness, Jana Pryde declutched her gyros and with a pulse of maneuvering jets pitched the *Turkina* ninety degrees back, so that it flew feet-first. To brake she fired the powerful main jump jets on her legs.

Greenfeather's feet hit so hard the enormously strong bulkhead perceptibly flexed. Malvina actually thought her audio pickups caught the ghost of a clang transmitted through the super-thin atmosphere still trapped within the hangar deck.

Flying full-speed, she had no choice but to plunge into the tunnel herself. In her three-sixty vision strip she caught a glimpse of the *Turkina*, its backward knees flexing deeply to absorb the impact. She hoped its structure might fail as she flashed into the passageway.

She fired the retropaks strapped to the *Shrike*'s sides. A kiss from Jana Pryde's PPCs had slagged one of the paired right-hand rockets. Overriding the collective controls, Malvina played the jets individually like a maestro as the machine shop lights sped toward her. Flames lit the passageway in garish flickering blue. If she misjudged by the slimmest sliver she would send Black Rose spinning out of control, bouncing off the steel walls. If she didn't stop in time, she would slam into the shop's after bulkhead.

The *Shrike* flew back into the light. Huge vertical mills

hunched to either side like quarter-sized BattleMechs, interspersed with multiaxial machining centers the size and general shape of hovervans. The path ahead was clear almost to the waiting bulkhead.

Malvina dropped her 'Mech's claws to the deck. They rang, sparked, tore through magnetized plastomer nonskid matting. She applied full downthrust as well as retros. Before her, a lathe with a two-meter-wide chuck stood almost to Black Rose's knee level.

Shrieking like a damned thing, swerving like a downhill skier under Malvina's iron control, the great machine came to a stop with its armored shins less than half a meter from the lathes.

Malvina's whole small body surged in a sigh.

She pivoted the *Shrike* as quickly as she could, applying subtle downthrust to keep her 'Mech's feet from losing their magnetic grip on the deck, which they had deeply scored in twin trails leading from the gangway. Crouched, she waited, weapons trained back down the black passage, should Jana Pryde choose to follow.

Nothing occulted the hangar deck glow. The battleship's metallic asteroid mass hid her enemy totally from her sensors. She had no idea where the *Turkina* was.

A moment longer she paused, breathing heavily. Her whole body was tightened like a finger on a trigger at the point of breaking. Her mind moved rapidly and methodically, taking stock of the damage her Rose had suffered.

To her annoyance she was sure she had got the worse of it. When she recalled the last stored wireframe schematic of Greenfeather it showed substantial weakening of the upper-right front armor on the *Turkina*'s fuselage, and a breach with possible systems damage to its left-shoulder LRM launcher. The battle computer did not think she had disabled either particle cannon despite tearing open the arm.

In return, Malvina had lost a couple of maneuver jets and three of ten LRM tubes. Her frontal-torso and right-leg armor had basically turned to lacy filigree: a good hard puff would blow it away, leaving the *Shrike*'s vitals exposed. One arm-mounted PPC sporadically flickered red in the

HUD, indicating only a single control circuit still functioned. And it was shorting unpredictably.

Grimly Malvina smiled. Drawing upon the wealth of *isorla* taken in the battles since leaving Skye, including the enormous bounty of the victory on Antares, her Black Rose had been restored three times. Now she was a wreck again, held together mainly by her mistress' titanium will.

Hold for me a little longer, girl, she thought. *Then you can rest for a long time.*

She gathered the massive 'Mech and leapt straight up through the roughly circular hull breach overhead. She used her leg jets' full upward thrust to pop out like a cork from a bottle, hoping to spoil her enemy's targeting solution should Jana Pryde be crouched waiting on the outer hull.

Instead she glimpsed the *Turkina*, blue jets spurting upward from its shoulders, running ponderously away along the hull. It flared blue as it crossed the terminator into the full hot glare of Sudeten's sun, and vanished.

"*Flee, then.*" For the first time Malvina broke radio silence—although it was unlikely her enemy heard her, unless one of Jana Pryde's seconds, watching from a craft beyond the Circle of Equals, bounced the message along to her. "*I will catch you, never fear.*"

She fired her own down-jets to kill her upward momentum, so that she hung apparently motionless above the pitted metal planetoid that was the *Emerald Talon*. Slowly, with a great creaking and groaning of protest through her BattleMech's tortured structure, she lowered the ornamental wings to full extension.

A pulse of down-jets; a kiss of upthrust. The magnetic pads on her *Shrike*'s feet engaged the hull with barely a bump. Then firing the down-jets again, she set Black Rose into the fastest run it was capable of, toward the nearest "horizon."

Sudeten's blue-white star rose fifteen degrees to her right. Malvina had her eyes at soft focus, taking in the totality of multiple sensor inputs and the view through her viewscreen as only a trained and skilled MechWarrior could do, seeking any sign of her foe. She guessed Jana Pryde would have put all the room between herself and her pursuer she could before turning to make a stand.

She could not question Jana Pryde's prowess as a Mech-Warrior—or her bravery. Despite the taunts she had thrown in her face, Malvina Hazen knew her enemy was very good indeed. Her insults were meant to provoke Jana Pryde, disrupt her normally keen thinking. As they had.

But if Jana Pryde fought with the fantastic skill and icy fury that exemplified the best of a Falcon warrior, she also fought very conventionally. So Malvina reckoned.

Wrongly.

Blue radiance flared from a ripped-open naval autocannon turret scarcely twenty-five meters to her left. The blackness of its shadow hid the crouching *Turkina*, huge as it was. The gun emplacement's contorted wreckage masked its ferric mass until Jana Pryde loosed all her weaponry at once in a furious alpha strike.

With steel-spring reflexes Malvina jumped, firing back. Tremendous heat sent her fusion reactor into shutdown as rockets, multiple-fragment LB-X slugs, and high-energy particles ripped open her 'Mech's left side.

With a screech of metal pushed beyond all limits the *Shrike*'s left leg came free. The viewscreen's metal frame glowed red from the heat. It was the only light inside the cockpit as Malvina was slammed around in her five-point harness.

Out of control, the Black Rose fell upward-outward from the WarShip, tumbling over and over into infinite night.

32

Galaxy Commander Beckett Malthus felt as if his stomach had gone into free fall. More: he had read somewhere how in Star League times some planets built elevators capable of carrying traffic clear into orbit.

His gut felt as if such an elevator had broken free and was plummeting to catastrophic reentry.

It took all his Jade Falcon will to keep his knees from buckling, though their failure would have no more than made him sway in the microgravity of *Bec de Corbin*'s bridge.

Manas Amirault raised his fists toward the darkened overhead, threw back his head and voiced a wolf-howl of despair.

Only Cynthy seemed unmoved, standing there with her teddy bear draped limply over her crossed arms, watching her captor and foster mother, the self-proclaimed Khan of All Humanity, plunging into interplanetary space in the shattered wreck of her once-proud BattleMech.

*　　*　　*

Though grounded, the SM1 bucked its front end clear of the hard-packed hilltop when it fired a burst from its immense main gun. The yellow flame that ballooned from the muzzle and jetted sideways from the brake was almost as big as the hovertank itself.

Crouched behind the haunch of an empty shop scarcely fifty meters away Rorion winced as the cannon's horrendous overpressure assaulted him. The noise didn't just threaten to implode his eardrums, blast waves slapped his cheeks like invisible palms and threw grit against his face and hands. And worse, into the face of his *patrão*, where he lay wrapped in his greatcoat with Rorion's jacket as a pillow.

Blinking concrete dust from his eyes he hissed over the ringing in his ears, "Quit mumbling to leave you. It won't happen."

He glanced at the small—if only in a relative sense—BattleMech crouched beside them. "It's not as if I must carry your bulk myself, anyway."

The older man scowled and shook his head. The tank destroyer fired again at its unseen target, across the northern fringe of the "civilian" spaceport.

"How—how did she get a BattleMech, anyway?" he asked when the shock wave passed.

"Don't you have better things to think about, old man?" came the voice from the *Piranha*'s loudspeakers. Senna Rodríguez had the modulation turned low, so that the two men could just hear her over the ringing in their ears.

"Under the circumstances," Heinz-Otto von Texeira croaked, "no." His cracked lips grinned briefly before twisting in a grimace.

"I'm broken inside, boy," he told his aide. "I still don't feel much, thank the Holy Spirit. But the pain is coming. . . ."

"I didn't rescue you from that *Dasher* just to lose you, old man," the voice from the machine said. "I said I would get you two out of here. And I will. I am Sea Fox."

"You told us not to trust Clanners," Rorion said.

In his mind he could see the woman's grin, lopsided and cynical. "A contract's a contract, after all."

"So where"—grimace—"*did* you come by a BattleMech?" von Texeira persisted.

"I knew where it was stored," the master merchant said, "having just sold it to the Falcons myself. They currently evaluate the design for a scout and anti-infantry 'Mech."

"And it was still keyed to your neural signature?" Rorion asked.

A rough-road chuckle emerged from the crouching metal humanoid. "Of course not. As I told you, I am Sea Fox."

"Meaning you built in a back door," Rorion said.

Senna said, "Uh-oh. Get ready—"

With no more preamble she picked up both men in her 'Mech's hands. The steel fingers closed about them with remarkable gentleness; for the first time it registered on Rorion that *Rodríguez* was a MechWarrior Bloodname. He had assumed that the MechWarrior rubric was a formality in the trade-focused Sea Fox Clan. But their ever-surprising ally was showing herself quite adept when it came to piloting a BattleMech.

Rorion deftly snagged his jacket as his master was lifted free of it. It got *cold* on this Christ-forgotten world for a hot-blooded Recife boy. . . .

Senna raised up just enough to peer around the curved flank of the building. By craning his neck Rorion could see the SM1 parked where the land dropped away to the landing field.

The ground erupted beneath it in a shattering ripple of explosions. The long-range missile salvo lifted the 50-ton tank destroyer two full meters. The SM1 jerked in midair as a huge ferro-nickel Gauss slug plowed into the starboard cockpit and transverse through the turret root at hypersonic speed. The sonic boom of its arrival was louder than its autocannon.

Stored autocannon ammunition exploded in white flashes that seemed to light the world. The big tank flew to pieces. Senna barely ducked the *Piranha* back down before metal shards, razor-edged and fast as rifle bullets, cracked overhead and clattered like metal hail against the shop's ferrocrete wall.

The SM1 was a pyre of orange flame and black smoke

when the 'Mech straightened to step around the shop. A Point of five conventional infantry in Falcon-painted full-head helmets crouched along the wall of the next building over. They wore green scarves knotted around their thighs and wrists as improvised recognition badges.

The Point commander shouted and pointed. Her four mates raised their laser rifles to aim at the helplessly dangling Spheroid civilians.

A green flash filled Rorion Klimt's world. The beam of Senna's left-arm mounted medium laser barely missed him. It did not miss the Slip Point commander. The whole front of her body simply vanished in the hideous glare of coherent light. She fell backward, arms outflung as if crucified. Her body puffed into yellow flame. She was already a lifeless husk with half her bodily fluids turned to steam.

The Sea Fox–built scout BattleMech sported no fewer than six miniguns along either side of its armored torso. These roared, belching long pale-blue and yellow flames. Their awesome muzzle blasts buffeted Rorion as he flailed at his own head with his jacket, trying to put out hair set alight by the *Piranha*'s laser.

The four Falcon foot soldiers were hosed backward by the ferocious close-range blasts. They fell in pink clouds, leaving great shockingly-bright scarlet smears on the wall behind them.

For a moment all was silent. Probably: all Rorion could hear through the ringing in his ears, now of cathedral-bell majesty, was a tiny musical tinkle as the last arcs of empty brass casings, glittering in the morning sun, fell into ankle-deep pools at the BattleMech's back and sides.

Stomach roiling to the smells of human insides spilled or flash-cooked, stronger even than the stink of his now mostly extinguished hair, Rorion looked around. The monster that had so summarily snuffed the tank destroyer and its two-man crew from existence lumbered straight toward them, up the hill from marshy flats north of the commercial spaceport. Huge explosions, possibly from Arrow IV bombardment missiles, made tall earth-fountains a quarter kilometer behind it.

"Santa merda!" Rorion exclaimed. "Where'd they get an *Atlas*?"

"Isorla," Senna said, ducking between the buildings and peering gingerly around. Rorion winced at the fresh sonic assault from her external speakers: she didn't bother keeping the gain down now. "Probably from you Steiners. The Jade Falcons don't favor them because they're such waddle-butts. They probably kept this one back for homeworld defense."

Rather than the somewhat trite skull with which Mech-Warriors had bedizened the *Atlas'* face, whose shape did strongly suggest it, since the 100-ton BattleMech had first rumbled off the Star League lines half a millennium before, the huge round head was painted in the likeness of Turkina herself. Its blocky upper torso was buff-colored like a jade falcon's breast, the shoulder armatures like emerald feathers. Even at this range—closer than Rorion found comfortable—it was a surprisingly detailed and beautiful paint job.

Gleaming green-paint feathers suddenly blackened, blistered, burned off in a twist of smoke as a blue beam struck the BattleMech repeatedly from its right. The *Atlas* turned to launch a spread of LRMs at a black-and-green painted *Vulture*. Elementals leaping like fleas loosed short-range missiles at the steel titan.

"Who *are* these people?" Rorion asked, as the *Piranha* turned away into the building's cover.

"No idea," said Senna. "The footsloggers I hit were Slips: that's what the green bandannas meant. Evidently they haven't had a chance to paint their faction badges on their machines."

"Who's fighting whom?"

Senna paused to peer around the far end of the cement half cylinder. "Slips and Jesses. Loremaster Buhalin, bless her pointed little head, sent her goons to arrest her rivals—not just troll in you two and murder my boys in the process." Bitterness sizzled in her words. "So to help defend Sudeten against Malvina's locusts she started a civil war. I guess that's the reason for the old expression."

She set the *Piranha* into a purposeful stride. Away from the spaceport, Rorion noted, with mingled relief and alarm. *How are we getting* off *this damned planet?*

"What old expression?" he asked.

"Jade Falcons are stupid."

"That's pithy."

He could sense her shrug. "What do you expect? We're Clan. Kerensky in His wisdom didn't have his scientists breed for wit."

"Where are we going?"

"Away."

"I can see that." He looked at his senior. Von Texeira hung limp in the BattleMech's grip, apparently unconscious. *I* hope *only unconscious,* he thought.

"We have to get the *chefe* to medical care."

"Not at the spaceport," Senna said. "It's shaping up to be a main event. No surprise, I suppose, but I hoped we'd get to my shuttle before fighting overran the port. Not happening."

"But what will we do?"

"Plan B."

"Plan *B*?"

"*Trust* me," Senna said.

With deft blue pulses of her maneuvering retros Khan Jana Pryde braked her massive *Turkina*. It approached a vast free-floating chunk of wreckage. It appeared to be the front half of a military aerodyne DropShip, probably parted from the stern when its power-plant containment failed. It was too distorted to identify the design.

That crazed surat *Malvina must have the Devil's own luck, as the Spheroids say*, Jana thought, carefully scanning the wreckage with sensors and Clan-keen senses. *For her* Shrike *to drift in here was a million-to-one chance, even with all this debris floating nearby*.

The thought brought a certain gratification. Because the bloodfoul's luck had now run out.

Jana hoped to find her rival dead inside her shattered 'Mech. Here at the end of things she felt not just the respect due a Falcon warrior of Malvina's. . . . *Call it mag-*

nificence, she thought. Despite all Malvina's unspeakable crimes, the unforgivable insults she had leveled not just at her khan but at Clan Jade Falcon itself, Jana felt even a tingle of affection for her rival.

You really were the best of us, she thought. *I'd like to credit Turkina's intercession for getting the better of you, but I know it was dumb luck.*

She laughed to herself. *Malthus told me sometimes it's better to be lucky than good.* She wondered what her renegade advisor was doing now. *Probably calculating the next turn of his coat,* she reckoned.

As she orbited the half ship with subtle nudges of her side-jets, Jana found herself thinking of the upheavals Malvina Hazen had tried to wreak in Falcon society toward the end. *I thought I was the radical reformer,* she mused, *but she put me in the shade.*

Might she be right? the khan of Clan Jade Falcon wondered heretically. Perhaps there was merit even to her most extreme notion: allowing the lower castes, honored in word and despised in fact, to aspire to join the warrior aristocracy.

"Look at Malvina herself," Jana said. Her voice sounded loud in her ears. "We're not doing such a grand a job with our breeding and upbringing programs, we Clans, to produce a monster like her."

Fear shivered through her as she maneuvered around the wreck's open end. Malvina Hazen had threatened not just the order of the Clans but humanity itself. Could another like her arise?

Perhaps a radical rethink—

Blue lightning broke her reverie.

≡ 33 ≡

The Casts
Hammarr Commercial Spaceport, Sudeten
Jade Falcon Occupation Zone
3 April 3136

Right beside them the concrete storage structure flew apart as a PPC bolt twisted into it like a plasma drill bit. *"Deus meu!"* Rorion shouted. He could not even hear himself as LRMs roared off around the fleeing *Piranha*.

Real fear filled his breast when he glanced over at his *patrão*. The older man's body flopped apparently lifeless in time to the pounding footsteps of the BattleMech as it ran at terrific speed, darting between buildings and around parked ground vehicles. Their only chance to survive this pursuit was the *Piranha*'s scout-'Mech speed. *Can the* Markgraf *survive the jostling?* Rorion wondered.

The *Thor* had appeared from around the side of a multiple-story stone structure that may have dated from Lyran days as Senna neared the outskirts of The Casts. It instantly fired on the *Piranha*. Rorion had no way of telling which faction the heavy 'Mech belonged to. Possibly it hunted them on purpose. Or perhaps, today on Sudeten, any unknown was an *enemy*.

They raced between storage buildings and semi-improvised

residences, most likely built for freebirths who had no place in the current Clan order—unless Malvina won. Ahead lay heath beneath a light coat of snow. Beyond that rose low hills spiked with conifers. Whether Senna thought she could find shelter among them, the Lyran had no way of knowing.

He was whipsawed cruelly in the steel fist as Senna veered left to avoid a spread of rockets from the *Thor*'s drum-shaped shoulder launcher. Though the *Thor* was fast for a heavy BattleMech, the lithe little scout machine should have been able to show it a clean pair of heels in short order. But it could not outrun rockets, must less particle beams. Senna had to trade speed for breakneck evasion.

The *Piranha* vaulted a hovertruck grounded crosswise in the street. Rorion's head snapped back. Apparently everybody else in Hammarr had gotten the word about the balloon going up before he and von Texeira did. The transport drivers in the seedy but busy spaceport district had all stopped their vehicles where they were, it seemed, and gone running off down the street—whether foreigners going to cover like rabbits or laborers lustily racing off to join the Revolution.

No MechWarrior from a Crusader Clan could have handled the *Piranha* any more skillfully than the master merchant. The jump jets barely hissed; clawed feet scraped paint on top of the truck's box. The 'Mech jolted back down in the street, slamming Rorion's jaws together.

Blue pulsations stitched the sky right overhead. The pursuer's large pulse laser would have ripped apart the *Piranha* and flash-cooked its passengers had Senna proven a whit less expert. Rorion set his aching jaws and made himself not glance at his boss. All he could do was torture himself with his inability to help his margrave. And he needed his wits about him; the situation could shift drastically at any time. It already had half a dozen times today.

A yellow glow grew against the clouds sky to his left. A comet slanted down the sky. Right at the bridge of Rorion's nose.

"Great," he said, his words whipped away by the wind and drowned by the thunder of another near-miss volley from the *Thor*. "Everyone else is shooting at us today. Why not God?"

But it wasn't God. Or if so, He used human proxies. Rorion made out a stub-winged shape tipping the glow. A shot-down aerospace fighter burned in on catastrophic reentry. But still it seemed to be coming right at *him*.

To his horror Senna braked, backpedaling and even firing retro jump-jets to halt the *Piranha*'s forward progress. "No! No!" he shouted, beating the metal fingers with his fists. "We have to get out of the *way*—"

Half a kilometer to the left the blazing fighter struck the planet. A blocky three-story building stood between the impact point and Rorion's horrified eyes. The wreck bounced, blasted through the building's upper half. Hypervelocity compression had superheated the air in front of the craft; it blew the building to pieces like a giant yellow glowing fist.

Tumbling, blazing, breaking apart, the fighter arced high over Rorion's head. Then darkness covered him as the *Piranha*, now stopped, knelt and bent its upper body protectively over the human cargo it clutched to its metal breast.

Hell hit them.

The *Thor* pilot, a second-line MechWarrior from the Jess faction, was locked-in on her quarry. She lined up her PPC sight for the kill. The hurtling aerospace fighter she ignored. A quick check of her battle computer showed it would miss her by three hundred meters.

The dynamic overpressure and thermal effect from the craft's smacking the planet at five kilometers a second did not miss her. Absent the ionizing radiation, they were little less than the effects of a kiloton-range tactical nuke going off at a quarter-klick's distance. Neither heat nor blast was severe enough to disable the 70-ton metal monster. They did however, catch the running giant mid-stride and knock it what von Texeira would have called *ass over teakettle*.

Though her five-point harness kept the garrison Mech-Warrior from serious harm, the jostling of cartwheeling a hundred whole meters and rolling another hundred, through three buildings, tumbled her gyros as thoroughly as it did her BattleMech's.

*   *   *

When the *Piranha* uncoiled, a pair of ground cars abandoned nearby blazed merrily. Rorion coughed, choking on the smoke. His cheeks felt sunburned and his ears rang.

Now he could not prevent himself looking to his master. To his amazement the big man stirred.

"I . . . love . . . a nice . . . vacation," von Texeira muttered. Then his eyes rolled up and his head slumped bonelessly.

Rorion cried out. His voice was drowned by the roar of rocket engines as an aerodyne lander swept down from the sky and flared to a jet-assisted vertical landing on the snow two hundred meters ahead. It hovered, spun, wobbling slightly on its axis. Miniguns snarled, casting tracer streams over Rorion's head. He registered the jaunty orange-and-blue Sea Fox emblem painted on the dark hull. Then he fainted too.

Heat filled the cockpit of Khan Jana Pryde's *Turkina*. Red lights flared in her heads-up display as systems failed.

A great arrowhead of steel crashed through the viewscreen to her left. She yelled in surprise as the *Shrike*'s talon crushed the front of her cockpit. Instrument panels flickered and died as the air rushed out.

"—*caught you*—" a hoarse vindictive voice said in her ear.

Malvina Hazen was not surprised when Jana Pryde came swimming out of the shattered cockpit to meet her. The khan of Clan Jade Falcon was no coward. Not one to wait like a rabbit in a hole to be dug out by a badger.

But if she was brave as a Falcon should be she was also that arrogant. Too arrogant in her moment of triumph to be as suspicious as she ought after the shattered Black Rose, apparently out of control, had conveniently disappeared into a tumbling hunk of wreckage.

Now the two BattleMechs were joined together by Black Rose's locked claw. And Malvina came, indeed, to dig her foe from her hole.

The taller woman wore a form-fitting green-and-yellow pressuresuit over cooling mesh and vest. Malvina's spacesuit was black and silver. Neither was armored to an appreciable degree; a BattleMech was a suit of armor, after all.

Jana Pryde was long and strong. Malvina was quick as a weasel. She snatched the laser pistol from Jana Pryde's grasp as it loosed a futile red blast into the void.

Then holding it before the faceplate of her enemy's pressuresuit Malvina Hazen crushed the weapon in her prosthetic hand. Which inside its glove was black as the space around them.

Floating free of the immobilized BattleMechs, the two warrior women grappled inside the shadowy half hull. Jana Pryde's strength told first. She pinioned Malvina's legs with her own, forced her arms to her sides. Futilely Malvina tried to head-butt her; Jana Pryde merely hugged her close with her chin on top of Malvina's pressure-hooded head. Had they not been forced to wear faceplates it would have exposed her throat to the madwoman's sharp teeth.

As it was, the khan held her foe helpless.

Malvina struggled wildly to break free. "And so it ends," Jana Pryde murmured, through jaws tight-shut to prevent Malvina's breaking them with a quick head bob. "You might have been a worthy successor. But you could not wait."

Malvina strained her head upward. Jana Pryde locked an arm around her throat, flowed behind her, caught her in a headlock.

"Good-bye, little Hazen," Jana Pryde said, twisting the smaller woman's head to break her neck. "Your Bloodline is overdue for a Reaving."

Malicious laughter rang in her ears. A hand reached up, caught her arm in a grip like an elemental battlesuit's, effortlessly peeled it from Malvina's throat. Jana Pryde grunted more in surprise than pain as the prosthetic arm twisted savagely, torquing her elbow from its socket. Malvina's legs scissored open; Jana's could not hold them. Malvina squirmed round and clamped her legs about her opponent's waist.

"I but toyed with you," Malvina said over their private channel, *"to make your failure sting the worse."*

Her flesh-and-blood hand seized her foe's right biceps. Her prosthetic reached for the faceplate of Jana Pryde's pressuresuit.

Pain exploded in her left side. Jana Pryde had drawn a knife left-handed and stabbed her. Unfortunately for Jana, the blade was vertical in relation to Malvina's ribs and could not slide easily between. Nor could Jana Pryde get leverage in freefall to punch the blade through.

The faceplate came away in Malvina's artificial hand. Jana Pryde's last surprised shout followed, condensing in a white cloud. Releasing her knife hilt she covered her mouth with her functioning gloved hand. It was a futile gesture. "Farewell, Jade Falcon khan," Malvina said in a musical, hateful voice. "The Chingis Khan has taken your place."

As Jana Pryde, once khan, stared at her enemy with eyes beginning to redden as capillaries burst within, Malvina Hazen reached up and opened her own faceplate. She pressed her lips against Jana's mouth in a deep kiss.

Then Malvina backed away. Her prosthetic arm forced her faceplate closed against the one-atmosphere rush of escaping air, sealed it again. Behind it she was laughing. Breaking capillaries had brought a maidenly flush to her cheeks.

Jana Pryde struggled to reseal her own helmet with her good arm. Malvina caught and held it with her prosthetic.

With her other hand she pressed something into Jana's glove. Through reddening vision Jana Pryde saw it was a black rose with a curled stem. Little splinters of ice drawn in the vacuum from its cells and flash frozen sparkled on the still-faultless bloom.

The fallen khan fought for air. But there was none. She weakened, weakened . . .

Laughing, Malvina unwound her legs from around Jana Pryde's waist. Drawing her knees to her chest she put her boot soles against the other woman's stomach and pushed.

The thrust sent Malvina backward deeper into the wreck. It propelled the suffocating Jana Pryde into open space, tumbling over and over toward Sudeten's distant sun, the black rose still clutched to her breast.

$\equiv$ 34 $\equiv$

Jade Falcon DropShip **Bec de Corbin**
Approaching Sudeten Orbit
Jade Falcon Occupation Zone
4 April 3136

Spurning assistance from solicitous naval crew, Malvina emerged from the shuttle onto the hangar deck of *Bec de Corbin*. Cynthy ran wordlessly toward her, wrapped her arms around her waist and buried her small face beneath Malvina's breasts. Wincing slightly at the pressure on her knife wound, in bandages beneath the midnight-black uniform she had donned in the rescue craft, Malvina hugged her back and kissed the top of her blond head. Then she straightened to face Beckett Malthus and Galaxy Commander Manas Amirault of Clan Hell's Horses.

"Loremaster Julia Buhalin has acknowledged the correctness of your victory in your Trial of Possession, my Khan," Malthus said gravely. "She reports all fighting has ceased in Hammarr and worldwide. Sudeten awaits you, my Khan."

"Does she follow my instructions?"

"To receive you in the Falcon's Perch in Hammarr rather than at the Eyrie? Indeed she does. Although she seems puzzled."

"Let her puzzle," Malvina said, "so long as she obeys."

Malthus cocked an eyebrow. "Be cautious of letting her hear you speak so, my Khan. Not even a Khan has authority to command a loremaster."

For a moment Malvina's eyes narrowed. Then they relaxed. She laughed.

"We shall soon see what authority the Chingis Khan has over a Clan loremaster," she said.

Manas Amirault frowned. "Surely you would not trespass upon a loremaster's prerogatives, Malvina Hazen?"

"I do as I please!" she flared. He stiffened. From a Falcon such an outburst would have drawn challenge if not immediate attack. But he only looked puzzled. *Perhaps it is a cultural thing,* she thought. Perhaps it was not. She made herself smile. *I have use for this one,* she thought. *And soon.* "I have run roughshod over all manner of Clan traditions," she said, "no few at your suggestion. Why hold back now?"

He continued to look troubled. She reached up to briefly stroke his tanned cheek. "Worry less, Manas Amirault. I have promised you glorious conquest. Have I not delivered Sudeten?"

She turned to take in the others—warriors of Falcon and Horse, naval personnel, technicians—assembled on the brightly lit deck.

"Have I not delivered Clan Jade Falcon to you, as I have promised?"

"All hail Chingis Khan!" Malthus cried. His voice rang throughout the deck like a tolling bell. Manas Amirault joined, and then the others. Only Cynthy, clinging wide-eyed to Malvina's hips, stayed silent.

When the cheering died away Malvina smiled. "Thank you," she said—in itself as uncharacteristic as apology. "You have all well earned your part in this glorious victory. And in what is to come!"

She turned to Malthus. "I wish to speak to Star Admiral Dolphus Binetti in my compartment. Have the connection made."

"At once, my Khan." Malthus turned to summon a technician. The ship was, after all, still nominally attached to his command.

Malvina beckoned the pair of technician-class minders who had escorted Cynthy here. Gently prying loose the girl's arms, Malvina knelt and took her face in her hands, the black and the pale. "There are things I must do now, child. I will see you soon."

Cynthy blinked several times. She nodded. Malvina smiled and kissed her cheek, then rose as the minders in their turquoise jumpsuits took her in hand and led her out.

"I would consult with you in private, Galaxy Commander Manas Amirault," Malvina said. "Please join me in my compartment in fifteen minutes."

She trailed flesh fingers across his cheek as she walked past and out.

In the cold, in the dark, Star Admiral Dolphus Binetti floated alone.

I die, he thought.

Not fast enough, old man, said a different voice of his thoughts. That was true enough: he had been slammed into a bulkhead of his CIC by the prodigious blast wave of a ship-killing missile, transmitted through the fabric of *Emerald Talon* herself. It broke him up severely inside, so that he must struggle to retain consciousness during the last of the space battle. As he drifted in and out of awareness, another giant missile exploded amidships, close enough to spall fragments from the bulkhead that had killed the rest of his command staff.

He had established communication with a backup command center—the flying bridge in the outer hull, which ironically survived unscathed. By that point little remained to do: Galaxy Commander Malvina Hazen had challenged Khan Jana Pryde, and the *Emerald Talon* was designated their dueling grounds. The fight was over for the once-mighty WarShip. She had covered herself with glory; and even if Binetti was uncertain of the rightness of the cause in which he fought, it had never been his place to question commands. He and his crew had served Turkina bravely and well.

Malvina Hazen's victory meant she would certainly be

khan of Clan Jade Falcon now. That made all right. *Quineg?*

Now her face appeared in flat projection, pale and aglow in darkness broken by a handful of blackout lights the color of dying suns. No air remained in the violated command center; he must strain to hear his superior's whisper over crackling star-song and the buzz of energy weapons as a few diehards continued to fight in space nearby through his pressure-helmet speaker.

What she said horrified him.

Yet that final directive exalted him as well. For good or ill *Emerald Talon*, and he himself, would win prominent place in the Remembrance of Clan Jade Falcon.

The corpse of a young yeoman, eyes bugged out and blackened tongue protruding from his green-mottled face, floated through the beautiful face of Malvina Hazen. Dolphus Binetti recoiled.

"Admiral?" His khan's voice was actually solicitous.

That snapped him to: the last thing he could abide was *pity* from his khan. And what he experienced now was indeed the *last thing*.

The dead body had floated from his vision's field.

He forced his gloved hand to snap to his helmeted brow in a machine-precise salute. It sent pain lancing up his right side. The pain was good: it helped him focus.

"I hear your command! I obey."

She smiled. *"I knew I could count upon you, faithful Dolphus Binetti,"* she said. *"You have always done your Bloodname great honor. Out."*

The image vanished. The screen darkened, plunging the death-filled compartment back into deepest gloom. Or was that only behind his eyes?

Ignoring fresh agony, he twisted his body until he could grasp a handhold and pull himself to a console. He had orders of his own to give.

The first was Abandon Ship. He owed his surviving men and women, however few, that much. His khan had not forbidden it.

The second he would key in himself, however sorely the

concentration cost him. Then, truly alone in a way few Falcons ever were, he would initiate the sequence to wake the still-functional main drives to carry him with the ancient WarShip *Emerald Talon* on her final sortie.

"You're awake," Rorion Klimt said.

Cocooned within the bed in *Gypsy Tailwind*'s sickbay, Heinz-Otto von Texeira groaned.

"Evidently you lacked the simple human decency to let me die back there on Sudeten."

Rorion felt a stab of encouragement. *The old man has enough of his fabled wits about him to know we're in space and under way.* He shrugged.

"Lack of basic decency's a useful trait in a Loki operative, as you no doubt remember. It's often said to be one in business as well, not that I'll ever know."

"Not the way *I* do business," von Texeira grumbled.

"We're Clan," said a voice from the entryway. "We have no sense of decency anyway. So I wouldn't know, myself."

Rorion rose. "Master Merchant."

She showed him a lifted eyebrow and came into the small compartment. "Sit down. No need for Spheroid formality here, and our Clan rituals mean even less to you than they do to me."

"A gentleman rises when a lady enters the room, Master Merchant."

"We've been through that routine before."

He sat. The magnetic strip in the seat of his burnt-orange shipsuit resealed itself to the chair.

"Rorion, my boy," von Texeira said from the bed.

Rorion looked to him. He still had little color save gray in his cheeks, which in one-gee boost looked puffy.

"Your glorified valet listens, my lord."

"Have you any thought for the future?" von Texeira asked.

Rorion had a keenly developed danger sense. One either got one or lived out the old saw about there being no old, bold Lokis. Alarm began to tingle his nerves and rumble in his belly, for no reason his conscious mind could identify.

"I suppose I'll continue serving *a família* von Texeira zu Mannstein, as my forebears have for generations. Perhaps one day when I'm old and stout as . . . *ahem* . . . certain parties who need not be named, I shall become head of security. If my incompetence on this assignment doesn't cause the *Markgraf* to discharge—"

"Oh, stuff that noise!" von Texeira roared.

"Steady, Margrave," Senna said. "If you make too much racket, Chief Medical Technician Ostia will come and nag me. Neither of us wants that, I promise."

Von Texeira cast her a grumpy look. She leaned her rump against a counter and crossed her arms. She smiled blithely back.

"If there has been any incompetence it has been mine," von Texeira said. "And I have made as complete a goat-sc— that is, muddle—of this mission as is humanly possible. It is a debacle. I'll be lucky if the archon lets me keep my title."

"Nonsense," Senna said. "Your mission was doomed from the get-go—involving, as it did, talking sense into Jade Falcons. The only Falcon with wit enough to listen went and got herself killed—not omitting to leave affairs of state in the hands of a nitwit exemplary even by JF standards. Your precious archon gave you a mighty screwing-over, if you'll forgive my assault on your virgin ears. And finally, as may one day soon become a catchphrase throughout human space: Malvina happened."

Rorion raised and lowered his eyebrows. "And there you have it," he said.

"And where does that leave us?" asked von Texeira.

"Running like bunnies," Senna said cheerfully, "for the nadir jump point. Leaving all those stirred-up Jade Falcons converging on Sudeten from zenith and pirate points far behind us. That's another great thing about not being Diamond Sharks anymore: no more Crusader-for-brains nonsense about gallant last stands and hoping our conquerors offer us hegira. *She who turns and runs away, lives to trade another day*, the saying goes."

"You could have run away and left us."

"I could," she said with a nod, "if Sea Fox honor let me

break a contract. That and the fact I reckoned your family might make trouble about paying off the balance if I failed to deliver you back to them in at least breathing condition."

She sighed. "And I owe a debt for Nestah and Petah. I could only discharge it in part. But I laid a good down payment on those treacherous Falcon bastards."

"Clan honor again?" Rorion asked.

"*My* honor. But yes, Rorion, I am Sea Fox. I may be a rowdy renegade even by Sea Fox standards, but I take my birthright and my Bloodname as seriously as any. And we Foxes do not survive in the company of our snarling pack-predator fellow Clans by letting them impose on us. Costs *will be* exacted. Time is long. And should I fall, my Aimag or even my Khanate will honor my debt to Turkina's nasty hatchlings."

"I would applaud, lady," von Texeira, "but my hands seem to be tied."

"For your own good. Or mine, anyway; my chief medtech hates to lose a patient."

She tipped her head and studied them through narrowed green eyes. "So where do I deposit you two?"

"Can you slip back across the border into the Commonwealth?"

Senna's crest bobbed to laughter. "Do you *really* want to imply that any Jade Falcon blockade could keep a Sea Fox from going where she will? *Or* your square-headed LCAF Navy?"

"Point taken," von Texeira said. "I am in poor shape to fight a trial, I fear."

"Once more: where do you want to go?"

"The nearest Steiner-held world will serve splendidly. But you're only going to drop off Rorion. I should like to accompany you on your travels for a while, if you will graciously permit."

"What?" said Rorion, after a moment's struggle for air.

"If you'll graciously pay, I'll ferry you all over the galaxy," Senna said. "Your surplus mass will of course call for a fairly steep surcharge."

"*Certo.*"

"Wait," Rorion said. "Where am *I* going?"

"Back home," von Texeira said, "to assume your new duties."

"What duties? I'm supposed to take care of you!"

"It is time you accepted the burdens of adulthood. Specifically, becoming a trader in your own right, and being groomed to succeed me as chief executive officer of Recife Spice and Liquors."

"What?"

"I have a confession to make, Rorion," von Texeira said gravely. "You are my son."

Rorion dropped his chin to his clavicle and tightly crossed his arms beneath it. He scowled blackly.

"I figured that out when I was nine," he said. "I'm not just a simple, thick-headed serving lad, you know. Also, Mom told me when I was thirteen."

Von Texeira rolled his eyes. "Women," he said. Then he looked in alarm at Senna.

"Inner Sphere women, that is. Present company naturally excepted."

"Sisterhood is powerful, Margrave," Senna said silkily. "But where do *you* intend to go? Or for me to take you?"

"Actually, wherever your normal rounds would take you next will serve splendidly," von Texeira said. "I wish to expand my horizons. And observe Sea Fox trading methods firsthand, unless that's a Clan secret?"

"If even *you* think you can beat us at our own game, you are most welcome to try, Margrave."

"Wait," Rorion said. "Wait."

His elders ignored him. "Don't you worry about your company," Senna asked, "not to mention your place in it?"

"Don Leopoldo will continue to do a workmanlike, if utterly unimaginative, job as CEO pro tem," von Texeira said. "As President for Life, Mamãe Luci will ensure that nothing dire befalls the company, least of all that *a família* lose control. Indeed, on my return I suspect she will take pains to reinstate me as CEO. If nothing else, she'll be well-pleased at being spared the prospect of poor Emilião running the company onto the reefs. And my first-born"—this with a meaningful glance at Rorion, who paled noticeably—"will be ecstatic that the cup will pass from his lips."

The tip of his tongue protruded slightly between bearded lips as he pondered. "Indeed, I think Archon Melissa herself will see fit to introduce my boy Emilião to Tharkad's top holovid producers. *Especially* once I blackmail her for double-dealing by letting loose that damned assault across the frontier. My fellow Lyran merchant princes may not be united in their love for me, but we do tend to pull together when the sovereign trifles with one of us."

"Blackmail is such an ugly word," Rorion murmured.

"I don't know. I've always thought it quite euphonious, myself."

"What of your wife?" asked Senna with half a smile.

"Dona Irmagilda will give birth to an entire brood of velociraptors," von Texeira said with a certain gloomy satisfaction.

"Which, given she's a San Luca, is no great stretch, genetically speaking," Rorion rallied enough to say.

"Indeed. She'll rage and screech and do an extraordinary amount of damage to the bric-a-brac. Which, in the fullness of time, I shall be called upon to replace at extortionate prices. Then she'll undoubtedly prevail upon her uncle Vittore, reigning *patrão* of the San Luca clan, to dispatch a team of assassins after me."

"See?" Rorion said, with the manner of a drowning man spying a rope in the water. "You'll need me to protect you against the San Luca bravos!"

"Not at all," his father said smugly. "I trust our captain and her doughty Fox crew to see to the safety of their high-paying passenger."

"You want *me* to cull *your* Spheroid gene pool of some Recifeiro thugs?" Senna asked. "Ah, well. Genetic hygiene is genetic hygiene. But won't these San Lucas declare vendetta against your family?"

"No," von Texeira said. "And there's the beauty of it all: their wrath, on behalf of Irmagilda's soiled honor, will focus tightly upon yours most truly. Without my substantial person on hand upon whom to wreak their vengeance, they won't confront the von Texeiras directly. Not even a dead-drunk San Luca who has just found his favorite mistress disporting with a coachman would dare cross Mamãe Luci."

"Word," said Rorion.

"In a year, perhaps two, my lady wife's righteous wrath at my 'cheating' her son will subside. She'll even repent setting murderers on my trail and cajole her uncle Vito to recall them. Should any survive."

"Unlikely. And junior here?" asked Senna with a nod toward Rorion.

"It will come as no surprise to Mamãe Luci that he's my son," von Texeira said.

"Mamãe Luci knows everything," Rorion agreed.

"Just so. And she knows that you're a devilishly capable young man. Taken aback as she may be at first—especially when the San Lucas puff and bluster and threaten war—she'll soon see that you're my ideal successor. Especially considering the alternatives."

"I believe she characterizes me as 'flighty and irresponsible,' " Rorion said hopefully.

Von Texeira beamed. "The very words she used to describe me when I was your age!"

Rorion looked at him. "I'm doomed?"

"Utterly."

Rorion raised his ashen face toward the overhead. *"No!"* His cry went on and on.

35

Jade Falcon DropShip **Bec de Corbin**
Approaching Sudeten Orbit
Jade Falcon Occupation Zone
4 April 3136

Their lovemaking was fierce and protracted. When it was done, Malvina Hazen and Manas Amirault broke apart to lie sprawled on the bunk in Malvina's small compartment onboard the *Bec de Corbin*, held fast by one-gee deceleration. They breathed heavily, bodies glistening with sweat in the muted yellow lamp glow.

Malvina glanced toward the amber numerals of the wall chron. Then she reached to the side table, leaning over the Hell's Horses Galaxy commander, who lay supine with his hands laced behind his head and his horsetail topknot laid across the rumpled damp pillow. Her bare breasts dangled in his face. He smiled and took hold of one.

Malvina pulled a single black rose from a round zero-gee vase on the table. The memory-synthetic membrane slid like enfolding lips down its twisted stem, flowing about thorns, to heal itself when the cut end sprang free.

She absently slapped Manas' hand aside as she sat back down, cross-legged, by his head. "Not now," she said. "Much as I admire your powers of recovery."

The frown that stamped itself on his handsome face softened and flowed to a grin. "I cannot stay angry with you, Malvina."

"No," she said. "You can't."

Smiling, she handed him the rose. He looked puzzled, as if not entirely sure what it was. Then his bright-white teeth shone from his dark-tanned face in a smile.

Malvina clicked the remote control she had fetched. An image materialized above the small holostage the *Bec*'s crew had placed past the foot of the bed: a marble of stirred blue and white.

"Sudeten?" Manas asked.

"*Aff*. The view ahead of this very ship. Now hush, and watch."

The image changed to the grievously scarred *Emerald Talon*, shown from "above" and astern, so that the great cigar form was foreshortened against the clouded backdrop of the world that filled the projection.

"Your Star Admiral Dolphus Binetti should be careful," Manas Amirault said thoughtfully. He took an apple from a fruit basket set on the deck beside the bed, bit into it with perfect Clan teeth. "If he does not change course he risks brushing the outer atmosphere."

He may have been no deep thinker, nor particularly knowledgeable of orbital mechanics. But he had the grasp of military operations required of a successful Galaxy commander. He understood the perils facing a WarShip that strayed too deep into a planet's gravity well.

"He is most careful indeed," Malvina Hazen said. "The honor of his Bloodname depends upon it."

The long, wiry-muscled man beside her relaxed slightly. But his keen features continued to harbor creases of concern.

The projection now showed a sprawl of city, snow-dappled gray, from perhaps three kilometers up. "Hammarr," Malvina said. "I have instructed aerospace fighters to overfly and observe."

The viewpoint became the broad plaza across from the spiny pile of the Falcon's Perch. Crowds milled before it, laborers and technicians mingling in an explosion of colors.

A pair of *Spirit* BattleMechs kept watch over them, as did a few mixed Points of armored elementals and conventional infantry. The crowd's mood struck Malvina as apprehensive yet exultant. The security forces seemed mostly tense.

She leaned forward. The projection shine played across features drawn taut as the string of an ancient steppe nomad's composite bow.

"Now watch," she breathed.

Sunlight falling through colored-glass panels in the tower soaring overhead lit the Grand Council Hall of the Falcon's Perch in dim polychrome. It turned the gaudy garb of the Falcon warriors gathered there a strange motley.

Staff in hand, Loremaster Julia Buhalin stood a few steps behind the podium in her full robes of office. Before her the survivors of the Slip and Jess factions stood or sat in distinct clumps as far apart as the chamber's dimensions allowed.

What is mad Malvina thinking? she wondered. She made herself amend it instantly to *Malvina Hazen.* Much as she despised the interloper, the renegade Galaxy commander had won the khanship fairly—on terms approved by the loremaster herself.

I must get used to the taste of that name in my mouth, she thought bitterly. She was safe, of course; even one so lost to proper behavior as Malvina would never dare act against her. Or Clan Jade Falcon would simply rise in revolt.

Let her feel the sting of the precedent she set, Julia Buhalin thought. Her full lips smiled.

An aide approached, still wearing the green Slip faction brassard. Julia would have to reprove her for that later.

"Yes?"

"Excellency," the warrior said, "planetary defense reports that the WarShip *Emerald Talon* has entered the atmosphere of Sudeten."

Julia Buhalin stared at her without comprehension. A murmur drew her eyes to the crowd. Upraised arms sent them skyward.

In a panel depicting the visage of Elizabeth Hazen a small yellow sun had appeared.

A yellow corona appeared around the *Emerald Talon*'s prow. In an instant it engulfed the whole huge ship. A bow wave of light blazed out around it.

"But a WarShip is not streamlined to enter atmosphere!" exclaimed Manas Amirault. Even as he spoke he saw the tremendous mass begin to break into pieces under stresses it had never been designed to endure.

"No," Malvina said. Her smile was mad wide. Her eyes shone like stars. "It isn't."

Again they saw projected the crowds gathered in Falcon's Way before the Perch. Someone pointed up into the sky toward the east. The viewpoint swung that way. This was clearly a news broadcast: the discreet green Jade Falcon Information Service logo was tucked at the bottom of the display.

For a moment Malvina saw nothing unusual. Then high up a yellow glow began to spread like a stain through a great fluffy mass of cumulus.

The cloud began to boil. The light grew brighter. Then an elongated mass thrust through, blazing like a meteor. It swelled rapidly, trailing a thick white contrail that writhed as if braided of vast serpents.

"Malvina!" Manas Amirault exclaimed, sitting up in alarm. "What is this?"

Impossibly her smile widened. She leaned into the hideous yellow radiance cast by the projection.

"Judgment," she said.

In its screaming descent the *Emerald Talon* broke into three primary sections. Inertia kept them close together on their downward trajectory. Lesser fragments flared bright and burned up like meteorites. But even the terrific heat could make little impression upon 1.2 million tons of mass.

The incandescent compressed air mass driven before the *Emerald Talon* struck the Perch like a bomb. As the battleship filled the sky the burning oxygen splashed across the plaza. Unprotected humans flared into momentary flame and vanished in a tidal wave of brilliance. Malvina saw a *Spirit* teetering, paint blistering, fuselage and metal limbs beginning to glow red before it was swallowed up.

Then the three main fragments of the great ship hit the heart of Hammarr like a close-grouped charge of shot.

The image went black. For a moment nothing showed above the stage. Then appeared a view from Sudeten orbit, just far enough to show the whole planet as a globe.

A dazzling white beacon shone from the midst of the southern landmass. White clouds rippled away from it like smoke.

"No," whispered Galaxy Commander Manas Amirault.

"Khan Malvina Hazen, Bridge," a brisk male voice said from a wall speaker.

"Bridge, Malvina Hazen," she said. "Speak."

"Our sensors report that the Jade Falcon Naval Reserve WarShip Emerald Talon *has suffered catastrophic reentry into the atmosphere of Sudeten. Impact point is calculated at Hammarr center, at approximately the coordinates of the Falcon's Perch."*

"Acknowledged," Malvina said. "Chingis Khan out."

A fiery globe rose from the surface. It sucked clouds up about it, transforming itself to a white mushroom.

"How could Dolphus Binetti do such a thing?" asked Manas Amirault as if his throat had swollen half-shut.

"Because I ordered him to," Malvina said breathlessly. "He was dying. His ship was dying. I offered him one final chance at history."

She jumped astraddle her partner. Her hand reached below her round-muscled buttock to find him. The artificial arm snaked round his neck.

"You grabbed for me before," she breathed into his neck. "Are you still in the mood? I want you now."

He threw her away from him with a cry of shame.

She fell through the image of the violated planet to slam against the bulkhead with her heels in the air. In an second she sprang into a crouch. Her eyes flamed at him from the midst of the projected globe. The parti-colored lasers painted pictures of devastation upon her bare belly and breasts.

"You dare?" she snarled.

"*You* dare?" he asked back. "You have destroyed a city!"

"It was mine to destroy! I am khan of Clan Jade Falcon. I am khan of all humankind!"

"But remember Edo! Remember Turtle Bay!"

"I do. I meant this lesson to eclipse that one. As it has." Strangely, debate had calmed her. The murderous rage had faded from her eyes. Her tone was reasonable now.

Almost.

"But Clan Smoke Jaguar was destroyed."

"By the Spheroids. They were weak. That was why they bombarded Edo from space—in angry acknowledgment of their weakness. I have burned Hammarr out of strength."

She gestured toward her naked body. "I have lit a bonfire to commemorate our triumph. Let the other Clans—and the puling Republic of the Sphere—look on and despair."

"But such wanton murder—" His face was drawn in horror. "Of your own! *Your own people!*"

"They defied me," she said. "Worse, when Sudeten was threatened by invasion, they fell to fighting one another like Spheroids in a tavern brawl. The Jade Falcon gene pool has languished long in need of cleansing. Now I Reave it with fire. Can you not see the glory?"

"No!" He jumped from the bed and began searching for his uniform, which he had discarded in haste shortly after entering the compartment. "I see—"

He shook his head. His black topknot whipped his bare, muscular shoulders. "I—see evil."

Malvina's expression was almost hurt. "But this is the Mongol doctrine. It is what brought you to the Falcon occupation zone, united your destiny to mine."

Again he shook his head, like a child refusing to go to bed. He still gripped the twisted black rose in his left hand as if unaware he did so. A drop of blood fell from his fist. One of the thorns had pierced his palm without him noticing.

"No. It was a parody of the true Mongol Way you practiced. We came to teach you the true Way: of the tactical doctrine, of the style of life Kerensky really meant his children to lead. And to steer you away from the false path you had strayed upon.

"Our Clan, Hell's Horses, had lost its purpose. We hoped to blend our deeper understanding of the ancient ways with the Crusading fire that burned within you. But never such a fire as *that*."

Her laughter was wicked silver music. "How can you set the cosmos alight if you scruple to burn a world?"

"How can I have been so blind?" he said. "You are lost to honor; lost to the Clan way. I pity you."

He stooped, caught up his brown-and-khaki whipcord trousers, straightened with them hanging from a dark hand. "I must ask to use your communicator, Galaxy Commander Malvina Hazen," he said formally. "I must inform my people: we withdraw to the Hell's Horses occupation zone at once."

"I challenge you," she said.

He stared at her as if she had spoken in some old tongue dead before the dawn of space travel. "What did you say?"

"I challenge you," she said, still crouched, naked and feral and clothed in desolation. "I, Malvina Hazen, Khan of Clan Jade Falcon, Chingis Khan, challenge you, Galaxy Commander Manas Amirault, to a Trial of Possession: of the Mongol doctrine, of Fire Horse Galaxy."

She stood erect, seeming to rise from the globe like a legendary sea-goddess from surf. "I bid myself as you see me. How will you defend?"

He only shook his head. "This is madness. I cannot—"

"But I can!" Like a leopardess she sprang. Once more she caught him around the waist with her legs, the white one and the black. Her hands clutched for his throat.

He dropped the rose, grabbed her forearms and held her off. "Your strength cannot match mine, Malvina Hazen," he said. "I permit you to unsay your challenge, if you allow us to withdraw unhindered."

Her hair, pale and unbound, whipped his face as she struggled. Her efforts were futile. His hands gripped her wrists, one flesh and bone, the other steel and polymer, like bands of iron.

Then she quit thrashing and smiled sweetly through the hair curtain hanging in her face. "You have no conception of my strength, Manas Amirault."

Her black prosthetic arm twisted in his grasp so savagely his thumb broke with an audible crack. He might have cried out then, in surprise if not pain. But Malvina's black ankle locked her white leg behind his back. Servomechanisms began to tighten it inexorably around his rib cage.

The breath was crushed from his body in a voiceless scream. She used the distraction to break her natural hand free. She caught his wrists in turn.

He writhed. Now it was he who could not break free. Her black hand closed on his wrist until the bones squealed and grated together. All this time he could draw no breath; her false leg continued to compress his ribs. Ominous cracking noises issued from his chest.

He tried to head-butt her. She lowered her face and took it on the crown. His noble nose flattened itself against the curve of her skull. He reared his head back, eyes rolling like a horse about to bolt. Blood gushing from his nostrils made matted red streaks in her near-white hair.

She laughed and squeezed harder. The veins stood out from his neck. His mouth gaped in a rictus of silent agony.

He plunged forward against the bulkhead, seeking to crush her with his weight. She grunted and took the blow. It was already too late: he had been too long without air. The vertebrae of his lower spine were beginning to displace beneath the relentless pressure of Malvina's black prosthetic leg.

He levered down his head. His brown eyes met hers with an unvoiceable plea.

She smiled and released the horrible grip of her black hand. His own hung like a wilted flower from his crushed wrist. Nonetheless hope flared in his eyes.

Malvina pressed her mouth to his in a fierce and lingering kiss. Then she seized his long topknot with her black hand and broke his neck with a single pull.

His body collapsed beneath her. She shuddered and cried out in ecstasy as she felt life flee him.

For a moment she lay sprawled across his unmoving torso. His skin felt waxen, already oddly cool. Then she rose, shook back the dripping tangle of her hair, went to pick up the rose he had let fall. She placed it on his muscular broad chest and crossed his unresisting hands across it. Then she stooped to shut his eyes with gentle strokes of her thumbs. Lightly she kissed both lids.

Then she stalked to the wall communicator with scarlet rivulets running down her marble-white breasts.

"Bridge, Khan Malvina Hazen," she said. "Send a crew to my quarters at once. There is a mess that requires cleanup."

When the cries of *Hail, Malvina Hazen! Hail, Chingis Khan* had died away on the flying bridge, Beckett Malthus alone stood unmoving, staring at her as from the bottom of a pit.

"What have you done?" he asked.

"Clear the bridge," Malvina said. The crew and staff, Hell's Horses as well as her own Falcons, obliged without question. The *Bec de Corbin*, after all, was really run from the CIC at its core. Their cheeks were still pink with triumph, and they chattered like songbirds.

The great viewscreen showed the blackness of space and Sudeten merely a bigger, brighter star among the multitudes, as well as floating holodisplays showing various aspects of the aftermath of the *Emerald Talon*'s final ride around and above the planet's surface. When they were alone she said, "What was necessary."

For one of the few times in his life he could find nothing to say.

Malvina moved to a console where two zero-gee vases sat clamped with instant-adhering patches—a precaution against violent maneuvers, since the DropShip was decelerating at one gravity on its approach to Sudeten. A single black rose sprouted from each.

She drew one out. Its stem was curled like a comma.

She flowed to Malthus like fog. Taking one of his great hands in her tiny one, she pressed the rose upon him. "You served Jana Pryde well until she cast you aside," she said. "You have served me well as I rose to seize control of Clan Jade Falcon. Now you shall serve me as khan of our Clan— and beyond!"

So saying she seized the lapel of his jacket and drew him down to kiss him on the lips. Then she released him.

The door to the flying bridge stood open. Two laborer women stood there with Cynthy standing between, clutching Burton Bear to the breast of her white-trimmed black dress. At a gesture from Malvina, the girl came forward. Her attendants remained in the corridor outside.

"You may leave us now, Bec Malthus," Malvina said, smiling and kneeling with her arms spread to embrace the girl, who ran to her.

Malthus allowed himself a thunderous frown. Malvina just smiled at him, slowly, over the girl's shoulder.

He turned on his heel and left.

Having got a look at the Galaxy commander's expression, the two laborers fled down the corridor before him as fast as they could without indecorum. He walked at a deliberate pace. It felt to him as if the ship—his ship!— were decelerating at two gravities instead of one.

She dismissed me like a mere laborer! he raged inwardly. *On my own ship! Is this what I have become, her lackey? I am Jade Falcon!* He threw the rose to the runner at his feet, raised his boot to crush it. And froze.

Aberrant as it was, his nature remained that of a Falcon warrior decanted. As such, it defined mercurial. And as quickly as he reminded himself of his own lofty heritage, his Bloodright, his anger turned to cold, sick despair that drained the strength from his knees. He lowered his foot and fought to keep from swaying.

I am Jade Falcon. The simple proud statement of fact rang horribly hollow in his brain. He had just helped inflict upon his Clan a wound greater than any ever dealt it by a foe. Not even Tukayyid could compare with the desolation of this day.

He did not ask himself what he had done: that was horribly clear, the moreso to a man who prized himself upon being a supreme realist. But he asked himself what it was that Malvina Hazen had become.

To ask was to answer.

After a lifetime, itself long for a Clan warrior, of cynical observation and appraisal of his kin and kind, there was one value he had always shared with the most unquestioning Jade Falcon zealot: that compassion was perversion and mercy a crime, and that the weak must be culled for the betterment of Clan and race. But this hour, watching the dome of white fire rise where once the capital of the Falcon zone had stood, some limit had been reached. Some cold bulwark he and every Falcon was taught from birth to erect against certain human feelings had been burned through by the sunlike heat of the *Talon*'s fall.

Now emotion flooded him. *Spheroid* emotions, which he had studied as cynically and disdained, if anything, more thoroughly than unthinking Clan passions. Misery. Despair. Horror. Sadness. *Pity*.

In that instant, standing alone in the DropShip corridor staring down unseeing at the black rose at his feet, Beckett Malthus died. And someone else rose from the muck of sick emotions to fill his shell and inspirit him anew.

The Clan ideal, which the Falcons exulted in taking to extremes, was to exalt oneself, win glory, smash foes on the battlefield and rake down rivals in order to rise as high as ability could possibly carry one. Yet, paradoxically, *selflessly*: for the good of the Clan, for the Clans and Kerensky's vision, to drive evolution closer to the perfection of the human genotype. In the end the individual, be she laborer or warrior, meant nothing. Turkina was all.

He had exemplified the opposite: caring nothing for glory nor visible rank but seeking power and influence, and all for himself.

But now he was dead to all that he had been before. A new resolve became an ember within him, burned brighter and hotter until he was surprised his beard did not catch fire and the paint of the bulkheads around him blister.

Slowly, carefully, he knelt and picked up the rose. Cradling it in his big palm, he stood straight.

I will serve you with all my skill and zeal, Malvina Hazen, he silently swore. *Until such time as my death can destroy you, and eradicate the blood-taint with which you have infected not just the Clans but all of humankind.*

The time was not now. He knew that. He could not yet envision, subtle and expansive as his imagination was, the circumstances in which he could do what he now knew must be done.

But Beckett Malthus, perhaps alone among Clan Jade Falcon, had cultivated patience as a skill.

He would wait. Until the lines converged.

Then blackness.

Almost girlish in her excitement, Malvina Hazen led her ward to the console. There she plucked the remaining black rose from the confining membrane. It alone had a long, straight stem, from which Malvina herself had stripped all thorns.

She knelt and folded Cynthy's hands across it against the girl's breast. She kissed her on the cheek.

"And thus do I seal your fate, my darling," Malvina said, "as I have sealed others' this day."

"Only yours differs from theirs. You I will always shield with all my wit and skill, with my very body if need be."

She stood to her full height facing the starry blaze in the viewport. "You shall rule all," she said in a voice that rang from the bulkhead. "You shall be the last."

Standing wordlessly at her side, Cynthy clutched her bear against herself in the crook of her elbow as she held the black rose gingerly in her two small hands. Tears welled up in her eyes and trailed slowly down her cheeks.

About the Author

I was born in Tulsa, Oklahoma, and spent most of my first couple years of life in Puerto Rico. When I was seven we moved to Santa Fe, New Mexico. Shortly thereafter my family relocated to Albuquerque, where I've lived, with a few interruptions, happily since.

As a kid I got hooked on the notion that it had to be possible to write thrilling action-adventure stories I didn't have to turn off my brain to enjoy. That's what I've devoted my whole life to doing: writing novels and stories aimed at exciting, rather than insulting, intelligent readers.

That's almost exclusively how I've made my living for more than thirty years. I've also been a cowboy, semipro actor, artist, bouncer, computer tech, and Albuquerque's most popular all-night progressive-rock DJ.

But writing is my first love. I'm coming up on ninety novels published, as well as a number of short stories. Pseudonymously I've written dozens of novels for adventure series, including The Guardians, Deathlands (most recent: *Vengeance Trail*) and Outlanders (most recent: *Lords of the Deep*). Under my own name I've authored various SF and fantasy novels, including the award-winning *The Cybernetic Samurai* and its sequel, *The Cybernetic Shogun*.

Along with writing I enjoy *taijiquan*, birding, ferrets, guns, and riding my recumbent tadpole tricycle through Albuquerque's scenic North Valley. I'm trying to overcome a lifelong black thumb and learn gardening. And, of course, I spend many hours indulging my lifelong passion for reading.

Currently I'm writing for Gold Eagle's new contemporary adventure novel series, Rogue Angel; my first entry, *Solomon's Jar*, came out in September 2006. My "classic" BattleTech story, "Callie's Call," recently appeared on the pay Web site www.BattleCorps.com.

My Web site, www.victormilan.com, offers free fiction downloads and a hopping forum. Look me up and say hi. Thanks for reading!

—**Victor Milán**